V Plague Book Twelve

DIRK
PATTON

Published by Reaper Ranch Press LLC

PO Box 856

Gilmer, TX 75644-0856

Printed in the United States of America

First Printing, 2016

ISBN-13: 978-1535027335

ISBN-10: 1535027339

Table of Contents

Fulcrum

Also by Dirk Patton

The V Plague Series

Fulcrum

The 36 Series

Other Titles

Author's Note

Thank you for purchasing Fulcrum, Book 12 in the V Plague series. If you haven't read the first eleven books, you need to stop reading now and pick them up, otherwise you will be utterly lost as this book is intended to continue the story in a serialized format. I intentionally did nothing to explain comments and events that reference books 1 through 11. Regardless, you have my heartfelt thanks for reading my work, and I hope you're enjoying the adventure as much as I am. As always, a good review on Amazon is greatly appreciated.

I have been remiss in thanking all the amazing people who help me deliver a completed book to you, the reader. Some of you wish to remain anonymous, and I will honor that, but you know who you are. Your insight and suggestions when I put a completed first draft into your hands are invaluable. For this, I thank you!

You can always correspond with me via email at dirk@dirkpatton.com and find me on the internet at www.dirkpatton.com and follow me on Twitter @DirkPatton and if you're on Facebook, please like my page at www.facebook.com/DirkPattonAuthor

Fulcrum

Down in a hole and I don't know if I can

be saved

See my heart I decorate it like a grave

Oh, you don't understand who they

thought I was supposed to be

Look at me now I'm a man who won't let

himself be

Alice In Chains – *Down In A Hole*

1

The female was slowly picking her way between the low dunes. Every few feet she would stop and test the air, take a quick look around, then continue slinking forward. The sun had set, and it was that between time of the evening when everything is lit by a hazy, blue light. Even with the high-powered sniper scope on the rifle I was using, it was growing harder to maintain my target.

I was at Groom Lake in southern Nevada, Area 51 if you will, and the infected female was on the hunt. She knew we were in the area, undoubtedly had smelled us, but she wasn't sure where we were. Yet. So I lay in the sand on the back side of a low hill, rifle resting on the crest, and tracked her.

She was still nearly 1,000 yards away, and I wasn't comfortable with taking the shot. Not now. Years ago, I'd probably have tried it. But then I'd spent a lot of time shooting at training targets anywhere from 100 to 1,200 yards. And I'd been pretty damn good.

Don't get me wrong. I wasn't one of those guys that could repeatedly hit a heart or head shot at 1,000 yards. No. I've never had the patience and temperament to be a sniper. But, there was a time when I could at least hit my target at that range. Now? I didn't have the confidence.

Sure, I'd been fighting everything from Russians to infected for months. And my skills with a battle rifle were as sharp as ever. Inside a couple of hundred yards. However, the skill to make a shot at 200 yards, versus a thousand, is like comparing high school gymnastics to the Olympics. They're doing the same basic things, but the execution couldn't be more different.

To add to the difficulty level, a breeze was blowing from left to right across the path the bullet would have to travel. It wasn't a strong wind, by any means, but at a thousand yards, a round is in the air for a long time. And the longer it's in flight, the more it will be affected by environmental forces. So, unmoving in the twilight, I waited.

Perhaps I should have been more confident with the rifle I'd found in the armory. It was an M2010 ESR or Enhanced Sniper Rifle, complete with a high power scope, night vision, thermal imaging and a sound suppressor. Chambered in .300 Winchester Magnum, the weapon was more than capable of taking out the female. It was just the rusty old soldier behind the trigger that wasn't so sure.

Fulcrum

Beside me, stretched out on the sand, Dog growled softly. Tearing my eye away from the scope, I glanced at him. He only growls when he catches the scent of an infected. And, there was no way he was smelling the one I was watching. The wind was wrong.

Dog was looking to our left, into the wind. Moving slowly, I pulled the rifle off the top of the hill and swiveled, activating the night vision scope. Settling the bipod's legs into the dirt, I carefully scanned for whatever had drawn Dog's attention.

The night vision scope let me see everything in the rapidly fading light. Several large, squat, concrete structures were sprinkled across the shallow valley of the dry lake bed that spread out below me. A dozen massive hangars were on the far side of a broad, extra-long runway.

Slowly panning across the scene, I paused when I saw movement between two of the buildings. A pair of females out for an evening stroll. They stalked along the base of one of the walls, heading for the entrance. With a sigh, I settled my cheek onto the stock of the rifle and clicked the safety off with my thumb.

The females weren't a threat to me or the building. They couldn't get through the door. But if one of the small group that was inside happened to walk out for some fresh air, they would be in trouble.

I checked the range to target. 700 yards. The wind was in my face, so I didn't have to worry about lateral movement of the bullet. But, I was shooting downhill, and that combined with the breeze would cause the round to drop more than normal.

Clicking an elevation adjustment on the scope, I hoped I remembered enough about long range shooting not to have completely fucked things up. Taking a breath, I moved my finger onto the trigger and squeezed until the first stage clicked. Exhaling, I timed my shot for the moment my lungs were empty, trying to fire the weapon in between heartbeats.

The big rifle bucked against my shoulder, seemingly impossibly quiet with the specialized suppressor. Watching my target through the scope, I cycled the bolt, loading a fresh round into the chamber. Squeezed through the first click of the trigger as I watched one of the females fly backward to slam against the concrete wall.

Shifting aim, I repeated the breathing process and fired again. The second female was looking around, trying to figure out what had attacked her sister when the big bullet arrived and blew a hole through her chest. Cycling the bolt, I watched through the scope for several seconds to make sure they were staying down.

Neither body moved. Before I turned back to check on the original female I'd been tracking, I noted the dual sprays of blood on the gray wall. A fist-sized divot was blasted out of the concrete in the center of each where the bullet had struck after passing through their bodies.

When I found her again, the first female appeared to have noticed nothing. She was too far away to have heard the suppressed fire, so had continued on, thinking she was alone. Checking the range, I noted she had drawn closer. 825 yards, now.

Adjusting the scope, I undid the elevation from a moment ago and made my best guess on the lateral setting, or windage. She was still drawing closer, moving a little faster now, and I would probably only have two shots at the most before she knew I was there. If the first one was off target, it had better not be far off. I didn't have time to keep playing with the scope.

Females are fast. No, not fast. Damn fast. If she took off, unless she happened to run directly at or away from me, I'd never hit her. I knew there were shooters that could. Had seen it done on targets even faster than a female infected, but I also knew I wasn't one of those freaky good trigger-men.

I fired and quickly cycled the bolt. An instant later, the female violently spun and tumbled to the ground. For a heartbeat, I thought I'd made a good shot, but knew I hadn't fully compensated for the wind when she jumped to her feet and raced away behind a dune.

No matter how many times I've witnessed it, it still amazes me. My bullet had drifted to the side and struck her shoulder. The socket had been completely destroyed, and when she leapt up, her arm was swinging loosely by only a few tendons. Blood was already soaking her filthy clothing.

I looked over when Dog yawned, no longer worrying about the female. The wound might not have put her down immediately, but it was mortal. She was running on adrenaline, but that will only take you so far when you're bleeding out. As she ran, her heart would pump harder, emptying her body. She might make it a few hundred yards if she was very lucky.

Eye back to the scope, I spent another twenty minutes scanning the surrounding desert. It was now fully dark, cold stars filling the sky. The moon wouldn't come up for another few hours, so other than possibly an owl, I had the best vision of any predator in the desert.

Fulcrum

A small pack of coyotes trotted across the far end of the runway. Other than them, nothing was moving in any direction. My stomach rumbled, but I ignored it. I briefly tried to remember the last time I'd eaten, but couldn't, so gave up. I knew it was before I'd given Katie a fatal dose of morphine, but other than that I didn't know. And didn't care.

Leaving the rifle propped on its bipod and stock, I sat up and looked a few yards away. In the faint starlight, I could just make out the hump of desert soil that was my wife's final resting place. We weren't religious, so there was no marker. I'd thought about finding a machine shop somewhere in the facility and making a crude headstone, but had yet to do anything more than think about it.

I'd left Katie's grave only twice since I'd buried her more than 24 hours ago. Once, when Igor had talked me off the edge of throwing in the towel and sticking my pistol in my mouth. But I hadn't been able to take the looks of sorrow from my companions, especially Rachel. Not that anyone was doing anything wrong, I just needed to be alone.

The second time had been to find and raid the armory. When I'd arrived at Groom Lake, there had been a cordon of Marines and Rangers providing security and preventing any infected from wandering in. But they were gone, and I'd begun seeing the occasional female show up. Needing something with more range than my M4, I'd been pleased to find the big sniper rifle.

Dog had stayed by my side. I hadn't called him or given any command. He just wasn't leaving me. Rachel had brought us food and water during the day yesterday but hadn't stayed long. I wasn't a very good conversationalist right now.

I'd drank the water, but Dog had gotten my food as well as his. At least one of us was well fed.

There was a soft bang from the direction of the closest building. Dog's head snapped up, but he didn't growl. Still, I grabbed the rifle and peered through the night vision scope. I spotted Rachel, looking at the two dead females. She had found a light-weight Air Force jacket and hugged herself against the chilly, night wind.

Turning away from the corpses, she looked in my direction, then began walking. The wind whipped her long hair around her face, and she had to forego holding herself for warmth to control her unruly mane. I scanned the entire area, making sure there weren't any infected stalking her. She was alone.

Several minutes later she sat down on the sand between Dog and me. After a couple of repositions, she was mostly sheltered from the wind by my body. Leaning out, she ruffled Dog's ears. He rolled onto his side and raised his front foot so she could scratch his belly. The sound of her nails was loud in the quiet darkness.

"How long are you going to stay out here?"

Rachel didn't stop scratching Dog, or look away from him when she spoke.

"Hadn't really thought about it," I said.

She was quiet, and I lifted the rifle to make another check of the area.

"Am I bothering you? Want me to leave?"

I thought about that before answering.

"No," I finally said.

"Want to get drunk? Nicole found a liquor cabinet in the base commander's office. It's pretty well stocked."

"Probably better if I'm not drinking right now," I said, even though the idea of losing myself in a bottle was kind of appealing.

Rachel gave Dog a final pat and turned to face me in the dark. I couldn't make out her expression. After nearly a minute, she twisted around on the sand and got to her knees.

Leaning forward, she wrapped her arms around me and pulled.

I resisted. Didn't return the hug. Tried to pull away as my throat began to constrict. But she was persistent. Didn't let go or stop pulling. Slowly, I let myself be drawn into her arms until my face was buried in her hair. I couldn't breathe at first, then I regained control and drew a shuddering breath.

My arms came up and circled Rachel. Neither of us said anything. I didn't cry. I'd already done that, and there was nothing left. We sat there in the night for a long time, not moving or speaking.

2

Once inside the building, Rachel steered me to a small cafeteria. The base had been well stocked with canned and freeze dried food, so everyone that had stayed behind was eating well. A large platter was waiting on the warming tray, and Dog dashed across the small space to thoroughly sniff the edge of the serving line.

"I'm not hungry," I said, trying to turn and head out the door.

"You need to eat," she said, grabbing my arm and pulling me to a table. "Sit your ass down and I'll get your food."

With a sigh, I pulled a plastic chair back and lowered myself. Half the weapons strapped to my body clanged and I stood back up and started removing them. Soon, there was a respectable pile of firepower on an adjacent table, and I sat back down. Rachel was already seated across from me, a steaming plate in front of my chair. I picked up a fork and poked at it, still not hungry.

"So, how are we getting to Australia?"

I shook my head and lipped a small bite of beef stroganoff off the end of the fork. It hit my pallet like a bomb, and I was suddenly starving.

"What does that mean?" She asked after watching me eat for a couple of minutes.

"It means that I don't know," I said in between bites.

Dog rammed his muzzle into my hip, and I scooped up a hunk of noodles, speared a piece of meat and held the fork out for him. He delicately pulled the food off the fork and swallowed after only chewing once. I picked up another bite and put it in my mouth with the same fork.

"OK, that's just gross!"

I turned to see Nicole standing in the entrance to the cafeteria. Her red eyes still startled me every time I saw them, but this time I managed to stop myself from visibly tensing. She walked forward, a smile on her face.

Navy Master Chief Gonzales followed her, most of his face swaddled in bandages. I hadn't seen the wounds but had heard that a female had bitten off much of the flesh on his lower face. He had to be in some pretty serious pain, but the man didn't reveal a glimmer of what he was going through.

"He's earned it. About a hundred times over," I said, feeding some more of my meal to Dog.

Fulcrum

As Nicole approached the table, Dog took a step away and growled softly. He still hadn't accepted her, but at least he wasn't attacking. I spoke to him, and he came back to sit by my side, keeping his eyes locked on the woman. He was no longer interested in the food.

Gonzales walked to a large, chrome urn and filled a ceramic mug with steaming coffee. Nicole had backed off because of Dog, and they took a seat a couple of tables away. It didn't escape my attention that they were sitting closer together than would be normal.

"So?" Rachel asked, prompting me to answer her earlier question.

"I still don't know," I said, sighing. "The Russians are patrolling the whole west coast to keep the Navy bottled up in Hawaii. There's no way they can pick us up."

"There has to be a way," Rachel said, staring at me.

"Not without the Navy's help," I said. "It's a damn long way and a whole lot of ocean between here and there. Besides, even if we could get there, the Aussies are protecting the Russians."

"Then you need to figure something out," Rachel said. "You always come up with something."

I looked at her for a long moment, then put my fork down. There was still some food on the plate, and I put it on the floor for Dog. His eyes flicked down as his nose twitched, but he didn't start eating. He didn't trust Nicole. Rubbing his head, I spoke softly in his ear, reassuring him. After a long pause, he slowly lowered his head and devoured the remnants of my meal.

"You're the resident genius," Rachel said, turning to Nicole. "Can't you come up with a way to get us there?"

Nicole looked at her, a flicker of resentment passing across her face before she answered.

"It doesn't matter how smart you are. There's only so many ways to make the trip, and as the Major pointed out, none of those are viable options."

Rachel stared back at her, then turned to me. For the first time, I realized how exhausted she was. Her eyes were puffy with dark circles bruising the skin beneath them. She was drawn and looked like she'd reached that point where even your hair hurts. She needed sleep.

And, so did I. After the food, my body was telling me it was time to shut down for a while. But, I was afraid to sleep. I feared the dreams that I knew would come. The loss of Katie had done more to me than the infected or the Russians ever could have. However, I knew my body needed to rest. To recover. How else was I going to be able to avenge my wife once the opportunity finally presented itself?

"Let's talk about this tomorrow," I said, standing and collecting my weapons.

Nicole and Gonzales nodded, staying where they were. Rachel stood, her and Dog following me out into the hall.

"Do you want to be alone?" She asked as we headed for the sleeping quarters.

"No," I said after a long beat.

She took my hand and led me to the room she was using. There was nothing special about it other than it had two single bunks. While I piled my arsenal in the corner and took my boots off, she pushed them together and spread blankets.

Rachel turned the lights off, and we lay down, holding hands across the gap where they didn't quite meet. Dog curled up on the floor, between us and the door, grunting as he got himself into a comfortable position.

I didn't think I'd be able to sleep. Expected this to be a frustrating exercise in futility. Planned to wait until Rachel drifted off, then take Dog and go back outside to hunt some more infected. But, as usual, my plan didn't work out the way I wanted it to.

Within minutes, Rachel was breathing slowly and softly. Sound asleep. Soon, Dog was snoring. I stared at the ceiling in the nearly perfect darkness, the only illumination coming from a faint light in the hall that leaked under the door. Several times I told myself to get up and put my boots on, but my body didn't cooperate. I went to sleep.

3

I was alone when I woke. Rachel and Dog had gotten up at some point and left the room. With no watch or clock, I had no idea what time it was and didn't really give a shit. I was content just to lay there for a while, staring at the ceiling and thinking.

Somehow, I'd made it through the night without dreaming about Katie. Well, at least if I did, I didn't remember having a dream. Now, I let my mind drift. Remembered our life together. Our dreams and hopes. The plans we'd made for the future. A future that would never come.

Then I thought about the reason that future would never happen. Not just for me, but for billions of other people on the planet that had died because of a madman in the Kremlin. All of the pain and loss that had been visited on the world in the past few months could be laid squarely on his doorstep.

Anger surged through me, both for my loss and the evil that had been unleashed on humanity. And now, the fucker directly responsible was sitting somewhere in Australia, living a life of luxury. Somehow, I was going to make the journey. Creep into his bedroom late at night and make him experience true terror.

Dirk Patton

The need for vengeance was invigorating, and I threw the thin blanket off and sat up. And got a whiff of myself. I was ripe. Well, maybe ripe didn't do justice to the smell coming off my body and clothing. The first order of business was to get clean.

Taking only a rifle and pistol, I grabbed my boots and headed out in search of clean clothes and a shower. Wandering down the hallway, I stuck my head into the cafeteria and spotted Nicole and Gonzales huddled at a table, talking in low voices. Her hand was on top of his, and he quickly pulled it away when he became aware of my presence.

"Relax, Master Chief," I said, smiling. "And, tell me where to find some clean clothes and the showers."

"Better I show you, sir."

He stood and stepped into the hallway, leading me in a direction I hadn't been.

"Sorry about what you saw, sir. I know it's not exactly…"

"Knock it off," I grumbled. "The world where you aren't supposed to fraternize like that is long dead. If you two want to be together, well then be together. And if your LT gives you any shit, come find me."

"Actually, sir," Gonzales chuckled. "He warned me about you."

"Me? Why the hell is he worried about me?"

"Just doesn't know you, sir. That's all. That, and from what we've heard you're pretty tight with Admiral Packard."

"Don't know if pretty tight is the right way to characterize it," I said as we entered a new hallway. "Never met the man. Only ever talked to him on the phone. There's just been a lot of shit I've been involved in that has been on his radar. Regardless, you do what your heart tells you. Before it's too late."

We reached a door marked *Quartermaster,* and he turned to face me. Held my eyes for a moment before nodding.

"Heard from a few of the Rangers that you were OK. Glad they weren't shining me on."

"I'm a gold-plated asshole," I grinned. "But I was an NCO, not an officer. I've got bigger things to worry about than who you're romancing."

He grinned back at me and nodded.

"Good supply of Air Force issue inside," he said, gesturing at the door. "Showers are about five doors down on your left."

"Thanks, Master Chief."

He nodded and walked away, heading back to the cafeteria with a spring in his step. I pushed through and turned on the lights. Stepping around a counter, I saw row upon row of steel shelving, loaded down with neatly folded and cataloged uniforms. Clean clothes in hand, I snagged a hygiene kit sealed in plastic and headed for the showers.

Opening the door, I was greeted with a billow of steam and the sound of running water. Putting my weapons on a bench, I stripped out of the offending garments that were stiff with blood and sweat. Picking up the towel, I stepped around the wall that divided the showers from the dressing area and came to an abrupt stop.

Irina stood under the closest shower, rinsing soap from her body. She was turned away from me and hadn't heard me enter over the sound of the water. I quickly retreated, wrapped the towel around my waist and pulled the door open to check. Yep. I was in the showers designated for men. Softly closing the door, I began gathering my clothes and weapons, intending to make a strategic retreat before she knew I'd inadvertently invaded her privacy.

Fulcrum

Before I had everything in my arms, the water shut off, and Irina stepped around the wall. She came to a surprised stop with a sharp intake of breath when she saw me, arms automatically covering her breasts.

"Sorry," I said, turning away and snatching up the last piece of my clothing.

"It is OK," she said.

I could tell from the sound that she had ducked back around the wall into the shower area. I was reaching for the door when she spoke again.

"Can you please hand me a towel?"

I paused, wanting to get the hell out of there. Yes, Irina is a beautiful woman, but the whole situation made me really uncomfortable.

Glancing around, I saw a stack of fresh, white towels. Picking one off the top, I edged up to the wall and held it around the corner. Irina took it from my hand and a moment later stepped back into view with it wrapped around her torso. The lower edge ended only a few inches below her hips.

"I am sorry," she said, appearing more composed with her nudity covered. "The showers for women do not have good pressure. I did not think anyone would be coming along."

31

She stepped around me and quickly disappeared through the door. I caught a flash of her ass as she moved, and all it did was make me think of Katie. I peeked around the wall to make sure I was alone, then dumped my stuff back on the bench and tossed the towel over a rack.

Nearly half an hour later I was clean and freshly shaven. Turning the water off, I stepped into the dressing area and came face to face with Rachel, holding a towel for me.

"Can't you women read?" I asked sarcastically. "It says, MEN. Right there on the goddamn door!"

I snatched the towel and wrapped it around my waist.

"Irina said you were in here."

"Yeah, well, she shouldn't have been in here, either," I groused.

Moving to the sink, I loaded a toothbrush with paste and began brushing my teeth. Rachel came to stand next to me, leaning her hip on the counter.

"Feel better?" She asked with a small grin.

"I'd feel better if I could take a shower without participating in a peep show," I mumbled around the brush.

"Suck it up," she said. Then, "You're going to be interested in what we found."

I turned to look at her, then had to spit toothpaste into the sink.

"What?"

"No one's sure," she said, still grinning.

That got my attention. Despite everything that had been going on, it hadn't failed to register on me that this was Area 51. If even a fraction of the conspiracy theories were right, there had to be some pretty fantastic things hidden in the massive, underground facility.

"If you tell me they found aliens," I stopped to spit again and rinse my mouth. "I'm going to take your rifle away before you hurt yourself or someone else."

"I'd like to see you try," she said.

With a smile, she stepped away and moved her slung rifle behind her back and put her fists on her hips. Despite myself, I laughed.

"OK, tell me," I said, turning to face her.

"Un-uh. You've gotta see this."

"Jesus Christ," I said under my breath. "Fine. Get the hell out and let me get dressed. I'll be right there."

Rachel stuck her tongue out, then left the room. Shaking my head, I stripped the towel off and pulled on my new clothes.

4

Rachel had waited outside the showers
for me, leading me to where Irina and Dog were
having a meal. When we walked in, Irina looked
up, then quickly away, a slight blush coloring her
pale cheeks. Despite myself, I smiled. If she was
embarrassed, it was her own fault. Rachel
appeared to be struggling to contain some
sarcastic remark, and I chose to ignore her.

It took us nearly fifteen minutes to make
it from the cafeteria to a cavernous hangar built
into the side of a nearby mountain. We'd
descended deep underground, then climbed
aboard an electric golf cart. Irina drove,
navigating a confusing maze of tunnels that
seemed to go on forever.

As we progressed, we passed countless
doors that were marked with only a number.
They were high-security slabs of chromed steel,
not unlike the vault doors from Los Alamos
where I'd first met Irina.

"Johnson had any luck with these?" I
asked.

Long and Johnson had decided to stay
behind with me, rather than evacuating to
Hawaii with Colonel Blanchard. I hadn't asked

them why. They'd made the choice, and I was happy to have them around.

"He's been able to open every door he's tried," Rachel answered. "There's just so many of them, and we've not been able to find anything to tell us which ones might contain something we can make use of."

"What have you found?"

"Very little we can make sense of," Irina said as she turned into a new tunnel. "Some Chinese and Russian tech that was being disassembled and inspected. That was pretty straightforward. Most of the rest is projects in various stages of completion, and no one can understand what they are supposed to do."

"Except the thing you're taking me to see?"

"Except that," she smiled.

"And, it is?"

"Something the GRU heard rumors was in development, but we were never able to confirm," Irina said. "Now, be patient. It is better if you see, rather than I try to explain."

I looked at her, then Rachel, but neither was giving anything away. Frankly, I was struggling not to get irritated with them. I don't like surprises.

Finally, we rolled through a broad opening at the end of a tunnel into a hangar large enough to easily hold a pair of 747s, with room to spare. Irina braked to a stop, and I stared in awe at an impossibly large aircraft. At least, that's what I thought it was.

Stepping out of the golf cart, I looked up at the skin of the craft, amazed when it changed color to match the difference in its background as I walked around it. I stopped, then reversed course, confirming my eyes weren't playing tricks on me. As the walls of the room behind it changed color and texture, the skin of the machine matched them, rendering it all but invisible.

"Watch this!"

I looked around at the shout to see Long with his hand on a large electrical lever. He pulled it down and brilliant lights set into the ceiling, far overhead, came to life. Suddenly, the entire aircraft became visible, and it was huge. Easily as long as a 747, it was wedge shaped with a sharp nose and blunt tail. Twin rudders stuck up from above and beneath the back, rectangular exhaust ports for the engines filling the entire rear surface.

"What the hell is it?" I asked.

"If it is what we heard of, and I am fairly certain it is," Irina began, then paused.

"What?"

"A hypersonic transport with adaptive camouflage. Faster than anything in the air, and invisible to both radar and visual sighting."

I turned to look at her. She'd gotten over her embarrassment and stared back at me.

"I am serious," she said after a pause. "Russia and China were both working on this, as were the Europeans. If it flies, it would seem you beat all of us."

"I don't get it," Rachel said. "I thought it was just a stealth jet."

"It is," Irina answered. "Only so much more. Imagine being able to go from New York to London in twenty minutes. And doing it in an aircraft that can't be detected or tracked. Or even seen."

"But we can see it," Rachel protested.

"Because of the specialty lighting," Irina said. "In a blue sky with only sunlight and maybe some clouds below? It would be invisible to the human eye."

I walked forward and reached up to touch the skin of the plane. It was cold and smooth, an unsettling difference from how it appeared. I was amazed when the surface around where my hand was in contact changed color to match my skin.

"Holy shit," I breathed. "Does it fly?"

"No idea," Irina said. "That is the one skill that none of us possess."

"Then why are you so excited about it?"

"Just think," Irina said. "If we can get Hawaii to send us a pilot, and this flies, we could make the trip to Australia in about ninety minutes!"

I stood there staring at the amazing airplane. The last time I'd gone to Australia, it had been a grueling, thirteen-hour flight from Los Angeles.

"Are you kidding me?" I asked.

Irina shook her head.

"Russia and China have already reached the speeds needed to record those types of travel times. But, only ever with unmanned, experimental aircraft. It appears this is well beyond experimental. There is a cockpit with controls. Seats for pilots. Seats in the back, as well as provisions for transporting heavy equipment."

"There's a whole equipment bay," Long said, walking up to stand next to me. "Easily room for a couple of Bradleys, and there's enough seating for an entire platoon. If she's right about this thing, that brings a whole new meaning to *Rapid Deployment Force*."

He grinned and reached up to touch the aircraft. The spot where his hand came in contact also quickly changed to match his skin color.

"Anyone talked to Hawaii about getting a pilot here?" I asked, stepping back and looking down the length of the wedge.

"Thought I'd leave that for you. Figured you could get directly through to the old man."

Lieutenant Sam appeared from around the far side of a large set of tires supporting the landing gear. I thought about what he said for a moment, then nodded.

"So, where's the comm room in this place?"

We borrowed the cart and headed back into the facility. Rachel and Dog stayed with Irina, both of them playing with the chameleon-like skin covering the plane.

Fulcrum

"The Master Chief said he had a conversation with you," Sam said as he drove.

I didn't know him and didn't know where he might be going with this, so all I did was nod. Sam glanced at me when he realized I wasn't going to say anything.

"He's a good man. Doesn't need to get his ass in a crack over fraternizing."

So, he was worried about his man. He just went up a couple of notches in my book.

"Don't know about the Navy, Lieutenant, but I can't think of any Army regs that would prevent him from becoming involved with a civilian, even if she is someone you rescued."

He nodded and turned into a new tunnel.

"Navy's got some unwritten rules. The result of some of the guys getting into shit in Iraq and A-stan."

"Don't really think any of it matters, now. How 'bout you, Lieutenant?"

"No, sir," he said. "I guess you're right."

We turned into another tunnel, this one stretching away so far it faded into a dark, distant point.

"Tell me about the infected woman."

41

"Nicole? We found her in Seattle. At the university. She was trapped in a nuclear physics lab when the alarm tripped and locked down the building. Scared the crap out of me when I first saw her."

"Me too," I chuckled. "How'd she survive?

"A well-stocked staff kitchen. Maybe the infection helped. Maybe not. But she's OK, and she's good for Gonzales. Strong as hell if we get in a scrap, and by the way, the females don't mess with her. I've seen them come to a hard stop and just stare at her before running off."

"No shit?"

"No shit, sir. Kanger couldn't explain it, but I'll take any edge we can get."

We made another turn, and the SEAL brought the cart to a stop next to a door labeled as *Secure Communications*. Stepping out, I noticed the keypad next to the door had been removed and dangled from a bundle of wires. Two new ones connected different points on a circuit board, held in place with tiny alligator clips.

"Johnson?" I asked, gesturing at the lock.

"Yep. Damn glad he's here. All of these doors are the real deal, and it's nice not having to blast our way through."

Fulcrum

I nodded and followed him into a large room. I'm a little old school and was expecting a more traditional radio-shack setup like the Canadians had at Alert station. Instead, everything was sleek consoles with computer screens and futuristic headsets. I stood there, looking around, with no clue where to start.

"Know how to operate it?"

Sam glanced at me and from the expression on his face, I knew what was coming.

"Make an Army joke and I'll have Dog shit on your pillow."

He looked surprised for a beat, a big grin finally spreading across his face. Sitting down in front of a console, he began working the keyboard. I didn't even try to figure out what he was doing.

After only a few seconds, he handed me a headset. As I slipped it on I could hear a soft, electronic tone, then a voice I recognized spoke in my ear.

"Hello, Jessica," I said.

"Sir! Good to speak with you!"

Her enthusiasm was infectious, and I couldn't help but smile.

"You too," I said. "What's the Russian situation?"

"They've pretty much got the Pacific sewn up. Their navy is severely degraded, but they're using what they have to keep us bottled up in Hawaii. They've set up a thousand-mile perimeter around the islands. Probably worried about us showing up in Australia and spoiling their party."

"Any chance of getting a flight to my location?" I asked.

"Don't see how. But, the Admiral might have something up his sleeve. You trying to get here?"

"Yes," I said, not wanting to advertise that I wanted to go on a hunting expedition in Australia.

Jessica lowered her voice.

"Might be better off where you are, sir."

"Why's that?" I asked, concern creasing my forehead.

"Lots of hungry people here," she said even softer. "Food stores are being rationed. The Admiral has people working with the local government to get production ramped up. It's starting to look like photos I've seen of America during World War II. Gardens are springing up in everyone's backyard. Seeds and fertilizer are worth their weight in gold. And don't even get me started on how we've already run out of soap, razors and toilet paper."

Despite myself, I started laughing. Jessica was quiet for a beat before speaking in a tight voice.

"It's not funny, sir. You should smell some of the people I have to work with. And the Admiral has already had to relax grooming standards for male personnel. It's going to look like Duck Dynasty around here before things get better."

I apologized, but I don't think she believed I was sincere as I was still laughing as I said I was sorry.

"Was there anything else you needed other than to amuse yourself over my hygiene issues?"

Jessica's words were tight, but I could hear the smirk in her tone as she spoke. I chuckled at her response, happy for a little relief.

"Actually, I need to speak with the Admiral. Think you can transfer me over to his office?"

"Stand by, sir," she said, all business again.

The line went quiet and stayed that way for some time. With a sigh, I plopped into a chair in front of the console. Sam was giving me an inquisitive look, and I filled him in on the shortages the people in Hawaii were dealing with.

"That'll ease as soon as we can break the stalemate with the Russians," he said. "Got to be warehouses full of all of that stuff, and probably plenty of cargo ships rusting at the docks all along the west coast."

I nodded as Jessica came back on the line.

"Sir, he's in a briefing at the moment, and his aide refuses to interrupt."

"Shit. OK, can you put me through to his aide?"

"He ordered me not to do that, sir. I think you scared him the last time you called."

She laughed as she said this. I shook my head and leaned back in the chair.

"Have him call me ASAP," I said. "Tell him I've found something here at Groom Lake that he's definitely going to want to know about."

5

Admiral Packard sat at the end of the large conference table, staring at the projected image on the far wall of the room. Commander Detmer had just completed a briefing he had prepared based on the Athena Project file that Major Chase had recovered from the Russians at Offutt Air Force Base. He was stunned at the information he'd just received.

"Do we have any way to verify this?" He asked after several minutes of silence.

"Sir, we have verified that there is what appears to be an oil production platform at the precise coordinates contained in the documents. Additionally, the information that a massive superconducting supercollider has been constructed beneath the seabed matches the mysterious ring we discovered with the NSA satellite. Short of an on-site inspection, I am of the opinion that we have enough verification to validate the file."

Captain Beasley, one of Packard's senior staffers, spoke up.

"There's no way this could be a Russian false flag operation? Dummy up a top secret file and use the information contained therein to draw us into the gulf? That's damn tight quarters in there if we had to fight."

"No, sir," Detmer answered, shaking his head. "I do not believe that to be the case. We also have the personal diary, taken from the body of a Spetsnaz officer, which references his unit being sent in search of records of the Athena Project."

Beasley nodded but didn't appear convinced. Still, he held his tongue.

"Something's not right," Rear Admiral Black groused. "If the goddamn Russians didn't get away with the file, then how did they know to be in the area and shoot down our reconnaissance flight? Can you explain that to me, Commander?"

"No, sir. All I can do is posit a theory. The Russians noticed the tankers we put in the area. They went to investigate, and the timing was bad for Lieutenant Commander Vance."

"I'm still not buying it," Black said sourly, turning to face Packard.

"Enough," Packard held his hand up before things got out of control. "I'm convinced there's something to this. I'm not sure I'm buying the whole black hole and warped space-time thing, but there's no way this was a plant by the Russians.

"They had no way of knowing the Major's flight was going to land in Omaha for fuel. It wasn't planned. The pilot didn't even know until an hour before they set down. No. I think the file is genuine."

He paused and looked around the room. Saw doubt in the eyes of many of the assembled officers, but also saw that they were going to keep any further disagreement to themselves. He turned his attention back to Detmer.

"Commander, have you had any luck trying to communicate with the platform?"

"No, sir. None. Comm protocols are one thing that is not contained in the file. We don't even know if they're capable of broadcasting or receiving on any of our channels. Perhaps they are, but are deliberately remaining EM silent to avoid drawing the Russian's attention."

"Do we have any confirmation that there's even anyone still alive on the platform?" Admiral Black asked.

"No, sir. We do not. We are able to confirm through satellite surveillance that the platform is powered up, as is the supercollider, but that could be automated systems. We are maintaining 24-hour watch from orbit, but so far have not seen any signs of activity."

"Could the infection have reached them? Fifty miles out at sea?" Packard asked.

"Yes, sir. Any number of ways. A transfer of personnel before the initial outbreak. Or, we know the virus has jumped to birds, and the platform is certainly within the range of a variety of species that inhabit the Texas coast."

The room fell silent again, each man thinking about the possibility that the personnel manning the platform were nothing more than raging infected. Every head turned when the door suddenly burst open, one of Packard's aides charging into the room.

"Sir," the Lieutenant nearly shouted. "Commander Vance is alive! We just found him!"

"Where?"

Admiral Black was the first to speak up.

"He's in the northern portion of the Sea of Cortez, sir. Between Baja and mainland Mexico."

"He's in the water?" Packard asked.

"Raft, sir. He must have punched out and was able to deploy the survival raft."

"That damn little puddle isn't that big. How far from land?"

"He's pretty much in the middle, sir. The closest land to him is 30 miles, and the wind is pushing him south. Keeping him in the middle of the Sea."

Admiral Black spun around in his chair and snatched a phone off a side table. He barked into it, then listened for a few moments before slamming it down.

"We'll never get an SAR flight in there," he growled. "Fuckin Commies got the area sewn up tighter than a frog's ass."

"Commander," Packard said to Detmer. "How far away is Major Chase? He's at Groom Lake in southern Nevada."

While Detmer pulled up a map, the Lieutenant cleared his throat, causing Packard to look at him.

"Something to say, Lieutenant?"

"Sir, Major Chase called for you earlier. I told him I'd have you call him back after your briefing concluded."

Packard glared at the junior officer from beneath his bushy eyebrows, turning back when Detmer spoke up.

"He's definitely in the neighborhood, sir. Four hundred miles, straight line. I'm not sure how far with the roads he'd have to take."

Packard was quiet for a beat.

"Alright. This Athena Project can wait. We've got a man in the water, and we need to get to him. Commander, get with Seaman Simmons and have her put together a route for him to the port closest to Vance's location, and also have her start looking for a boat the Major can use once he gets in the area."

Detmer acknowledged the order, gathered his files and hustled out of the conference room.

"Lieutenant, get the Major on the line," Packard said.

The man leaped forward and set to work on the secure phone resting in the middle of the conference table. There was a series of electronic tones, then Major Chase's voice came over the speaker.

6

Sam and I had been swapping stories about events since the attacks. He'd had some hairy experiences of his own. I resisted the temptation to one-up with what I'd dealt with. When the comm console beeped for attention, he was telling me about the trip through the locks in Seattle with Dr. Kanger.

"Major, I hope all is well," Admiral Packard said when I answered.

"As it can be, sir," I said.

"Good. I hope you understand why I couldn't allow any infected into Hawaii. How is your wife?"

I was quiet for a moment, giving my throat a chance to unconstrict before I answered.

"She passed away, sir," I finally said.

There was a long stretch of silence before Packard spoke again.

"I'm truly sorry for your loss, Major. I wish there was something I could have done."

"Me too, sir," I said.

"We have a man in trouble, and he's not far from you," Packard transitioned smoothly, and I was happy to talk about anything other than Katie.

"Someone still in CONUS?" I asked in surprise.

Sam's eyes locked onto me when he heard my question.

"Close enough," the Admiral said. "He's adrift on a... Sea...tez..."

"Admiral, repeat your last," I said, flapping my hand at the Lieutenant for assistance.

Sam leaned forward and yanked the headset's plug out of the console, transferring the audio to a built-in speaker. We heard an electronic squeal that made both of us cringe, then Admiral Packard's voice returned for a brief moment.

"...forty mile.. sou..west ... Penasco..."

"Admiral, I do not have a good copy on your message. Please repeat!"

I shouted into the microphone though I knew that wouldn't do any good. Sam manipulated the console without any success.

"Kill it and open a new circuit," I said.

He nodded and entered some commands, grunting when several indicators on the screen remained red.

"What's wrong?" I asked when he didn't seem to be in a hurry to fill me in.

"We aren't connecting to the satellite," he said. "Either it's being jammed, or it's gone."

"Any way around it?"

He shook his head as he tried a few different commands.

"We're limited to the NSA satellites. Everything else was knocked out by the EMP. There is no around."

"You sure it's a satellite failure?" I asked.

"Pretty sure."

"What if it's Hawaii? The Russians lob another nuke?"

He was shaking his head before I finished speaking.

"Not that that isn't possible, but our problem, for the moment at least, is we can't connect to the satellite. If I had to guess, it's the Russians doing something."

"Fuck! Sounds like we've got a man in the water and the Admiral wanted us to go get him."

"In the water? We're in the middle of the goddamn desert," Sam said, turning to look at me.

"It was broken up, but I'm pretty sure he was saying the Sea of Cortez."

Sam shook his head.

"Gulf of California," he clarified. "Between Baja and the main part of Mexico. About 600 miles long and a hundred or so miles wide. That's sixty thousand square miles. How the hell are we supposed to find someone in that?"

"You heard the last part he said? Penasco? Forty miles southwest. That's got to be Puerto Penasco. Rocky Point if you're an American. It's only about 80 miles south of the border."

I looked around the room for a map but didn't find one. Sam stared at me, doubt on his face.

"What?"

"That's pretty fuckin thin, Major. How many towns do you think there are in Mexico that have Penasco in their name?"

"Got no clue," I said. "But, probably a few. That just happens to be the one I know of."

"He didn't try to give any coordinates?"

"That was probably coming," I said, shaking my head.

I didn't blame him for being dubious. We were a good distance from Mexico and had nothing more to go on than a broken transmission. An idea dawned on me, and I slapped my pants pocket. I still had a handheld sat phone. Jumping to my feet, I headed for the door.

"What are you doing?" Sam asked, getting up and following.

"Got a sat phone," I said over my shoulder. "Going to give it a try. Make sure we don't just have an equipment problem."

We hopped in the golf cart, and Sam accelerated away with a squeal of tires on the smooth concrete. Several minutes later we had successfully negotiated the maze of tunnels and emerged into warm sunshine.

Stepping well clear of the cart, I brought the phone out and powered it on. It took a long time to boot, then began searching for a signal. After nearly five minutes, it was still in search mode. I said a couple of choice words and powered it down before shoving it back in my pocket.

"It's gotta be one of our pilots," Sam said. "Had to eject and came down in the water."

"The Admiral said he's adrift," I said, trying to remember the exact words. "Adrift would mean he's on a raft. Right? He'd say something different if he was just in the water?"

Sam nodded, thinking.

"There're single occupant, inflatable rafts built into the ejection seats of our fighters," he finally said. "And yes, you're right. If a Navy man says *adrift*, he means a vessel that isn't powered."

"No doubt about that?" I asked, turning and checking the area around us for infected.

"An old warhorse like the Admiral wouldn't make that mistake."

Sam spoke with certainty, then waved me to the side as he raised his rifle. I moved and turned to see a female sprinting towards us. He fired a single shot, and she flopped lifelessly to the desert sand.

"What if he's in the water?" I asked, getting a shake of his head.

"The Admiral wouldn't even have called us. Someone in the water isn't going to last very long."

"This is Mexico," I said. "The water's warm."

He looked at me and shook his head.

"The season is changing, and the water temp will be down. Not cold, but cool enough. It will just delay hypothermia. And, I was at Coronado near San Diego. That water ain't warm. Trust me. Maybe a little warmer in the Gulf of California, but survival time would be in hours, not days. Besides, if the water doesn't get you, the sharks will."

"So, we've probably got a pilot on a raft, drifting around the middle of the Sea of Cortez. And we've got a starting point."

He nodded but appeared less than enthusiastic.

"What?"

"No disrespect, sir, but you're Army. You ever tried to find something the size of a man on a tiny inflatable somewhere in the ocean?"

I shook my head.

"Well, without air support, or at least satellite observation, it's damn near impossible. There're waves, and even little ones will hide the target from a surface vessel. You can be thirty yards away and never even know what you're searching for is just right there."

"You sound awful negative, Lieutenant," I said, peering at him.

"Sorry, sir. You misunderstand me. I'm ready to go. I just want to be sure *you* understand our odds of finding and rescuing this pilot are pretty fucking anorexic."

"I think I got that, Lieutenant," I grumbled. "Dad was in the Navy, so I've heard the stories."

"How'd you wind up a ground pounder?" He asked in surprise.

"Black sheep of the family," I grinned. "Sometimes, I wish I would've listened to Mom. I'd be a plastic surgeon in Beverly Hills, up to my neck in tits and ass."

He looked at me for a beat before laughing and heading for the golf cart. As we started driving, he contacted Gonzales on the radio and ordered him to gather everyone into the cafeteria.

7

"Major? Major!" Packard leaned forward over the speakerphone, then when he got no response, turned to his aide. "What the hell is going on?"

"Don't know yet, sir," the man answered, an internal phone already pressed to his ear.

"Never mind," Packard said, getting to his feet. "I'm heading to the CIC."

The senior officers surrounding the conference table had shot to their feet when the Admiral stood. By order of rank, they followed him out of the meeting room for the short walk. When Packard pushed through the doors, the duty officer turned and faced him.

"Sir, we've lost all comms with our satellites. Best guess is Russian jamming."

"Everything?" Packard asked, glaring around the room.

"Yes, sir. Everything. We're deaf and blind. All digital comms are down. We can't uplink to the satellites, and the Battlespace network is offline."

"Bullshit, Captain," Admiral Black stepped forward. "We're jam proof, just for this reason."

"That may be, sir," the Captain answered cautiously. "But we're still down across the board. We're trying to restore the links, and I've got a team working on dusting off some analog radio gear so we can talk to our ships, but so far the secure digital system isn't coming back up."

"Why?" Packard mused, cutting Black off before he could continue grousing.

"Sir?" The Captain asked, not understanding Packard's question.

"Why jam our comms now? We've ceased hostilities. Their elite have evacuated to Australia. It makes no sense. Unless..."

Packard rushed past the surprised duty officer, making a direct path to Jessica's station.

"Seaman. Any luck restoring the uplink with the satellite?" He asked as he approached.

"No, sir," Jessica answered without turning around.

"Where was the Russian fleet when we lost surveillance?"

"Which one, sir?" She asked, turning to look up at him.

"The one in the Pacific."

Fulcrum

Jessica turned to her keyboard, her fingers flying. After a few moments, she pointed at a large monitor in the front of the room. A broad, aerial shot of the ocean was displayed, the timestamp showing it was footage from fifteen minutes ago.

"They haven't really moved, sir," she said. "They're standing off at 1,000 miles, and have us pretty well surrounded."

Packard's eyes moved across the view, noting and cataloging every enemy vessel within sight. All warships and all positioned to prevent the US Navy from entering or leaving Hawaii.

"What's going on at Midway?" The Admiral pointed at a small cluster of large planes on a tiny atoll. "Can you zoom?"

Jessica worked on her keyboard, the image tightening on a small point in the north Pacific, nearly 1,400 miles from Pearl Harbor. When the screen refreshed and sharpened, everyone in the room cursed.

"Captain," Packard growled at the duty officer. "Can you explain exactly how we missed the Russians massing troops and equipment on Midway?"

"No, sir," the man swallowed audibly. "I don't have an explanation."

Admiral Black stepped closer to the screen, intently watching the activity for a few moments.

"What do you think, Chet?" Packard asked.

"I think it's a goddamn invasion force. We thought they were pulling back to restore order within their borders, but this must have been their play."

Packard took a deep breath, staring at the screen. After only a brief moment, he began barking orders.

"Captain, get a reconnaissance flight in the air. We need to know when the Russians start moving. Chet, take command of coastal defense. Coordinate with the civil authorities."

"The civilians aren't going to be able to help," Admiral Black said, a sour expression on his face.

"We've got plenty of rifles. If someone wants to fight, give them one. We're going to need every body we can muster."

"Aye, sir," Black said, turning and striding out of the CIC.

"Commander!" Packard shouted for one of his aides who was on the far side of the room.

"What's the status of the fallback positions in case the enemy is able to make landfall?"

"Sir, those bunkers were built in World War II. And they were thrown together in a hurry and sat abandoned for seventy years. The concrete is crumbling, the power doesn't work, and there's no water. No comms, either. Half of them were home to all variety of wildlife."

"And?"

"They'll be ready, sir. I've had teams cleaning them out and getting them ready for several weeks. The Marines have been digging in in the hills around them. Dense jungle, and we'll own the high ground. But, if we have to go there, it's going to be primitive."

"Understood, Commander. Just make sure they're ready when we need them."

"They'll be ready, sir."

Packard nodded and turned his attention to Jessica.

"Seaman, is there any chance you can find a way to defeat the Russian's jamming?"

Jessica looked away in thought before answering.

"Maybe, sir. I've studied their tech, but it's been a while since I reviewed any of the data. Theoretically, it's possible. But..."

"No buts, Seaman," Packard said, staring at her.

"I can't do it from here."

She gestured at the console where she was seated and gave the Admiral a timid smile.

"Captain West!" He bellowed without taking his eyes off Jessica.

Packard's senior aide was standing right behind him and answered immediately.

"Captain, I want you to ensure personally that Seaman Simmons is allowed immediate access to any and all systems she may need to utilize, and she is provided with any support she requests."

"I'll make it happen, sir!"

He stepped around the Admiral and bent to speak with Jessica. Packard stepped away as Jessica leapt to her feet and departed the CIC with his aide in tow.

When the Admiral was young, he'd read the history of the battles in the Pacific following the bombing of Pearl Harbor. He'd watched some of the epic movies that chronicled the amazing resilience and determination of the US Navy in defeating the Japanese and protecting the Hawaiian islands and the west coast of the United States.

He'd marveled that all of this had been accomplished in the vast, empty stretches of the Pacific without the benefit of satellite imagery, jet engines, radar or sonar. It had been nothing more than a butt in an airplane seat flying reconnaissance missions, and a bunch of tougher than nails Admirals making decisions that could have won or lost the war for America.

Now, closing in on a century later, he was just as deaf and blind as those same Admirals who had risked everything to stop an enemy fleet. But he had one thing they didn't have. A young woman who had so far managed to work miracles with her keyboard. He just hoped she had one more rabbit left in her hat.

8

Fifteen minutes later we were all gathered in the cafeteria. Gonzales and Nicole sat close together, as did Igor and Irina. Long and Johnson were both stuffing their faces with something they'd found in the kitchen, holding Dog's undivided attention. Rachel, Sam and I found some coffee before sitting down near the middle of the assembled group.

I spoke for a few minutes, relaying the information to them. Though Igor's English was steadily improving, Irina translated for him. She spoke softly, making sure he understood all of the details I was relaying.

As I wrapped up my monolog, Johnson tossed the last bite of his food to Dog and leaned back to rest his boots on the table where he was seated. Dog swallowed without chewing, then waited a moment to see if there were any more tidbits coming his way. With nothing forthcoming, he made the rounds of the room, bumming ear scratches, then flopped down on the tile floor at my feet.

"So, what are we waiting for?" Long asked. "Let's go get Squidward."

Sam and Gonzales both turned to glare at him over the term he used to refer to a sailor.

"What?" He asked innocently when he saw them looking.

"We are," I said, having had time to think this through. "Or at least I am. But I think some of us should stay here and see what else is behind door number 3."

"You think it is a good idea to split up?" Irina asked. "Every time we have, something bad has happened."

I nodded, acknowledging her comment.

"No disrespect to the Master Chief, but he's still healing."

"Sir, I'm good to…"

He stopped when I held a hand up.

"Not open for discussion," I said firmly. "Odds are we'll end up in the water at some point. That's the last thing your wounds need. And, I really don't want to be swimming next to you if one of them opens up, and the sharks get a whiff of blood. Besides, someone that knows how to fight needs to stay behind to protect the rest."

He stared back at me for a beat, his eyes finally sliding to Lieutenant Sam. The SEAL officer nodded his agreement with my decision, even though it wasn't necessary.

"Johnson," I said, turning to face his table. "I want you opening every door and vault you can. Get an inventory of what else is here that we could use. And pay attention to electronics and comm gear. We need to find a way to burn through the Russian jamming. I've got a bad feeling."

"Copy that, sir," Johnson said.

"Irina and Nicole, I'd like it if you would assist him. Catalog what you find if you can make heads or tails of it."

The two women exchanged glances before nodding their agreement.

"Good. Sam, Rachel, Igor, Long, Dog and I will go after the pilot. I'm hoping he's not injured and can fly that thing we found."

Heads nodded all around the room.

"Any questions?"

"What if I open a vault, and there're aliens inside? Do I ask them for help?"

Johnson was grinning as he spoke. Nicole sighed and shook her head.

"Ask them who really killed JFK," Long quipped.

"Might want to make sure they don't have any anal probes," I said, smiling at the look on Johnson's face.

Everyone looked at him and chuckled. He looked like he had a witty reply ready to go, but it was time to get serious.

"OK. Johnson and Gonzales, I saw a bunch of up-armored Humvees in one of the hangars. Get three of them fueled and make sure there's plenty of ammo, food and water on board."

"And a medical kit," Rachel said.

I nodded.

"Everyone who's going, get some chow and put your gear together. I want to be on the road in half an hour. We've got 400 miles to cover, and I want to be out of this valley before dark."

There was silence for a moment, then chairs scraped on the floor as people began moving. Johnson and Gonzales hustled out of the door. Irina grabbed Nicole's arm and spoke to her briefly, getting a nod.

"All of you go get ready," Irina said loud enough for everyone to hear. "We will prepare some food."

I thanked her and headed out into the hall. Everyone that was going to be making the trip fell in behind and followed me to the armory. We spent a few minutes gathering additional weapons and ammo. Igor looked doubtfully at the M4 rifle I handed him, then expertly broke it down for a quick inspection.

"Not good as Russian," he grumbled.

I ignored his complaining and headed for the small room where I'd slept. Dog tagged along, and I quickly gathered my pack and vest. Everything loaded, I returned to the cafeteria.

Irina and Nicole were carrying steaming plates of microwaved food out of the kitchen as I walked in and Dog nearly tripped both of them in his urgency to sniff.

"He's not afraid of me!"

Nicole had stopped in the middle of the room, holding two large plates at shoulder level, out of Dog's reach. He sat in front of her, no more than a foot away, eyes glued to the food and nose twitching.

"He's a food whore," I chuckled and told Dog to go lay down.

He completely ignored me and Nicole finally stepped around him and put the plates down on my table. Rachel was the next to arrive, joining me. The rest of the team trickled in, and we all devoured the mostly tasteless, freeze-dried mystery that passed itself off as a meal. At least it was hot.

Fifteen minutes later, the entire group stood in a large hangar next to three Hummers that Gonzales and Johnson had pulled out. The engines were idling, loud in the cavernous space.

"Orders? In case you don't make it back, sir?" Johnson asked in a low voice as I tossed my pack in the back of the lead vehicle.

"Survive."

I was at a loss for anything more insightful than that. He nodded and stepped away to say goodbye to Long.

Rachel, Dog and I climbed into the first Humvee in line after I had made sure the fuel cans strapped to the rear were full. Long and Igor climbed into the second, Lieutenant Sam riding solo in the third. I performed a quick radio check to make sure we could communicate between the vehicles, then shifted into gear and nodded at Johnson. He hit a button on the wall, and the pair of massive doors began trundling open, late afternoon sunshine streaming through the slowly widening gap.

Rachel waved to Irina, and I drove through as soon as it was wide enough to accommodate the Hummer, glancing in the mirror to make sure Long and Sam were staying tight. Turning north on the almost impossibly long runway, I swerved to run down a pair of males, then accelerated on the smooth pavement.

"Think we can really save this guy?"

Rachel squirmed to get comfortable in her seat. Dog was stretched across the back seat, panting softly and staring out the side window.

"Maybe," I said. "But we've gotta try. Without a pilot, we're pretty much stuck here."

We were quiet for a moment, the tires humming loudly on the tarmac.

"That sounded wrong," I said. "That's not why I'm doing this. I'd go after him even if he couldn't fly a plane."

"I know that."

Rachel smiled and reached over, placing her hand on my shoulder. Dog shuffled around and a moment later thrust his head between the front seats, knocking Rachel's hand with his muzzle. She absently scratched his ears as I drove. Well, some things hadn't changed.

9

We followed a well-maintained dirt road that cut through the desert north of the installation. Every few miles we would pass a sign facing southbound traffic that warned drivers they were trespassing on US Government property and were subject to arrest. The road followed a track at the base of a small mountain range and frequently there were electronic surveillance devices visible on the slope overlooking us.

"What was Johnson talking about? Aliens?" Rachel asked after half an hour.

"Seriously?"

"Yeah. What?"

"Area 51? You've never heard of it?"

I looked at her in surprise. It was hard to imagine that there was a person that hadn't heard at least something about the place. It had been a staple in fiction novels and movies for decades.

"Nope," she shook her head. "Never had much time for, or interest in, TV or books. Kind of hard to waste hours in front of the boob tube when you're in medical school."

"Still…"

"I was a nerd," Rachel smiled. "All I did was study, go to class and go to work."

"OK," I said, my voice trailing off.

"What?"

"Nothing."

"Bite me."

Rachel smiled, began laughing and smacked me on the arm.

"Of course, I've heard of Area 51," she said. "What'd you think? I lived under a rock?"

I just shook my head, not willing to get sucked any further in.

We pushed on at a steady fifty miles an hour. I'd given up checking the rear-view for Long and Sam. The Humvee's tires were throwing up so much dust that they'd backed way off, and I couldn't see them. Glancing at a cheap, digital clock stuck to the dash, I noted it had been ten minutes since the last check-in. I called each of them on the radio, satisfying myself they were still back there.

"Sir, did you know that both the car and the airplane were actually invented in Russia?" Long asked when I called him.

I rolled my eyes and didn't bother to respond. Apparently, he was managing to communicate with Igor.

Twenty minutes later I slowed as we drove across a cattle guard that protected a narrow, paved highway. Turning south, I accelerated past a sign that welcomed us to Rachel, Nevada.

"Good town," Rachel said, deadpan.

"They've probably never heard of Area 51, either."

"And they're probably stunningly beautiful with well above average intelligence."

"Must be aliens, then."

That earned me another smack, then I had to focus on my driving as a small group of males stumbled from behind a building and onto the highway. The heavy grill guard bulled them aside, then I was able to push our speed up to 60. The wheel vibrated, and the whole vehicle squirmed side to side. Not too bad, but it was going to be a damn long 400 miles.

"We aren't going through there, I hope," Rachel said, hooking her thumb at the side of the road.

We had just passed a sign that said Las Vegas was 137 miles.

"Don't know how much choice we're going to have," I said. "This is a pretty desolate area. Not a lot of roads that don't go through Vegas. I'm planning to stop in the next town to find a map."

Rachel nodded, looking around at the bleak landscape. The sun was setting, painting the desert with a golden light. Other than the asphalt, there wasn't a single indication of civilization. It was going to be a very dark night.

The town was tiny, and we were through it in only a couple of minutes. There was nothing ahead or to either side of the road other than stark, empty desert. Rachel watched the landscape as the light began to fade, leaning back in her seat and sighing.

"What?" I asked, checking in the mirror to make sure Long and Sam were close.

"It's so bleak. Barren. It's... I don't know. Spooky?"

"Really? This feels like home to me."

"How do you stand it without some green? Some trees, or even some bushes and grass?"

Fulcrum

"Guess it's what you're used to," I said. "I grew up in west Texas, which is just as desolate as this, and Arizona isn't any different. I actually prefer this to a forest. At least here, you can see what's coming for you before it's in your face."

Rachel thought about that for a minute, scratching Dog's head as she kept looking around.

"You've spent a lot of time in forests, though. Right?"

I nodded as I answered.

"Yep. Jungles, actually. Central America. Africa a little bit. Wherever there was something going on that needed a little special attention. And there were a few deserts thrown in for good measure. Personally, I'll take the deserts. Can't stand all the bugs that live in jungles, and I'm not a fan of humidity."

"What about snakes and scorpions and spiders? I thought the desert was full of them?"

"They're there. But I wouldn't say *full*. And you learn to look before you step or sit. Generally, there's nothing in the desert that will come after you. Leave it alone, it'll leave you alone. Just remember rule number one."

"What's that?" She asked, turning to look at me.

"Never put on a pair of boots that you haven't shaken out. Scorpions like tight, dark places, like the inside of a boot."

"I've noticed you do that. Thought it was just some kind of ritual, knocking them against something like that."

"Nope," I shook my head. "I was maybe five years old when I learned that lesson. Was messing around in my parents' closet and thought I'd put on Dad's boots. Just stuck my feet in. Scorpion got me on my big toe. That's one of those mistakes you'll only ever make once in your life."

"How bad are the stings?"

"Bad enough, if you aren't allergic. You'll be in pretty bad pain for a week. If you have an allergy, like to bee stings, it can kill you quick."

Rachel shuddered and fell silent. The light was fading fast, and I lowered the pair of night vision goggles I'd taken from the armory. We were going to run dark and hopefully not draw the attention of any passing Russian planes. Sure, they'd spot us if they were using a thermal scanner, but unless they were out patrolling specifically for vehicle traffic, we'd probably go unnoticed. At least, that's what I hoped.

Fulcrum

We drove for another half an hour without seeing a single sign of civilization, other than a lone road sign. Rachel had settled in and seemed to be on the verge of drifting off. Dog had retreated to the rear seat and was on his back, legs up in the air, snoring loud enough that I was sure the windows were vibrating.

"Major!"

Long's voice in my radio earpiece startled me out of the near hypnotic state I was in from driving.

"Go," I answered.

"You got a civilian radio in your vehicle?"

I glanced around but didn't spot one. They weren't standard equipment in military vehicles, but a lot of the guys would strap a cheap boom-box in for a little entertainment on long patrols.

"Negative. What's up?"

"You should hear this."

"Copy. We're stopping."

I lightly touched the brakes and slowed the Humvee, staying in the middle of the road. Rachel sat up straight and looked around.

"What's going on?"

"Long's got something on a civilian radio frequency he wants me to hear."

Dog woke up and scrambled to his feet as the vehicle came to a stop. I left the engine running and looked all around before opening the door and stepping out, my rifle in my hands. Rachel and Dog followed a moment later.

Long had stopped within a couple of feet of my back bumper, Sam tight behind him. The SEAL officer stepped out when he saw me, scanned the area behind us, then walked forward to meet at the middle vehicle.

The armored window was slid open, and I could hear a voice as I approached Long's Hummer. He and Igor stayed inside, staring at a small radio that was rubber banded to a grab bar. The voice was slightly static covered, but clear enough to tell it was an English speaking woman.

"... will repeat."

I only heard those two words, then there was nothing but static.

"What was that?" I asked.

Long held up a finger to tell me to hang on, keeping his attention focused on the radio. A few seconds later, the voice returned.

Fulcrum

"We have moved to sector five. Sectors one, three, four and six are overrun. Charlie and Delta are in sector two. All units report at designated times. This message will repeat."

"How long have you been hearing that?" I asked.

"Found it just before I called you," Long answered.

The voice returned, and we all listened as the same message was repeated.

Sam turned and scanned around us.

"What the hell is it?" Rachel asked.

"Did it just start up, or were you rolling through channels and found it?" I asked, ignoring Rachel for the moment.

"Igor was rolling through," Long said.

The message started again. I listened closely, trying to tell if it was a live broadcast and the woman was repeating herself, or if it was taped and on a loop. This time, she paused in a different spot to take a breath. The same words but they were being broadcast live.

She finished speaking, and we stared at the radio, waiting for her to start again. This time, she didn't. Instead, there was a sudden increase in static as the transmitter went off the air. I checked on Sam, who was still keeping watch.

"Survivors?" Rachel asked.

I shrugged, standing there in the dark and thinking.

"They have to be close, right? For us to hear them?"

"Not necessarily," I said. "AM radio and the sun is down. That transmission could be coming from hundreds of miles away, especially now when there aren't any competing signals."

"Or, they could be in the next town," Sam said without taking his focus off the surrounding desert.

"Right," I said.

"Any chance it's military?" Rachel asked.

"Possible," I acknowledged. "But I doubt it. There's more than enough radio gear lying around that's in good working order."

"And this is a one-way broadcast," Long said. "There's no way to answer. But she's telling units to check in. That means they've got two-way comms. So why the hell are they transmitting in the clear?"

I shook my head again. It didn't make any sense to me. But it did make me nervous. We were approaching Vegas. If there was somehow a group that had survived the virus and the infected, they might be a problem. There was no reason to think they'd be friendly at this point.

"She said *report*," Sam said. "We may be wrong in assuming they are going to do that over a radio. Maybe they don't have any comm gear and all they can do is listen for a broadcast and take action on what they're told."

"Then how do they report?" Rachel asked.

"Maybe they send a runner. Or flash a light. There're all kinds of ways to communicate," I said, thinking about what Sam had just said. And agreeing with him.

"OK," I said after another minute of thought. "This doesn't change anything. We've still got a man to rescue. Next town is Crystal Springs. I'm going to stop if I see someplace that looks like it'll have a road map. Stay tight and keep your eyes open. Let me know if there are any more broadcasts."

Sam and Long nodded, the SEAL heading back to his waiting vehicle. Rachel, Dog and I piled in our Humvee, quickly getting back up to speed.

Fulcrum

We reached Crystal Springs in less than fifteen minutes. It was slightly larger than the last town, sitting astride the junction of two minor highways. No infected greeted us as we passed a faded welcome sign. Everything was dark and abandoned.

"Keep your eyes moving," I said to Rachel in a low voice.

She was wearing a set of night vision goggles. Between us, there shouldn't be much we couldn't see.

I slowed as we approached an intersection with a road sign pointing the way to Vegas. Beyond, a small truck stop loomed in the night. Driving through the intersection, I wheeled into its lot and came to a stop a hundred yards from the closest building. Taking my time, I slowly scanned the entire area.

"Front's clear," I transmitted after checking to see if Rachel had spotted anything.

Long and Sam responded in turn, neither of them seeing anything of concern.

"Dismount," I ordered, shutting the engine off.

We all got out, meeting next to the middle Hummer. Dog's nose was up, testing the air. I paused a moment, giving him time, but he just kept sniffing without indicating there were any infected in the area.

"Long and Igor, stay with the vehicles," I said. "The rest of us, let's see if there's a map inside."

I would have preferred to have everyone stay together, especially in the event we ran into any problems, but I wasn't about to leave the Humvees unguarded. All you have to do to start one is turn a small lever, and it would take a matter of seconds for one, or all, to be stolen. There are normally steel cables, mounted to the dash, that can lock the steering wheel in place and prevent theft, but for some reason, they had been removed from these. So someone needed to keep an eye on them.

I led the way across the lot, Dog close to my side. Rachel was right behind us, Sam hanging back a few yards and covering our rear. The dark building ahead was small, large panes of glass looking out over the fueling area of the truck stop. There weren't any vehicles at the pumps, but in a large, dirt lot to the side were half a dozen abandoned 18 wheelers.

As we approached, the night vision allowed me to see the interior of the building. Everything appeared orderly. Whatever the locals were doing when the virus hit, they apparently hadn't been inside.

Fulcrum

Reaching a pair of glass doors, I paused and stared inside. Nothing was moving. There were a dozen rows of merchandise, as well as glass fronted chillers stocked with beverages. A small register area was right next to the doors. I could see a display for road atlases.

Signing for Rachel and Sam to stay put, I gently tugged on the door. It didn't budge, which surprised me. The people here had enough advance warning to lock up and leave. Maybe because the area was so isolated.

Taking a step back, I fired a couple of bursts from the suppressed rifle through the safety glass in the door. The entire pane shattered but was held in place by the layer of tough plastic. I kicked it out and paused long enough to make sure there wasn't an infected inside the building that was coming to greet me. Still seeing nothing, I stepped through, snatched an atlas off the counter and ducked back out into the night.

"Light to the east, on top of the ridge."

Long's voice over the radio jolted me, and I spun to look in the direction he'd indicated. The cover over the gas pumps blocked my view, and I quickly moved to an area that had a clear line of sight. And didn't see anything. I waited a few seconds, scanning back and forth, but couldn't spot it.

"Negative visual," I said, not taking my eyes off the ridge.

"It's gone now," he replied. "Only saw it for a few seconds. Series of quick flashes, then it went dark."

I turned around and looked to the west. Half expected to see an answering signal, but after nearly a minute of watching I turned back to the east.

"Let's move," I mumbled to Rachel and Sam.

We hustled back to the waiting vehicles. Igor had taken the sniper rifle I had been using at Groom Lake and was peering through the thermal scope at the ridgeline to the east.

"See anything?" I asked, stepping up next to him.

"Nyet," he said without taking his eye away from the scope.

I checked to the west again, then turned a slow circle, looking for anything that was out of place in the barren moonscape of the Nevada desert. Nothing.

"We'd better get on the road," I said, not liking the situation even one little bit.

Fulcrum

We all climbed into our vehicles, the engines starting in near unison. Hitting the throttle, I led the way onto the road that headed south to Vegas.

"Keep your eyes on the desert," I said to Rachel, glancing over my shoulder at the ridge. "Don't worry about the road. If we're going to have a problem, it'll come from the sides."

By now we were at maximum speed, barely over 60 miles an hour.

"Think it's Russians?" Rachel asked, her head slowly traversing across the surrounding terrain.

"Possible, but I don't think so," I said, shaking my head. "With that broadcast, I think we've found some survivors, and I think they've found us."

Rachel glanced at me for a brief second, then resumed her scan of the surrounding terrain.

"Long. Copy?" I called on the radio.

"Go."

"Have your passenger see if he can raise the rest of our party on the radio. Tell him to use his native tongue and speak to the blonde woman. Warn them of probable hostiles in the area."

"Copy that," he replied a moment later.

"You think they're listening in?" Rachel asked.

"Not going to take the chance," I said.

Rachel nodded and didn't say anything else. Dog, picking up on our tension, had his nose pressed against the side window behind Rachel, staring out into the darkness. I was opening my mouth to ask her to reach back and slide the window open so he could smell the night air when a loud bang sounded on the window right next to my head.

"Taking fire!"

I shouted on the radio and pressed harder on the accelerator. The damn pedal was already tight to the floor. There was the sound of another impact somewhere on my side of the vehicle.

"What the hell is that?" Rachel shouted, wildly looking around.

"Bullets!"

I began cranking the wheel, whipping the ungainly Humvee back and forth across the highway. Hopefully, this would make it harder for the sniper to zero in.

"I'm taking fire, too!"

Sam's voice over the radio, then a second later Long confirmed he was being shot at. As I continued to try and make us a more difficult target, a part of my brain acknowledged that whoever was shooting at us was one hell of a shot. A vehicle moving at 60 miles an hour, at night, and he'd put a round directly on my side window. If it wasn't for the additional armor, he'd have taken my head off.

"Got movement!"

I looked at Rachel, then through her side window. A couple of hundred yards away, a jacked up Chevy pickup was racing across the desert on an intercept course with us. It was running blacked out, and I couldn't tell if the driver had night vision or was just winging it in the moonlight.

"Contact at my three!" I shouted over the radio. "Long, tell Igor to take them out!"

"Copy," came a quick response.

It was only seconds later when the Chevy suddenly swerved hard to its left. The front tires dug into the soft sand, then it went airborne and cartwheeled several times, disappearing in a huge cloud of dust. Igor must have shot out a front tire with the rifle.

"Contact on Sam!" Came over the radio almost immediately. "Two vehicles on my six, closing fast."

"I'm slowing! Change places!" Long called.

In the rearview, I saw Sam swerve into the oncoming lane and stay there, the nose of Long's Hummer dipping as he hit the brakes. He was positioning himself for Igor to fire on the pursuing vehicles, but I couldn't watch. Ahead, a large truck completely blocked the road.

The Governor of Hawaii stood at the entrance to a massive tunnel cut into the side of Mt. Kaala. He was accompanying a young Navy Commander named Meghan Glass. She had been assigned by Admiral Packard to coordinate defensive efforts with the civilian authorities.

Mt. Kaala is the highest point on Oahu, near the western edge of the island. On the eastern side is Schofield Barracks, an Army base. The west side slopes down to the northwestern beaches and is heavily forested with tropical vegetation.

The tunnels were left over from World War II, leading into bunkers housed deep within the mountain. At the peak, with a commanding view of miles upon miles of coastline, were a multitude of abandoned coastal defense battery stations. In their day, most housed 155 mm guns, but now they were empty and overgrown.

"This is going to be a target for the Russians."

The Governor's voice was whiny as he stepped farther away from the gravel road. A large truck carrying an anti-aircraft missile battery rumbled past and into the tunnel. Behind it was a long line of heavily laden trucks, grinding their way up the primitive trail that was carved into the side of the mountain.

"Yes, sir. It probably will, but there will only be military personnel inside. You and your staff will be in Battery 405. It's 200 feet below ground and will probably be the safest place."

"Then we should go there," the Governor said, sounding relieved. "I don't know why you're bothering to show this to me."

Glass took a deep breath, trying to hide her exasperation with the man. The Admiral had asked her to give him a quick tour of the defenses that were being set up to protect the island, but the Governor seemed only to be concerned about his personal safety. Not once had he brought up the topic of the plight of the civilian population during the coming Russian invasion.

"I'll take you there next, sir," she said in a tight, professional voice. "But we have to wait until these trucks have cleared the road. There's no other way down."

"Can't you have a helicopter or something come get us?"

She looked at the man. At the obvious fear on his face.

"No, sir. There aren't any available."

Fulcrum

As if to punctuate her statement, a flight of several Apache helicopters roared overhead. They were escorting a dozen heavily laden Chinooks that were transporting equipment and personnel from Pearl Harbor to the mountain top. Turning away, she looked out at the ocean stretching away from the island.

Hundreds of boats of every size carved white scars into the blue water. The other islands were being evacuated, the people being consolidated on Oahu. There weren't enough ships, planes or men remaining to defend all of the islands in the chain. Meghan didn't think there were enough to protect the one island which was the last outpost of America.

It was only a few minutes later when one of the trucks ground to a halt next to where she was standing. A large radar antenna rested in its bed. The passenger door opened, and three men who had been crammed into the cab climbed down. With a grinding of gears, the truck moved away, and they quickly crossed the gravel track to where she was standing.

Glass came to attention when she saw the eagle on the Army uniform of the man leading the way. He waved at her to relax as he walked up to face her.

"Colonel Blanchard," he said.

"Sir. Commander Glass," she responded, taking his outstretched hand.

The quarantine that had been imposed on Blanchard and the troops he'd brought from Nevada had ended as soon as Packard saw what the Russians were planning. The Admiral had placed the Colonel in charge of the island's ground defenses.

"Are you in charge here, Commander?"

"No, sir. I'm escorting the Governor on a quick tour of our preparations."

Blanchard's eyes slid over her shoulder and took in the nervous man standing a few feet away. As quickly as he looked, he dismissed him and returned his attention to the naval officer.

"Carry on, Commander," he said.

Turning, he looked into the tunnel, then stepped close to Colonel Pointere, who had a large pair of binoculars pressed to his eyes as he surveyed the surrounding jungle.

"Brutal terrain," Blanchard commented.

"Damn brutal. For the fucking Commies," Pointere growled, then lowered the glasses and raised his arm to point. "We put men all along the top of these two ridgelines. That gives us control of the valley leading up here."

Blanchard took a moment to look over the terrain, then nodded.

"Agreed. But, we've got seven more locations to defend, plus Battery 405 and the harbor."

"We're going to be thin on the ground, that's for sure," Pointere said. "At least we've got plenty of arms and munitions."

"OK. Let's use your Marines for the static defensive positions. We can supplement with Navy and Air Force. Use them for observation and runners. I'll have some Rangers down in the valley. They'll set up some surprises for our guests and keep them harassed so they can't move fast."

Blanchard turned to the third man in the group. He was a Navy Captain, wearing a SEAL trident on his uniform.

"Captain, I'm rethinking your suggestion, and I agree with you. SEALs planting mines on the Russian ships. There's just not enough of you to make a difference in the jungle, but if you can clog up the harbor with burning enemy ships, it'll make it damn difficult for them to keep landing troops."

The man smiled and lowered the binoculars he was using to survey the harbor below.

"Figured you'd come around," he chuckled. "I already told my men that's what they were doing. They'll be ready."

"Good," Blanchard said without hesitating. "Colonel, get orders issued to your Marines and let's move. I want a look at Battery 405, then the north shore."

"You're going to Battery 405? Can I get a ride with you?"

The three men turned to see that the Governor had stepped close behind them. Blanchard glanced at Commander Glass before looking back at the man.

"Shouldn't you be coordinating with your state police or something? Get your civilians someplace safe? Arm the ones that can fight?" Blanchard asked.

"My aides are handling that," the man said in a pompous tone. "I'm supposed to be evacuated to the shelter."

Blanchard sighed and turned his back on the man. Pointere and the SEAL officer had already moved away, radios pressed to their ears as they issued orders. The Colonel called his aide who was on his way in a Black Hawk. When he arrived, the Captain would take command of the installation's defenses. Blanchard and the two officers would depart in the Black Hawk.

The Colonel had just lowered his handset when the radio beeped. Answering it, he didn't like the news coming from the CIC at Pearl Harbor.

"Russians have sailed from Midway," he said after the call completed.

"How long?" Pointere asked.

"Forty hours at their present speed," Blanchard said. "We've got a crippled carrier, two Aegis cruisers and an attack sub going to engage them in a few hours. Try and slow them down, but we're severely outgunned."

The three men looked up as a Black Hawk swooped over the top of the mountain and came into a hover over their position. They were standing on a slope, and there was nowhere for it to land.

A moment later a crewman looked down before tossing a heavy bag through the open side door. A thick, fast-rope line unspooled as it fell, thumping onto the edge of the gravel track. A man appeared at the opening, sliding down and stepping away. He was quickly followed by three more soldiers. The crewman leaned out again, then started pulling the rope back into the hovering Black Hawk.

Blanchard spoke briefly with the Captain and a Lieutenant, both men turning and jumping onto the running board of a passing truck. They would set up a command post within the mountain. The two men remaining stepped forward when the Colonel looked in their direction.

"How do you two keep turning up?" He asked with a grin.

Drago and Chico both shrugged their shoulders and smiled back at him.

"OK," Blanchard said, getting serious. "We've got to defend this approach. The Marines are going to take the ridgelines on either side of the valley. When the squads show up, start setting up some welcome presents. You got into the armory without any problems?"

"Yes, sir," Drago said. "One thing about Hawaii, it's well stocked. We've got enough to keep them bogged down for a while."

"Make it happen," Blanchard said. "Captain Forest is in command until I get back."

"Yes, sir," Drago said.

He and Chico turned away and headed down the steep slope. Within seconds, they had completely disappeared in the thick foliage.

Blanchard looked up as Pointere was helped into the helicopter by a crewman. He'd been winched up once the fast-rope was clear. The steel cable immediately started back down to pick up the next passenger.

"I have to go up that?"

The Governor stepped forward and grabbed Blanchard's arm. The Colonel calmly reached over and removed his hand. The cable had made it back to the ground, and the SEAL officer stepped into the harness and twirled his hand at the watching crewman.

"No," Blanchard said. "I'm sure there's a vehicle coming."

The man looked at him in surprise, his mouth hanging open for a beat.

"I was promised I'd be taken to the shelter," he shouted. "I demand you take me with you!"

"Military only in the aircraft," Blanchard said, stepping forward to snag the harness swinging at the end of the cable.

"Admiral Packard will hear about this!"

The Colonel bit back a less than respectful response as he snugged the harness around his hips, grabbed the cable with one hand and twirled the other.

"What was that all about?" Pointere asked when Blanchard stepped into the Black Hawk.

"Threatening to call the Admiral if I didn't bring him with us."

"Fuck him," the SEAL said. "Goddamn politician!"

"Should have brought him," Pointere said.

"You serious?" Blanchard and the SEAL both asked in surprise.

"Sure. We could have thrown his ass out the door, over the ocean, and told everyone he slipped."

12

"What else can we throw at them, Captain?"

Admiral Packard was standing in Pearl Harbor's CIC, feet spread as if he were astride the heaving deck of a ship at sea.

"Sir, we've got two Coast Guard cutters and an Arleigh Burke class destroyer that's barely sea-worthy. Other than that, everything still floating is too far away to reach us in time. The bastards truly caught us with our pants around our ankles."

Packard nodded, glaring at a massive display that showed the current position of every American ship on the globe. Well, the best guess current position. Since the Russians had begun jamming their communication signals, the CIC was no longer getting a constant feed from every Navy asset that was in service.

Arrayed across the screen, and still over a thousand miles to the northwest of Oahu, was the Russian fleet. And there were a lot of ships. A squadron of Marine pilots had flown a daring reconnaissance mission, all but one of them falling prey to the CAP being flown over the enemy armada. The final man had managed to evade and escape, making it most of the way back to Hawaii before running out of fuel.

He'd punched out of the aircraft and been picked up by a small Coast Guard boat. The crew had taken the 25-foot craft, intended for use in the protected waters of bays and harbors, over two hundred miles out into the open ocean to retrieve the downed pilot. His report on the positioning of the fleet, and observed speed and heading, was the basis for the plotting of the enemy on the display.

"How long until Falcon flight is over their fleet?"

"Estimated thirty minutes, sir. We lost comms with them as soon as they were out of line of sight."

"Any progress on finding the source of the jamming?"

The Captain shook his head.

"No, sir. Our senior engineer's best guess is it's orbital. But we can't pinpoint a satellite if it is."

Packard took a deep breath to compose himself. Frustration threatened to overwhelm him, but he managed to push it aside. For a commander who had always been able to depend on instant communications and satellite surveillance, the situation he found himself in was maddening. It was only a step above fighting with a blindfold.

"Captain, find me the moment we get any update on the status of Falcon," the Admiral said, turning and stalking out of the CIC.

"Yes, sir," the man said, struggling with his own frustration.

Falcon flight was four B-2 stealth bombers, escorted by two squadrons of Navy F-18s. The bombers each carried a payload of airburst, chemical dispersion bombs that were loaded with MX-489 nerve agent.

Once they reached the Russian fleet, they would drop their payloads, which would detonate at 1,000 feet over the surface of the ocean. An atomized mist of nerve agent would then drift down over the enemy ships. Admiral Packard didn't hold out much hope for the success of the mission, but he had to use every tool at his disposal.

There were numerous civilian cargo ships in the fleet, almost certainly loaded down with ground troops and equipment, but there were also many warships. Unless the Americans got incredibly lucky, they'd just seal all their hatches and ignore the deadly, chemical rain. Once the last bomb delivered its contents, all they'd have to do would be to follow standard decontamination procedures. The same process for dealing with the presence of radioactive fallout.

Massive pumps would be started, sucking in thousands of gallons of seawater. From dozens of strategically placed nozzles all around the exterior of each ship, high-pressure water would rinse the vessel clean of the nerve agent. Packard's hope was the chemical would have a chance to reach the interior of the ships before the captains realized what was happening. But it was a slim hope.

Striding beside the manicured lawns of the sprawling naval base, the Admiral headed for the giant building that housed the equipment and personnel responsible for the secure communications networks on which the US Navy relied. Reaching the entrance to the facility, he, and his six heavily armed Marine guards, breezed through security without breaking stride.

Several floors below ground, he barged into a cold, dark room filled with computer terminals and several dozen sailors sitting idle. The first one to spot him shot to his feet and shouted that there was an *Admiral on deck*. The rest of the room immediately fell silent and leapt to their feet, all except for one person.

Fulcrum

Packard's eyes zeroed in on Jessica, and he quickly made his way to where she was bent over a multi-screen terminal. Several manuals were open on the work surface, and she was intently peering at one of the screens. His senior aide, Captain West, stood as the Admiral approached.

"Any progress?" Packard asked quietly.

Captain West tilted his head in Jessica's direction.

"Not yet, sir," Jessica said without looking away from the monitor. "But, I've got an idea."

"Tell me, Seaman."

"Well, sir," Jessica said slowly as she leaned back and looked up at Packard. "I've learned a few things. First off, this isn't frequency jamming, like we thought. The Russians aren't flooding the EM spectrum with radio energy to block our comms. This is much more sophisticated."

"Explain," the Admiral said, a small bloom of optimism warming his chest.

"This is some sort of cyber-attack, sir. Are you familiar with the old FLTSAT network?"

"The satellite network from the 80s?"

"That's the one, sir. It was abandoned because some Brazilian ham radio operator found a way to break in and use the satellites to re-broadcast his signal all around the world. Well, believe it or not, some of those birds are apparently still up there. And operational. That's how the Russians got in."

"Are you kidding me?" Packard exploded.

Lack of sleep and mounting frustration finally got the best of him.

"I wish I was, sir," Jessica said, not at all perturbed by his outburst.

"Captain," he said, turning to West. "We still have anti-sat capabilities, correct?"

"Excuse me sir, but that won't help," Jessica interrupted before West could respond. "They aren't connected in or anything. They broke in, planted a worm in the software that controls all of our comms, then got out. That's the problem. The damage is done. Taking the satellites out won't have any impact."

"It will keep them from doing it again, once you fix this. Right?"

"Yes, sir. If I can fix it."

Packard looked at her a moment before turning to Captain West.

"Issue the orders. Identify and destroy all of the legacy FLTSAT birds."

"Sorry, sir. Our remaining ships with anti-satellite capabilities are too far away to communicate with. There's no way to contact them."

The Admiral took a deep breath and turned back to Jessica.

"Seaman. How long will it take you to fix this?"

"I literally just identified the issue, sir. I don't know how deep the worm has gotten. Our first step is going to be to dump the entire operating system and restore from the last *known good* backup."

"Will that restore our comms?"

"Maybe. Theoretically, yes. But I've seen some pretty inventive stuff come out of the Russians in the past couple of years. However, it's our first logical step."

"Well, by all means, don't let me delay you further," Packard said. "Captain, I want an hourly status update. Again, whatever resources the Seaman needs, she gets."

"Yes, sir. I'm staying by her side," Captain West answered.

13

"Road's blocked! Stay on my ass!"

I shouted into the radio as soon as I saw the truck parked across the pavement. Cranking the wheel to the right, we went airborne for a moment when the Humvee blasted over the low berm that bordered the road. Dog bounced around the back seat like a ping-pong ball as we came down and began roaring across the desert. There were multiple, loud impacts from bullets striking the vehicle's armored hide, and I hoped they didn't get a lucky shot on a tire.

"They're with us!"

Rachel was twisted around, looking through the rear window to make sure Long and Sam weren't being left behind. That was good, as I couldn't take my attention off the terrain. Thankfully, I was wearing night vision goggles that let me see as if it were the middle of the day. Holes, ravines, large rocks and occasional stunted trees would have caused us a serious problem if I hadn't been able to spot them in time.

The ride was rough, but this was what Hummers were made for. I steered at a ninety-degree angle to the highway, heading away from our ambushers. Keeping my foot on the floor, the engine roared as I cut through the sand at 50 miles an hour. I had no idea who was attacking us, or why. Right now, we needed to open some distance.

"Are they following?"

I had to shout to be heard over the bellowing engine and roar of the sand that was being thrown against the undercarriage by the tires.

"Yes," Rachel said after a moment. "But they're losing ground. They can't keep up."

I breathed a small sigh of relief. There are a handful of civilian vehicles that can stay with a Hummer across desert terrain, but there aren't many. And they're pretty damn expensive. Not that these guys probably didn't have their pick of vehicles that had been left abandoned, but I wasn't going to complain that we had an edge. But it sure would have been nice to have the grenade machine gun I'd used at Offutt Air Force Base.

My attention was focused on the ground directly in front of the vehicle, and on battling the wheel as we jolted across the uneven desert. When I looked up, I slammed the brakes on and cut the wheel hard to the side. Rachel and Dog were both thrown forward, several un-lady-like curses, and a couple of yelps, loud in my ear.

The Hummer came to a stop, dust boiling around us and obscuring our view. There was a hard bump as one of the two following vehicles came to a stop with its front bumper crashed against us.

"What the hell?" Rachel shouted.

"Big canyon. Damn near drove off a cliff!"

I shoved my door open and jumped out. My hands automatically brought the rifle up into low ready as I moved through the dust cloud to the other two vehicles. There wasn't any breeze and the damn stuff was taking its own sweet time before clearing.

"What the fuck, sir?"

Long and Igor loomed suddenly in the blinding dust. Sam ran up from the side.

"Big ass canyon," I said, hooking a thumb over my shoulder. "We're cut off."

I led the way a few yards to where the dust was thinner and looked to the east. Half a dozen sets of headlights were approaching, bouncing up and down as the vehicles navigated the rough terrain. Sam ran to the edge of the canyon, and after a few moments of looking around returned to where we were standing. Rachel and Dog had joined us.

"Not going that way," Sam said. "It's running for as far as I can see in each direction."

"There a way down?" I asked, eyes glued to the approaching headlights.

"Not in a vehicle. Slope's damn near vertical."

"That's why they're not in any hurry," Long said. "Must know it's here."

I nodded, then turned and looked at the three Hummers.

"Long and Igor," I said. "Get these parked in a wedge. Igor, up on the roof with the sniper rifle. Sam, flank right, I'll take left. On my order, we take these fuckers out."

Everyone nodded, Long and Igor dashing to the closest vehicles and starting their engines. Sam ran off into the desert, and I turned and led Rachel and Dog to the left. I was counting on these guys not having gotten their hands on any night vision. Hopefully, since they were driving with their lights on, they hadn't. Otherwise, they'd see Sam and me heading out to set up flanking fire.

One hundred yards to the left, I stopped behind a small outcropping of boulders. They stuck up from the sand like some giant had been playing marbles and just left them there. Dog hesitated, looking at the base of the rocks and growling. A second later, I heard the warning sound of a rattlesnake. Rachel let out a gasp of fright and jumped back.

It took me a moment to spot the little bastard. He was curled up beneath a small growth of sagebrush, only a few inches of his tail out in the open. Scooping up a fist-sized rock, I tossed it into the bush, then followed it with another. I was reaching for a third when the snake slithered into view, turned away from us and quickly retreated into the desert.

Hurrying forward, I knelt behind the rocks, Dog joining me. I looked around in surprise when Rachel didn't kneel down on the other side of me.

"Get over here!" I hissed.

"There might be another," she said, fear in her voice.

"Probably not, since Dog is OK," I said in exasperation, looking back at the headlights. They were getting close. "Now get down before they see you."

A few seconds later, Rachel moved so that she was crouched down behind Dog. Several sarcastic comments came to mind, but I kept my mouth shut and focused on our pursuers.

Fulcrum

"I'm in position," I said over the radio.

Sam confirmed he was ready, then Long answered for both he and Igor.

"I count eight vehicles," I said. "Don't have eyes on occupants."

Sam and Long confirmed they didn't see anything different.

I watched for another few seconds. The sound of the engines was loud in the still desert air, dust swirling in the wake of the trucks and Jeeps. They slowed when they were close enough to pick out the stopped Hummers in their headlights. Soon, they were only moving at an idle, spreading out in a line to make use of all of their lights. I waited until they were abreast of my hiding place.

"Igor, take out the drivers," I said, pulling my rifle tighter against my shoulder.

The big rifle was suppressed, and I couldn't hear the report over the noise coming from the vehicles. My first indication that he had started shooting was when men began leaping out of one of the trucks and shouting that they were being shot at.

I knew Igor wouldn't be able to see the drivers behind the glare of the headlights, but that didn't really matter. All he needed to do was put a round through the windshield where a driver would be sitting. And I was pretty sure that was what he did. Quickly and efficiently.

Two of the trucks swerved towards each other, fenders crunching as they came to a stop. More men began leaping out of cabs as other vehicles changed course and slowly idled away. Soon they began firing in the direction of the Hummers, the reports from all variety of rifles harsh on the night air.

"Sam, open fire," I said, squeezing my rifle's trigger.

I'd like to say it was a battle. Or, at least a fight. It wasn't. It was wholesale slaughter. One vehicle almost got away, but Igor made an improbable shot on the driver, and it crashed against a large rock. All the rest were hit, the trucks coming to a stop when they idled into softer sand or a depression in the ground.

The men that jumped out and started firing at Igor and Long's position didn't know enough even to go prone and reduce their profile. They just stood in the open and fired blindly at our vehicles.

Sam and I methodically worked our way through them, our suppressed rifles unheard by our targets. Quickly, there were only three men still standing. One of them looked around at all the bodies on the sand, and I had a perfect view of his face through my scope. He was terrified. Almost all of his friends had died in less than a minute, and he hadn't heard anything other than his own weapon.

"Cease fire!" I called on the radio.

The three men that were still standing had thrown their weapons onto the ground and raised their hands in the air. An eerie silence descended over the desert in the absence of gunfire. Other than the idling of the vehicles that were still running, it was quiet.

"I count three targets surrendering. All others down," I said into the radio.

"Confirmed," Sam said.

"Da," Igor answered after a long pause.

"Everyone stay put, and watch my ass," I said. "I'm advancing on the targets."

When I received three confirmations, I stood and stepped around the rocks, my rifle trained on the men. Dog moved with me, tight against my left hip, Rachel bringing up the rear.

"Move and you're dead," I shouted before stepping into the light of the closest vehicle.

Dirk Patton

Their heads swiveled in my direction, but I was still masked by the night. I took my time advancing, checking each body I encountered. My focus wasn't on the three men with their hands high in the air. I trusted Igor, Long, and Sam to put them down instantly if any one of them made a grab for a weapon.

The third man I checked was still alive. Barely, but his eyes were open, and blood was trickling out of his mouth and across his chin. He must have taken a bullet through a lung. I pointed my rifle at his head and pulled the trigger. It was a bit of mercy, but mostly I didn't want him behind me on the off chance he could summon up enough energy to pick up a rifle and start shooting.

Several more bodies, all dead, and I moved into the light and stopped ten yards in front of the men. Dog stayed close, Rachel moving to my right.

"Tell Rachel move," Igor said over the radio. "She in way."

I glanced around and gestured for her to step to the side. To her credit, she did as I asked without questioning why. I made a mental note to talk to her about making sure she didn't step into someone's line of fire.

Fulcrum

Turning back, I faced three very frightened men. Two of them were young, no more than their early twenties. They were literally shaking in fear. The third, standing closest to me, was nearer my age. He was severely overweight, squeezed into a pair of Army surplus BDU pants and an OD green T-shirt. He was sweating heavily, even though the night was cool.

"Who are you?" I asked, keeping my rifle trained on his jiggling belly.

"M-m-m-mark Ames," he stammered in fright.

"What the fuck did you think you were doing, Mark?"

"I'm a Captain in the Nevada Militia. We're just protecting our territory."

I snorted and shook my head.

"How is it none of you are infected?" Rachel asked.

"Don't know," he said, glancing at her before cutting his eyes back to the muzzle of my rifle. "We just aren't."

I could feel Rachel look at me, but I didn't take my attention off the fat man.

"How many of you are there?" I asked.

He stared back at me for a moment, nervously licking his lips. He didn't want to answer. Without warning, I fired a round into the ground at his feet. The report of the rifle was muted, but he still jumped like a cattle prod had been rammed up his ass.

"I'm not fucking around," I said. "And I'm not asking again."

"About four hundred," he said.

I stared at him, trying to determine if he was telling the truth. Finally, I decided he was too scared to be anything other than honest.

"And what the hell did you want with us?"

"We're supposed to stop any survivors. Find out what they're doing in our territory."

I didn't like the tone in his voice when he answered the question.

"And what are you supposed to do with survivors?"

He stared back at me, sweat trickling down his jowls and staining the collar of his shirt. His silence answered my question.

"Watch them," I said to Rachel and moved out of the prisoners' earshot.

"Local militia," I said into the radio. "Big boy here says there's 400 of them. Igor and Long, find some high ground and see if there's any more out there."

"Copy that," Long answered.

"No infection?" Sam asked.

"Negative. No sign of it. They seem perfectly normal."

One of the Humvees started up and headed north towards a low bluff. Igor and Long should have a commanding view of the area from the top.

"What are you going to do with them?" Sam asked.

I turned and looked at the three men being guarded by Dog and Rachel.

14

"Can they be immune?" I asked Rachel.

Long had returned, leaving Igor on the high ground to keep watch over the surrounding area. The three men were tied up and sitting in the sand in front of one of their trucks.

"I don't know," she said, shaking her head. "Sure, it's possible, but I can't see this many people, unrelated, all with immunity to the virus."

"No," I agreed. "I'm going to have a chat with them, then we've got to get back on the road. Clock's ticking for our pilot."

Everyone nodded as I turned to look at the frightened prisoners.

"Separate them," I said to Sam and Long. "Each of you take one of the kids. Move them far enough away that they can't hear my conversation with tubby."

They walked over, each grabbing an arm. The younger men protested, fearful they were about to be executed.

"What are you going to do?" Rachel asked, staying me with a hand on my arm.

Fulcrum

"Going to ask some questions," I said, looking into her eyes.

She stared back at me for a few moments, then lowered her hand. I held her gaze for another beat, then walked to where the man was sitting. Slinging my rifle, I squatted down in the sand in front of him.

"Here's the deal," I said in a calm, reasonable voice. "We're not a militia. We're the real deal. US military. And you made a big fucking mistake trying to stop us."

He bobbed his head up and down in agreement, the wattles of fat under his chin jiggling with the motion.

"So, I'm going to ask you some questions, and you're going to answer me. If you don't answer, or I think you're lying to me," I paused as I drew my Ka-Bar. "I'm going to start carving off body parts and feeding them to that dog over there. Then, if you're still not telling me what I want to know, that's OK. He'll have a taste for you, and I'll let him come over and take the parts he wants. Tell me you understand."

I was looking at the knife blade as I spoke, twisting it slowly in the air. Turning it over and examining it before holding it up above eye level to peer at the edge.

"Whatever you want, mister. And I'm sorry. We didn't know there was any military left. Thought you was some outlaws or something."

"Hmmph," I grumbled, gently pressing the point of the blade into the sand and looking up to meet his eyes.

"How have you survived the virus and the infected?" I asked.

"We're the militia. We hid out until they left."

He spoke in a rush, the words tumbling out of his mouth.

"Hid out? Where?"

"We was in bunkers. Bunch of us been preparing for years. Then a couple weeks ago we started coming out."

"400 of you? That's a lot of bunkers," I said. "Lot of food and water to have been holed up for months."

"Like I said, we been prepping for a long time. The General's got this big property and we been getting ready."

I kept my expression neutral, but the mention of someone called, *The General*, worried

126

me. I'd already met *The Reverend*, and I wasn't in any hurry to meet any more nut cases.

"Tell me about the General," I said.

"She's our leader. Without her, we wouldn't have survived."

"Her?"

I was surprised. Not that a woman couldn't be their leader, but it sure wasn't what I expected.

"Where'd she come from?"

"What?"

"Was she an Army General? Maybe Marines or Air Force?"

"I think maybe Army. She's got a uniform and medals and a couple of them pistols like Generals wear."

"What pistols?" I asked.

"You know. Big ones. .45s, I think. With pearl handles?"

"Like Patton?"

"Yeah," he smiled, happy I'd figured it out. "Just like in the movie!"

Just fucking great. This was all I needed. Some fuckwit in the middle of the Nevada desert who thought she was Patton.

"Now, tell me again," I said without revealing my thoughts. "Why were you trying to stop us?"

The man hesitated, and I could see him trying to come up with an answer.

"You've done good up until now, Mark," I said, raising the knife. "You don't want to start playing games at this point. It wouldn't be fun for either of us."

His eyes were once again glued to the blade as I slowly waved it around in the air.

"We was out scouting," he said, swallowing hard. "Saw you rolling into Crystal Springs. Figured you'd have food and water. Maybe some medical supplies, and some..."

"Some, what?"

He didn't want to answer. Stared at the knife and swallowed hard again. When his eyes flicked to Rachel, I knew what he was going to say. Fortunately, she wasn't paying close attention. Otherwise, she'd probably have shot all three of them on the spot. I looked into his eyes and nodded.

"I understand," I said in a quiet voice. "So, you saw us in Crystal Springs. Were you getting your instructions from that broadcast?"

"What broadcast?" He asked.

I narrowed my eyes and looked at him.

"The broadcast on the AM radio. A woman telling different units to check in."

He was shaking his head before I finished speaking.

"I don't know what you heard, mister, but it weren't us. We got some walkie talkies, but no transmitter like you're talking 'bout."

I glared at him for a few moments, satisfying myself he was telling the truth. Shit! That meant there was another group out there.

Standing, I took a look around, verifying that Long and Sam were not only watching the prisoners but keeping an eye on our surroundings.

"Igor," I said into the radio.

"Da?"

"Any movement?"

"Nyet. Is quiet."

I turned another circle, trading looks with Rachel, then squatted back down in front of the man I was interrogating.

"Where's this General?"

"I can't tell you that," he said nervously. "You're military. You know how it is."

I stared hard at him for a moment.

"First, don't ever compare yourself to me. We're not the same. Not even close. Second, the rules haven't changed. You answer my questions unless you want to start losing body parts."

Holding the knife up, I turned it so the headlights glinted off the blade. He stared at it, transfixed.

"Angle City," he finally said, looking down at his lap.

"Get the map out of the Hummer," I said to Rachel.

A moment later she handed me the glossy atlas. I flipped pages until I found the one for Nevada and held it in the light so the man could see.

"Show me," I said.

His hands were tied behind his back, and all he could do was tell me where to look. It took a few moments, but I finally spotted it. Standing up, I moved next to Rachel.

"Middle of nowhere," I said, staring at the map.

Angle City appeared only to be accessible by a primitive forest service road. It was at the base of a solitary mountain called Mormon Peak and was about 40 miles across the empty desert from our current location. Far enough that I wasn't too worried about more of the militia suddenly appearing.

"Tell me about Vegas," I said to the man.

"What about it?"

"Is it full of infected? Are the roads passable?"

"That's where you're going? Vegas?"

"Doesn't matter where I'm going," I growled. "Answer the fucking question."

"The last squad we sent down there reported there was a lot of infected still in the city. Roads are clogged. They had to walk in. Barely made it out. Why you want to go to Vegas?"

I ignored the man and walked a few yards away into the dark. Rachel came to stand next to me, Dog remaining close to the prisoner. Calling Sam and Long, I had them bring their two guys back so we could all talk.

"These guys are part of a prepper militia outfit," I said when we were all standing in a tight group. "And they aren't the same ones that we heard on the radio."

"How the hell are there survivors?" Sam asked.

"Beats the hell out of me," I said, shrugging my shoulders. "He says they were all in bunkers and only came back above ground a couple of weeks ago. Seems they were out scavenging for whatever they could find. Saw us and thought we'd be an easy target."

"Dumb shits," Long muttered.

"That's not the worst. Infected in Vegas, and the roads are jammed. We're going to have to find a way around. Probably off-road, but I'm worried about the river crossings."

"What river crossing?" Rachel asked in surprise.

"The Colorado. Hoover Dam is just south of Vegas. There's a roadway on top of it, but I think it was permanently barricaded after 9/11. That leaves a bridge just downstream, but who knows if it's still standing."

"What are our options if it's out?" Sam asked.

"Follow the river down into California and hope to find a bridge that will get us into Arizona. We could just follow the river all the way to the sea in Mexico, but that will add several hundred miles."

"What do we do with these guys?" Long asked, gesturing at the three men.

I turned to look at them. Considered the options, not the least of which was just putting a bullet in each of their heads.

"Turn them loose," Rachel said after watching my face for a couple of seconds. "Give them some water and send them on their way."

"Might not be a good idea," Sam said, looking intently at me.

I knew what he was thinking. Turn these guys loose and they hook back up with their buddies. Because of my questions, they knew where we were headed. It wasn't hard to imagine a whole bunch of them loading up and coming after us. But, leave their corpses in the desert, and even if they were found, no one would know for sure where we'd gone, or even who had killed them.

"We don't do this!"

Rachel stepped between me and the SEAL, glaring at both of us. After a long pause, I nodded.

"Disable all the vehicles, make sure they've got water and cut them loose," I said.

Long and Sam looked at me for a beat, then turned away to do as I'd ordered.

"And take their shoes," I called after them.

"Their shoes?" Rachel asked.

"They won't be going anywhere very fast without them," I said. "Not in the desert. It'll buy us some time to get out of the area."

It was pitch black in the desert as we resumed driving south. The moon was just a tiny crescent and didn't provide enough light to see your hand in front of your face. We were running without any lights showing. Fortunately, the night vision goggles allowed us to navigate the rough terrain without having to worry about driving into an unseen canyon.

We had about 90 miles to cover before we reached Vegas, and it was going to be slow going if we stayed off the lone highway that crossed the desert. I didn't want to go back to the pavement where the likelihood of being ambushed again was much higher, but was about to convince myself it was necessary. We were just moving too damn slow.

Sure, the Hummers were tough and capable, but we were having to keep our speed around 30 because of the rugged moonscape of southern Nevada. That meant three more hours just to get to Vegas. At a minimum. And that was just too much time.

I had no idea what condition the pilot was in. About all I knew was that he was adrift in a tiny life raft. Did he have water? Was he injured? Would he survive the coming day, baking in the sun on the surface of the sea? We needed to get there as fast as we could. But then what?

The SEAL was right. It was going to be next to impossible to find him somewhere in thousands of square miles. It would be like looking for a specific grain of sand on a beach. If we didn't know where to look, the chances of us finding it were pretty damn slim. I shook my head as I made my decision.

"We're getting back on the highway," I said over the radio.

Neither Sam nor Long responded, but they stayed close behind as I steered towards the narrow strip of asphalt.

"Why aren't we staying off-road?" Rachel asked.

"Moving too slow," I said, grunting as we hit a depression in the desert floor that momentarily sent the big vehicle airborne.

She nodded and braced herself as we bounced over a series of rocks. I had to slow to negotiate a deep drainage ditch, then we were back on the marginally smoother asphalt. Quickly I had us up to the vehicle's top speed, the needle bouncing somewhere between 60 and 65.

"So I've been thinking," Rachel said after several quiet miles.

"About what?" I asked when she didn't continue with her thought.

"The virus and why these people aren't infected."

"Because they were in bunkers. Protected. Right?"

"Maybe. But remember the Canadians when we landed at Offutt. As soon as they were exposed, some of them started turning."

"Ok..."

"I think it might be environmental."

"I'm not following," I said.

"Alright. Remember how the Canadians were okay because the virus couldn't survive in the extreme cold?"

I nodded.

"Well, it gets pretty hot here, right?"

"Very," I said. "Maybe a little cooler than where I'm from in Arizona, but it'll still reach 110 in the summer. You think that's it? The virus can't handle extreme temperatures?"

"It makes sense," Rachel said, nodding slowly as she thought. "Besides, that's normal for any virus. They like a nice, temperate environment. In general. I mean, just look at this place! When's the last time it rained? Weeks? Months?"

"Maybe. Probably," I said. "But, if that's the case, why are there infected in Vegas? The attacks were in the summer. If it can't survive the heat..."

"Humans can't survive the heat, either. That's why we have air conditioning and easily available water. Our planes, cars, trains... all of them are cooled and would make a perfect environment for the virus. Perhaps it was people that had been exposed but hadn't turned yet, maybe fleeing California, that brought it here.

"It would be on their clothing. Their personal possessions. Everything they touched or breathed on would become contaminated. If it was an object outside, in the sun, the virus probably wouldn't survive more than a few minutes at best. After all, how hot do things get in direct sunlight when it's 110?"

"Door handles are hot enough to blister your fingers if they're in the sun," I said.

"There's probably no way the Chinese could have hardened the virus to the point that it could survive that. But, all it would take would be one infected person to walk into a hotel or casino, or a convenience store to buy a drink, and the environment suddenly becomes hospitable. That's probably why there are infected here."

I thought about what she was saying as I drove. Checked the mirrors to make sure Long and Sam were still back there. Returned my attention to the road ahead.

"So, this place was free of contagion, but now that winter is coming, and the weather has cooled off, it'll be back?"

"Not necessarily," Rachel said, shaking her head. "I don't know if the infected remain contagious. Maybe, maybe not. I'm sure Dr. Kanger could tell us, but that's not something that ever came up when I was around."

"How does this help us?" I asked after several more miles of quiet.

Rachel shook her head, biting her lower lip in thought.

"I don't know that it does," she finally said. "It's just a puzzle that I was trying to work out in my head."

We lapsed into silence at that point. Only the hum of the tires on pavement and the constant rumble of Dog's snoring from the back seat broke the quiet.

"Major."

I was startled when Lieutenant Sam's voice came over my earpiece. Rachel noticed me jump slightly, and grinned.

"Go," I answered, ignoring her.

"How close are we going to be to Nellis when we pass through Vegas?"

He was referring to Nellis Air Force Base. I knew it was near the city but had no idea where it was located.

"No clue," I said. "What are you thinking?"

"That we could use some heavier weapons. How about a quick stop to raid the armory?"

I thought about that for a moment, liking the idea. But, would we be able to get to the base?

"Check the map," I said to Rachel after telling Sam to standby. "You're looking for Nellis Air Force Base. It's somewhere near Vegas, but I've got no idea where."

Rachel dug around on the floor, lifting the road atlas into her lap a few moments later.

140

"Check around for a red-lensed flashlight," I said, stopping her from turning on a small light that would have washed out my night vision goggles.

She rummaged some more but didn't find one.

"What do you want me to do?" She asked after searching the interior of the vehicle.

"Hang on," I said to her, then activated the radio. "Anyone got a red lens?"

It turned out that Igor had some red cellophane in his pack for this exact purpose. With a sigh at having to lose more time, I called a halt and braked to a stop in the middle of the road. I hated losing even a minute but wasn't about to turn on the vehicle's lights so I could see while Rachel read the map. That would be as good as sending up a flare for any of the groups in the area that might want to intercept us.

We'd only been stopped for a couple of seconds when Igor appeared at Rachel's door and handed her a sheet of the stuff before running back to his vehicle. Rachel wrapped the noisy plastic around the lens of her flashlight, commanding Dog's immediate interest and undivided attention. It crackled like the kind of plastic used to wrap food, and it took him an extended session of thoroughly sniffing every

141

object in Rachel's lap to satisfy himself he wasn't missing out on a treat.

"Found it," Rachel said almost a minute later. "Looks like it's just south of I-15 as we come into the north part of town."

"We can get there without having to go through the city?" I asked, confirming what I'd hoped I was hearing.

"Yes. The highway we're on connects to the 15, then it's maybe about 10 miles or so to the base."

I nodded and relayed the information to the other vehicles, accelerating away immediately. Quickly, Long and Sam were back on my ass. Ok, so it didn't take *that* much time.

If there was a large contingent of infected when we got there, I wasn't going to stop. We didn't have time to fight our way in and out. But if it looked clear, and we could make a quick run onto the base and secure some heavier weapons, it was worth the time.

16

Admiral Packard snugged down his seatbelt as the big Seahawk helicopter lifted off the ground. He was on his way to Mt. Kaala for a personal look at the defensive positions that were being prepared. Fifteen minutes before, he'd gotten word from an observation flight that the Russians had successfully intercepted and shot down all of the bombers, and most of the escorting fighters, that were part of Falcon flight.

All of the main communication systems were still down, Jessica working furiously to restore the Navy's servers. As a stop gap, high-speed boats had been sent out into the open ocean to form a daisy chain of repeaters that would carry a radio signal from Pearl Harbor to a severely degraded Carrier Strike Group that was steaming to meet the invaders.

The CSG was merely a shadow of what it had once been, now not much more than a ragtag collection of ships and damaged submarines, which were preparing to engage the enemy fleet. The Admiral well knew they had no hope of stopping the Russians. That wasn't the point. The brave men and women on those ships and subs were sacrificing themselves to buy time for the defenders on the shore. Time that was desperately needed.

The latest estimate was that the first Russian ship would be coming over the horizon in slightly less than 40 hours. Not much time when the positions his people were preparing were moldering and overgrown with dense, jungle foliage due to decades of neglect.

No, not neglect, he reflected. Dismissal. The belief that technology and the military might of the US would stop any potential aggressors well before they could make landfall. After all, land invasions of this sort were something from the distant past. It had been a very long time since anyone in the Pentagon had seriously considered the possibility of an enemy landing troops on American soil. Certainly not since the Cold War ended.

With a shake of his head, Packard acknowledged to himself that only a year ago he would have dismissed the possibility out of hand. The days of assaults like the invasion of Normandy by the allies in World War II were nothing more than the occasional movie to the modern military. A military that was almost totally dependent on its technological superiority.

Not that all of the advancements of the past 70 to 75 years weren't quantum leaps forward in how war was fought, but sometimes it came down to the simplest of terms. Strip away all the tech and what was left? A man in a foxhole with a rifle. With a sigh, the Admiral realized they weren't far from that becoming the new normal. Until current stores of ammunition were exhausted. Then what? Bows and arrows? Rocks and sticks?

It was a very real concern for the Admiral and his staff. There were no factories in Hawaii that manufactured rifle ammunition, or anything else that was needed. And, with the Russian presence along the west coast of the mainland, he couldn't send scavenging crews to replenish their stores. Fortunately, there were tons upon tons of ammo and munitions stockpiled on the island. But, once the enemy arrived, they'd burn through those reserves in a hurry.

"Admiral, Fulcrum has been successfully picked up by the North Carolina. The team is on board, and they're proceeding at best speed to the target."

Packard's aide's voice coming over the noise canceling headset startled the Admiral out of his reverie. He turned his head, met the Commander's eyes and nodded.

Fulcrum was a team of SEALs he had dispatched in a last ditch effort to stop the impending Russian invasion. They had been flown out of Pearl Harbor in a B2 stealth bomber, heading southwest in a large circle to keep plenty of distance open between them and the Russian fleet that was sailing from Midway. They'd jumped from 30,000 feet, 600 miles due south of the Solomon Islands, into the vastness of the empty south Pacific.

Once the team was in the water and formed up, they dove beneath the waves to a waiting submarine, the North Carolina. A Virginia class, fast-attack boat, it was hovering at periscope depth, waiting for the SEALs. They were quickly aboard, entering through an airlock specifically designed to support special operations personnel. Once they were aboard, the Captain sent a burst transmission from a slender mast that was the only part of the boat showing above the surface.

The B2, loitering in the area, received the message as the North Carolina retracted the antenna and dove for the protection of the ocean depths. The signal was repeated by the bomber and picked up by a KC-135 tanker that was flying a racetrack pattern 800 miles to the northeast. It was waiting to refuel the SEALs' plane, as well as act as a radio relay.

From the tanker, the message bounced through another aircraft patrolling south of Hawaii, then was repeated by half a dozen small boats that were positioned to act as relay stations. It eventually arrived in Pearl Harbor's CIC and was immediately passed on to Admiral Packard's aide.

Fulcrum

As the North Carolina dove, it accelerated to 35 knots and set a heading of 180 degrees, or due south. Their destination was 1,300 miles away, and if the speed could be maintained, they would arrive in slightly less than 33 hours. Once at their target, the SEALs would *lockout* of the submerged boat and deploy two RIBs housed in a specially constructed addition to the hull of the submarine. Once on the surface, they would begin a fifty-mile journey to shore under the cover of darkness.

Entering Sydney Harbour, they would navigate to Elizabeth Bay before making landfall at 0200 local time. From there, a short, one-mile walk would bring them to the luxury penthouse apartment that was the new home of President Barinov. Their mission was simple, and they had been unleashed by the Admiral. No rules of engagement. They were to locate and capture the Russian president.

With Barinov in their custody, they would bring him back to the North Carolina. Once aboard the sub, they were to convince him to order all Russian forces to stand down. Admiral Packard had personally spoken with the Commander leading the SEAL team, ensuring he understood that success in his mission was the only concern. The Russian president had to be convinced to cooperate. By any means necessary.

"What do you think their odds are?" Packard mused as the helicopter gained elevation to reach the top of Mt. Kaala.

"Honestly, sir, if I was a betting man, I'd have to put money on them failing."

"Why?"

Packard was of the same opinion but was curious what the younger man was thinking. He turned when there wasn't an immediate reply, correctly reading his aide's expression.

"That's a sincere question, Commander. Not a trap."

He tried to smile, but the weight of everything that was pressing in on him killed it before it started.

"Well, sir," the man began, then took a deep breath. "There's Russian Spetsnaz pulling security all over that neighborhood. They've got three distinct, concentric rings of protection set up around the building. Over two hundred of their best troops."

The man paused, watching the Admiral to make sure he wasn't overstepping his bounds. Packard nodded encouragement for him to continue.

"Then there are the Aussies. Barinov apparently put a good scare into their PM. He has their Navy guarding the entrance to the harbor and patrolling all of the bays. Assuming Fulcrum Team can get past them, undetected, there's a large contingent of SASR troopers on the ground.

"I'm sure part of their task is to keep an eye on the Russians, but they're also going to protect them. There's no doubt they have orders to assist and support the Spetsnaz if there's an attempt on any of the high-ranking Russians living in the area.

"So, no sir. I don't like their odds one bit. But, if there's anyone that can do it, it's these guys. They're the best. A little bit of luck and they just might pull it off."

Packard nodded in thought. The Commander had voiced the same concerns he had, nearly word for word. His attention was pulled away as the Seahawk slowed and came into a hover.

Looking through the window in the side door, he could see the antique fortifications on top of the mountain. Workers crawled over nearly every square foot, hacking off dense vegetation which was then dragged away.

Several of the gun emplacements were already cleared, exposed to the sun for the first time in decades. Each location was a ring that had once housed massive shore defense batteries. Now, they were nothing more than six-foot tall, concrete walls that were permanently stained black by the mold and algae that flourished in the tropical environment.

Two of the cleared rings were hives of activity as crews completed the installation and testing of anti-aircraft missile systems. Several tall barrels, part of an artillery unit, thrust into the sky from a third. There were many more rings to clear, and in the distance, the Admiral could see several heavy-lift helicopters approaching the mountain. Hanging beneath each were more missile systems and big artillery guns.

"Take me to the entrance," Packard said to the pilot over the intercom.

The helicopter immediately banked away, slipping down the eastern slope. In the valley below sprawled Schofield Barracks. A long line of trucks stretched down the side of the mountain into the Army base as men, supplies and munitions were transported up the primitive road.

"Nowhere to land, sir." The pilot's voice came over the intercom as he brought them into another hover.

Beneath, a truck disappeared into the mountain as it entered the large mouth of a tunnel. Packard watched as three more followed, then saw two men walk out of the entrance and look up at the helicopter.

"Sir, that's Colonel Blanchard below us. He's on the radio asking if you'd like a tour."

Packard hesitated. He was sorely tempted. Wanted to see the progress in their preparations. But his presence would add nothing. In fact, it would be a distraction, and the last thing anyone needed right now was another distraction.

"Thank him for me," the Admiral finally said. "But tell him I'm needed elsewhere. Let's go back to Pearl."

"Aye, aye sir," the pilot answered.

A moment later the big helicopter spun and headed south, following the eastern slope of the mountain range.

17

"What the hell," I muttered, bringing the Humvee to a stop.

I spared a glance in the mirror to make sure Long wasn't about to crash into the vehicle's rear end, glad to see him pulling to a stop a few yards behind. We had reached the northern edge of Vegas. For the past few miles, I'd had to lower our speed to negotiate abandoned cars and trucks that dotted the freeway. Following the signs, I'd taken the exit marked for Nellis Air Force Base and had only traveled a few miles on a surface street along the perimeter fence. Now, we sat in the darkness as I stared at a hive of activity and a huge group of infected.

The activity was on the other side of the tall, chain link fence that surrounded the base. An even dozen trucks were lined up alongside a series of squat buildings that were immediately recognizable as armories. All of the vehicles had their lights on, and half a dozen portable, generator powered floodlights were set up. The entire area was lit like it was mid-day.

At least a thousand infected were pressing against the fence. Pushing in. Screaming. The females trying to climb over to reach the uninfected humans on the other side. A couple of dozen men were watching them, frequently shooting into the heaving mass of bodies.

But, these weren't Air Force personnel. They had found fully automatic rifles, and were shooting down the climbers with long bursts, burning through full magazines to put down a single female. The sound of their firing was loud on the still, night air, and, I had no doubt, was carrying for a long distance. Checking the immediate area, I stepped out when I saw it was clear. Dog followed quickly, Rachel getting out the far side a few moments later.

"What are we doing?" Rachel asked, turning to watch Dog as he trotted to the closest bush.

"Those idiots are making enough noise to raise the dead," I said.

"And the lights, too. Bad idea," Sam said as he came to stand next to me.

"Long," I said when he and Igor joined us. "You two keep an eye out. There's going to be infected attracted to all that activity. Let's not get caught with our dicks hanging out."

Long nodded and stepped away as Igor climbed onto the roof of their Hummer and began scanning the surrounding area with the scope on the sniper rifle.

"Think they got in?"

Sam was referring to the armories. They're built tough because of what they house.

"They're in, or are confident they're going to get in," I said. "Either way, they got their hands on some military hardware, somehow. They didn't pick up full auto rifles at the local Walmart."

He nodded as another long, chattering burst of fire sounded.

"Think this is the group those guys we talked to are from?" Rachel asked.

I shrugged, then turned and walked over to Igor's Hummer and scrambled onto the roof with him. He handed over the rifle when I asked. I extended the bipod legs and peered through the high-power scope. A few adjustments and I had a crisp, close-up view of the goings on inside the air base. The optics were top-notch, good enough for me to see individual faces clearly.

First, I looked over the group that was defending the fence. Definitely not Air Force. They were wearing a variety of military surplus and civilian camouflage clothing, some with their features darkened with face paint sticks. Like that would do one bit of good in helping them hide from an infected.

Fulcrum

Most were seated on the lowered tailgates of pickups, and as I watched, cans of beer were being passed from a large cooler. Moving on, I scanned down the line of idling trucks nearer the armories.

These weren't civilian pickups. They were Deuce and a Halfs, painted in Air Force blue. So they'd found the motor pool. I was a little surprised to see them. The military had been transitioning to a replacement truck, called the LMTV, for well over a decade, but here they were.

A driver sat behind the wheel of each truck. Half a dozen guards were strolling up and down the side of the convoy closest to me. I took a few moments to look carefully, noting they were all armed with military issue rifles. A couple of them wore honest to God bandoliers of ammo, trying to look like Rambo. Instead, they looked fucking ridiculous.

Moving on, I focused on a small group gathered around the entrance to one of the armories. The door was off its hinges, lying on the ground a few yards away. It was heavily damaged, the way a high-security door that has been forced open with explosives is damaged.

The group of men standing at the opening looked like they were waiting for someone or something. Curious, I kept the scope focused on them and watched.

"What's up?" Sam asked from below.

"Looks like some sort of half-assed militia," I said without taking my eye away from the scope. "They've got at least one armory open, and I'm guessing their leaders are inside deciding what they want to take. Got a group just standing around, like they're waiting to be told what to go get. There're twelve Deuce and a Halfs waiting to be loaded, so they're planning on taking a lot."

Sam grunted as he thought about the information.

"What's the Air Force going to have in an armory?" He asked after a long pause.

"Not sure," I said. "Probably not what you and I are used to, but they're still going to have a lot of shit. Base defense in a combat zone means a lot of rifles and ammo. Probably a good amount of light and heavy machine guns. And no doubt some SAMs (Surface to Air Missiles) for protecting the airspace. Beyond that, your guess is as good as mine."

Sam kept speaking, but I wasn't listening. A small group had just emerged from the armory, the woman in the lead drawing all my attention.

Fulcrum

Neither young nor old, she was probably somewhere around my age. Well-fitting jeans were bloused into a pair of highly polished jump boots. A brown, Army issue T-shirt was stretched tightly over her large breasts. Thick, brown hair flowed down to mid-back. Appearing tall, I had to admit, she cut a stunning figure as she stood speaking to the group of men.

But what caught my eye was a web belt cinched tightly around her narrow waist. On each hip, it supported a holstered, pearl handled Colt .45, just like the man I'd interrogated had described when he told me about *The General*.

Watching her stand there and issue orders to the waiting men, I could believe she had spent some time in uniform. Her demeanor and bearing as she addressed her underlings weren't those of a civilian. She was accustomed to giving orders and having them followed. Not that she couldn't have attracted plenty of men to do her bidding with just her looks, and perhaps that was why they had first joined her, but she wasn't using her femininity to control them.

"Found The General," I said, still watching the woman.

"Seriously?" Sam asked.

"Yep. Climb up and take a look."

I rested the rifle's stock on the roof and slithered down the windshield as Sam scampered up the back. He was quickly in place, and it didn't take him long to spot the woman. Watching for a few moments, he let out a low whistle before passing the weapon to Igor.

"What?" Rachel asked.

"Let's just say she doesn't fit the mold of what you think of when someone calls her The General," I said.

Rachel looked at me for a beat, then Sam when he jumped down next to me with a grin on his face. After a short time, she rolled her eyes and turned around to check on Dog.

"OK," I said to Sam and waved Long in. "We don't have time to screw around with this. Need to get on the road. We're way outnumbered with just what I can see. We'll bypass the base and cut through the desert to avoid the city, then pick up the highway south of town. Hopefully, the bridge is still standing."

They nodded, and I headed for my vehicle. Rachel and Dog were standing near the back, waiting for me. Before I climbed in, I looked over my shoulder to make sure the rest of the group was ready to roll. Igor had climbed down and was having an animated conversation with Long. Apparently, he was describing The General as he was holding cupped hands in front of his chest as he spoke.

"Not sure I want to know how they talk about me," Rachel said as she got into the Hummer.

"They'll never talk about you like that," I said, shifting into gear and turning the wheel to accelerate away from the base.

"Why not? Because of you?"

I shook my head as I steered us onto our new course.

"No. Because you're one of them, now. You've fought with them. Bled with them. Sure, they'll notice you're a woman, but you're their sister now. Anyone messes with you, you'll have a whole bunch of big brothers with bad attitudes defending your honor."

"Uh huh."

Rachel sounded like she didn't believe me, but I didn't say anything else. Finally, she turned to look at me. I met her eyes briefly and nodded. She was quiet for a long time, staring out her window at the dark landscape.

"Is that how you see me? Your sister?" She asked after several more miles had passed.

I wasn't ready for that question.

"I... It's just... I don't know what to say to you," I stammered.

My heart ached over the loss of Katie. I've lost a lot of people I cared about over the years, but nothing compared to this. It was only through sheer determination and the burning need for vengeance that I was up and moving, not curled into a ball with a bottle in my hand.

"I'm sorry," Rachel said softly when I didn't say anything else.

She reached across and gently rubbed my arm before placing her hand on my shoulder. I couldn't look at her. Didn't want her to see the tears in my eyes.

18

From the Air Force Base, we stayed to the east of Las Vegas. There were plenty of roads through the area, but if they weren't clogged with wrecked vehicles, they were thick with milling infected. For a short time, we were able to move out into the desert, but soon reached a series of low, rocky hills that fronted a small mountain range. They were impassible with the Humvees. I had to call a halt when we came to a point where there weren't any infected in the immediate area.

Telling Long and Sam to sit tight, I pushed the NVGs off my eyes and took the map from Rachel. Turning on the flashlight with the red cellophane covering the lens, I started trying to find our approximate location. As I was poring over the map, Dog woke up and thrust his head into the front.

It took me a couple of minutes, but I figured out where we were, then looked over our options. I didn't like the idea of continuing south, even though we were skirting the metropolitan area. There were just too many residential areas to pass through, and they all butted up against the base of the hills. If we ran into a problem, say a herd too big to push through, our options would be limited to retreating, or turning west into the city.

I didn't doubt the accuracy of the intel I'd gotten from our prisoner. He'd said the city was jammed with abandoned vehicles and roaming infected. This fit with every other city I'd seen, so I was comfortable with taking him at his word.

What I did know was I had no desire to approach the more densely built-up and populated areas. A road that headed due east, crossing the mountains before turning south towards Lake Mead, caught my eye. We had already passed it and would have to backtrack a couple of miles, but I decided it was worth it. On the map, at least, it appeared to go through the middle of nowhere. Perfect for avoiding infected.

Handing the map book back to Rachel, I turned off the light, lowered my NVGs and filled in Long and Sam over the radio. Making a U-turn, I led the way back north and turned east onto Lake Mead Boulevard. Quickly, we began climbing, leaving any sign of civilization behind.

The road was in good shape, relatively smooth, and ran straight as it climbed. On either side of the asphalt were fairly steep slopes of sun-blasted sand and rock, only the occasional cactus breaking up the monotony. As we progressed, a sense of unease settled over me. Soon I was scanning the passing terrain with the night vision, paying more attention to it than the road in front of me.

"What's wrong?" Rachel asked.

"Nothing, really," I said. "Just don't like being bottled up like this. Perfect place for an ambush if someone was so inclined."

She nodded without saying anything. After another moment, Sam's voice sounded in my earpiece.

"Not liking this terrain," he said.

"Agreed," I answered.

"How far to the crest?"

"Maybe another three or four miles," I said, picturing the map in my head.

"Copy."

The radio fell silent at that point, and I pressed harder on the accelerator. It didn't do any good. We were climbing a steep grade as we approached the pass that was in a saddle between two jagged peaks, and the Humvee was already moving as fast as it could. I didn't bother to glance at the speedometer. There was no point.

"There!" Rachel cried, her arm extending towards a point near the top.

163

I had seen it too. A brief flash of light. Very brief.

Now was decision time. Did we stop? Turn around? Press ahead and trust in the Humvees' armor? I made the decision without hesitating. You never knowingly drive into an ambush unless you already know what's waiting for you and are prepared to overwhelm your attackers. We had no information and no weapons other than rifles and pistols.

Calling a warning on the radio, I hit the brakes and brought us to a quick stop. Long and Sam, both experienced warriors, kept some distance between us this time. If you're about to be attacked, bunching up just makes it easier for the enemy and hinders your ability to turn a vehicle around and get the hell out of the area.

"They've gotta have night vision," Long said over the radio. "No way they saw us otherwise."

"Sound," Sam countered. "These engines were making a lot of noise climbing the hill. Besides, if they had night vision, they'd probably have radios, too, and wouldn't be using a light to signal."

The SEAL had a good point. But just because they might be short on technology didn't mean they were short on weapons. Our

Hummers might be up-armored, but that hardly meant they couldn't be disabled by some well-placed shots. The armor was intended to protect the occupants, not the vehicle. A few high velocity rifle slugs and we'd be driving on flat tires that would eventually shred off until only steel rims remained.

And that was if we weren't facing a truly devastating weapon, such as a .50 caliber rifle. With the right ammo, our armor wouldn't be enough to keep us safe.

"Think these are the same guys that were flashing the light right after we left Groom Lake?" Rachel asked.

"Doubt it. That's a long way away, and there's no way they could have gotten here ahead of us and set up a trap. Hell, we didn't even know we were coming this way until a few minutes ago."

"What's on the other side of the mountains?"

"Nothing," I said, thinking about the map. "Just more desert."

"Long," I called over the radio. "Send Igor up the slope with the rifle. Tell him to use the thermal scope and see if he can tell what's

165

waiting for us. Rest of us dismount, but stay by your vehicles."

I shut off the engine and stepped out into the night. The air had been cool down near the city, but it was downright cold at this higher elevation. A steady breeze was blowing, making it feel even colder.

Rachel and Dog joined me near the rear bumper of our Hummer. I turned a slow circle, carefully looking over our surroundings with the night vision. Igor was silently scrambling over rocks to gain some elevation, finally finding a spot he was happy with and placing the rifle on top of a small boulder.

Checking on Sam and Long, I was happy to see they had their rifles up, scanning the area. Dog, standing next to me, lifted his muzzle and sampled the breeze. His nose twitched for a long time, his head turning slightly as he caught the scent of something. But he didn't growl or seem concerned over what he'd detected. Lowering his head, he sniffed the ground, then followed the trail of something to the edge of the pavement where he lifted his leg and marked a struggling bush.

"At least no infected in the area," Rachel said, watching him.

"Not upwind, anyway," I said, turning to look at Igor when I heard his broken English in my ear.

"Seven people," he said. "Two thousand meters. They not move. Maybe infected. Not tell."

"Vehicles?" I asked.

"Nyet."

The breeze was coming from the direction of the unknown people, and Dog had taken a good snootful of the night air. These weren't infected. I trusted his nose.

"Can you see any weapons?" I asked Igor.

"Da," he answered immediately. "All have rifles."

Seven people with rifles didn't cause me undue concern. What did was what might be waiting for us that Igor couldn't see. More people concealed in caves. Heavy weapons. Vehicles on the other side of the pass that could block the road.

"Do we go back?" Rachel asked. "Work our way around the city?"

I didn't have to give it much thought. There were other ways to go without having to risk the unknown waiting for us at the top of the mountain. Nodding, I was opening my mouth to call Igor back down when Sam's voice sounded over the radio.

"Contact! Nine o'clock. Thirty degrees up-slope."

I spun to face the hill looming over the left side of the road, snapping my rifle up and searching the area Sam had identified. It only took a second for me to find the target and I paused in surprise. A young woman, no more than 18 or 19, was peering around a boulder with a rifle in her hands.

19

"Hold your fire!"

I spoke quickly over the radio before someone put a round in the girl's head. Other than having surprised us, she wasn't doing anything threatening. Yes, she had a rifle in her hands, but it wasn't aimed at us. She was just holding it, the muzzle nowhere near pointed in our direction.

"Igor, check the rest of the slope," I said, keeping the girl's face centered in my rifle's scope.

"Clear," he said after a long pause.

"Copy. Keep an eye on the pass."

"Da."

"Come down!" I called to the girl. "Nice and slow and keep the muzzle of that weapon pointed away from us."

After hesitating, she slowly stood and began picking her way down the slope. I told Sam and Long to keep checking the area around us without taking my attention off the girl.

She was wearing jeans and hiking boots with a couple of jackets layered over a flannel shirt. Long hair was pulled back into a severe ponytail, and her face was filthy with streaks of dirt. Moving easily, she descended to the edge of the road. Reaching level ground, she paused and looked us over before stepping closer.

"Are you the real military?"

"Yes, we are," I said, lowering my rifle's muzzle but keeping the stock to my shoulder. "The people ahead. At the pass. They yours?"

She stared at me for several beats before nodding.

"OK," I said after watching her eyes. "If you've got some way to communicate with them, tell them to relax. We don't want to hurt anyone. We're just passing through."

Her eyes tightened slightly as she peered at me in the darkness. Finally, they slid to the side to look at Rachel and Dog, then farther back at Long and Sam, who had their rifles up, scanning the surrounding slopes. Slowly, she reached into a jacket pocket. I tensed but didn't raise my rifle.

"Just a flashlight," she said, correctly reading my body language.

With exaggerated caution, she brought her hand out, and I could see the small light gripped in her fist. Aiming the lens up the road, towards the pass, she began flashing out a message. I thought it was Morse code but couldn't understand the language.

When she finished, there was a long pause, then a series of flashes answered. She started to send another message.

"Hold on," I said, taking a step closer to her. "Let's not get carried away with the conversation. What did you say to them?"

"Your military and you don't know Morse?" She asked.

"I know Morse," I said, "But I don't know the language you were using."

She looked at me for a moment before laughing.

"Texting," she said, looking at me expectantly.

"Excuse me?"

"Texting." She smiled, waiting, then sighed when I didn't get it. "Just like tapping out a text message, it's faster and easier to signal without spelling out every word."

I thought about what she was saying for a moment, then smiled in surprise. She was right. If you could send a message with less than half the characters, and it could be understood, why bother to tap out all the extra letters?

"Maybe you'd better tell me your name, and exactly what your friends up top have in mind."

"I'm Chelsea," she said, glancing up the slope as she spoke.

"Movement. Come our way. Two people," Igor spoke over the radio.

"Who's coming, Chelsea? Not a good idea to try and surprise us," I said, hoping the warning was clear in my voice.

"I'm just a lookout," she said after a pause. "My brother's coming. No surprises."

I nodded and told Igor to keep an eye on the people approaching, but not to engage unless they did something threatening. He acknowledged, and I motioned for the girl to move farther up the road so I could watch for the new arrivals and still keep an eye on her.

"What are you doing out here?" Rachel asked the girl.

Chelsea looked at her for a beat, then shook her head.

"My brother will tell you if he wants to," she said.

We stood there, no one speaking, for what felt like a long time. When I finally detected movement on the road with my NVGs, I mumbled to Rachel, telling her to keep a close eye on the girl. She stepped several yards away from me, rifle held tight in front of her body. Dog, picking up on the elevating tension, took up station between us.

The two figures quickly resolved into a male and a female, each carrying a rifle. When they approached to within thirty yards, I called out for them to stop. Neither had night vision, and both were startled when they heard my voice. They stood in the middle of the road, looking around.

"Come forward slowly. Keep your rifles pointed at the ground," I yelled to them.

"Chels? You OK?" The male shouted without moving.

"I'm fine," the girl said. "Just do what they say. There's a sniper on the slope, watching you."

I could see their heads turn to look at the hill where Igor was sitting. After a long pause, they cautiously stepped forward and approached the front of the lead Humvee.

"Close enough," I said, moving forward to meet them.

The boy, well, man, was about 20. He was tall and thin and held the rifle like he was familiar, but not quite comfortable with it. His right arm was heavily bandaged and in a sling. The girl next to him was much shorter, barely five feet tall, with a figure that showed even through the warm clothing she was wearing.

"Hi," I said. "I'm Major Chase. US Army."

I wasn't getting a bad vibe from these kids. If anything, I was a little concerned that they had so casually just walked up, apparently trusting us without a second thought. I watched them, watching me, rocking sideways when Dog leaned against my leg. The two kids looked down at him briefly, then back at me.

"You're really Army? Not that militia?" The boy asked.

"Yes. We've seen the militia. They look like bad news. What did you have ready for us at the pass?"

I could see an embarrassed grin spread across his face before he spoke.

"We thought you were some of those militia assholes. Got some rocks ready to drop down on any vehicles that try to come through."

I nodded, staying silent so he would keep speaking.

"I'm Caleb. This is Tiffany," he gestured at the shorter girl standing next to him."

"What are you doing out here, Caleb? Any adults with you?"

He bristled slightly but held his tongue when I asked the question.

"Sorry," I said. "That wasn't a slight against you. Is there anyone older than you?"

"I'm the leader if that's what you're asking," he said, clearly offended.

"Leader of what?"

"Don't really know," he finally said. "Us, I guess. We're just trying to survive and stay clear of the militia, so they don't take anyone else."

I paused when I heard that little tidbit. A moment later, Rachel stepped up next to me, no longer watching Chelsea. If I wasn't confident Igor was keeping an eye on things from above, I would have warned her to stay focused.

"What do you mean, take anyone else?" Rachel asked.

Caleb sighed and looked over at his sister. She met his eyes and after a few seconds, nodded.

"They took six of us."

"Just girls?" I asked, a sinking feeling in the pit of my stomach.

"Yeah, but I was the only guy to start with," he said.

I looked around to make sure Sam and Long were still scanning the area. They were doing their jobs. I checked with Igor, who reported that other than the five people still at the top of the hill, we were alone.

"OK, Caleb," I said, lowering my rifle to hang on its sling. "You'd better tell me what's going on."

A few minutes later we were seated on several large boulders at the side of the road. Dog had decided that Tiffany was his new friend and sat at her feet with his chin in her lap as she ruffled his ears and talked baby talk to him. He has this uncanny ability to spot a dog person immediately and uses it to his full advantage.

"The girls are all part of a softball team," Caleb began speaking.

Chelsea was squeezed close to her brother on the same boulder.

"Are you from Vegas?" Rachel asked.

"No ma'am. Thousand Oaks. Right outside of LA. Anyway, our Dad is the coach. We were at this big tournament in Albuquerque when the attacks happened."

"Where's your dad?" I asked.

"Wasn't with us. He came down with the flu the night before they were leaving and couldn't make the trip. I've been helping him coach for years, so when he got sick, he asked me to drive the van and coach the girls during the tournament."

"How many girls?" Rachel asked.

177

"Eleven," Chelsea spoke up.

Caleb looked at her and nodded.

"Eleven girls on the team, plus me. And two little sisters tagged along to help with the equipment, water during the games, stuff like that."

"Fourteen of you?" I asked.

Caleb and Chelsea both nodded.

"Tell me about the six that are missing."

"We were on our way home from New Mexico after the attacks. Things were going crazy in Albuquerque. Fortunately, I'd filled up the van the day before when I made a run for water and snacks. We got the hell out of there, but heard that southern California had been attacked."

"How'd you wind up here?" I asked. "Vegas is kind of out of the way if you were on I-40."

He nodded.

"We made it to Kingman, Arizona, a little before the state line. The police had closed the freeway and were forcing everyone off. They said that the military was at the border to stop infected from coming out of California. We tried to get a motel room in Kingman, but they were all full, so we just found a place on the edge of town. All of us slept in the van that night.

"The next day, we went into town for some food. There were mobs at every store, looting the shelves. The cops weren't anywhere around. Don't know if they left, or were all at the roadblock, or what. People were shooting other people, setting buildings on fire and we saw a couple of women get dragged away by groups of men.

"I figured it was a good idea to get the girls someplace safer. Saw a road sign for Vegas and thought a big city would be better off. You know. More cops. So we headed north. Rolled into town on fumes and it was worse than Kingman. The strip was burning. People were going crazy. I had to run down a guy that was trying to take the van. We made it out of town and up into the hills, then ran out of gas."

"How have you survived?" Rachel asked.

"We didn't eat for almost a week. I'd just bought a bunch of water for the tournament, and it was still in the van, so we had that. When we couldn't stand it anymore, we walked down to town one night. There were still fires burning in the distance, but there's a sub-division at the bottom of the first hill.

"There were lots of empty houses. We broke in and stole food. Took as much as we could carry. We go back when we start running low, or if we need more water. There's still some gas stations with bottled water. Just gotta be careful an infected doesn't get you while you're gathering supplies."

"So how did the girls get taken?" I asked.

"A few months after we started hiding in the hills, we headed into town for supplies. By this time there was nothing left but infected, and we'd figured out how to get around them. The males are easy. The women? They're dangerous as hell if you're not really careful."

I nodded in agreement, encouraging him to continue.

"So we were in a new neighborhood. The one we'd been raiding was picked clean. No food, or anything worth taking, was left. Anyway, we'd split up into a couple of groups so we could go through the houses faster. There were six girls that were kind of their own little group inside the team, if you know what I mean.

"They were trying to break into one house while the rest of us were going through the kitchen in a little restaurant. First, we heard a bunch of vehicles coming. We tried to get to our teammates, but there were at least twenty men, and they all had guns. They rounded up the girls and loaded them in their trucks.

"I could hear them talking. Bragging on a radio about having captured a bunch of women. They were kind of dressed like soldiers, and one of the trucks was flying a big, black flag that said they were the Nevada Militia. Had a snake on it. There was nothing we could do other than watch them drive off with the girls."

The pain and anger in Caleb's voice were clear to hear. I didn't blame him and was regretting not having put a bullet in the heads of the militia members we'd captured.

"You didn't have the rifles then?" I asked.

"No," he shook his head. "We hadn't even thought about finding guns. But after that, we found a police station. Didn't even have to break in. The doors were unlocked. Found plenty of guns and ammunition. Took us a while to figure out how to load and use them, but we've got it down, now."

"What's with the flashlights?" I asked.

"We took radios from the police station, but the batteries died pretty quick, and we didn't have any way to charge them. So Chelsea came up with the idea of the lights. Use Morse code to talk to each other."

Dirk Patton

I looked at Chelsea, and she smiled in embarrassment.

"Where'd you learn Morse code?"

"I'm kind of a geek," she said, shrugging and looking down. "I'm a math major. I saw a movie a few years ago where they were using it and looked it up on the internet. Learned it in an afternoon. Remembered it, and taught it to the others."

"You learned Morse code in an afternoon?" I asked, more than a little surprised.

No, Morse code isn't rocket science. But to look it up and learn it on your own, in a single afternoon, is pretty damn impressive.

"She's a genius," Caleb said when she didn't answer. "Without her ideas, we'd either be dead or captured by now."

I looked back at the young woman and for about the thousandth time since the attacks, reminded myself to never underestimate anyone.

"I've seen this militia," I said after a few moments of silence. "We had a chat with a few of them out in the desert. Earlier tonight, saw a whole bunch of them raiding the armory at an Air Force Base. They're going to be well armed now. And probably have night vision and a few other things that will help them hunt you down."

"I don't think they know about us," Caleb said.

"You don't think the girls they captured told them?"

"I do!"

Chelsea answered before her brother could speak. He looked at her for a moment before meeting my eyes and nodding agreement. I was glad to see these kids weren't viewing the world through rose-colored glasses.

"Can you get them back?" Tiffany spoke for the first time.

Dog had pulled his trick of slowly lying down while being petted. When his victim of choice leans down to keep rubbing him, he rolls over and suckers them into scratching his belly. Invariably, they wind up seated on the ground next to him, and he's on his back soaking up every ounce of attention. It had worked on Tiffany, who looked up at me from where she was sitting in the dirt.

"There's only four of us," I said.

"Five!" Rachel corrected me.

"OK. Five," I conceded. "And there's hundreds of them."

I kind of felt like a heel, making excuses.

"Why couldn't the SEALs have found us?" Tiffany pouted.

"Young lady," Rachel said, her tone stern. "That man right over there *is* a SEAL. And that one's a Ranger, and he's a Delta Force trooper. And that one up there in the rocks? He's Russian special forces. This isn't a video game or a movie. This is reality. I've seen these guys do some absolutely amazing things, but you don't put four against four hundred. That's not how things work."

I appreciated Rachel jumping to my defense, but it didn't make me feel any better. Glancing over my shoulder, I saw that Sam was close enough to have heard our conversation. From the look on his face, he wasn't feeling any better about it than I was.

Tiffany didn't flinch under Rachel's glare, and I had to give the girl credit. She had some iron in her spine. But then, these kids had managed to survive all this time on their own. You don't do that if you're not made of some pretty stern stuff.

"Look," I said, cutting off the retort that was about to come out of Tiffany's mouth. "There's bigger things going on in the world than six girls captured by the militia."

Fulcrum

I held up my hand to forestall the angry protests that started to come from all three kids.

"Let me finish. I'm not saying those girls aren't important. But, here's the situation. The world as you know it is gone. I know you've been pretty isolated, so you may not know what's happened over the past several months.

"The US is dead. The whole world is dead, for that matter. All except for Australia. The man who started this is hiding out there, and I plan to do something about that. First, I've got to get to Mexico and try to rescue a downed pilot. He's adrift in the Gulf of California right now and probably won't survive another day if we don't get to him. That's where we're headed.

"But, we're coming back. We have friends not too far away that we have to pick up. When the pilot is safe, and we get back, I'll do everything I can to rescue those girls. You have my word."

I stared into each of their eyes to see if what I'd said had registered.

"Why not now?" Tiffany asked, not willing to give up.

"How long ago were they taken?" I asked.

They all thought about that for a minute, Chelsea finally answering.

"Seventy-three days," she said, surprising me that she was so precise.

"Math major. Remember?" She grinned at my expression.

"That's a long time," I said, turning to face Tiffany. "I understand how you feel, but two more days will almost certainly mean the pilot will die. Two more days after seventy-three for the girls? I'm sorry, but they're going to have to wait."

Tiffany glared back at me and started to open her mouth, but Caleb reached out and placed his hand on her shoulder.

"Tiff. I don't like it either, but the man's right."

She stared at him for a long time, her hand never ceasing its rubbing of Dog's belly. Finally, she looked down. Her hair fell and hid her face, but not before I saw a tear trickle down her cheek. After several quiet moments, Rachel stood and motioned at Caleb.

"I'm a doctor. Let's take a look at that arm. And is there anyone else that needs medical attention?"

21

Fifteen minutes later we were all crammed into the three Humvees. The kids were coming with us. It had actually taken some convincing, but not that much. They were tired, hungry, dirty and scared. I wasn't surprised that the final holdout was Tiffany. She'd moved away from the group and crossed her arms over her chest.

First Caleb, then Chelsea tried talking to her, but she was having none of it. They'd signaled the remaining girls who had come running, but Tiffany wasn't listening to any of them, either. Finally, Rachel walked over and put her arms around the girl, speaking softly to her. They stayed that way for several minutes.

"One of the girls the militia took is her sister," Caleb said to me in a quiet voice.

That explained a lot, but we didn't have time. I wasn't going to force Tiffany to come with us, but I also wasn't going to stand around in the middle of the Nevada desert with my thumb up my ass while people tried to convince her. We'd already lost too much time and needed to be back on the road. Finally, whatever Rachel said worked, and she escorted the girl to our Hummer.

Now, as we drove down the backside of the mountains, our vehicle was full. Caleb and Tiffany, apparently a couple, had stayed together and elected to ride with us. Dog was thrilled, planting himself between them and resting his head in the girl's lap.

Behind us, Long and Igor had Chelsea and another girl with them, the remaining four riding with Sam. With all the gear, food and water we'd brought along it was a tight fit, but the kids were hungry and very quickly started going through our supply of MREs.

None of us were much in the mood to talk, and it wasn't long before Dog's snores turned contagious, and our two passengers were sound asleep. How they could sleep with Dog doing his best to imitate an asthmatic steam engine, I'll never know, but somehow they did. Rachel turned around in her seat to check them, then looked at me with a smile on her face.

"How tired do you have to be to sleep through that?"

She hooked her thumb at Dog. I grinned and shook my head.

"You think you'll be able to get those girls back?" Rachel whispered some time later.

"Maybe," I said after glancing in the back to make sure everyone was still sleeping. "But I doubt it. Seventy-three days is a long time. And that's just one thing that's bothering me. The militia guy I interrogated said they'd only started coming out of their bunkers a couple of weeks ago. I'm pretty sure he was telling the truth. So... who really took those girls?"

"He could have been lying."

"Sure, he could have. But why? Why lie about something like that? It doesn't make sense."

I shook my head.

"How many people did he say were in the militia?"

"Four hundred. Why?" I asked.

"Maybe they weren't all in bunkers. Maybe some of them stayed above ground. Or came out earlier than he knows about."

I thought about that for a minute. Rachel was right, at least about the possibilities she had suggested.

"We may have other problems, too," I said.

"What?"

"The voice we heard on the radio. Maybe that was the militia, and the guy didn't know about it. Maybe not. Then there were the lights we saw up in the mountains not long after we left Groom Lake. I've got a bad feeling there's a lot more going on here than we've realized."

"Why here? What's special about this place?"

"Hot, dry and isolated. Maybe the virus died out quickly here, and there's a whole lot more survivors out there than we thought."

"What about where we're going? Arizona and Mexico. Just as hot and dry?"

I nodded, not liking what Rachel was thinking. The infected were bad enough. We didn't need a bunch of post-apocalyptic assholes running around thinking they were some kind of end of the world warrior like on a bad, made-for-TV movie.

We each lapsed into our own thoughts as I drove. The road curved gently, descending, then after twenty or so miles it dead-ended at a T intersection. I thought I knew which way to go but took half a minute to double check the map. It was a good thing I did. I would have turned in the wrong direction and wound up somewhere in the middle of nowhere on the north side of Lake Mead.

Fulcrum

Heading the right way, the road narrowed as we moved through some particularly rugged terrain. On the right were steep, rocky slopes. To our left, I could see the dark, calm waters of the massive lake through my night vision. That was a good sign. At least Hoover Dam was still standing.

I had worried about the dam having failed. Right off, I couldn't remember how much water it held back, but did know it was the largest reservoir in the United States. The bridge we needed to cross was no more than a quarter of a mile downstream, and in the event of a failure at the dam, there was no way it would survive the flood that would be released.

We followed this route for several miles until reaching US Highway 93. Now I was at least somewhat familiar with the area and didn't need to check the map to know which way to turn. Of course, the road sign pointing the way to Arizona didn't hurt, either.

The highway was clear of any abandoned vehicles, and perhaps that should have encouraged me. It didn't. This was the only way across the Colorado river for a very long way in either direction, and it didn't make sense to me why it wasn't clogged up with cars and trucks.

Braking to a halt a few dozen yards short of the bridge, I saw why. It was gone. A hundred feet out into the river gorge, the bridge deck ended in a twisted mass of steel and concrete. It had been dropped into the river, 800 feet below. This had probably been an effort by the authorities to prevent the infected from easily crossing in large numbers. The road had been clear because there'd almost certainly been a road block stopping traffic before it could even get close.

"What's wrong?" Caleb asked from the back seat.

He didn't have the benefit of night vision and couldn't see what I was looking at.

"Bridge across the river is out," I said.

"Are there other bridges to the south?" Rachel asked.

"Yes, but they're a long way, and if this one got destroyed, they're probably down too."

"What do we do?" Caleb asked.

"Try the dam," I said, cranking the wheel and making a U-turn.

We'd passed an access road for the Hoover Dam a couple of miles back, and that might be our best option.

"What dam?" Caleb asked.

Fulcrum

I glanced in the mirror and sighed. Almost said something about the public school system he'd been educated in, but bit my tongue. It wasn't his fault he hadn't been taught some of the basics about the very country where he'd been born.

"Hoover Dam," I said patiently. "It's what creates Lake Mead out of the Colorado River. Built in the 1930s, if I remember right."

"Oh, yeah. I saw some signs for it when we were driving up from Kingman. I just figured it was an old monument or something. It's still there?" Caleb asked in surprise.

Rachel and I exchanged glances, then both of us shook our heads.

"What?" He asked, sounding slightly miffed.

I slowed and turned onto the access road, which at one time was the only highway across the river as it wound along the top of the dam. Keeping my thoughts to myself, I drove slowly, glancing at the mirror to make sure Sam and Long were staying close.

We passed several large signs that warned we were entering a secure area where vehicles were subject to search. Not a bad thing. I'm glad we never got to find out what a few hundred pounds of plastic explosives in a terrorist's truck would do if detonated on top of the dam.

Slowing more, I drove through a chain link gate that had been violently ripped aside and torn from its hinges. Around a sharp curve, the road narrowed, and I stopped. Just ahead, a jacked-up Chevy pickup lay on its side, blocking the way. Beyond, I could see where the asphalt transitioned to the concrete road surface on top of the dam.

"Everyone stay put," I said, opening my door.

Long, Sam and Igor didn't need to be told to join me. As soon as I stepped out, their doors popped open. The four of us spent a couple of minutes scanning the surrounding canyon walls but didn't see anything of concern. Igor used the thermal scope on the sniper rifle, and I waited to get a final *all-clear* from him before turning my attention to the crashed truck.

Walking closer, I could see the sheet metal was riddled with bullet holes. The glass was blown out of all the windows, and three of the four tires were flat. I leaned down and looked in the cab, spotting two bodies. I think they were both men but couldn't tell for sure. The decomposition was significant.

194

"We can move it with my Hummer," Sam said, standing next to me. "Got a winch on the front bumper."

"Let's take a walk and check the dam, first," I said. "If it's not passable, there's no point in wasting time on it."

I called to Igor and Long, telling them to stay with the vehicles. Moving around the truck, Sam and I spread apart, our rifles up to our shoulders. The first thing we encountered, no more than thirty yards on, was a dual line of thick bollards that stuck up several feet from the road's surface. These were just like the ones that had protected the entrance to the lab in Los Alamos where I'd met Irina and Igor.

Sam walked up to one, which was nearly as thick as he was, and placed his hand on the rounded top. It was above his waist, and the two rows of them effectively blocked any vehicle traffic from making it onto the dam.

"Shit," he said quietly. "No way we're moving these things."

I looked at him, remembering how Tech Sergeant Scott had been able to lower them in Los Alamos. They're hydraulically controlled, and he'd found a maintenance hatch where he could access the system and release the pressure. They'd retracted most of the way under their

195

own weight, at which point we'd been able to drive across them.

"Know anything about hydraulics?" I asked Sam.

He looked at me, then turned back to look at the bollard he was touching. After a beat, he shook his head.

"No, but how complicated can it be?"

"Let's check the dam," I said, waving him forward.

We moved past the barricades and out onto the top of the dam. To our right was the downstream portion of Black Canyon. Sheer rock walls and 700 feet straight down to the river. To our left, the contained waters of Lake Mead. I glanced at the lake as we walked, then slowed and looked closer. After a moment, I moved to the railing and looked down the upstream side of the dam.

"Something wrong?" Sam asked, coming over to stand next to me.

"The water," I said. "It's way too high."

"How much too high?"

"Been here a few times," I said. "Never seen the water even close to where we're standing. It was always at least 60 feet below the top, usually more. That's what? No more than 5 feet?"

Sam looked down and nodded agreement with my guess.

"OK, but what's your point."

"Don't know that I've got one. But think about it. If the lake is this full, probably because there's been no one to monitor and operate the spillways, that's a hell of a lot of pressure on the structure that it may not have been designed to hold. Besides. We're standing on almost one-hundred-year-old engineering."

"You're not giving me a warm fuzzy," Sam said. "Are you saying we shouldn't try to drive across?"

"No," I shook my head. "I'm saying we'd better get our asses across before it fills up anymore. If this dam goes, there won't be a bridge across the river left standing, even if there is one that didn't get blown. And, I'm worried about coming back."

"You're just a cheery fucking soul, aren't you," he said with a grin.

I shrugged my shoulders, and we walked the rest of the roadway. On the Arizona side, we found another set of bollards blocking the way.

Taking a few minutes, we scanned the surrounding cliffs, then turned and headed back to rejoin our group.

"So what do you want to do?" Sam asked as we walked.

"The bollards aren't part of the dam. They're in the approaches. They were added sometime after 9/11 happened. That means there'll be maintenance hatches we can access without having to go inside the dam. We're going to see what we can do to release them."

Sam was starting to say something when we both froze as a deep, mournful groan sounded from all around. We looked down as vibrations traveled from the concrete up through our boots. It only lasted for a few seconds, but it spooked the hell out of both of us.

"Look at that," Sam whispered, pointing at the water.

I turned and caught my breath. The formerly calm surface of the lake, where it met the dam, was distorted by millions of tiny ripples. It reminded me of how water looks when it vibrates in a sonic cleaner. This continued for almost half a minute, then quickly dissipated, the water returning to a smooth, reflective surface.

22

"That's what we heard?"

Long looked freaked when I told the group about the dam vibrating and the ripples on the surface of the water. Everyone glanced around nervously when a low frequency rumble started up, seemingly coming from everywhere at the same time. It wasn't loud. In fact, I'm not sure I so much heard it as felt it.

The kids began talking to each other in frightened voices as the rest of us looked at each other with the realization that our path across the river was in danger of disappearing. After a few more seconds, the bass rumble subsided. Making up my mind, I yanked open the rear of my Humvee and dug through the gear in search of a toolkit.

"Long. You and Sam go find the maintenance hatch for the closest set of bollards," I said, still digging. "Igor. Find a high spot. You're on overwatch."

"What can I do?" Caleb asked.

I spied the tool kit I was looking for and pulled it from under a pile of ammo cans.

"Keep your group together and close to the vehicles. When we get these bollards retracted, we're going to have to move fast."

He nodded, and I took off at a trot to where Long had found and opened a large steel plate set into the side of the road. Rachel and Dog came with me, and I was surprised when I noticed Tiffany running with us.

"What are you doing? You need to stay with your group," I said.

"You might need me. I was an engineering student at Cal Tech. I've worked with hydraulic systems before."

If I hadn't been running, I would have stared at her in surprise. She was a beautiful young woman, and also a softball player. I would have guessed just about anything other than an engineering student at one of the best schools in the country.

"Chauvinist," Rachel mumbled beside me.

I didn't take the bait, just shut my mouth and slid to a stop next to the large opening in the ground. Long and Sam were already down in the hole, flashlights illuminating what, to me at least, looked like a very complicated system of thick hoses, pumps and tanks.

Fulcrum

"Think you can lower the bollards? Without power?" I asked Tiffany.

She nodded, took the tool kit from my hand and with the easy movement of youth, dropped into the cramped pit. Sam and Long looked at her in surprise, then up at me.

"Give her room," I said. "She knows what she's doing."

To their credit, they didn't hesitate to move aside. Tiffany took Sam's light and squatted to inspect the hydraulic system. Long stood behind her, adding additional light to each area she looked at.

"Contact!"

Igor's voice over the radio. I spun to look in the direction of the parked Humvees.

"Talk to me," I said, frowning in concern when I heard a faint report from the suppressed sniper rifle.

"Female coming fast." Two more shots. "Large group."

"Long and Sam, get your asses up here! Infected attacking!"

Two more shots from Igor in close succession.

"Go! I'll stay with her," Rachel said, pulling her rifle around on its sling.

I nodded and ran for the vehicles, not waiting for Sam and Long. Steady fire from Igor continued as I dashed around the crashed pickup. The kids were lined up behind the Hummers, rifles at the ready. As I approached, I could see Caleb moving from girl to girl, giving them instructions and encouragement.

Beyond was a group of at least forty females, charging directly at them. They were still outside 100 yards, and as I came to a stop next to Caleb, Igor fired again, sending one of them tumbling to the pavement.

"We're ready," he said.

"I see that," I answered, oddly proud of the young man.

I glanced around at the sound of running boots, seeing Long and Sam come around the wreck.

"Have everyone hold their fire. None of your rifles are suppressed and will make too much noise. We'll take care of the infected."

While Caleb spread the word, Long, Sam and I spread out and opened fire. Igor kept shooting as well, and the numbers of infected still alive quickly began to dwindle.

"More coming," Igor said as a well-placed shot from Long dropped the last of the first group.

"How many?"

"Many. Shitload."

Despite the situation, I couldn't stop myself from grinning at Igor's use of the English language.

"Caleb. Bigger group coming. Can these girls really shoot?"

"Yes they can," he said with complete confidence.

"OK, get them into the rocks on either side of the road. Have them hold their fire until I yell for them to start shooting."

He nodded and quickly split the girls into two groups. After a brief set of instructions, he sent them on their way, remaining in the middle of the road next to me.

"Rachel, any progress?" I called on the radio.

"She's found the release, but we can't turn it. The wrench is too short, and neither of us are strong enough."

Shit! I glanced down at Caleb, noting the sling supporting his right arm.

"I'm going to help with the bollards," I shouted over the radio and to Caleb. "Keep me updated."

As I turned away and began running, Igor fired the first shot at the new group of infected. I briefly wondered what the hell they were doing all the way out here, but it didn't matter. They were here.

Another loud groan sounded as I pounded down the road. I spared a brief glance to my left, not liking it when I saw the surface of the lake. It was dancing again, the same ripples as before distorting the usually calm water. I had no idea if this was normal, or a precursor to the dam failing. For that matter, this could go on for months or years before anything catastrophic happened. Or the whole thing could collapse in the next ten seconds.

Shutting my thoughts off, I skidded to a stop next to Dog, who was guarding the opening into the maintenance pit. Rachel and Tiffany were shoulder to shoulder, both gripping a small wrench as they tried to turn it.

"Make room!" I shouted, jumping down a moment later.

Fulcrum

They scrambled out of my way, Rachel holding the light for me. Beneath a nest of thick hoses was a large tank with a complicated valve. Several of the lines were attached to it at the top, a thick bolt sticking out of the side. A small, chrome wrench was hanging from the bolt head.

"This will let the fluid out of the system. Right?" I asked Tiffany.

"Not out," she said. "It releases it into that tank and depressurizes the whole system."

I didn't have time to ask any more questions. Thrusting my arm into the tight space, I grasped the wrench and tugged. It didn't budge. Taking a breath, I re-gripped the tool and pulled with all my strength. It didn't budge. Sweat popped out on my forehead as I kept up the pressure, but I soon backed off with a creative string of curses.

"Sam. Sitrep?"

I was pushing hoses out of the way so I could get better access to the wrench and took advantage of the moment to check on the team. As soon as he answered, I could hear suppressed rifle shots being fired very quickly.

"There's a whole mess of 'em, sir! We're engaging the leading edge, but we're going to need every rifle we've got in a minute. Sure would be nice if you could hurry."

I reached for the valve, starting to say something to Sam, when the next groan from the overstressed dam sounded. Maybe this one was worse, or perhaps it was because we were below ground, but it was intense enough to rattle my organs against my ribs. There was a gasp from Tiffany and Rachel both, but I didn't have time to look at them.

Grasping the wrench with both hands, I pulled with a grunt of effort. At first, it wasn't budging, then it suddenly released with no warning. My knuckles banged into several things that hurt like hell as I stumbled backward, then there was a loud rushing sound, like water in pipes, as the hydraulic fluid flowed into the tank.

The groan subsided as I stuck my head out of the hatch to check the bollards. They hadn't moved. Was Tiffany wrong about how to release them?

"They're not moving!" I shouted.

"Mechanical locks in the shafts," Tiffany yelled back.

I looked down to see her grab a hammer out of the tool kit and worm her way past a couple of hoses. Looking at the ceiling, she extended the hammer and hit something with a sharp blow and quickly stepped back. The bottom of a bollard appeared, descending rapidly until it came to a stop with a dull thud I could feel in the concrete floor. Checking outside, I confirmed that one of the bollards had indeed retracted.

"You've got eleven more. Can you get all of them?"

"No problem," Tiffany said as she headed for the next one, hammer swinging from her hand.

"Go. Sounds like they need help," Rachel said. "I'll call if we need you."

I met her eyes briefly, then climbed up onto the road. Telling Dog to stay and protect them, I ran for the vehicles. Before I reached the crashed truck, I heard the unsuppressed rifles the kids were carrying start up. That wasn't good news. There must be a lot of infected coming if Igor, Long and Sam couldn't hold them off on their own.

Reaching the lead Humvee, I cursed when I saw how many females were bearing down on the group. Two hundred, at least. Bodies littered the road, but there were still more infected charging towards us than there were lying dead on the asphalt.

Taking position behind one of the Hummers to use its hood for a shooting rest, I joined the fight. Putting down three females, I paused when I saw several run at an angle into the rocks. The same rocks I'd had Caleb send the girls into.

"Females are going into the rocks!"

I shouted into the radio, pulled the trigger on two more, then slapped Caleb on the back.

"Go pull your girls out of the rocks before the females get to them!"

He nodded and disappeared as I engaged another fast runner.

"Igor. Is your position secure?" I called.

"Da," he said, continuing a long string of invective in his native tongue as he kept firing as fast as he could cycle the bolt on the sniper rifle.

I kept firing, but the females were pressing in. I'd like to say that every shot each of us was putting downrange was dropping an infected, but that just wasn't the case. We were easily missing as many as we were hitting, and more were cutting away from the asphalt and heading into the desert. I couldn't tell if they were zeroed in on the girls, or if they were trying to flank us.

Fulcrum

The volume of unsuppressed fire from my right dropped as Caleb rounded up the girls and moved them back onto the road. Seconds later, the first group joined me at the vehicle and resumed shooting. Caleb ran past, shouting for the rest of the girls to come down to the Humvee.

"We got the last one. Heading across the dam!" Rachel's voice over the radio.

"Watch your ass," I said in between shots. "Got a lot of females and they're trying to flank us. Some may leak past and get to you."

"We've got Dog," she said, her voice bouncing as she ran. "We're good."

I didn't like the idea of them heading to the far side by themselves, even if Dog was with them. By now, Rachel was at least as good with a rifle as many trained Soldiers I'd worked with, but there were still only the two of them. However, there wasn't a choice.

What I'd thought had been only about 200 females was still coming. Apparently, there had been some slightly slower ones behind them. But only slightly. They raced around the curve in the road, coming into view, and the bitches just kept on coming.

I had just changed magazines when a scream to my left snapped my head around. A female had made it past us and raced onto the road to tackle one of the girls to the ground. Rifle still in my hands, I took a long step and swung the stock. The high-impact plastic solidly struck the side of the female's head with enough force to snap her neck and send the body tumbling away from the frightened girl.

Well, maybe frightened wasn't the right word. She couldn't have been more than 17, but she leaped to her feet, bleeding from several wounds and delivered a solid kick to the corpse before turning and continuing to fight. Damn. I was starting to like these kids!

Moving around behind her, I spotted and killed three females who were picking their way amongst the rocks. One of them was coming up behind Igor, who hadn't been aware of her approach.

"Igor, get your ass down here!" I shouted as I fired on another infected that was trying to reach him.

He fired two more shots then jumped up and half ran, half slid, down the hill. A female charged him before he reached the pavement, leaping to wrap herself around his upper body. The big Spetsnaz soldier grabbed her by the throat and twisted, slamming her head against a rock and ending her fight.

Fulcrum

"Rachel, you OK?" I shouted, stepping farther back and scanning the rocks for more females.

Two on the right side managed to avoid my fire, the bullets blasting chunks out of a couple of boulders instead of putting them down. They ducked, using the rugged terrain to their advantage and I lost sight of them.

"We're fine," Rachel answered, panting.

It's nearly a quarter of a mile across the top of Hoover dam. Not really that far, but when you're racing the clock, and attacking infected, it can feel like forever. They were probably running flat out for the far side.

"Females are starting to leak through. Keep your eyes open."

The volume of fire coming from my team and the girls was ferocious, but we were barely holding our own. And I was starting to worry about our ammo situation. Dropping a charging female, I dashed to the back of the Humvee that was carrying most of our ammo, screaming for Caleb to join me.

Yanking the hatch open, I grabbed several cans of loaded magazines and dragged them out to fall to the ground. By this time, Caleb ran up. He'd apparently had an up close and personal battle with a female as his face was covered with blood from a scalp wound. Didn't matter. He was still on his feet, he could still fight.

"Start distributing ammo," I said, pointing at the cans before running to the opposite flank.

Caleb nodded and grabbed one with his good arm, racing away towards Long and Sam. More females were in the rocks, and I was getting worried they'd either attack us from the rear or keep going and run down Rachel and Tiffany.

They were staying in small groups as they worked their way to our sides, and I decided to go for a more aggressive response than just a rifle. Retrieving grenades from my vest, I started pulling pins and tossing them into the areas where I saw movement. The detonations were brutally loud, even over the fire from the girls' rifles, and must have startled them. When the first one blew, they stopped firing and looked in fear to see what had happened.

My own stupid fault. They had reacted exactly the way anyone unaccustomed to battlefields would. Despite showing themselves to be quite adept at fighting the females, they were thrown for a loop by the ear shattering detonations.

"Keep firing!" I shouted.

Fulcrum

Slowly, first one, then all of their rifles picked back up. But that little lull had allowed the small herd of females to draw closer. By now it seemed as if they were already on top of us, but they started dropping quickly again when the girl's got back into the fight.

I was running for a Humvee to get more grenades when the loudest groan so far started up. The road vibrated under my feet, and the sound was like a physical force. It was everywhere around us, the hard stone of the canyon picking it up and amplifying it.

As the volume and pitch rose, it felt like my bones were resonating right along with the rocks. Reaching the back of the vehicle, I started grabbing more grenades, pausing when the rifle fire around me sputtered into silence. I've been on battlefields where this happens, and it's rarely good news.

Expecting the worst, I stepped to the side and looked down the road. All of the females had come to a halt, looking around as the groaning from the rock slowly faded. What the hell?

For a long beat, every female I could see just stood there. They looked at the ground, the sky, the surrounding rocky terrain. Many of them tilted their heads back and sampled the air. Then, slowly at first, they began backing away.

Soon they were turning and running in the opposite direction.

"What fuck?" Igor exclaimed from a few feet away.

Everyone had stopped shooting, too stunned at the completely unexpected reaction of the females.

"The," the girl who I'd saved from the infected said to him.

He looked at her with a confused expression on his face.

"What *THE* fuck, not what fuck," she said, reaching up and wiping blood off her face.

In another time, I would have enjoyed watching an American teenaged girl teach a Russian Soldier how to curse properly. But now, I was more than worried. It's been documented for a long time that animals somehow know when a catastrophic event, like an earthquake, is imminent. No one knows how, though theories abound.

Now, I'd just witnessed humans react like an animal. Was I reading too much into this, or had the infection reawakened something primal in the females? A dormant instinct that warned them when something really bad was about to happen?

214

"Rachel?" I called on the radio, fearing the worst.

"We just made it to the far side," she said, her voice tight with exertion. "We're trying to raise the access panel, but it's heavy as hell."

"Any infected near you?"

"No, but Dog's freaked out about something."

"Not infected?"

"Don't... think so. Oomph," there was a loud clang of metal. "He's not growling. And we can't move the hatch. We need help."

"On my way," I said, turning. "Lieutenant, get this truck hooked up and dragged out of the way! I'm heading across the dam to get the bollards down."

"Copy. We'll drive across as soon as we get it moved."

I skidded to a halt and turned back.

"Negative! Stay off the dam until the roadway is clear. The way it's moaning and groaning, you don't need to be sitting on it, waiting. I'll call when it's clear, then you come fast."

He looked at me, glanced at the lake pressing against the dam, and nodded. Without another word, I turned and ran.

I was about halfway across when the concrete beneath my feet began vibrating again. This time, there was no accompanying sound, but if anything it felt stronger. The lake's surface was doing its dance, and with a bad feeling in the pit of my stomach, I ran harder.

As I neared the far end, Dog ran out to meet me. Rachel was right, he was definitely freaked out, and I was afraid I knew why. I nearly fell when he rammed his head into my hip, trying to steer me, or stop me. Pushing around him, I kept running, Dog so close to my side I had to concentrate to not trip over him.

"I think this dam is about to go!" I said to Rachel as I ran up and dropped to my knees next to the access panel.

It was a four-foot square piece of heavy, sheet steel, hinged on one side. Strong enough to support a vehicle driving across its surface. Probably intended only to be lifted by a crew with a winch or something similar. I hadn't paid attention to the other one since Long and Sam had opened it, but looking at this one, I hoped I had the strength to move it.

Fulcrum

Tiffany had jammed a screwdriver into the holes that would be used to attach a chain, creating a makeshift handle. Moving into a squat, I gripped it with both hands and pulled. The panel shifted and began to swing open. And it was fucking heavy! Grunting, I held on with everything I had and slowly stood, my legs shaking and the muscles burning from the exertion.

When I had raised it a foot, first Rachel, then Tiffany rushed to either side of me and placed their hands flat on the underside and pushed. With a screeching protest of rusty hinges, it rose to vertical, and I gave it a final shove. With a hard bang, it flopped all the way over and impacted the asphalt, bouncing once.

Breathing like a steam engine, I stepped aside as Tiffany dropped into the hole and began looking around with her flashlight. I heard a few decidedly inappropriate words come out of her mouth, then she stood up in the opening and looked at me.

"We've got a problem. This is a newer system. The depressurization valve is inside the tank and requires a specialized tool to operate."

Of course it did.

"What about just bleeding the fluid out?"

I remembered how Scott had bypassed the hydraulics in Los Alamos. Tiffany was shaking her head before I finished speaking.

"Nope. It's designed with a bleed valve inside the tank, so fluid isn't spilled when you're purging air. There's no way to do this without the right tool or power to run the pumps."

"Wait a sec," Rachel said. "We're standing on top of a hydroelectric generator. Right? Shouldn't there be power?"

I looked at her for a beat, then turned to Tiffany. She might be young, but I'd never been an engineering student. That put her one up on me.

"The lake's high because there's no water going through. See those towers?" She pointed at four massive, cylindrical structures sticking out of the lake. "Those are the intakes for the turbines that generate electricity. They must be closed, because there's no water coming out the downstream side. No flow, no power."

"Do we go back?" Rachel asked after a long pause.

The two women looked at me, waiting for a decision.

"Will an explosion set hydraulic fluid on fire?" I asked.

218

"Depends," Tiffany said. "I have no way of knowing what they're using. There're fluids that are water based, and won't ignite, but there's also a whole range that will burn."

I squatted at the edge of the pit, thinking for a moment. Dog nearly knocked me into it, shoving against my side with his head. He wanted us to get moving. I didn't blame him.

"OK. What if we release all the mechanical locks, like you did at the other end, first? Once they're open, tell me where to place some explosives so that the system is breached and drains of fluid. That should work. Right?"

Tiffany thought about it for several long seconds. Rachel, squatted next to me, looked back and forth between us as the young woman thought about my idea.

"It should, yes. And even if it ignites the fluid, we don't care."

"Exactly," I said, smiling.

"Guess we've gotta try," she said, grabbing the hammer and disappearing into the pit.

In a few seconds, I heard the muted bangs of her releasing the first lock. Standing, I turned to look at the dam and the dark surface of the water.

"Is this a good idea?" Rachel asked. "Is it worth the risk, or should we back off and head south on the other side of the river?"

She had voiced the thoughts that were going through my head. Sure, crossing here and heading through Arizona to Mexico would save us hundreds of miles and many hours the pilot probably didn't have, but was it worth it? If this dam went as we were driving across... But then, if the dam failed...

"Here's the problem," I said. "Unless we head all the way to the other side of the coastal mountains in California, we're in the flood zone if the dam breaks. There will be a wall of water sweeping all the way down the Colorado into the Gulf of California. We don't want to be anywhere near that if it happens."

"Is it any better in Arizona?"

"Yes. We head east before turning south. Any flooding would be contained well away from us by the terrain. Not so in California."

Tiffany was still hammering away, and it took all of my self-control not to shout at her to move faster.

"What happened with the infected?" Rachel asked.

Fulcrum

"Spookiest damn thing," I said, shaking my head. "That last big groan freaked them out. Froze them in their tracks, then they turned and ran."

"That's not good," Rachel whispered, staring at me in surprise.

I nodded, then shrugged my shoulders.

"Ready!"

We turned when Tiffany shouted. I quickly dropped into the pit and looked where she was pointing with her flashlight.

"There and there," she said. "Take out those two valves and the whole system will drain. What are you going to use?"

I reached into my vest and pulled out two of the grenades I'd restocked with while fighting the females. Her eyes got big for a second, then she handed me the flashlight, turned without another word and scrambled out of the pit.

Shining it around, I didn't see what I was hoping to find. Ripping open pockets on my vest, I dug through, but couldn't find what I needed. A simple roll of duct tape. That's all I needed to hold the grenades in place.

"Rachel!" I shouted. "Got any medical tape with you?"

"No," she answered a moment later.

Crap. OK, make do with I've got. Cutting two, one-foot lengths of paracord, I tied the grenades in place. It took the right touch, and tape would have worked much easier, but I got it done. Making two more, much longer lengths of line, I threaded them through the grenade's rings before carefully straightening the pins so they would pull easily.

Moving gingerly, I climbed back to street level, paying out the two lengths of line as I went. Waving the girls back, I moved as far from the opening as I could and waited until Rachel had gotten Dog to join her. He whined and sat on her feet, looking around with his ears folded against his skull.

"Fire in the hole," I said, giving the two cords a sharp tug.

There was slight resistance, then they fell free. I heard the faint tinkle of the pins on the concrete floor of the pit as I scrambled away to open more distance. Five seconds later, the grenades detonated so close together that it was hard to distinguish the separate blasts.

We were well shielded from the concussive force and shrapnel but still felt it in our feet. A heartbeat later, flames shot out of the open hatch as the hydraulic fluid ignited. They receded briefly, then quickly grew in intensity as the system drained and fed the fire. The heat was intense, but we were all well back.

Tiffany's attention was focused on the bollards, which after a few seconds began slowly retracting into the road's surface. She turned to face me with a big smile on her face, jumping up to wrap her arms around my neck and give me a hug.

"We did it!" She shouted.

I hugged her back, then turned to look across the dam. I couldn't see the rest of the group, and hoped they'd been able to move the crashed vehicle.

"Sam, you copy?" I called on the radio.

"Go for Sam," he responded quickly.

"Clear on this end. You ready?"

"Yes, sir. We moved the wreck enough that we can squeeze by. We're coming to you."

"Copy," I said.

I got Rachel, Dog and Tiffany moving, heading away from the dam. The bollards had fully retracted, the road now wide open for the rest of the team. There was no point in standing this close to the dam while we waited for them, so I led the way towards a large parking lot that had been built for tourists.

It was only a short distance, in a vehicle, across the top. I expected Sam would be leading the way, coming fast. We should be seeing the first Hummer at any moment.

Calling a halt once we were clear of the road, I turned to watch for them just as another moan started up. Dog whined, moving next to me and shoving his whole body against my leg. Rachel caught her breath and reached for my hand.

This sound was unlike any of the previous. It had the same low frequency, bass rumble, but there was also a high pitched scream, like the tortured souls of the damned. I spotted the lead Humvee, racing along the narrow roadway atop the dam. The moan suddenly stopped, leaving only the scream. An instant later, a crack sounded, so loud and violent it made me take a step back. Then everything went still and quiet.

The straining engine was loud in the night, and I breathed a sigh of relief. I could clearly see Sam's face behind the windshield, and he was going to make it safely across. Only a couple of hundred yards separated us.

Fulcrum

I heard the roar of jet engines an instant before a brilliant streak of fire rushed through the darkness to a point on the face of the dam just below the road surface. There was a thunderous explosion, an intense ball of fire instantly spreading to consume the Hummer. An instant later, a second missile flashed in and detonated within the fireball.

Screaming a warning into the radio, I snapped my head up in time to see a Russian Yak fighter bank sharply and turn to continue over the lake. Spinning, I grabbed Rachel and Tiffany and started running away from the dam. Dog raced ahead of us, and I looked over my shoulder as we opened up some space.

The fireball was subsiding, and I could just make out the road along the top of the dam, and the Hummer on it, through smoke and a cloud of pulverized concrete. Then, the entire top of the dam began tilting towards the empty, 700-foot-deep gorge on the downstream side.

"Oh my God, no," Rachel breathed.

She was looking over her shoulder, too, and was slowing. I yanked on her arm to keep her running, desperate to reach cover before the fighter jet returned. We were in the open and would be sitting ducks for a strafing run. I risked another glance, hoping that Sam would make it across.

But, the tilt was increasing. Then, a huge section of the top began to slide. At first, it was a barely perceptible movement. The roadway was slipping towards open air, but the Humvee was still coming towards us, emerging from a thick cloud of debris that had been blasted into the air.

In slow motion at first, but rapidly accelerating, the upper thirty feet of Hoover dam broke free and began to tumble into the canyon below. Billions of gallons of water, suddenly free to flow, pushed against the indescribably massive chunk of concrete. Another second and everything was obscured by a cloud of roiling mist as the waters of Lake Mead rushed through the gap left behind.

Commander Jason Talbot, Captain of the North Carolina, wasn't a happy man. For that matter, he was rarely in a good mood, or so it seemed to people who didn't know him. But, he was one of the best submarine skippers the United States had ever put to sea. Meticulous attention to detail, and demanding near perfection from the men and women under his command and pushing them harder than they'd ever been pushed in their lives was the only way he knew how to operate.

Traits such as these can easily lead to resentment amongst the ranks, but he had repeatedly shown that he lived by the same high standards he expected from everyone aboard his boat. And while he might seem a rigid taskmaster to an outsider, he was the most upfront and fair officer any of them had ever encountered. He didn't accept excuses, but he understood valid reasons. His crew loved him.

Times had been hard since the attacks on America and the spread of the virus across the world. Based out of Pearl Harbor, the majority of the crew had been able to talk to family members who lived in Hawaii. Not that there weren't parents and siblings, and a few spouses and children who had perished on the mainland, but for the most part, none of them were dealing with the complete and total loss of their entire family.

That had softened the blow to morale, yet hardly eliminated it. The Captain himself had lost his wife, who was visiting friends in Denver when the attacks happened. His two daughters, both in their teens, had stayed behind in Hawaii to work summer jobs. Living in officer housing on the base, they had been watched closely by the Navy wives that lived around them. And, he'd gotten to see them once, briefly, when the North Carolina had put in for a restock of food stores.

A nuclear powered submarine can stay on patrol indefinitely, except for one small problem. The crew has to eat. The reactor provides endless propulsion and electricity, also powering a desalinization unit that produces unlimited fresh water from the surrounding sea. But, food. The only thing, other than the psychological pressure of being in a steel tube deep in the ocean for months on end, that could force a sub to return to port.

The North Carolina had been near the end of a planned 60-day patrol in the South China Sea when the nukes went off in New York, DC and LA. They had received new orders, scrapping plans to return to Pearl Harbor within the week. Joining with the hastily created NATO armada, they had fought the Chinese invasion fleet. By the time the battles were over, Captain Talbot had expended all of his torpedoes and Tomahawk missiles, accounting for seven of the enemy ships that were sunk. And the cooks were getting pretty creative with what remained in the mostly barren pantry.

A quick trip to Hawaii to restock their stores was necessary. Surfacing near the entrance to Pearl Harbor, just after sunset, the North Carolina had taken aboard a pilot who was responsible for navigating the waters of the harbor and delivering the 8,000-ton boat safely to the dock. A veritable army of sailors was waiting with truckloads of provisions, ready to start loading the moment it was tied up. Food and medical supplies were brought aboard by hand, the Navy utilizing the tried and true method of a bucket brigade.

While the men sweated in the hot and humid night, a full complement of torpedoes and Tomahawks were loaded. Along with them came crates full of M4 rifles, 9mm pistols and thousands of rounds of ammunition. An American submarine typically only has a very limited armory with only a handful of rifles and pistols. Enough for the senior officers and NCOs to arm themselves in extraordinary circumstances.

But things had progressed well beyond extraordinary, and it had been decided that every crewman should have a weapon available in case the sub had to put to shore in a hostile environment. Which was pretty much anywhere other than Hawaii.

For the officers and crew who had family in Hawaii, their loved ones had been gathered by the Navy and brought to the dock for a brief visit while the submarine was in port. Wives and children were still in shock over what had happened but understood the necessity for them to put back to sea as quickly as possible.

Not knowing how long before they could return, enough provisions to feed the crew for eight months had been taken aboard. There was so much that berthing areas, passageways, and even the Captain's cabin, were stacked high with boxes of rations. Emotions running high, the crew had boarded as soon as the loading was complete, and lines had been thrown.

The pilot took them back to open water, wished the Captain well and departed on a small boat that had trailed behind to pick him up. Twenty minutes before sunrise, the North Carolina slid beneath the waves of the Pacific and dove for the security of deep water.

Since that day, they hadn't been back to port. Hunting and killing Russian ships and subs had been their mission, and the Captain and crew had carried it out with deadly efficiency. Then, they'd received a new set of instructions over the ELF (Extreme Low Frequency) radio. The system, the only way to communicate with a submerged submarine, wasn't impacted by the worm the Russians had introduced into the Navy's digital Battlespace communications system.

But it was inherently inefficient, only able to transmit a few bits of data per minute, and the sub is unable to respond as an ELF transmitter is incredibly large. So, the North Carolina had received a message that took over an hour to download, instructing them to proceed to a set of coordinates in the Solomon Sea and wait at periscope depth to pick up a SEAL team.

Captain Talbot had received the message, but with no way to reply, it was taken on faith that the North Carolina would be at the correct location, on the proper day and time. The SEALs had jumped into the vast emptiness of the south Pacific Ocean without any confirmation there was a ride hanging around to pick them up.

But the sub had been there. Now, they were racing towards the southeastern Australian coast with the SEALs aboard, and Captain Talbot had just finished reading the orders delivered to him by the Commander in charge of the team. The orders were directly from Admiral Packard himself and had left no doubt that time was of the essence. That was the reason for the North Carolina currently running at flank speed. And it was why Captain Talbot was unhappy.

"So, what's so damn important, Commander?"

He was addressing the SEAL officer, seated across from him in his cramped cabin. A stack of boxes containing creamed corn separated the two men, like a tall, square table.

"We're making more noise than my daughter's stereo, running this fast. If there's a Russian within fifty miles, they're going to hear us. And, we're deaf at this speed, too. We won't hear a Russian, or Australian, until there's already a torpedo in the water."

"I understand, Captain. And I can assure you that Admiral Packard does as well. But, here's the situation."

The SEAL talked for several minutes, providing details that weren't in Talbot's orders. He briefed him on the last ditch effort to capture Russian president Barinov and force him to call off the invasion fleet before they landed in Hawaii.

Talbot listened carefully, a grim expression on his face as he thought about what might happen to his daughters if the Russians succeeded in defeating the defenders and capturing the islands.

"Are you planning to bring Barinov back aboard when you capture him?"

"Yes, we are. We need to be able to control the environment, and will need to use your comm gear once we break him."

"What if you can't break him?" Talbot asked.

"We'll get him to cooperate," the SEAL growled. "My only concern is the tight schedule. We're going to reach point Alpha off the Australian coast in just over 32 hours. That leaves us roughly eight hours to make it to shore, capture Barinov and bring him back to the North Carolina. Any longer than that and the Russians will be sipping Mai Tais in the sand on Waikiki."

Talbot leaned back in his chair in thought, then turned and picked up a sound powered phone. He ordered his XO, Executive Officer, to join him in his quarters. Less than a minute later there was a knock on the door, and he called out permission to enter.

Lieutenant Commander Adrienne Cable stepped into the room and softly closed the door behind her. She was the first woman to ever become the XO of an American nuclear submarine, and despite the doubts of the crew, had managed to fit in very well. Every bit as sharp and determined as her skipper, she had been at the top of her class at Annapolis and continued to impress him with her logical mind and nearly encyclopedic knowledge of every system on the boat.

Talbot introduced her to the SEAL, then spent a couple of minutes bringing her up to speed. He didn't fail to notice how the man looked at her, but would deal with that outside her presence. She was a naval officer, the XO of the boat, and he was going to make damn sure that was clear to the SEAL. He wasn't going to tolerate any lack of respect.

"So, XO, the Commander here is going to be on a very tight clock once he and his team lockout. Alpha Point is fifty miles from the entrance to Sydney Harbour. I was thinking that perhaps we could get him a bit closer and cut down their transit time in the RIBs. Thoughts?"

Adrienne opened the secure iPad that was her constant companion and began tapping on the screen. A few seconds later, she leaned forward and laid it flat on Talbot's desk. On the screen was a navigational chart, the broad opening to the harbor at the extreme edge.

"Point Alpha is here," she said, tapping a spot in the ocean directly east of Sydney. "It's the last deep water before the seabed rises dramatically. At Alpha, we've got 2,500 meters of water. Move closer by ten miles, and we lose half of that. 1,200 meters. Another 10 miles, 346 meters and it just keeps getting worse until we reach the mouth of the harbor."

She tapped on the point, and the iPad displayed the depth. 30 meters.

"If the Aussies, or Russians, are conducting any ASW sweeps, they'll find us. And there's nowhere to go deep if we need to run."

She was referring to Anti-Submarine Warfare.

"So you're saying you can't get closer," the SEAL grumbled, leaning back.

"I didn't say that at all," Adrienne locked eyes with him. "I was just explaining the situation to the Captain. We've operated in shallower water than this in the... well, never mind where. Anyways, with the skipper's permission, I'll park this big bitch right here, in the middle of Bate Bay. And, unless they get really lucky, the Aussies will never know we're there."

She touched a point on the map just to the south of the harbor entrance. A semi-circular bay cut into the coastline, and if the SEALs disembarked there, it would take them less than ten minutes to sail the RIBs around the headland and enter Sydney Harbour.

"That would save us at least three hours, maybe more, depending on the sea state," the SEAL said, leaning closer to the iPad.

"Agreed," Adrienne said, smiling for the first time. "And if we get spotted, which we won't, but if we do it's a straight run to deep water."

She traced a path to the southeast with a perfectly manicured nail. Talbot followed her finger with his eyes, then looked up.

"Thank you, XO. Have a plot ready for my review in half an hour."

"Aye, aye sir," Adrienne snapped, picked up the iPad and quickly departed.

"She's something else," the SEAL said when the door closed.

"What she is, is a naval officer and the XO of this boat. I would advise you to not lose sight of either of those facts, Commander."

"Captain?"

"Don't play dumb, Commander. I saw your expression when she walked in. You don't like a woman in command."

"Not at all, Captain," the SEAL said, a surprised look on his face. "You've got me wrong. I was simply wondering if she's married."

24

We stood in shock, staring at the impossibly massive plume of water pouring through the gaping hole in the top of the dam. A heavy mist was created as it rushed past the shattered concrete and fell 700 feet to the canyon floor. That mist quickly soaked us to the skin, as if we were out in a pouring rain.

I could hear the Yak fighter, circling overhead, but at the moment knew that we were safe. There was so much water vapor saturating the air all around the dam, there was no way he could see us. Not even with thermal imaging. For the moment, we were safe.

The roar of the lake emptying itself was tremendous, and the ground vibrated from the impact of millions of tons of water as it struck the rocks below. The sound was intense, completely enveloping us in its embrace. It was mesmerizing, watching the raw power of the water.

Tiffany was crying, and started to move closer to the dam, but Rachel grabbed her and pulled her into her arms. There was another crack, loud enough to be heard over the pounding roar. I couldn't see anything through the heavy mist, but suspected another piece of the top of the dam had been torn away by the unimaginable force of the water.

I looked up as the Russian jet screamed overhead again, sounding much lower this time. He was trying to find another target. We were still in the cloud of mist, getting a steady drenching, but I urged the girls into a run, wanting to reach some cover before he decided to start blindly shooting up the whole area.

"Are here?" Igor's voice over the radio startled me.

Rachel also had a radio earpiece, and by the look of surprise on her face I could tell she'd heard the transmission.

"Igor! You big Russian bastard! You're OK?" I shouted as we ran.

"Da. Who with you?"

"Sam didn't make it. He was on the section that broke free. Is Long with you?"

"Nyet. No. Sam lead. Long follow. I no see Sam go over. Dam broke right in front me after missile strike. Long and Humvee fall. I stop and go reverse."

By now we had reached the relative safety of a jumble of massive boulders that overlooked the road leading to the dam. We worked our way in, and I looked up involuntarily as the Yak fighter passed overhead again. At least I think it was the same jet. Maybe there was a whole squadron of them up there. I looked around to see Rachel telling Tiffany that Igor had survived.

"Ask him who's with him!" Tiffany cried, hope blooming on her face.

"Igor. Who do you have with you?"

"Caleb, Chelsea, and girl name Sara. Who with you?"

Tiffany slumped against a boulder in relief when Rachel told her who else had made it.

"Rachel, Dog and Tiffany," I answered. "What's your status?"

"Vehicle good. Not injured. What we do?"

"We wait for that goddamn jet to leave. After that, I don't know yet. Stand by."

I thought about his question for a minute. Lake Mead was huge, stretching for more than forty miles to the east and north. Then there was a little thing called the Grand Canyon. It would take days, probably close to a week with current conditions, for him to circle around and reach our location.

Fulcrum

The Yak flew over again, the bellow of its engines loud, echoing in the canyon. Amazingly, it was clearly audible even above the all-enveloping rumble of water pouring out of the lake.

"What the hell happened?" Rachel asked, pushing wet hair out of her eyes.

"Goddamn Russian fighter," I said, pointing at the sky. "Fucker put a couple of missiles into the dam. It sounded like it was in trouble, and those munitions just finished it off."

"What are we going to do?"

"Hold on," I said, cocking my head to listen.

The roar of the water was loud, but I could no longer hear jet engines. Maybe the pilot had gained altitude or moved into a wider orbit. Or maybe, if luck was with us, he was low on fuel and had been forced to head home.

"Igor," I called on the radio. "Can you hear the fighter?"

"Nyet," he replied after almost a minute. "Think he gone."

"OK. Get your ass back to where we came from. He'll be back, or he's put out a radio call, and others will be coming."

241

"What you do? I come to you!"

"You can't," I said.

He was quiet for a long pause. I stood there and stared at the water still pouring over the dam. Thinking. Glancing to my right, I checked the level of the lake. Despite how much had already rushed through the breach, it wasn't noticeably lower. Of course, there was so much water in the reservoir, it would take a long time for enough to drain out to have a significant impact.

"Negative, Igor. Get out of the area as fast as you can before more fighters or helicopters show up. There's no way for you to get to me with the flooding."

"What you do?" He repeated.

Turning around, I checked the parking lot where tourists would leave their cars when visiting the dam. It was empty. Closer was a secured area where employees could park, but the fence had been torn down, and there weren't any vehicles in the lot. Rachel, hearing both sides of the conversation with Igor, was watching me expectantly.

"We're stuck," I said to Rachel after several minutes. "This is a damn big, desolate part of the southwest. It's been a few years since

I've driven between Phoenix and Vegas, but there's only one road. The one we're standing on. And it's at least 30 miles south before there's a goddamn thing other than rocks and cactus."

"So what's there? We can walk 30 miles in a few hours."

"Tiny little wide spot in the road," I said. "Can't even remember the name. Nothing but a gas station and a few mobile homes. I do remember that it's the only place to get gas for a long way in either direction."

"Igor," I said into the radio.

"I here."

"We're walking. There's a small town to the south. We'll pick up a vehicle there and continue on."

He was quiet for several seconds, and I suspected he didn't like having to turn around any more than I would have.

"I go south. Follow river."

"Negative," I said, shaking my head. "Listen to me. You need to return to where we left the others. The only way around the flooding would be to go west to the coast, then turn south. That's a lot of heavily populated area. Probably lots of infected."

Dirk Patton

The southern California coast was pretty much one big metropolis from Santa Barbara, through LA and San Diego to the Mexican border. And just on the other side of that border was Tijuana, which had a population of nearly two million before the attacks. No, there was no way anyone was going to make it through all of that mess.

"Da," he said resignedly, after a very long pause. "We go back. Dos Vedanya."

"Be careful and good luck," I said, wishing there was a way to get him across the canyon.

I turned and looked at my companions. Rachel was watching me, through tangled, dripping hair. Tiffany was seated on a wet rock, her arms wrapped around Dog's thick neck. His head was lowered and pressed against her chest as she hugged him close.

The earlier relief over the news that Caleb was alive had been replaced with tears. I was sure she was thinking about her teammates that had been lost. At the moment, I would have been happy to sit down and hug Dog, too. Lose myself for a while in mourning over the loss of Katie, Sam and Long and the girls. But I didn't have that luxury. Maybe once I'd exacted vengeance from Barinov.

"Time to move," I said to Tiffany.

"Where?" She looked up without releasing Dog.

"We're walking south. There's a small town, and I hope we can find a car."

"What if the Russians show up?" Rachel asked, standing.

"I don't think they're going to be worried about three people walking across the desert," I said, hoping I was right. "They probably spotted the Humvees and attacked because they're US military vehicles."

"If you're wrong?" Tiffany asked.

I looked at her and shook my head. On foot, in open terrain, there would be nothing we could do if Russian aircraft took an interest in us. But we couldn't stay where we were. Finally, I shrugged and gestured towards the road. Slowly, she removed her arms from Dog's neck, sniffed and wiped her eyes. Without another word, she stood up and followed as I led the way.

We'd been walking for a couple of hours, and none of us were in the mood for conversation. I was setting a fast pace, one I hoped was averaging out to about five miles an hour. The farther we got from the dam, the better I was feeling. Not that an aircraft couldn't easily range the few miles we'd covered and find us, but if the Russians were coming back, I strongly suspected they'd be looking for vehicles.

Still, I kept a sharp ear out for the sounds of approaching aircraft. I'd already prepared the girls on what to do if we heard one. On either side of the road was open desert with the occasional outcropping of rock. If I gave the word, we were going to do our best to burrow into the sand, hoping it would block enough of our heat signature from Russian thermal imaging that we would be overlooked. It was a desperate measure, and probably wouldn't work, but it was all I had.

It was still dark, which was a good thing. Even though it was well into fall, it could still get very warm in the Arizona deserts. We didn't have any water or food, or much of anything for that matter. Our packs had been in the Humvees, along with all of our provisions and medical supplies. And spare ammo, which was another concern. After the battle with the females, I was down to two full magazines and a partial. Rachel had less than two, and Tiffany only had ten rounds total. We weren't in good shape if we had to fight.

The only good news was that none of us were burdened with the weight of a pack, and we were making good time. Getting to a vehicle quickly was a very real concern. The clock was ticking for the pilot, and now for us. We had to worry about the enemy returning. And getting caught out in the middle of the day with no shelter and nothing to drink.

The night was cool, and we were doing OK without water, though I'd have loved a tall, cold beer about now. A real beer. Ice cold with a nice golden glow and a frothy head. None of this bohemian, hipster micro-brew shit that had become so popular. Or the flavored crap like blueberry or, God help me here, root beer. What the hell was wrong with a beer that tasted like beer? That made you spit it out when you were a teenager and got your first taste? You want fruity flavors, buy a goddamn soda pop.

"How much farther is it?" Tiffany asked.

Her question startled me out of my thoughts. Maybe thinking about beer wasn't the most productive use of my mind, but it beat the hell out of dwelling on the deaths of people I cared about. I'd been down that road before and knew it wasn't a good thing to keep thinking about. Sure, I will always remember the people I've lost. But concentrating on them is distracting, and will eventually result in compromised decision making because you're afraid of losing someone else.

That's fine, if you're not a Soldier. I suppose it's good, in fact. But when you're in combat, the lower risk decision is rarely the correct one. Things have to be done, and if you're all knotted up worrying about sending someone into harm's way, you're not doing your job as a leader.

"Something like 20 miles," I answered. "Maybe another four or five hours."

Despite the toughness the young woman had already displayed, I expected her to complain. Whine that she was tired, or her feet hurt, or she was hungry or thirsty. She didn't do any of that. Simply nodded and kept plodding right along, matching me stride for stride with her much shorter legs.

Rachel was on the far side of her, and she met my eyes with a grin. That little smirk conveyed her message perfectly. I smiled at her and turned back to the front, scanning across the barren landscape for threats. I saw nothing other than a perfectly straight ribbon of asphalt and empty desert. Dog walked beside me, ears at full mast and nose in the air as he, too, kept watch.

Starting to think about beer again, I forced myself to focus on the situation at hand. If there wasn't a vehicle in the little town ahead, we were pretty much screwed. There were a couple more, tiny outposts of civilization farther south, but the closest one was at least another forty miles beyond our destination. Probably even farther, as I hadn't driven this highway in a long time and was working off of memory. The map had been in the Humvee Sam was driving.

But I had to think positively. There would be a vehicle in the first town we reached, and it would have gas. And I'd be able to get it started. I regretted not having taken the opportunity to have Long teach me how to hotwire a car. In the end, it hadn't been exactly difficult to start the Ford truck Rachel and I had used to escape from Atlanta, but I also knew I'd gotten lucky. It was a several generation old model and didn't have any built in anti-theft features.

Moving past those concerns, I thought about the route we'd take to get to the pilot. I knew the area well enough not to need a map. It was fairly straightforward, and the only part of it that concerned me was skirting the Phoenix metropolitan area. Maybe it would be free of infected, or it could be overrun. Only one way to find out.

Then I remembered that we'd pass very close to Luke Air Force Base on the west side of the city. Whatever we found that would get us that far, we could make a stop and switch to another Humvee, and hopefully, replenish the ammo and supplies that we'd lost. Thinking about the air base, another idea occurred to me.

"Tiffany, you don't know how to fly a plane, do you?"

At this point, I wouldn't have been surprised if she'd said she was a pilot and could fly anything in the Air Force inventory. But, I never get that lucky. She just looked at me and shook her head.

We kept walking. One foot in front of the other. Maintaining our pace, and ignoring the complaints from our knees and ankles. Well, at least mine were complaining. I had no idea about Rachel and figured Tiffany was too young to have joint problems. Regardless, I sucked it up and walked.

Half a mile later, I came to a sudden stop and held up my hand to tell the girls to remain quiet. Turning my head from side to side, I was able to hear the occasional roar of a jet engine. It

was distant, fading in and out as the plane
changed perspective to my position.

Closing my eyes, I focused on the noise. It
was coming from the direction of the dam and
sounded like at least two different aircraft were
in an orbit. More jets had probably arrived and
were searching.

"Russians?" Rachel asked, moving next to
me and staring to the north.

"Has to be," I said, looking to my left at the
desert floor. "Let's get ready, in case they come
this way."

We moved onto the sand, each of us using
our hands to scoop out holes in the shape of
shallow graves. If the Russian fighters began
approaching, we'd lay down in them and cover
our bodies as best we could. I wasn't worried
about Dog. If they saw him on thermal, he'd look
just like a coyote and wouldn't draw any
attention.

The holes were dug quickly, and we each
got on our knees, ready to dive into them as we
listened. It seemed like it took forever, but
eventually the noise of the jets faded away. It
happened slowly, as if they were incrementally
moving their search towards Vegas. I hoped Igor
was driving like hell and could avoid the militia.
And, even though they were Americans, part of

me hoped the Russian fighters spotted the militia. They'd almost certainly take out all of their vehicles at a minimum.

When several minutes had passed without me hearing the fighters, I got to my feet and headed for the pavement. Before I could reach the edge of the road, the beat of a helicopter rotor caught my attention. I whirled around and scanned in the direction of the sound, but couldn't spot anything. Listening for a moment, I dashed for the hole I'd dug when I realized the noise was coming closer.

"In your hole! Pull sand over your body, just like we talked about!"

I shouted as I flopped onto my back and began using my arms to sweep piles of sand on top of myself. Dog, thinking it was a game, came and stood over my face. I had to push him away when he kept trying to lick me.

Quickly covered in several inches of sand from the chest down, I craned my neck and checked on Rachel and Tiffany. They were both concealed as well as I was, and I lay my head back and shoveled some more until I was buried to my neck, then lay still. The rotor was still approaching, apparently following the road we had been walking on, transiting from north to south.

Fulcrum

As it drew closer, Dog came back to stand over my head. The view was less than pleasant as I stared up.

"Dog, so help me, you piss on my head and I'll cut your balls off," I said.

He turned and stuck his nose in my face, gave me a big, wet lick then lay down and plopped a big paw onto my forehead. Worming an arm free of the sand, I moved it off my face, scratched his neck briefly then put it back under cover.

The rotor was growing loud, and I could now tell there were two helos coming our way. From the sound of them, both were Hinds, which was to be expected.

"What do we do if they see us?" Tiffany called.

"Stay behind him and do what he says," Rachel answered before I could speak, and there wasn't anything I could add to that.

A minute later a pair of Mi-24s passed directly overhead. They were no more than 500 feet above the ground, and I got a good look at them through the night vision. They didn't slow or deviate from their course, going right by and continuing south. I let out a sigh once they were another mile down the road.

"Stay put," I said to the girls. "They may turn back."

There was no response, but they didn't get up. We stayed where we were, buried in the sand as the Russians flew far enough south to pass out of earshot. I didn't think they'd go much farther. This had to feel like a futile search to the pilots, and I decided to give them ten more minutes before moving. Time was nearly expired when I picked up the sound of their rotors again. They were coming back.

"They're coming back!" Tiffany said, panic in her voice.

"It's OK," I said, calmly. "They're in a search pattern. They've gone as far south as they're going to, now they're heading back north. Nothing to worry about."

I don't know if I made her feel any better, but she didn't say anything else. Fortunately, I was right. A few minutes later they passed overhead again, heading north. This time, they were much higher and moving faster, apparently bored with searching an empty road and ready to head home. The only question I was left with was, where the hell were they operating out of?

Dismissing that thought, I climbed out of the hole and started shaking sand out of my clothing. Rachel and Tiffany followed suit, without saying anything, and we quickly resumed our southerly trek.

Two more hours passed in silence. Nothing but the sounds of our feet on the asphalt and Dog's soft panting. The temperature suddenly dropped noticeably, going from cool to downright chilly. I knew this meant the sun would be rising soon, and glanced over my left shoulder to the east.

The sky was just perceptibly lighter than it was directly overhead. We had maybe another forty minutes before the sun peeked over the mountain tops. When it did, the temperature was going to go up fast.

I wasn't really sure what month it was, but knew North America had settled into late fall/early winter. I tried to figure that out for a few minutes before giving up. Maybe Chelsea, with her mathematical mind, could tell me, but I'd been too busy running and fighting to worry about what the date was. All I knew, with any degree of certainty, was that it had been early summer when the attacks occurred.

Trying to figure out the timeline based on everything that had occurred since turned out to be an exercise in futility. I finally gave up and guessed it was somewhere around late November. That made me think of a Thanksgiving meal, and my stomach rumbled long and loud. Tiffany looked at me and giggled. I made a face at her, seeing Rachel shake her head from the corner of my eye.

Even though it wasn't summer, the daytime temperatures in the open desert can easily reach 90 degrees Fahrenheit. If we were out in the sun for any extended period, the lack of water was going to become a serious problem. But that shouldn't happen, I reminded myself. We had been walking for over four hours, and must have already covered 20 miles. That left ten to go, with less than that by sunrise. As long as we didn't have to keep going to the next town, or get stalled hiding from Russians, we'd be fine.

Realizing I'd fallen into a near trance as I walked, I silently cursed myself and took a long look at our surroundings. Everything looked exactly the same as it had since we'd left the dam. Sun blasted, barren desert. Not even a bush visible within the range of my night vision goggles.

"Where do you think all those females came from?" Rachel broke the silence.

"Probably Boulder City," I said after thinking about it for a minute. "It's a town that sprang up for the workers who built the dam. Not a big place, but the only population center in the area that I can think of."

"How'd they know we were there?"
Tiffany asked.

"They have hearing like a bat," I said.
"Most likely the noise of the vehicles as we drove in. We were moving faster than they can, but once we'd been stopped for a while, they caught up."

Tiffany and Rachel came to a stop when a high pitched howl floated across the night air from somewhere to our right. Dog's head snapped in that direction, but he didn't react in any other way. When I realized he and I were walking alone, I stopped and turned around.

"What the hell is that?" Rachel said, sounding spooked.

"Coyote," I said, trying not to smile. "They won't bother us."

"They?" Tiffany asked, still frozen in place.

"They run in packs," I said. "Don't worry. They aren't going to mess with three adult humans and a big, furry dog."

Neither of them looked terribly convinced that we weren't in imminent danger, and I had to coax them into resuming our trek. I didn't fail to notice that they were both walking much closer to me than before, their rifles held tightly to their

257

bodies as they nervously scanned our immediate surroundings.

The coyote howled again. This time, an answering voice came from the opposite side of the road. Soon the pack was yipping and singing all around us, and Rachel and Tiffany moved even closer. This continued for more than ten minutes, then they fell silent. It was probably a good thing the coyotes moved on as both girls were pretty freaked out by then.

The eastern horizon had continued to lighten, and I pushed my night vision goggles away from my eyes. There was more than enough early light to see without them. The sun rose quickly, the way it tends to do in deserts. I caught a brief glint of light reflecting off something far in the distance, directly to our front. It was several miles away but almost had to be chrome or glass to have flashed as brightly as it did.

Neither of the girls had seen it, and I kept the information to myself. I'd probably just seen the town that was our destination, but there was no guarantee that it was a vehicle that had caught the sun. It could just as easily have been the window of a mobile home. I didn't want to get their hopes up.

26

The town was called White Hills. Calling it a town was being generous. The first thing we came to was an aging gas station that billed itself as the *Last Stop*. A small restaurant and a few pumps, and that was it. No vehicles. But, first things first. We needed to find some water.

Dog and I carefully entered the building while Rachel and Tiffany kept watch outside. The instant I pulled the swinging door open, I was hit with the sickening stench of rotting corpses. Pausing, I gave Dog a moment to sniff the air. He didn't growl, but I didn't see any way he could scent an infected over the horrible smell of decomposition.

The building didn't have any windows, the exterior cinderblock walls painted with the likeness of flags from dozens of different nations. It was dark inside and, breathing through my mouth, I lowered the NVGs. I took my time scanning the interior.

Females had been here. Nothing else tore through people the way they did. There were more than a dozen bodies scattered around the cramped space, sprays and splashes of blood decorating the walls, the floor almost completely covered with black stains where it had pooled and dried. The only thing missing was a seething mass of flies, feasting on the remains and spilled body fluids. I didn't understand why they were absent but didn't have time to give it any thought.

Seeing and hearing nothing, I stepped into the structure, Dog tight against my leg. Behind us, the door sighed shut. Stepping over the dead, I was careful where I placed my feet. There might not be a swarm of insects, but I had no doubt that all variety of bacteria were thriving in the remains and on every surface. A simple mistake, like a misstep that caused me to stumble and cut myself, could very easily result in a fatal infection.

There were a dozen vinyl upholstered booths lining the front wall, a scattering of tables filling the space between them and a long counter. Almost every piece of furniture was turned over, except for the counter stools which were bolted to the concrete floor. Behind the counter was a long grill, beyond that a swinging door that opened into what I suspected was a pantry.

Hoping to find some bottled water, I stepped around the end of the counter and paused short of the door. Dog sniffed but remained silent. Exercising an abundance of caution, I whistled loudly, then waited with my rifle aimed at the door. A full minute later,

nothing had come charging, so we went forward
and pushed through.

The food storage area was small, not
really much more than an oversized closet. It
only took a few seconds for me to see that it had
been stripped bare. Nothing other than cheap
plastic shelving remained. Cursing, I went back
outside, pausing long enough to turn the valve on
a sink, just in case the water was still on. It
wasn't.

Turning it back off out of habit, I headed
for the exit. Taking a deep breath when I
reached fresh air, I shook my head when Rachel
looked at me. She nodded, understanding my
message.

Behind the restaurant was another block
building, garishly painted with childlike images
of a green alien, a monster truck and a couple of
belt-fed machine guns. A sun bleached sign
advertised Grand Canyon monster truck tours
and a shooting range where tourists could fire a
real machine gun. Getting the girls' attention, I
pointed at it, and Dog and I started walking.
They fell in behind, doing a good job of keeping
an eye on our rear.

The front door was a stout slab of steel,
solidly locked into the surrounding walls. If I'd
had a bit of C4, I would have used it, but that was
another item lost in the Humvees. Circling

around the building, I paused in surprise when I came up against a tall, solid fence. It was made of what looked like sheets of scrap iron and was at least 10 feet tall. Coils of barbed wire lined the top and there was a single, wide gate secured with a heavy chain and padlock.

A quick check of Dog, who was alert but calm, and I stepped up and peeked through the gap in the center where the two sections of the gate met. There were only a couple of inches to see through, but that was enough to spot four huge pickups. They were all lifted ridiculously high, riding on massive tires and painted outlandish shades of purple, green and yellow.

Telling Rachel and Tiffany to stay where they were, I led Dog around the perimeter of the fence, hoping to find an easy way in. There wasn't, and that's probably why it looked like no one had been inside. Going back to the gate, I stood in the sun for a moment, staring at the obstacle.

There was no way to climb the smooth iron plates. And even if I could, the coils of barbed wire would be a problem. The chain was too thick to be broken with a bullet or grenade. Walking back to the front door, I checked it over again to make sure I hadn't missed a weakness that I could exploit to gain entry. It was just as solid and impenetrable as the first time I'd looked.

Fulcrum

When I came back around the corner, Tiffany was standing at the gate, examining the padlock. She turned when she heard me coming.

"Need to get through to get to those trucks, right?" She asked.

I nodded.

"Can I borrow your knife?"

I looked at her for a moment before drawing the Ka-Bar, then pulled it back when she reached for it.

"What are you going to do? It can't cut through or break that lock."

I didn't care if she wanted to try a crazy idea, I just didn't want my knife damaged.

"Trust me."

She smiled and held her hand out. After another pause, I extended the weapon, hilt first. She took it and without saying anything else, rushed to retrieve a plastic cup that was trapped in a small bush. Holding it against the fence, she pressed the blade against the metal and began slowly scraping down, towards its mouth. A fine powder of rust fell into the cup with each stroke.

"What's she doing?" Rachel asked, staring curiously as Tiffany kept working.

"I think I know," I said, smiling.

"Yeah? So?"

"Just wait," I said.

Rachel shook her head and checked the area around us before going back to watching Tiffany.

The girl worked for several minutes, finally stopping and looking into the cup. Apparently satisfied, she put it on a rock and started searching the ground. Spying what she wanted, she hurried over to a shallow drainage ditch and plucked out a crushed beer can. Standing, she searched some more and found a large, flat rock and another the size and shape of a baseball.

Carrying the rocks to where we were standing, she put them on the ground and used my knife to cut the ends off the can, then slice it into narrow strips. I cringed at the damage being done to the edge of the blade, but held my tongue and let her work. When she had all of the strips neatly lined up on the flat rock, she stood and handed the Ka-Bar back to me.

"Sorry about the edge," she said, digging through a pocket in her jeans.

She pulled out two large packs of chewing gum and handed them to Rachel.

"Chew these," she said. "All of it. Get it nice and wet and sticky."

Rachel stared at her a moment, then turned to look at me. I shrugged and took one of the packs from her. One by one, I unwrapped each stick and stuck it in my mouth. I was parched from the long walk without anything to drink, but eventually, I had what felt like a golf ball sized wad of gum rolling around in my mouth.

While we chewed, Tiffany attacked the strips of the beer can with the round rock. First, she pounded them even thinner than they already were then, with a twisting motion, began grinding them between the two stones. It took some time and effort, but she eventually managed to reduce them to a coarse powder.

Using the edge of her hand, she carefully wiped all of the powder to one end of the rock. Picking up the plastic cup, she poured the finely powdered rust onto the other. Comparing the two piles, she brushed away a small quantity of rust, then pushed both into the cup and shook it to mix the contents thoroughly.

Looking up at us, she held out her hand. Rachel and I deposited two balls of well chewed gum. Tiffany pressed them together, then dropped the larger mass into the cup. When she pulled it out, it was coated with the powder mixture she'd created. Kneading the ball like it was dough, she worked the powder into it. She kept repeating this process until all of the mixture had been used up.

Holding the ball up, she looked at it and nodded in approval. It was probably fifty percent larger due to the added powder and was nearly dry. Picking up one of the foil wrappers I'd dropped on the ground, she rolled it into a tube, and after poking a hole in the ball with a small stick, she inserted an end deep inside.

"Can you open a bullet?" She asked, looking up at me. "I need the gun powder."

I grinned at her and, using the Ka-Bar, quickly separated a bullet from its brass casing and held it out to her. Carefully, she poured the powder into the foil tube.

"You made a bomb?" Rachel asked uncertainly.

"Thermite," I said.

Tiffany looked at me, nodded and smiled.

"What's Thermite?" Rachel asked.

"Iron oxide, or rust, and powdered aluminum. Mixed in the right proportions and ignited, they burn in excess of 4,000 degrees Fahrenheit," she said, standing and moving to the gate. "More than hot enough to melt the shackle on this padlock."

"Really?" Rachel asked in surprise.

"Who's the chauvinist, now?" I asked as Tiffany molded the ball of thermite gum around the padlock's shackle.

"Oh, fuck off," Rachel said, but she was teasing.

"So here's the problem," Tiffany said, stepping away from the gate. "This will burn really hot, and it tends to spray molten metal. Whoever lights it had better be ready to run."

She was looking at me, and after a moment Rachel turned to face me. With a sigh, I reached into my pocket and pulled out a disposable lighter. Rachel smiled, then followed Tiffany to a safe distance, making sure Dog was staying with them.

Taking a deep breath, I moved to the gate and looked at the padlock. The foil tube containing the gunpowder stuck up from the ball of chewing gum at a forty-five-degree angle, waiting for me to light it. Once I touched flame to it, the powder would flare and burn hot enough to ignite the thermite.

I knew how hot and violently thermite grenades burned, and had no reason to think

Tiffany's creation wouldn't do the same. All things considered, I'd rather have a nice long fuse so I could set it off from a safe distance. Shutting down my internal bitching, I flicked the lighter and held the flame to the tube.

At first, nothing, then the gunpowder flashed violently. I yanked my hand back and ran, a loud sputtering sound starting up behind and a wave of intense heat washing over me. When I reached Rachel and Tiffany, I turned to watch and shielded my eyes as they were already doing.

Thermite not only burns extremely hot, but the flame is bright enough to damage your retinas. Ideally, to watch it burn, we should have been wearing welder's goggles. But, we didn't have any, so as the metal violently combusted, we settled for occasional, quick peeks through our fingers.

The fire hissed and popped for several seconds, then a fist sized lump of glowing, molten steel dropped to the ground. The two ends of the thick chain swung free, lightly scraping across the iron plate. With a smile, Tiffany bounced on the balls of her feet in excitement.

"I sure am glad we brought you along," I said, smiling at her.

She looked back at me, her face beaming.

27

There was a back door into the building, inside the fenced lot, that wasn't nearly as stout or secure as the front. It popped open easily enough with a little persuasion from a long crowbar I found in the area that was used to maintain the monster trucks.

I might not have bothered to break in if any of the vehicles' keys had been in them. But, they were locked up tight. They were also too tall for me to be able to see through the windows. I had to lift Rachel up on my shoulders so she could check. While I was doing this, Tiffany had poked around the garage area and found a stepladder.

Pausing in the open door, I stared at the darkness for a moment, then lowered my NVGs. Dog, close at my side, remained quiet. Slowly scanning with the night vision, I didn't see any danger. Leaving the girls outside, Dog and I crossed the threshold and began searching the place.

It wasn't large, even smaller than the diner, and was cluttered so badly I idly wondered if the owner was a hoarder. Boxes covered almost every inch of floor space and were stacked to the ceiling. There was a cramped area by the front door where customers could stand, if they wanted to stand very close to each other, and a battered wooden desk facing the entrance.

The desk was so piled with papers that I couldn't see the surface. Raising the goggles, I clicked on my flashlight and began pulling drawers open. They were also stuffed with papers. Finishing the left side, I tugged the shallow center drawer open. Light reflected off four sets of keys. Scooping them up, I shoved them in my pocket and turned for the door, the light flashing across a box that caught my eye.

Bottled water! Of course. It made sense. This place operated vehicles that took tourists out into the Arizona desert. You don't do that without also taking along plenty of water. In fact, it wouldn't surprise me if the tour companies hadn't been required by law to have enough water on the trip to last a full day in case they broke down in the middle of nowhere.

Shining the light around, I could see the printing on the boxes that hadn't been visible through night vision. What I had thought was hoarding was actually box after box of water. Grabbing the closest one, I wormed my way through the maze and outside where the girls were waiting. I put it on the ground and ripped the top open, grabbing a couple of bottles.

Fulcrum

Rachel and Tiffany saw what I had and rushed over. Each of them drained a bottle without pausing, then reached for more. I took a minute to search around, finding an old drip pan in the open area used as a garage. I washed it out with one of the bottles, then put it on the ground and poured water for Dog. While he was noisily drinking, I downed three bottles in rapid succession.

We spent several minutes re-hydrating ourselves, then I went back inside and grabbed two more cases. Sitting them on the ground, I stood beside the girls, looking at the monster trucks.

"Which one?" I asked.

"That one," Tiffany said without hesitation, pointing at the purple one.

It was an older Ford pickup with four doors and a long bed, and it wasn't just purple, it was *purple*. Maybe it was triple purple or orgasmic violet, but it was one hell of a shade of paint. There were two rows of molded plastic seats in the bed, and the rear window of the cab had been removed so those passengers could communicate with the ones inside.

Using the stepladder, I climbed up and tried keys until I found the right one to unlock the door. Getting behind the wheel, I glanced around for a moment, amazed at the feeling of being on top of the world. The interior was well worn but in decent shape. I just hoped the damn thing had fuel, and the mechanicals were in good working order.

Starting the engine, I couldn't help but smile at the bellow of raw power. I guess I shouldn't have been surprised. It takes a lot of horsepower to move four tires that are nearly as tall as me. A quick check of the gauges showed there was slightly less than half a tank of gas. The way this thing most assuredly drank fuel, there was no way we'd make it to Phoenix and the Air Force Base.

Shutting off the engine, I scrambled down and spent a few minutes moving the step ladder and checking the other trucks. None of them were any better off. Shit. Back at ground level, I explained the problem to the girls.

"What about the gas station?" Rachel asked, pointing through the open gate.

I reflexively turned to look and cursed when I saw a pack of females charging towards us. Where the hell had they come from?

"In the truck!" I shouted, racing to grab one of the cases of water.

Fulcrum

Rachel and Tiffany scrambled up the ladder and into the cab, Rachel turning and extending her arms as I skidded in the dirt. With a heave, I tossed the box into her waiting arms. It was heavy and unwieldy as hell, but somehow she managed to snag it and pull it inside.

Dog had caught scent of the females and was slowly stalking towards them, head lowered as a rumbling growl emanated from his chest. I appreciated his sentiment, and would have preferred to fight, but we were too low on ammo. Bending, I scooped him into my arms and, one wobbly step at a time, went up the ladder.

I nearly fell off when an unsuppressed rifle sounded right over my head, but managed to maintain my balance. Rachel was back at the open door, reaching out and grabbing Dog's front shoulders as I pushed his big, furry ass. A moment later I was up and in.

A quick glance told me I didn't have time to screw around with the step ladder. Slamming the door, I fumbled the keys out of my pocket and started the beast. Shifting into gear, the exhaust bellowed as I hit the accelerator and cut the wheel to aim for the open gate.

Right in front of the truck was a dead female, and I realized that the shot Tiffany fired had probably saved my life. The giant tires rolled over the corpse without so much as a bump being felt in the cab.

The rest of the females reached the gate at the same time we did. Several leapt at us, bouncing off the fenders. Blasting through, I ran down a slower moving one, then nearly turned us over when I made a sharp turn onto the highway. I had to remember how this thing handled and not make a sudden maneuver that would ruin our day.

"Help!"

Tiffany's shout came an instant before two females screamed, seemingly inside the truck with us. Rachel and I both snapped our heads around to look over our shoulders. Tiffany's rifle was tangled in a seat harness, and she was shrinking away from the first female's grasping fingers. Dog bounded over the back of the seat and slammed into the one reaching for Tiffany. The second was crawling through the opening at the back of the cab.

Rachel ripped my pistol out of its holster on my thigh, raised the weapon and fired in one motion. The report inside the cab nearly deafened me, but it was worth it to see the female flop dead into the bed of the truck. Dog quickly finished off the female he'd attacked, leaving the corpse to bleed all over the back seat.

Fulcrum

"You OK?" Rachel shouted to Tiffany over the roar of the engine and tires.

"I'm good," the girl said, finally freeing her weapon from the seat belt.

"Where the hell did they come from?" Rachel turned to me and put my pistol back in its holster.

"Probably there," I said, pointing at a small cluster of dilapidated mobile homes sitting on the side of the road. "I started the truck to check the gas and it made enough noise to attract them."

Thinking about gas, I looked at the gauge to make sure we at least had as much as I'd thought. The needle was just below the half mark. A quick scan of the rest of the instruments and I was satisfied we weren't about to have any engine trouble, though that could change in a heartbeat.

"How the hell are they living out here? There's no water. No food. How are they surviving?"

Tiffany scooted forward and hung her arms over the seat back to make it easier to talk to us.

"Don't know," I said when Rachel didn't seem inclined to answer. "We keep seeing shit like this. Keep hoping they're going to start dying off. But they don't."

"They seemed slower," Rachel said.

"What?" I looked at her in surprise.

"They were moving slower. It's a good thing, too, or we might not have made it."

"You think they're weakening?" I asked.

Rachel shrugged her shoulders before looking at me.

"I've got no idea," she said. "But, I'm with Tiffany. How the hell are they still alive and a threat?"

"Shouldn't there have been some males in that town?" Tiffany asked.

"I'd think so. Maybe they just couldn't get to us fast enough when we started making a lot of noise."

"Maybe," she said.

Rachel turned in her seat to look at the younger girl.

"What are you thinking? You have an idea why there weren't any males?"

Fulcrum

Tiffany shook her head as if deciding whether to say something or not. Finally, she wrapped an arm around Dog's neck and sighed.

"They're still human, right? Which means, they've gotta eat to survive. So, since they're still alive, it follows that they have to be eating *something*. Right?"

We entered the outskirts of Kingman, Arizona about an hour later, and though I'd never particularly cared for the town, I was very happy to see it. We'd driven about 60 miles, with a quick stop to dump the two dead females, and the truck had consumed nearly all of the fuel in its tank. With the heavily modified engine and monster tires, I wasn't surprised.

"Are we getting gas, or changing vehicles?" Rachel asked as I slowed for a curve in the highway.

"Changing will be a problem, unless we find something with the keys in it," I said, stopping myself from mentioning Long.

"So is gassing this thing up, unless you've got a plan."

I shook my head and looked in the rearview mirror at Tiffany.

"What about you, MacGyver? Any ideas how we can get fuel out of an underground tank without a pump?"

"Who's MacGyver?" She asked.

I paused for a beat, looked at Rachel, then shook my head.

"Never mind," I said with a sigh. "Before your time."

"Well, whoever she was, I don't have any bright ideas," Tiffany said.

"He."

"He? He who?"

"MacGyver was a... aw, Christ. Forget it, already. You're making me feel old."

There was quiet for a long beat, then Tiffany began giggling. Rachel glanced at her and after a moment started laughing, too. Shaking my head and grumbling, I ignored them and drove, keeping my speed low.

Kingman is a small city that straddles Interstate 40 in northwestern Arizona. There is a ton of traffic that passes through, heading to and from California. Well, there used to be, but anyway, I knew there were numerous large truck stops in town and felt they were our best chance to find a different vehicle. Or to refuel.

"How far to the air base?" Rachel asked when the merriment died down.

"About 200 miles to Phoenix," I said, hoping I remembered correctly.

"Can this thing make it on a single tank, before we hassle with trying to fill it up?"

"Don't think so. We just used almost half a tank to go 60 miles."

I slowed when I saw an abandoned wreck on the road ahead. So far, I hadn't seen any infected. We'd passed several small neighborhoods with cheap, squat, block homes and a few businesses that looked like they'd been hanging on by a thread. They were all devoid of life. A steady wind blew dust and tumbleweeds down the empty streets.

I accelerated gently after steering around an overturned school bus. The pavement skirted another neighborhood to our left, nothing but endless desert to our right. Towering dust devils dotted the horizon.

"This is really creepy," Tiffany said in a quiet voice, pulling Dog close as she looked around.

I had to agree with her. But then, I'd gotten used to the ghost towns that had been created after the attacks. They no longer made the hair on my arms stand up. Much.

"No infected," Rachel said after another half a mile.

"Let's hope it stays that way," I said.

Fulcrum

A minute later we topped a small rise and got a good view of the small valley where Kingman nestled between two rugged mountain ranges. A mile ahead were the twin ribbons of asphalt that were I-40. Beyond, the town stretched away to the southeast. From our vantage point, it looked perfectly normal. If only...

At the bottom of the gentle hill we were driving down was a massive truck stop. An asphalt parking lot covered several acres of desert, and I was surprised to see that it was packed with both 18 wheelers and passenger vehicles. With a quarter of a mile remaining, I pulled to a stop.

"What are you doing?" Rachel asked.

"Just want to watch for a bit. See if there's anyone or anything moving."

She nodded, staring through the windshield at the mass of vehicles. There had to be at least a hundred trucks, and three or four times that many cars and pickups.

"It was like that when we came through," Tiffany said from the backseat.

Her comment reminded me of the conversation I'd had with Caleb. They'd left Albuquerque, trying to get home to California, but the Interstate was shut down. That's how they'd wound up near Vegas. Now I knew why there were so many vehicles that had congregated at this one location, but that didn't tell me if there was a whole bunch of infected, or survivors, waiting for us at the bottom of the hill.

After five minutes, I hadn't seen a single indication of life. No movement other than a tall, skinny dust devil that whirled across the sand and into the parking lot before losing its energy and disappearing. Taking my foot off the brake, I let gravity do the work and roll us down the hill.

"Stay sharp," I said to the girls. "A maze like that is prime territory for infected."

Neither of them said anything in return, but I could tell their attention was glued to the parking lot ahead. Reaching an entrance, I stopped again and sat for a few more minutes. Even at idle, the truck was loud as hell, and I was counting on it drawing out any infected that were in the area. When none showed, I pulled in and idled around the perimeter of the paved lot.

It was apparent that people had been living in their vehicles. There were also a large number of tents crowded into the empty spaces between parked cars. Many were tied to bumpers, which was probably the only reason they'd survived the wind and were still in place.

But even the ones that had lasted were damaged and tattered from nature's constant assault.

Or the assault of females that must have raged through the stranded people. There were a lot of blood stains on the tent fabric, the cars' sheet metal, and in numerous cases the inside of vehicle windows. There were a lot of bodies, many of them savagely dismembered. And the ripe smell of decomposition was heavy in the air, even with the stiff, desert breeze.

Just like in the *Last Stop* diner, the scene was made even more surreal by the complete absence of flies. I had convinced myself they hadn't been present in the diner because they couldn't get inside, but there was nothing here to stop them. Glancing skyward, I looked for vultures. None to be seen. That alone was disturbing, even more so since there was a veritable banquet just waiting for them.

"This doesn't make sense," Rachel said as she stared at a pile of corpses huddled against the side of a sedan.

"What do you mean?" I asked.

"The state of decomposition. If these people were killed fairly soon after the attack, months ago, the bodies should be much farther gone."

"How much farther?"

"A lot, especially considering we just went through a summer. It's very hot and dry here. Right?"

"Yep," I said.

"So, maybe that explains it, but it feels... I don't know. Off."

"You know what else is wrong?" I asked.

Rachel shook her head after thinking about my question for several seconds.

"No scavengers. No insects. They should be carpeted with flies. Vultures and crows should have been at them. Rats. This is a feast for all of them. Coyotes, too, for that matter."

"But there's coyotes around. We heard them!" Tiffany protested.

"We did," I said, nodding. "And I don't get it. They'll eat anything. Don't understand why they'd pass this up."

"The virus," Rachel said. "Maybe the bodies are contaminated, and the coyotes can smell it? The same way Dog reacts to an infected."

"Maybe," I said, unconvinced. "But where are the insects? Maybe that's what feels off. The hot and dry environment slowed decomposition, and there weren't any scavengers feeding on the corpses. It is off."

We fell silent at that point, each of us lost in our own thoughts. I circled the lot once, at idle. There was still nothing that caused me any concern. Well, undue concern. The whole damn scene was a gut twisting reminder of what had happened to the world. Pulling to a stop, I took a final look around, then shut off the rumbling engine.

The quiet was startling at first after over an hour of the constant barrage of harsh noise. Now we were left with the moaning wind and the hiss of sand being pushed across the asphalt. Several tents were partially torn loose and flapped in the breeze, their ends occasionally snapping hard enough to sound vaguely like gunfire.

"OK," I said. "We're all getting out, and we're staying close together. People were living in their cars, and that probably means a lot of them will have the keys inside. I hope. You two keep watch on our flanks and rear. I'm going to look for anything that will start after sitting in the heat all summer, and hopefully it'll have enough gas to get us to Phoenix."

Rachel nodded and performed a quick check of her rifle to make sure it was ready to go.

After a moment, Tiffany did the same thing. I remembered that she was dangerously low on ammo, and handed her one of my full magazines. Then I rethought things and told her to swap rifles with me.

"Why?" She asked.

Despite questioning my request, she was already working the sling over her head.

"You're on watch. If you need to fire, I'd rather you have a weapon with a suppressor so we don't alert the entire town to our presence. I'll take yours. I'm going to be busy checking cars, so if there's more infected than you two can handle, it won't matter much if I fire an unsuppressed rifle."

She nodded as we traded weapons. Another slow look around and I popped the driver's door open. Damn, it was a long way down without a ladder. Twisting around, I swung my feet out into space and, tightly gripping the seat harness, lowered myself until I could drop without worrying about injuring an ankle.

Immediately, I held up a clenched fist, telling Rachel to stay in place as I scanned a full 360 degrees with the rifle. Still quiet as a tomb. I spun another slow circle, then looked up. I expected to see Rachel staring down at me, but movement in the bed of the truck caught my eye. Stepping back, I could see both girls standing back to back, keeping watch. Dog hung his head over the side, panting as he watched me.

OK, so I don't have the market cornered when it comes to good ideas. With the height of the monster truck they had a commanding view of our surroundings, with the added advantage of it not being easy for even a female to reach them. I decided to leave them where they were, but I wanted Dog's nose and ears with me.

There was no easy way to do this, so I had Rachel lower the tailgate as I came to stand below it. Dog walked to the edge and looked down, then whined and stepped back. I called him, but he wasn't stupid. It was a long way to the hard pavement below. But, finally, between my coaxing and some urging from Rachel, we got him to make the leap.

I caught him in my arms and can't really say how I managed to stay on my feet. He weighs more than a hundred pounds and hit me solidly in the chest. I staggered back several steps, caught my balance and squatted to put him on his feet. He looked at me for a beat, then trotted to the truck's rear tire and lifted his leg.

"You would have left me down here by myself if you didn't need to take a piss," I said to him when he was finished.

He snorted, ignored me, and raised his nose to test the wind. It was coming from the west, out of the open desert, and he didn't detect anything that caused him to growl. That was good, but the town was downwind from our location and could be full of infected that he couldn't smell.

Nearly an hour later we pulled out of the parking lot in our newly acquired vehicle. It was a Chevy Tahoe, and Dog was taking full advantage of the roomy back seat. Stretched out on his back, he had his head resting in Tiffany's lap while she gently rubbed his belly.

It had taken some effort to find the SUV. The first challenge had been to locate a vehicle that didn't have a corpse inside, or the interior wasn't washed in blood. Then I had to find one with keys in the ignition. The alternative was to start searching the dead, but I'm not too keen on sticking my hands in the pockets of a body that has been rotting for a few weeks.

Fortunately, I found the Tahoe without too much difficulty. To my great surprise, the engine had turned over and started easily. But the gas gauge didn't deliver the same good news. The needle was below the big, red E, and a chime warning of low fuel began sounding as soon as I started the vehicle.

Putting Dog inside, I cut away a couple of tents that were secured to the bumpers, then climbed behind the wheel. There were a lot of corpses in the area, and I didn't have any option other than to drive over them. I wasn't happy about it, but I got it done and drove to park next to the monster truck.

Shutting off the engine, I told Rachel and Tiffany to stay put while Dog and I went in search of a hose. The best option I had was to siphon gas out of the other vehicles to fill the Tahoe, and I planned to start by emptying the truck's tank into my new ride.

It took longer to find a hose than it had to procure the SUV, but I finally located one. I started by draining the truck, then drove from vehicle to vehicle to continue the fueling. It was a slow process as the Tahoe's tank was higher than most of the other vehicles to which I could get close enough to siphon.

This meant I had to stop what I was doing and go find something that could be put on the ground that I could drain gas into. Finally, I hit the jackpot when I came across a pickup with a trailer that held four ATVs. Four, red plastic gas cans were strapped down in its bed.

Using them, I was able to work much faster and soon had put as much gas into the Tahoe as it would take. Filling the cans, I stacked them on the carpeted floor behind the rear seat and drove back to the monster truck. Parking beneath the open tailgate, I got on the roof and helped Rachel and Tiffany climb down.

Fulcrum

The Tahoe was running, but it sounded like shit. Modern gasoline, with all of the environmentally mandated additives, doesn't store well. It will quickly start losing its octane, which is simply the measure of how much compression a fuel can withstand before igniting. The higher the octane rating, the less likely the fuel is going to pre-ignite at higher pressures and damage an engine. That's why performance cars with higher compression engines require higher octane fuel.

So, as the fuel we were burning had sat for several months, it had degraded and was igniting much too early for the Tahoe's engine. This throws off the delicate timing balance of when valves open and close, and will destroy the engine. Hopefully that wouldn't happen before we got where we were going.

Now, we were on I-40, heading east, the engine making a horrible pinging sound as it labored with the old fuel. It wouldn't be long before we'd reach the turnoff for the highway that headed down to Phoenix. There were only a few small towns to go through, and I was slightly optimistic that we were finally going to start making good time.

The day had warmed up, the sun coming through the windows almost hot on my skin. Rachel was apparently feeling the heat, too. She adjusted the air conditioning and leaned back in the leather seat.

"Maybe we should just keep going in this," she said.

"Not if we can get a Humvee. Or better," I said.

"What's wrong with this? Besides the noise from the engine?"

"It's made for soccer moms. That's what's wrong with it," I said. "The windows are regular glass and the sheet metal wouldn't even stop a pellet rifle. We don't know what's ahead. And it may decide to die on us at a really inconvenient time. Besides, if we can get onto the air base, there're a few other things we lost that I'd like to replace."

Rachel thought about what I said.

"And what if we get another Hummer and a Russian plane spots us? Didn't you say they probably attacked the dam because it was military vehicles that were moving?"

I thought about that for a moment. It's always annoying when someone is right, and they're right because they're using your logic against you.

"We'll see what we find when we get there," I finally conceded.

"What about an octane booster?" Tiffany suddenly asked from the back seat. "Pretty much any auto parts store, or even a truck stop, should have some bottles of it."

I looked at her in the mirror and shook my head.

"What?"

"You're just not what I remember teenaged girls being," I said with a smile.

"I'm 20," she said, sounding slightly offended. "And besides, why the hell wouldn't I know this stuff?"

I wasn't about to touch that one with a ten-foot pole. She glared at me for a few seconds before her face split open into a big smile.

"I'm just screwing with you," she said. "Caleb's into cars, big time. He's got this Honda he built into a street racer and it takes really high octane fuel or it won't run. He can either buy racing gas for ten bucks a gallon, or regular gas and throw in some bottles of octane booster. It's not perfect, but it will work if you don't have a lot of money."

I ignored the smile on Rachel's face and kept my mouth shut. Hitting the brakes, I turned hard for an off-ramp. There was another truck stop at the exit, and I was willing to try Tiffany's suggestion.

The scene was mostly identical to where we'd stopped and changed to the Tahoe. A parking lot full of vehicles that had been lived in. And died in. There still weren't any infected, and within a few minutes I'd found a whole case of octane booster and added a couple of bottles to the tank. Tossing the rest into the cargo area, I got us back on the freeway. Within a few miles, the pinging from the engine stopped.

I looked at Tiffany in the mirror and she smiled at me, then rested her head on the seatback. Soon, Dog was snoring like a wood chipper. When I looked around, Tiffany was sound asleep with her hand still on his belly. I started to say something to Rachel, remaining silent when I saw that her head was tilted to the side, eyes closed and lips parted as she dozed.

Other than occasional drifts of sand, the freeway was clear. I pushed our speed close to 100, not comfortable going any faster in a high-profile vehicle. We had quickly left Kingman behind, and I hadn't seen any sign of infected or survivors.

Fulcrum

The wind picked up as I drove, blowing hard enough to occasionally shove the Tahoe around. It also brought dust with it, reducing visibility, but not by enough to cause a problem. Besides, I'd lived in Arizona for a lot of years and was used to driving in dust storms.

Our turn came quicker than I remembered, but then I'd never driven this route at nearly 100 miles an hour. Slowing to make the transition, I pushed our speed back up as soon as we were on the new highway. The road was every bit as rough as I remembered, but the softly sprung SUV made for a comfortable ride.

The miles, and a few towns, rolled by quickly. I slowed for each outpost of civilization, not wanting to be blasting through at a high rate of speed and have an infected suddenly stumble into my path. But as we progressed, and drew closer to the Phoenix metropolitan area, I had yet to see a single infected. I hoped it would be the same in the city.

The Phoenix area, prior to the attacks, was home to about five million people. Even with the Russians using their sound control to attract and direct the infected, I'd learned from experience that it wasn't effective on all of them. Too many cities that had supposedly been emptied still had large contingents, just waiting for a warm meal.

I knew where Luke Air Force Base was, and at one time it had been well removed from any population. But Phoenix and its surrounding cities had experienced explosive growth over the past couple of decades. Now, Luke was more of a suburban air base than one out in the desert. That meant a higher probability that we'd encounter infected as we approached. Finally reaching the first, far-flung edge of town, I dropped our speed to navigate around abandoned vehicles and the occasional downed utility pole.

Phoenix sits in a massive valley, surrounded by desert mountains, and we were coming into the extreme northwest corner. The thought went through my head that I should go to my house. Years ago, Katie had claimed a shelf in my large gun safe, filling it with things like our passports, marriage license and stacks upon stacks of photos. I knew our house had burned, but that safe had cost me an arm and a leg and was rated as fireproof for up to three hours. Those pictures were probably still in it, undamaged, and I knew there were a lot of Katie.

"You OK?"

Rachel's voice startled me. The last time I'd checked on her, she'd been sound asleep. I hadn't realized she'd woken up.

"Fine," I said. "Just thinking about Katie."

She reached over and gently took my hand.

"What were you thinking?"

I took a deep breath, trying to get my emotions under control.

"Wish I could go by my house and find a photo of her," I finally said.

"Then let's do that," Rachel replied immediately.

"No time," I said. "It's all the way on the far side of the city. Would probably take at least 90 minutes to get there, if there were no problems on the way, then we'd have to backtrack the same amount."

She was quiet for a few moments, and I became aware that she was intently watching me.

"What?"

"You'll probably never have another opportunity," she said.

I nodded. She was right. But the round trip drive and time spent while we were there would easily add four hours to our trip. Possibly much more if we ran into infected or survivors.

That was time the pilot didn't have. His life was worth more than a photo of my dead wife.

"Maybe someday," I said, making my decision. "Right now, the pilot is our priority."

Rachel squeezed my hand and didn't say anything else. She continued to surprise me as I kept waiting for her to press the issue and want to have a discussion about what the future might or might not hold for us. I was thankful she hadn't done that because I didn't have any answers for her. There wasn't much I could think about until after I'd stared into Barinov's eyes and watched the life depart his body. Slowly and painfully.

I headed deeper into the city, then turned south on one of the giant freeways that looped around the metro area. We were now moving no more than 30 miles an hour, driving a slalom through the wrecked and burned out cars that had been left behind. More often than not, I had to drive in the median to pass.

Some time later, I slowed even more for the exit to Luke Air Force Base. It was to our right, but the sight out of the left side windows drew my attention. The giant enclosed stadium where the Arizona Cardinals football team had played. It had burned, or partially burned, and the roof and most of one of the sides had collapsed inwards onto the field.

Fulcrum

In the acres of parking lots that surrounded it, thousands of cars baked in the midday sun. There were half a dozen large trucks with FEMA (Federal Emergency Management Agency) painted on the sides, a veritable forest of tents surrounding them. Stepping on the brakes, I came to a stop on the elevated ramp and stared. Nothing moved. There was no sign of life, infected or otherwise.

"Think it's going to be like what we ran across in Kingman?" Rachel asked.

"Maybe. Too far away to tell."

Shaking my head, I accelerated down the ramp and turned onto the broad street that would take us to the air base. From the back seat, I heard Tiffany yawn, then a moment later Dog snorted before letting out with a sneeze so violent he startled her. She squealed in surprise, then began cooing to him and rubbing his head. I could see him watching me in the mirror as he soaked up her attention. Any second, I expected him to smile and wink.

SEAL Commander Teller Sam sat back and thought about the updated plan that had just been presented to him. The North Carolina's XO, Lieutenant Commander Adrienne Cable, watched him expectantly, even though she knew it was a good plan. She'd run it by the skipper first, and with his blessing had sought out the SEAL to brief him.

She hadn't failed to notice the man's interest in her, and while she was reticent to admit it, he had caught her eye, too. Sitting in the officers' wardroom, she anxiously awaited his response as he stared at the ceiling. Her eyes drifted across his chiseled features, but she stopped herself from looking any lower in case he caught her stealing a glance.

"So why the change?" He finally asked, snapping her out of a daydream. "I thought you said you could bring the boat right into Bate Bay, and we'd lockout from there."

"I checked some other charts that aren't digitized. Old school stuff, you know? Paper? And it's a good thing I did. There's a notation about rip tides and their timing. If we'd gone in there, you and your team would have emerged into a 15-knot current that would have carried you to New Zealand. This is much better."

"Ballsy as hell, too," he said with a grin. "You ever done something like this before? That close?"

"A couple of times in the Med. Yes. Damn near got caught, but we pulled it off."

He looked at her for a moment before nodding.

"So, will this work for your team?"

"It adds a degree of risk, but not too much. The water's going to be turbulent, and visibility will absolutely suck because of sand stirred up from the sea floor, but it gives us good cover. Any idea about ASW activity around the harbor from the Russians or Aussies?"

Adrienne shook her head. The North Carolina had trailed an antenna attached to a buoy long enough to listen in on radio traffic from Russian ships approaching Sydney, but had not had any success in intercepting any military signals.

"No. Without satellite comms we've got no way of knowing until we get there. Sorry."

He nodded, trying to think of something to say to extend his time with her. They were still several hours away from Sydney, and there were things to do with his team, but he could afford fifteen more minutes.

"Where were you when it happened?" Adrienne asked, surprising him.

"On board the Washington. We were getting ready to go into North Korea for a sneak and peek. See what the crazy little bastard in charge was up to. Never made it more than a couple hundred miles from Pearl. You?"

"Here," Adrienne said. "We were at the end of a patrol. Did you lose anyone?"

"Parents, I'm sure," he said. "They lived in Virginia Beach. Dad's a retired Admiral. Heard Virginia got hit pretty hard, so I'm hoping they went quick and didn't suffer."

She could see the pain in his eyes for a moment before he shut down that specific thought.

"What about you?" He asked.

"Didn't have anyone." She shook her head. "My folks were killed in a plane crash a couple of years ago, and I didn't have any siblings."

"No husband?"

Adrienne snorted and barked a quick laugh.

"I'm the Executive Officer of a nuclear submarine. I sometimes don't even have time to eat, let alone try and hold a relationship together."

She blushed when he stared intently at her, finally lowering her eyes.

"You? A wife?"

"No," he chuckled. "XOs on fast attack boats don't have the market cornered when it comes to no time for relationships. The only other family I have is a little brother. He's a Lieutenant in the teams. He survived, and the last I heard he's running around CONUS with some crazy Army major."

"He's a SEAL?"

"Yep. Kind of runs in the family. Dad was a frogman when we used to be called that. Guess neither of us had much choice, though I did consider the Marines for about three seconds before I came to my senses."

The door to the wardroom clanged open, and they looked around in surprise, quickly coming to their feet when Commander Talbot walked in.

"Carry on," he said, waving them back into their chairs and heading for an urn of coffee. "What do you think of the XO's plan, Commander?"

He filled a spotlessly clean, white ceramic mug and turned to face their table.

"Captain, I think it's a little bit crazy and a little bit genius. And, probably enough of each to work."

"Glad to hear it," Talbot said, taking a careful sip. "We've picked up some assistance from the East Caledonian Current, and should be approaching Sydney Harbour an hour ahead of schedule. XO, is that going to help us, or are we going to be sitting and waiting?"

Adrienne quickly pulled out her iPad and tapped furiously on its screen for nearly a minute. She read some data, then tapped some more as she worked on a calculation.

"Actually helps, sir," she said without looking up. "There's a big Russian container ship that should be transiting the area within a very few minutes of our arrival."

"Excellent," Talbot said, taking another sip. "XO, Lieutenant Hale has the watch. I'd suggest sleep for everyone. We're going to be very busy in a few hours."

Fulcrum

He stared at them over the rim of his coffee cup until they stood and excused themselves. Watching them leave, he felt a minor twinge of guilt at having interrupted. He'd seen the way they were looking at each other when he walked in.

The Captain didn't care if a romance blossomed between the two officers. In fact, he'd be happy for them. But now wasn't the time for his XO to be distracted, nor did the SEAL need to be thinking about anything other than the mission. With a sigh, he stepped out of the wardroom and headed out to take a walk around his boat.

31

Admiral Packard didn't bother looking up when the knock on his office door sounded. Shouting for whomever it was to enter, he kept his focus on the paper he was reading. It was a transcript of Russian military communications that had been picked up by a B2 bomber specially equipped with a sophisticated ELINT (Electronic Intelligence) suite.

The plane, very stealthy to begin with, had overflown the advancing invasion fleet well above its publicly published service ceiling of 50,000 feet. At nearly 75,000 feet, it had been invisible to the enemy's radar and infrared defensive systems. The only problem was that he'd had to wait for it to return to Hawaii and download the intelligence it had gathered, so he was reading a transcript of a conversation that had occurred several hours ago.

At first, the conversation seemed innocuous. It was the Admiral in command of the fleet and the General responsible for the tens of thousands of Russian troops that constituted the landing force. The first few pages were the General ensuring that they were ready to meet the depleted American fleet that stood between them and Hawaii. The Admiral assured his counterpart that they were ready.

Packard grimaced when he read that line. Two hours after the conversation, before the transcript had reached his desk, the Russians had rolled over the ragtag collection of ships he had sent to slow them down. Yes, they'd bought some time for the islands, though not much.

What had piqued the Admiral's interest was the conversation the two senior officers had after discussing the readiness of the fleet. They were worried, that much was obvious. There was dissension in the ranks as the fighting men were unable to reconcile pressing an attack against an adversary that was already beaten.

The Motherland was in pieces. Millions had died from the attacks launched by the Americans, and those that hadn't were facing the swiftly approaching Russian winter without even the basic necessities of food and fuel for heat.

Specifics weren't discussed, but the General referenced three occasions in which outright rebellion amongst the troops had to be put down. Apparently with the ruthless use of lethal force. The Admiral had commiserated, revealing there had been attempted mutinies by the crews aboard two of his warships. He was concerned that as they continued to approach Hawaii, more malcontents would try to take control.

His eyebrows rose dramatically when he read the line where the General mused that perhaps the men were right, and they should turn around and head for home. He read the line two more times to make sure he wasn't missing something.

Following the General's comment were several marks on the paper, denoting the passage of time before the Admiral responded. His words caused Packard's pulse to begin racing. Rather than railing at the General, the Admiral had said they shouldn't be having the conversation over a channel that could be monitored, then broke the connection.

Slamming forward in his chair, Packard stabbed the intercom button on his desk phone. A young Lieutenant, manning the outer office, answered immediately.

"Get me the actual audio of this transcript, and a Russian translator in here. And I want someone from NIS with everything we know about Admiral Padorin and General Toklov. Now!" He shouted.

His aide acknowledged the order and Packard cut off the intercom.

"Bad news, sir?" Captain West asked.

Fulcrum

The Admiral looked up in surprise, having forgotten that someone had knocked and entered his office. The Captain had waited patiently, standing in front of his desk.

"Read this!"

Packard thrust the sheaf of papers across his desk. West took them and quickly scanned the first few pages. Reaching the part that contained the conversation, he stiffened in surprise before flipping back a page and re-reading.

"They're ready to throw in the towel!"

He placed the papers on the Admiral's desk and smiled. Packard met his eyes but wasn't as convinced.

"Perhaps," he said. "I want to hear the conversation for myself. Listen to their voices as they have the discussion, even if I can't understand what they're saying."

"Seems pretty clear, sir. They're about to have a full blown mutiny on their hands. If they've already got problems amongst the ground troops *and* on two of their warships... well, that's damn good news for us."

"Don't forget, Captain. These are the Russians. Their military, at the enlisted level, has never been terribly professional. It was better during the Cold War, but since the Soviet Union fell, they've pretty much filled the ranks with any warm body they could find. Discord amongst their enlisted isn't all that uncommon."

"Agreed, sir," Captain West said. "However, discord is one thing. This sounds like an outright revolt against the officers who are ordering them to keep fighting."

Packard nodded, looking up when his door opened. It was his receptionist, escorting a man carrying an iPad.

"Commander Marx, sir," the new arrival introduced himself. "I have the audio file you requested and am also a translator."

"Marx? Russian heritage?" West asked as the man stood at attention in front of Packard's desk.

"Yes, sir. My father was a Soviet diplomat in Cuba in the early 80s. When Andropov died, and Chernenko assumed power, he had to get out or face recall to Moscow. He apparently had some history with the new Premier, though he never shared the details with me. I was three years old when he and my mother took me and boarded a refugee boat leaving Cuba for Florida. We were granted asylum, and I grew up in the US, but learned Russian before English."

West traded a glance with Packard. Both men already knew the details that Marx had just related. Early on, once Russia was revealed as the architect of the attacks, NIS had taken a very close look at every person who had even the most tenuous of ties to the enemy. Commander Marx had been front and center in their investigation, having been born in the former Soviet Union. Even though nothing was found to indicate he should pose any concerns, his was one of a handful of files that had been forwarded to the Admiral for his review.

Packard cleared his throat.

"Play the file for me Commander. The part where they're discussing the attempted mutinies. Just let me hear it. If I want it translated, I'll ask."

"Yes, sir."

The man tapped the tablet a couple of times, then swiped his finger to cue up the part of the conversation the Admiral had requested. A deep, Russian voice began coming from the tiny speakers.

"The General is the one speaking, sir," Marx said quietly.

They listened intently, Packard following along with the written transcript. When there was the click as the Admiral disconnected, the Commander stopped the playback and waited for further instructions.

"What do you think, Captain?" The Admiral peered across his desk.

"I hear a man that is exhausted. War weary. Both of them, for that matter. I would expect some emotion in their voices as they discuss rebellion in the ranks, but I didn't hear that. They almost sound like they're sympathetic. The tone matches the words I read. This wasn't a joke or sarcasm, in my opinion."

Packard thought about what he'd just heard, then turned to Marx.

"Commander. You've listened to this several times now. Being a native Russian speaker, what's your take?"

"Sir, I concur with Captain West. These two men are not happy with the situation in the least. There is no apparent anger towards the mutineers, which is what I would expect. Instead, there is only resignation. As if they are just going through the motions."

The Admiral stared at him for several long moments.

"What would push them over the edge? What could I say to convince them to do just what the General suggested? Turn around and go home."

"Sir, Russians are a very feeling people. I grew up an American, in a Russian household, and got a firsthand look at the differences between my parents and my friends' parents. What I learned from that is there seems to be a depth of emotions present in Russians that is not there in Americans."

"You're saying they care more about their kids than we do?" Captain West asked, sounding slightly offended.

"No, sir. Not that. I'm not sure how to explain this, but I'll try. If you attack America, we get mad as a society and generally retaliate against the aggressor, but in general, we get on with our lives. In World War II, Germany and Japan were our mortal enemies. Thirty years later they were two of our greatest allies. That wouldn't happen with Russians. They take everything personal. Deeply personal. They don't move on, and they don't forget. It's one of the traits that makes the Russian people great, but is also one of their greatest weaknesses."

"I don't understand what you're trying to say, Commander." Packard leaned back in his chair. "Are they pissed off because we attacked their home? Or are they only thinking about their loss and wanting to see their loved ones?"

"Probably some of both, sir. But, what I'm trying to say is that I believe they feel continuing to prosecute the war is pointless. Both sides have been devastated. As they sail into battle, their families are starving. Attacking us further will not lessen the misery at home, nor will it prevent additional Russian deaths. In fact, it will have the opposite effect. They want to go home and save the ones they can. However, they won't. At least not the senior officers. They're too… Russian."

Packard stared at the Commander for a long time, saying nothing. His gaze was intense, and after more than a minute a sheen of sweat formed on the younger officer's forehead. Finally, the Admiral looked away and picked up a mug of coffee that had gone cold.

"Commander, put together a message. Video and a separate audio-only version. I want you to explain, in Russian, where Barinov and his cronies are. How they're living. Use some of the footage we received from our Consulate in Sydney.

"At the end, make it clear that the United States no longer has a quarrel with the Russian people. We just want to be left alone to survive. There will be no further attacks unless we're attacked first. Your target audience are the enlisted men in that fleet. Can you have that ready in an hour?"

"Yes, sir. I can do that!"

Marx smiled as he thought about the probable reaction by the men aboard the Russian fleet if they heard and saw how their president was living, while their families were either dead or dying.

"Captain, as soon as that message is ready, let's start transmitting it at the Russian fleet in any and every way we can think of. If we're lucky, a few incidents of mutiny will turn into a wholesale insurrection."

There weren't any infected as we drove from the freeway to Luke Air Force Base. The road was broad, which was good as there were frequently wrecked or abandoned vehicles blocking the way. Not so we couldn't make progress, but they slowed us more than I liked.

The area had been in a transition period as urban sprawl took over. We alternately passed established neighborhoods, empty fields that had once grown crops, and more than a few developments that were under construction. But, no infected.

"Why aren't there any?" Rachel asked, looking around nervously.

"No idea," I said, steering around a National Guard deuce and a half that was on its side, straddling two lanes.

"Maybe the heat here, too?"

"What are you talking about?" Tiffany asked from the backseat.

Rachel spent a few minutes filling her in on the theory that the virus couldn't survive extreme temperatures. She nodded when the explanation was over, not asking any more questions.

Ahead and to my left, I caught sight of the air base's perimeter fence, glittering in the sun. I was encouraged to see that it was still standing. Well, at least the part within my view.

"Luke coming up on the left," I said to alert Rachel that we were approaching our destination.

Soon, we reached a section of the road where the fence ran parallel to the pavement. I followed it for a few minutes, coming to a stop short of the main gate.

"Are you fucking kidding me?" I asked in frustration.

Several bollards extended up from the cement apron leading to a stout bar that controlled vehicle access to the base. I sat staring at them for a long moment, debating just abandoning our attempt to change to a military vehicle and getting back on the road. As it was, it would be dark by the time we made it to Puerto Penasco.

But we needed other things, too. If we didn't change vehicles, it wasn't that big of a deal. However, the state of our ammo supply hadn't improved. We really had to find an armory. I knew there was a Cabela's in the other direction, near the burned out stadium, but I had little doubt it had been stripped bare in the days after the attacks.

"Want me to lower them?" Tiffany asked, shoving Dog aside so she could push her head forward, between the seats.

There really was no other decision. In addition to ammo, we needed supplies. Rachel had brought a well-stocked medical kit from Groom Lake, fully expecting the man to be in rough shape. It had been lost in one of the Humvees when the dam failed. Sure, we could probably find a civilian hospital, but they hadn't been protected the way one on a military base would have been. There was too great a chance they would have been stripped clean.

"Yes," I said with a sigh. "Sit tight for a second. Let me and Dog check the area."

I took a long look around, seeing nothing that even resembled a threat. Gripping my rifle, I stepped out onto the asphalt, Dog jumping down right behind me. He lifted his nose and sampled the gentle breeze, but didn't react to anything he may have smelled. Walking forward, I cautiously checked the gatehouse, finding it empty. Another slow circle and I was confident we weren't in imminent danger.

Fulcrum

Waving the girls forward, I stepped over to a large metal plate set into the concrete. The three of us quickly had it open. Tiffany jumped in without hesitating, and within a very few seconds, the bollards began retracting.

I reached in and grabbed her hand, lifting her back to ground level. We had to drive across the opening to the maintenance pit, so I muscled the hinged cover up and let it drop into place with a loud clang.

"What about that?" Rachel pointed at the red and white striped gate arm.

I walked over and tested it. It was some sort of metal, probably aluminum. Not secure, by any stretch, but I didn't want to crash it with the Tahoe and risk damaging our vehicle. There was no guarantee that we'd find a replacement on the base.

Tiffany had followed me over and wasted no time in attacking the bolts that held the arm to the motorized swivel that would raise it. I supported its weight as she removed the final two bolts, then turned and tossed it to the side, instantly regretting my action.

Between closing the access plate, and now dropping a metal pole onto the concrete, I was making enough noise to alert every infected even remotely close to our location. Irritated with

319

myself for getting sloppy, I herded everyone back to the Tahoe.

I drove through the opening and down a long access road that paralleled part of the runway system. Another fence protected the very long stretches of tarmac, and in the distance I could make out the forms of dozens of aircraft parked beneath sunshades.

Luke was a training base, and there was everything from F-16s to F-35s, and even a small group of Ospreys. One of the latter would have been perfect if I only knew how to fly. Fast as a plane, but with the ability to hover like a helicopter. I couldn't think of a better platform to use in our search for the pilot. Those thoughts made me think about Martinez, and I forced myself to focus on something else before I started remembering all the people I'd cared about, and lost.

Pausing at an intersection long enough to read the signs, I turned for the base hospital. Driving across the sprawling air base was surreal. Other than the complete absence of any life, it was untouched. No buildings were burned out or fences torn down. There were no wrecked vehicles, left abandoned for all eternity. No bodies on the ground or even a hint of violence. Nothing.

Fulcrum

The only things out of place were the pieces of trash that had collected along the base of chain link fences. You'd never see that on a functioning military base. If you did, you could be assured there was a General about to be relieved of his or her command.

Passing the gate for the flight line, I pulled to a stop for a longer look. It was closed and locked. I briefly surveyed the parked aircraft on the far side of the runway, then turned to look at the motor pool on the opposite side of the road.

"Why aren't there any vehicles here?" Rachel asked. "Everywhere else we've been, there's always been plenty left behind."

Tiffany's interest was piqued, and she squeezed past Dog to push her head into the front so she could listen to our conversation.

"There was no release of nerve gas in this area," I said. "And if your theory about the heat is right, the virus may not have been able to survive here long enough to take hold. This is one of the few places in the country that's hotter than Vegas in the summer.

"It's starting to make a little more sense. Those FEMA trailers at the stadium? The locals weren't fighting infected. They were just trying to survive the summer and each other. And with there not being a single vehicle on the base, I'm guessing there was an evacuation."

"Then why did they leave all the planes behind?" Tiffany asked, pointing across the runway.

I took another look, mentally cataloging the aircraft sitting in the shaded parking spots. Looking further on, I saw several massive hangars with their doors standing wide open. They were all empty, and there were two large areas of tarmac close to them that were also empty.

"There's only combat aircraft remaining," I said, re-scanning the flight line. "No cargo or transport planes left. Anything that could carry supplies or passengers is gone."

"Does that make sense to you?" Rachel asked.

I shook my head, trying to figure things out. I may tell jokes about the Air Force, but then that was part of the oath I swore when I enlisted in the Army. But it didn't make sense for an obviously functional Air Force Base to just pack up and leave. Unless there were some pretty strange circumstances that I didn't know about. Something that had caused them to run.

Fulcrum

"Could they have gone to Hawaii?" Rachel asked.

"And leave all those fighters behind?" I asked, though it was a rhetorical question.

"Could they make it that far?" Tiffany asked.

"Easily. As long as they were able to refuel in flight, and I've got no doubt there were several tankers at this base."

We sat there thinking about the mystery for another minute. Rachel started to pose another question, but I cut her off. It was time for us to start moving. We still needed to find the hospital, but after seeing how there was seemingly an orderly evacuation, I was concerned it would have been completely stripped of medical supplies.

I drove forward to an intersection and followed the sign to the base hospital. It wasn't terribly large, but then it only had to serve the few thousand military, and their dependents, that were assigned to the base. Besides, being on the edge of a major metropolitan area meant there was plenty of advanced healthcare right outside the gates.

There were no vehicles in the parking lot, and I wheeled into the space closest to the entrance. A large sign warned that it was reserved for Lt. Colonel Adams, who had probably been in command of all of the medical staff and facilities on the base.

"Tiffany, swap rifles with me again. Remember to keep your finger off the trigger unless you have a target and are ready to shoot. And don't shoot unless there's no other option. Understood?"

"I got it," she said, sounding slightly miffed at my instructions.

We spent thirty seconds trading weapons, and I was glad to note that as I began checking mine for readiness, she copied me. She might still sound like a teenaged girl from time to time, but she definitely had her head on straight. But then, that's probably why she was still alive.

"Dog and I lead. You two have rear security. Once we're inside and find the supplies, Dog and I will provide security while you collect what you need. No talking unless there's a threat, and no noise that can be avoided. Questions?"

Neither of them had any, so we stepped out into the parking lot. I turned a circle, looking for any danger, but other than the sound of a gentle breeze, it was eerily silent. Dog's nose was up, but he remained quiet.

Fulcrum

I began leading the way to the pair of glass doors at the entrance but pulled to a stop with a raised fist. I hadn't seen or heard anything, but something was bothering me. The little hairs on my arms were standing up. It felt like I was being watched.

Pulling the rifle scope to my eye, I turned slowly, giving our surroundings another look. Nothing. Raising the weapon, I scanned every rooftop that overlooked the area. Still nothing. Taking a deep breath, I glanced down at Dog. He was on full alert but showed no signs of having detected anything of concern. Letting the breath out, I got us moving again, unable to shake the feeling.

"We need to do this fast," I said in a mumble when we paused at the doors.

"What's wrong?" Rachel mouthed silently.

"Just a feeling. Let's go."

I pulled on the door, mildly surprised to find it locked. Pressing my face against the glass, I peered into the dark interior, looking for infected. Not seeing any, I stepped back and fired a short burst through the door. Battering the damaged glass out of the way, I took another look, then reached through and released the lock.

Opening the door, I kept my rifle aimed at the interior as Dog stepped forward to check the air. Again, he remained quiet and, seeing nothing moving, I led the way into the building.

We found the ER with no difficulty. I wished I'd had the conversation with Rachel before we came inside. If I'd known the Emergency Room was our destination, I would have parked in the ambulance bay. Oh well, my own fault for not asking.

One thing about the military, they aren't shy about posting very visible signage that will easily direct someone to a specific location within a building. As long as it's not a security concern. And a hospital certainly doesn't qualify, so it was simply a matter of following the proverbial *yellow brick road*.

The hallways were empty and clean. There was no smell of death, rather a mustiness with a sharp, underlying tang of disinfectant. We moved quietly, Dog's nails making more noise on the hard floor than the soles of our boots. Well-worn running shoes in Tiffany's case. I needed to find her a pair of boots, but that wasn't a priority.

Reaching the ER, we cautiously cleared the space. Gurneys were neatly draped with sheets and pushed against the wall. Treatment areas were clean and orderly. Whatever had prompted the Air Force personnel to depart, they'd most certainly had plenty of time to prepare. It was almost like they were expecting to come back.

When I was satisfied there weren't any lurking infected or survivors that would jump out and try to harm us, I motioned for Rachel to start gathering what she needed. Tugging on Tiffany's arm, she had the girl follow her into a cramped space behind the nurses' station. I made another scan of the area, then glanced at them.

Rachel met my eyes and nodded as she began grabbing supplies out of a tall cabinet. Tiffany held open a large, plastic waste bag and Rachel deposited the items into it. They worked for several minutes, then moved to where Dog and I were standing, keeping watch. Each of them held a heavy plastic bag, bulging with medical supplies.

"Find everything you need?" I mumbled without taking my eyes off a long hallway.

"We're good," Rachel said, adjusting her burden on her shoulder.

Turning, I retraced our steps through the hospital. It only took a short time to reach the entrance doors, and I brought us to a stop when I saw a flicker of movement. It had come from behind a row of low-growing bushes that bordered the parking lot, neatly separating it from a broad area of desert-scaped ground that fronted the entrance.

I was well back from the doors, standing in shadow, and was comfortable that anyone outside in the bright sunlight wouldn't be able to see me. A quick glance over my shoulder confirmed that Rachel and Tiffany had frozen in place. Dog was directly beside me, but I didn't think he'd spotted whatever had caught my eye. Staying as still as a statue, I kept watching. Waiting.

Sure, it could have been a bird. Or a rabbit. Or even a dog. But I didn't think so. Other than hearing the coyotes, and the small family of burrowing rodents that Dog had enjoyed hunting at Groom Lake, I hadn't seen any indication there was any wildlife remaining. I didn't dwell on this as the implications were almost too horrifying to contemplate.

After nearly five minutes, I saw it again. This time, I happened to be looking in exactly the right spot and recognized what I'd seen as a man's arm. He'd been scratching an itch on the back of his neck. An inch at a time, I slipped sideways to gain a better viewing angle. Now I could see the son of a bitch.

He was prone on the sandy soil of the landscaping, almost completely concealed behind the spreading branches of an ocotillo cactus.

What appeared to be a civilian deer rifle rested on the ground, the muzzle thrust into the hedge and aimed at the entrance doors.

We were very lucky this wasn't a trained sniper who had the discipline to remain perfectly still. Only a flash of movement had alerted me to his presence. He was dressed in desert tan camouflage clothing, and with the screen from the cactus, was basically invisible. Unless he gave his position away. Fortunately for us, he had. If we'd come strolling out the front doors, he would have been completely hidden from view and could have put bullets through us before I even knew he was there.

I spent several more minutes searching the area with my eyes. My head didn't move as I looked for more people waiting in ambush. Eventually, I gave up. Either there weren't anymore, or they were in locations that I couldn't see. Slowly, I retreated deeper into the hospital, waving Dog ahead of me.

Rachel and Tiffany had taken up positions in two doorways, watching our backs with their rifles up and ready. I stopped next to Rachel and told her what was going on.

"Just one?"

"That's all I can see, but I can't imagine he's alone. Can't get a good view of the surroundings, and can only see a corner of the Tahoe. There could be thirty more of them out there for all I know."

"What are we going to do?"

"Back to the ER and find a good hiding place for you two and Dog. I'm going out through the ambulance bay and see what I can do."

By now, Rachel had learned there was no point in protesting or arguing when I told her I was going to do something. She liked to tease me, calling me Rambo in situations like this. It had irritated the hell out of me at first, but I'd come to realize it was just how she dealt with the stress of not knowing if I'd return.

We went back to the ER, and the girls settled into the small alcove behind the nurses' station. I told Dog to stay with them, and he obeyed, but still gave me a look that said I was foolish not to take him along. I ruffled his ears, reminded Rachel to stay absolutely quiet, and headed for the ambulance bay.

The doors were two large panels of sliding glass that would open wide enough to admit a gurney with medics walking on either side. I approached cautiously, staying to the deeper shadows. Several minutes of careful observation didn't reveal anyone lying in wait, so

I stepped forward and carefully pried them apart.

When the opening was wide enough for me to slip through, I moved fast. The ambulance bay was a broad concrete apron with a high ceilinged overhang to protect it from the weather. It was the last place I wanted to be dragging my feet as there was absolutely nothing to conceal me from an enemy.

Dashing across the area, I threw myself to the ground behind a thick clump of dwarf date palms. Waited for a bullet to come my way, or a shout of surprise at my sudden appearance. But neither happened.

Controlling my breathing, I crouched behind the rough trunks of the trees and listened as hard as I could. I couldn't hear anything over the scraping of palm fronds that were being rubbed together by the breeze. That didn't make me feel any better.

The front corner of the building was thirty yards to my right, and the hedge the sniper was using for concealment followed the pavement right to where I was hiding. I had no idea what kind of plant had been used to create the border, but it was close to three feet high. Jagged shaped, waxy green leaves grew densely, and even from several feet away I could see the branches were lined with small thorns. Pushing through it would be impossible without using a sharp blade and making a lot of noise.

But, I didn't want to push through. I wanted to use it for cover to reach the man waiting to ambush us. So far, I hadn't seen or heard any sign to tell me he wasn't alone. However, I was counting on him having some friends along. Well, the first step was to spot everyone. Then I could decide on the best way to handle them.

Once I had taken another careful listen, trying to pay close attention between the scrapes of the fronds, I began crawling on my knees and elbows. After about the third rock that jabbed into me, I was becoming nostalgic for the days when I would have had pads on my joints to protect them. But, I didn't have any, so I sucked it up and kept going until I reached the concealment of the hedge.

Another pause to listen. Nothing. Moving slower, I worked my way to the corner, stopping to peer around and listen again. Still quiet. Once I was sure I wasn't in imminent threat of attack, I took a moment to remove my rifle scope. Holding it like a monocular, I stuck my head up and carefully scanned all of the rooftops in the area. If the guy had any buddies with him, they hadn't moved to high ground to keep watch.

Moving slowly to ensure I didn't make any sound, I reattached the scope and turned the corner. The guy I was hunting was on the opposite side of the hedge, about 100 yards away. Halfway between us, a sidewalk cut through, leaving a three-foot gap in the foliage. If I transitioned at that point, I would be able to approach the sniper from behind.

I came to a stop a couple of yards short of the sidewalk. This was potentially the riskiest part of stalking the man. If he had anyone else watching his ass, they'd see me when I appeared in the break in the hedge. Hell, it was broad daylight.

Taking my time, I listened some more, then slithered on my belly to the edge of the concrete walkway. A millimeter at a time, I extended my head at ground level to get a view of the other side. There was a short, neatly landscaped area, then pavement. The parking lot extended to the road that ran past the hospital, and it was completely stark and empty, other than the Tahoe.

Raising my eyes, I spent another five minutes patiently scanning the rooflines that overlooked the parking lot. Seeing nothing, I rolled onto my back and slowly checked the hospital's roof. Finding it empty, I took a breath and began a slow, careful crawl onto the sidewalk.

Fulcrum

As I moved into the open, and became as visible as a streaker in church, a spot on my back began twitching and itching. Even though I'd looked carefully, I still expected a bullet to come screaming in and pin me to the ground. But, fortunately for me, that didn't happen.

The hedge was about two feet wide at this point, and when I reached the far edge, I stopped. Stretching my neck, I poked my head around the corner for a quick look before jerking it back. I wanted to make sure the sniper was still in the same position, and also that he hadn't turned around and was waiting to blow a new asshole into my forehead as soon as I crawled into view.

I caught a glimpse of him before I pulled back. He was still in the same position, but that was all I could tell with such a brief look. Believing I was still undetected, I moved forward until I could see around the hedge, stopping when I had him in sight.

The sniper was slightly less than fifty yards away. He lay on his belly, tucked in between a large ocotillo and a patch of prickly pear. I was going to have to be careful that I didn't wind up getting skewered by either one of the cacti. Ocotillo aren't too bad. They're covered with thorns that are similar to a rose bush. Sure, it would hurt like hell, but that's about it.

But, a prickly pear can be a whole different experience. The thorns are thin, strong, needle sharp, and are usually several inches long. I've known people who have had one of those little spikes go all the way in and become embedded in a bone. That kind of pain I can do without, not to mention the really nasty infection that typically comes along with it.

Crawling around the edge, I began worming my way through the sand. The twitchy feeling on my back was getting worse and for not the first time I wished it was dark. But it wasn't, and at least the daylight would help me avoid coming face to face with a snake.

I got a better look at the sniper as I slowly drew closer. He wasn't a large man, probably no more than five foot six or seven. Thin, with a receding hairline and black rimmed glasses, he actually looked more like an accountant. And as I kept watching, he was acting like one. He certainly wasn't behaving like a trained warrior.

It was a warm day, and he was frequently mopping sweat off his forehead. If he wasn't doing that, he was scratching his neck. Or his arm. Or his ass. What the hell? Did this guy have the crabs, or was he just in serious need of a shower?

Shutting down thoughts that didn't matter, I kept coming. Move five yards on my

336

belly, then stop and listen and watch. Then move some more.

I was using my elbows to pull myself along, the rifle gripped in my hands. It would have been very easy to put a few rounds into the guy and get on with my day. In fact, I was sorely tempted to do just that. After all, that sure seemed to be what he had planned for me. But I wanted to know what he was doing.

Finally, I was within ten yards of his feet. He wore boots, but it was obvious from the soles that they weren't military issue. Most likely they'd come from a sporting goods store. So had his camouflage clothing. And his rifle.

He was still scratching like hell. In fact, he was almost constantly reaching for some part of his anatomy. Then he slapped the back of his hand and looked down at the sand he was lying on. He cursed loud enough for me to hear and began to squirm backward. As he moved, I saw the problem. The dumb son of a bitch had stretched out right beside an anthill.

He kept moving, pulling his rifle with him and carefully avoiding the two cacti. OK. Time to announce my presence.

"There's a rifle pointed at the back of your head," I said in a low voice.

Someone experienced with having weapons pointed at them would have frozen. He didn't. Letting out a gasp of surprise, he rolled onto his side to see who was behind him, managing to jam several of the prickly pear needles into his leg in the process.

He gasped again, reaching for the spot where it hurt. There was a pistol holstered on that leg, and his hand was getting too close to it for my comfort. With a sigh, I pulled the trigger and fired a burst into the ground, inches from his face. Sand fountained, raining down on his head, and he finally stopped moving.

"Don't. Fucking. Move." I said slowly.

This time, the message got through. He lay on the ground, cactus needles poking out of his leg and sweat pouring off his face, but he didn't move another inch. I stared at him, trying to decide what to do.

There was no way this guy was a soldier. For anyone. He had to be a civilian survivor. Frankly, that conclusion was the only thing that was keeping me from just shooting him and getting on with my day.

"Now, *very slowly*, you're going to remove that pistol and toss it deep into the hedge. Don't forget there's a rifle aimed at your head and my finger is on the trigger. If the muzzle of that

338

pistol even starts to swing my way, I'll put you down. Got it?"

"I got it," he said, his voice quavering. "Please. Don't shoot."

He followed my instructions, or close enough. The pistol actually wound up on the ground on the far side of the hedge, but for the moment that was fine with me. Standing, I kept the rifle trained on him. Every instinct was to scan my surroundings for danger, but I wasn't about to take my attention off the man.

"Come on out of there and..."

His eyes suddenly snapped to the left, looking past me, growing wide with fear. Screams from several infected females tore through the air a fraction of a second later.

I didn't like the idea of turning my back on this guy, but I didn't have a choice. There were numerous voices screaming out their rage, and they sounded close. Too damn close.

Spinning, I brought the rifle on target and immediately fired. A young female, wearing an Air Force uniform, flopped dead in the parking lot. The group was close, and there were too many for me to stand my ground. I had to retreat and fire at the same time. The problem with that was the three-foot-tall hedge behind me.

Getting over it would waste precious seconds I didn't have. The females would be able to close too much distance while I was hopping my happy ass over to the far side. Very aware of my limited supply of ammo, I clicked the rifle's selector and aimed for their legs. My best option was to slow them down.

I raked fire across the charging infected, destroying knees and shattering femurs. It would have been nice if this did anything more than slow them down, but it didn't. As soon as a female tumbled to the ground, no longer able to run, the bitch would start pulling herself along with her arms. And they weren't exactly slow without their legs, either.

Fulcrum

Dropping an empty magazine, I slapped in a new one and fired two more bursts which put the last pair on their faces. Clicking into single shot mode, I had to step back to avoid the swipe of a claw-like hand. I fired a round into her head, then moved around the perimeter of the group and delivered multiple coup de gras with my knife. I didn't have enough ammo left to shoot all of them.

Their determination to reach me never wavered. This was one of those times I would have appreciated the more intelligent ones who had demonstrated a fear of weapons. But, at least they were all on the ground, and I didn't have to worry about any escapees stalking me once the battle was over.

When I killed the last one, I whipped around to face the sniper and came face to face with the muzzle of his pistol. Instead of helping with the fight, the fucker had jumped the hedge and retrieved his weapon to use on me.

I let the rifle hang from its sling, freeing up my hands, and stared into his eyes. And didn't like what I saw. He might not be trained, but he sure as hell looked determined. There was fear visible, but it wasn't paralyzing him or even weakening his resolve.

"Don't move," he said, his voice breathy from a pounding heart.

"What are you going to do? Shoot me?"

His eyes widened in surprise when I spoke.

"You *are* an American," he blurted. "I wasn't sure I heard right before."

"No shit," I said, lacing it with heavy sarcasm. "What were you expecting?"

"Russian," he said, squinting at me.

The pistol was still aimed at my face, and I had grown tired of playing with this asshole.

"US Army," I said, lowering my voice and glaring at him. "You aren't military. I can tell that much. Now, lower your fucking weapon."

He stared at me for a long moment, then shook his head. That was when I moved. The pistol was in his right hand. My left hand shot out and grasped the weapon between the trigger guard and the muzzle, pushing it out of alignment with my head. At the same time, I struck the inside of his wrist with the heel of my other hand. I had a firm grip on his gun, and it neatly popped out of his hand before he could tighten his finger on the trigger.

He had half a second to stare at me in shock before I landed a solid right hand in the center of his face. I felt his nose, and maybe a couple of teeth, crunch, then he stumbled backward and fell on his ass. His glasses flew off, and he sat there looking at me with blood pouring across his chin and onto his chest.

Dropping the magazine, I racked the slide to eject the round in the chamber. The brass glittered briefly in the sun as it tumbled through the air. Pistol empty, I shoved it into my waistband.

"How the fuck have you survived this long? You're about as stupid as a bag of hammers."

I stood over him, glaring. He held his nose with one hand, trying to stem the flow of blood, and glared back. With his other, he picked up his glasses and put them on.

Taking a step away, I looked around to make sure there weren't any more infected charging in on the party. Seeing nothing, I pushed the radio into my ear and called Rachel, telling her to come outside.

"Are you really the Army?" The guy on the ground asked.

"Told you I was, didn't I? What the hell did you think you were doing, you stupid fuckstick? Hiding there with a rifle, waiting for us to come out of the hospital? You're goddamn lucky all I did was punch you in the nose!"

"Didn't know who you were," he said. "We've been hiding in one of the houses here on base since the Russians left."

"We? Who's we?"

His eyes told me he'd let some information slip that he would have preferred to keep from me.

"I meant me," he said quickly. "I'm all alone."

"I'll hit you again if you keep lying to me," I said.

He watched me closely as if trying to decide if I was telling the truth. While he was thinking about what I'd said, Rachel, Tiffany and Dog came jogging up. Dog stopped next to my left leg, staring at the man on the ground. He didn't growl, but his upper lip curled back, revealing a pretty intimidating set of teeth. The guy's full attention shifted to Dog, and he shrank away.

Rachel stood next to me and looked down at the man before turning and checking the area around us. I glanced over my shoulder to see Tiffany staring at the females I'd killed. I focused back on the man, then shook my head again.

Fulcrum

We needed to go, but our ammo situation was now even more critical than it had been. I should be able to find some, somewhere on the sprawling air base. But, I didn't want this guy going and getting whoever he was hiding out with and coming after us. We definitely weren't in a position to fight another battle at the moment.

"OK," I finally said to the guy. "It's your business what you're doing, as long as you don't interfere with us. We just stopped off for supplies, then we'll be on our way."

The surprise on his face was immediate. I had no doubt he'd been sitting there, expecting to die. And, to tell the truth, the thought had crossed my mind. I couldn't get a read on him, which bothered me. He had been stupid, there was no doubt about that. And his stupidity had put him into the very small club of people who have pointed a weapon at me and lived to tell the story.

Still, something just didn't sit right. A guy like this just shouldn't still be alive. Shouldn't have been able to survive all the predators in the world, both infected and uninfected. Yet, here he was, staring up at me with blood covering his face and chest. For a moment I seriously considered just putting a bullet in his head and getting on with things. All that saved him was Rachel and Tiffany's presence. I didn't want to put him down in front of them. Rachel might understand, but Tiffany? I didn't need the problems.

"On your feet," I said.

"Why? What are you going to do to me?"

"Nothing, if you do as your told," I said. "Now, get off your ass and show me where the closest armory is."

Slowly he stood and dusted off the seat of his pants before delicately pulling the cactus needles out of his leg.

35

Half an hour later we drove out of the main gate and turned west, heading for the highway that would take us to Mexico. We were loaded up with ammo, and a few other little toys I'd found in the armory the man had taken us to.

I hadn't learned anything about him, but hadn't pressed the issue. Once I'd gotten him on his feet, I thoroughly searched him and we'd piled into the Tahoe. I'd put him in the cargo area, and Dog had sat in the back seat, facing to the rear to keep an eye on him. He hadn't asked us any questions, and when Rachel had tried to find out more about him, he'd just looked away and kept his mouth tightly shut.

That was fine with me. I had several theories rolling around in my head about him, but since he was cooperating, I decided to let him keep his secrets. He'd only spoken to give me directions to the armory, and when we arrived, I found the door had been forced open already. Expecting to find it cleaned out, I was pleasantly surprised when we entered and found it well stocked.

It seemed as if a few crates of ammo and some rifles and pistols were missing, but without an inventory sheet, there was no way to know.

Regardless, it didn't matter. I put a crate of ammo into the back of the Tahoe, then another of empty magazines and told Tiffany to start loading them. While she worked and Rachel kept watch on the man and our surroundings, I went back inside.

I found some fragmentation grenades, pistol ammo and loaded up a small ammo can with smoke grenades. The real prize was an M249 light machine gun, or SAW (Squad Assault Weapon). It fires the same round as an M4 rifle, but from a linked belt of ammunition and can make all the difference in the world in a firefight. One of the best things is that it can be carried and fired like a rifle in a pinch, even though it's a little heavy and cumbersome.

After it was loaded into the Tahoe, I added half a dozen crates of ammo belts and closed the rear door. The man was standing a few yards away, watching me nervously. He was probably expecting a bullet, or for me to sick Dog on him. I probably would have been having the same thoughts if I were in his shoes.

Reaching inside the SUV, I brought out his rifle, and after making sure it was empty, walked over and handed it and his pistol to him. He tentatively took them, watching me closely as if he expected it was a trick.

Fulcrum

"If you're smart, you'll go in there and get yourself an M4 and a bunch of ammo. That bolt action deer rifle is only good if you want to play sniper."

He stared back at me without saying anything, finally nodding as I backed away and waved Rachel and Dog into the Tahoe.

"What do you think his story was?" Rachel asked as I steered around a smashed city bus.

I shrugged.

"Whatever it is, it's amazing he's made it this long."

"So, those infected," Rachel said.

"What about them?"

"We haven't seen any all the way into town. The base seemed empty, then they showed up out of nowhere. Doesn't that strike you as odd?"

"It does," I said. "And look around us. None. This is the first time we've been in a city of any size that there wasn't a greeting party."

"Does that mean anything?"

I shrugged my shoulders, again. Yes, it was bothering me, but we didn't have any information that would let us even begin to come up with a theory.

"Did you notice they were all wearing Air Force uniforms?" Tiffany asked from the back seat.

I glanced at her in the mirror. Her head was down as she continued to load magazines.

"I did, yes."

"Makes me think they were trapped in one of the buildings and got out," she said.

"Or someone let them out," Rachel offered.

"Not our problem," I said. "Not anymore, at least. For now, we've got to haul ass for Mexico. It's going to be dark by the time we get to Puerto Penasco."

"Are we going to start searching tonight?" Rachel asked.

"No." I shook my head. "Going to be hard enough to find him in the daytime. We'll get some rest when we get there, then find a boat in the morning and head out."

Rachel sat there thinking about that. From the back seat, I could hear a rhythmic clicking as Tiffany continued to work. Dog sat on the seat next to her, watching every movement. If you didn't know him, you might think he was fascinated by what she was doing. I knew he was just waiting for an opportunity to lie down and put his head in her lap.

"How would the Navy find him, if they could get there?" Rachel asked after several more minutes.

"He'll have an EPIRB," I said, referring to an Emergency Position Indicating Radio Beacon. "They'd put up a couple of helicopters and home in on the signal."

"OK, yeah. The Navy pilot I went down with in Idaho had one of those sewn into his flight suit."

"Did he have a strobe of any kind?" I asked, an idea taking shape.

"Not that I saw," Rachel said after thinking for a moment. "Why?"

"Because this guy's supposedly on a small inflatable raft that was built into his ejection seat. And, it seems to me, it would make sense for there to be an infrared strobe as part of the raft that would activate when it inflated."

"You think?" Rachel asked.

"I don't know," I said. "Maybe. Naval aviation is a whole different world than what I ever operated in. But, it makes sense. Think about it. A rescue helo responds to the general location of an EPIRB signal at night. If the ocean is rough, its got to be a bitch to find a tiny little raft amidst all the waves. But, if there's an IR strobe flashing away, it'll be very easy to spot with their night vision."

"So, he might actually be easier to find in the dark?" Rachel asked.

"Maybe," I said. "I wish Lieutenant Sam was here. He'd know the answer."

"Should we take the chance and go out tonight?"

"Probably," I said, turning the idea over in my head. "I'll decide by the time we get there."

We fell silent at that point, each lost in our own thoughts. There was only the sound of the tires on asphalt, and the clicking of ammunition going into magazines. I concentrated on my driving, pushing our speed up at every opportunity.

Reaching a small state highway, I turned south, heading for Interstate 10. Once there, we'd follow it a short distance west, then turn south onto the road that would take us to Mexico and on to Puerto Penasco. There was only one town still to pass through, Gila Bend, Arizona, and I hoped it was as empty of infected as the Phoenix area had been.

"Ever been to this place before?" Rachel asked after we were on I-10.

"Puerto Penasco?"

She nodded.

"Lots of times," I said, my chest tightening as a flood of memories came rushing in. "It's called Rocky Point in Arizona."

"Vacation spot?"

"Yeah," I said, my voice husky. "Big party spot for people in Arizona. It's an easy drive from Phoenix. We used to go down there all the time. Camp out on the beach and get drunk and set off fireworks. There're some pretty good bars in town, too. And, go down the right time of year and you can buy fresh caught shrimp right off the fishing boats. We'd bring pounds of it home and spend a whole day having a shrimp boil."

"So this was a good part of Mexico?"

I snorted at that.

"Well, it kind of was. You still had to be careful and pay attention to your surroundings. But at least then, pretty much the worst thing that would happen was you'd get robbed. We quit going several years ago. Same problems as everywhere along the border. I didn't feel like going into a war zone for a vacation. Kind of a shame. We had some really good times there."

By this time, we had reached the highway that cut due south to the border, and I made the transition to it. The sun was low, and it was maybe an hour before it would dip below the mountains to our west. Tiffany had completed loading every one of the magazines and was dozing with her head tilted back. Dog had stretched his head into her lap and was snoring so loud I couldn't imagine how the girl was sleeping.

We breezed through Gila Bend twenty minutes later. It was just like Kingman and Phoenix. Devoid of any activity. I had to slow slightly for several wrecks, but the road was surprisingly clear. Passing beneath Interstate 8, I pushed our speed up again. Less than an hour later, light quickly fading, I slowed as we approached the border crossing into Mexico.

Several small buildings had constituted the sum of both the American and Mexican presence at the portal. And they had all burned. Debris from the fire and a couple of gutted

Border Patrol vehicles completely blocked the pavement. Slowing more, I shifted the Tahoe into four-wheel drive and plowed through the soft sand to the side, bypassing the wreckage.

A hundred yards into Mexico, we bounced back onto pavement. There were several small towns that had grown up on the southern side of the border, and we had to pass through them. The light was almost gone, and I elected to use my night vision for driving, rather than turn on the SUV's headlights. Driving slowly, we began passing a huge variety of shops that lined the highway, solely to serve American tourists on their way to Rocky Point and beyond.

Less than half a mile into the first town, we began encountering females. Responding to the noise our vehicle was making, they emerged from within businesses and homes that either no longer had a door, or the door was standing open. Some of them stood and watched us pass, while others charged at full speed to slam into the front and sides of the Tahoe.

The impacts were brutal, and I was worrying about the vehicle's ability to withstand the onslaught. As badly as I wanted to accelerate and get out into the open desert, I forced myself to hold our speed at a sedate pace. Too fast and all of the bodies could damage the Chevy to the point that we'd be stuck.

Though she wasn't voicing it, Tiffany was freaking out in the back seat. In concert with nearly every blow from a female, I could hear a small gasp of fright escape her mouth. She was breathing hard, panting even, as if she'd just run a race. I risked a glance in the mirror, seeing that she had her arms tightly wrapped around Dog's neck, her face pressed against him for comfort.

"You notice the smart ones?" Rachel asked.

"The ones just standing back and watching? Yeah, I saw 'em."

"What do we do if it's like this when we get to Rocky Point? There's too many for us to fight through and find a boat."

"Deal with it when we get there," I said through gritted teeth.

I yanked the wheel to avoid four females who suddenly charged from behind a building and were on a direct path for our front bumper. The maneuver was mostly successful, avoiding three of them, but the other one made a mighty leap and landed on the hood.

For a moment, it seemed as if she paused to stare at me through the windshield. I couldn't see the red eyes, colors not coming through in the NVGs, but I could clearly make out the mask of rage that distorted her features. With a scream, she pulled on the edge of the hood and lifted her hand to smash the glass separating us.

In slow motion, I saw something in her hand. A rock large enough to shatter the only thing protecting us from her. As she began the blow, I jammed my foot on the brakes. The nose of the Tahoe dipped, and everyone was thrown forward, equipment in the cargo area loudly clanging as it shifted.

The female was caught off-guard. With only one hand grasping the hood, she was thrown free before the rock could contact the windshield. The instant she disappeared, I hit the gas, and the engine roared as we surged forward and bounced over her body. She had still been tumbling on the asphalt, not having had time to regain her feet.

There was a loud bang from the back, then the sound of breaking glass. Rachel whipped around in her seat, cursing when her rifle barrel got stuck on the center console. Jerking it free, she thrust it over the rear seat, ready to fight.

I looked in the mirror, seeing that the back window was shattered, but still held mostly in place by the layer of plastic that made it safety glass. A female running behind us had apparently been able to catch up when I braked hard to lose the one on the hood. She was still right there, preparing to hit the undamaged part of the window with a rock.

"Don't fire!" I shouted, jamming the accelerator to the floor.

The Tahoe surged, the female missing us and screaming in frustration as we pulled away. Keeping our speed up, I did my best to avoid the charging infected while swerving around debris and wrecked vehicles that were on the road.

"What the hell?" Rachel said when she turned to face forward. "We haven't seen that before!"

"They're getting smarter," I said. "We'd better remember that when we're on foot."

I pushed on and fortunately, it didn't take long to pass out of the last small town and into the desert. The really good news was that we left all of the females behind. Holding our speed down, I drove several miles before pulling to a stop in the middle of the road.

"What are you doing?" Rachel asked, looking around in alarm.

"Making sure we didn't take any damage before I push our speed up," I said, popping my door open and stepping out into the night.

Fulcrum

Dog jumped onto my seat, then followed me out. While I scanned a full circle with the night vision goggles, he raised his nose to test the breeze. Immediately he began growling. I checked him, and he was facing into the wind, which was coming from the direction of the towns. He smelled the infected we'd just driven through. I hoped.

Not seeing any danger in the immediate area, I made a quick circle of the Tahoe. I was most concerned with the tires. We'd driven over numerous bodies as well as debris fields I hadn't been able to avoid. I was worried that a tire might have been damaged but breathed a sigh of relief when they all appeared to be intact. A quick look at the grill to make sure our radiator was ok and I called Dog back into the SUV. He leapt in, and moments later I was accelerating on the perfectly straight, two-lane highway that ran to Rocky Point.

It's only sixty miles, or so, across flat, open desert, and we drove in silence. I was lost in thought, considering the implications of females having grown smart enough to pick up a rock to smash their way inside our vehicle. Up until now, even the smart ones could be managed. But if they'd reached the point where they could reason and use tools...

"There weren't any males," Rachel said, her voice startling me in the quiet.

I thought for a minute, then realized she was right.

"The ones standing on the side of the road watching us were pregnant."

"What?" Rachel and I both said in surprise after Tiffany spoke.

"They were pregnant. They didn't run after us. They just stood there, watching."

I traded glances with Rachel, thinking about the implications.

"Are you sure?"

Rachel turned in her seat to face Tiffany.

"Yes. Every single one of them. And most looked pretty far along, like they've only got maybe three or four months to go."

We were quiet for another mile, thinking about the new development.

"How long since the attacks?" Rachel asked in a quiet voice.

"I don't even know what month it is, for sure," I said, shaking my head. "But I think it's been about six months or so. Feels like years."

Rachel nodded.

Fulcrum

"Remember when we went to the casino to rescue Katie? The two infected on the ground that kind of freaked us out?"

She was talking about a male and female infected we had seen having sex. The male was either too brain damaged or uncoordinated to do anything other than lie on his back, but the female on top appeared to have successfully mated before she killed him.

"You think that's why we aren't seeing as many males? Or any, for that matter?" I asked.

"What are you talking about?" Tiffany asked.

Rachel spent a few minutes filling her in, then looked at me and answered my question.

"It could explain it, yes. We've been wondering what the females are eating. Maybe that's the answer. They kill the male after intercourse, then there's plenty of meat available to sustain them."

"Are you serious?" Tiffany asked. "You really think the females are trying to get pregnant? OK, I'll buy that they might eat the males. I've seen them eat just about anything. But, sex?"

"We don't have any idea how the virus has impacted their brains, other than to induce rage.

Perhaps there are some researchers that do, but... Anyway, reproduction is a base level instinct, hardwired into every animal. Humans are included in that. Just because the females' higher cognitive functions have been stripped away, it doesn't mean..."

Rachel trailed off as another thought came to her.

"What?" I prompted when she didn't say anything.

"The babies," she said. "What will they be like?"

I looked at her and couldn't manage to suppress a shudder.

"Don't think I want to find out," I said in a quiet voice.

"What do we do?" Rachel asked quietly.

We were standing on the edge of a small bluff that overlooked the town of Rocky Point, Mexico. And, it was crawling with infected. Even at a distance, it was impossible not to notice them. Females, stalking about, seemingly in search of prey. Many more females standing in the streets and on the sidewalks, watching their sisters hunt.

"Not sure, yet," I said. "The marina is right by downtown, and we aren't getting through that. The whole area is lousy with them."

"What's that?"

I turned to see where Tiffany was pointing. It was a tall building, north of town, situated on the beach.

"Tourist hotel," I said, remembering it had been under construction the last time I'd been here.

"A beach hotel for tourists should have some boats, shouldn't it?" She asked.

I looked at her and smiled. She was right. They most likely would have something, and it would probably be in better shape than many of the floating rattletraps I'd seen that were part of the fishing fleet.

We climbed back into the Tahoe and, after engaging the four-wheel drive system, I headed across the desert, carving a path around the perimeter of town. The going was slow, but the big SUV handled the terrain and soft sand without any problems.

It took us most of fifteen minutes to navigate to within a half a mile of the hotel. There was nothing around for at least three miles, and I was feeling good about Tiffany's suggestion. Shutting the engine off, I took a moment to check my rifle over.

"Why are we stopping here?" Tiffany asked.

"Noise," I said without looking up. "If there's infected hanging around, I don't want to come any closer and alert them to our presence. We go on foot from here. Quiet and dark."

Not bothering to wait and see if she had anything to say to that, I stepped out onto the sand. Dog came out right behind me, and a moment later the girls emerged from the far side of the Tahoe.

I could smell the sea on a gentle night breeze, and the dull roar of surf faintly reached my ears. Dog lifted his nose, growling a moment later. The wind was coming directly across the large resort complex, and he was smelling infected. Hopefully, they were all in and around the buildings and not on the beach.

We didn't need to go into the structure to get a boat. If there was one, it would be on the beach. There was probably also an outbuilding where the keys were locked up, somewhere on the sand. I was hoping it was going to be that easy.

Taking some time to survey the area, I signaled to Rachel the path we were going to take. She nodded, and I headed out with Dog at my side. Tiffany walked next to Rachel, the pair keeping an eye on our rear as we moved.

The sand was soft and loose, making walking difficult. Frequent clumps of dry grass rustled in the wind, but there wasn't anything else moving or making noise. As we drew closer, the roar of waves crashing on the beach intensified. The Sea of Cortez may not be large, but it has strong tides and surprisingly intense surf.

We gave the resort grounds a wide berth, skirting them on the north side, well away from the town. Every hundred yards I'd stop to scan carefully, then resume our advance after checking to make sure Rachel hadn't spotted something of concern.

Past the hotel, we transitioned onto the beach. The only real difference was there were no longer clumps of grass. Now, it was only pure sand. And it was very deep. With each step, my boots sank several inches before reaching solid purchase. I didn't like this. If we had to run, we would be severely hampered. Hopefully, the females would have the same problem.

I'd yet to spot any of the infected that Dog had scented when we got out of the SUV. But, that didn't make me doubt him for an instant. It just told me that we'd been lucky so far.

Stopping a few yards short of the water, I took another long look around. No infected in sight, and a hundred yards south I spotted a small building sitting on stilts, close to the surf. Beyond it, on the sand well away from the waves, were several shapes that looked like boats. Checking on the girls, I signed our new direction and led the way.

The going was slow, partially because of the footing, but also due to my growing paranoia that infected were going to spot us at any second. My head was on a swivel, and I frequently stumbled in the sand as we moved. Dog, on the other hand, seemed to have no problem and flowed easily along the beach.

Fulcrum

With a silent curse, I took us closer to the water to walk on sand that had been compacted and smoothed by the waves. It was a relief to reach it and be able to walk normally, even if our feet were getting an occasional soaking.

We covered the remaining distance quickly, then slowed as we approached the elevated building. On the far side, both a set of stairs and a long ramp led up from the beach to what I assumed was its entrance. Circling through the soft sand to go around, I kept my rifle up and ready as the other side came into view.

There was a door, and a waist-high window facing a small balcony that ran its length. Both were tightly shuttered, the padlocks that secured them swinging gently in the wind. I double checked to make sure there wasn't an infected hiding beneath the building, then turned my attention to the boats I'd seen.

They were about 25 feet long with sharp, high bows and squared off sterns. These weren't pleasure craft; they were rescue boats that could quickly get through pounding surf to reach swimmers in trouble. There was only one problem. None of them had a motor.

Cursing silently in my head, I turned a slow circle, looking for a likely storage place for the motors. Other than the main hotel buildings, there were only two structures. One was the building on stilts right behind me. The other was much larger with a tattered awning and a dozen tables scattered around. It sat at the upper edge of the beach and had to be a bar so guests had easy access to their next margarita.

Dismissing the bar, even though a frosty cold beverage would have gone down really good at the moment, I signed for Rachel and Tiffany to stay put and keep watch. With Dog following, I climbed the stairs on the front of the stilt building.

I'd wondered about the reason for the ramp. Mexico didn't place a high priority on providing accommodations for people with disabilities. A ramp like this in the US wouldn't even draw attention, but here, now that I thought about it, it was out of place. Especially on a soft sand beach that could never be traversed in a wheelchair.

Boat motors are heavy, even the small ones. When the lifeguards shut down for the night, they probably brought them inside so they didn't walk away in the wee hours of the morning. And, I was willing to bet they had some sort of specialized hand truck, with fat tires for the sand, that they would use to wheel them up the ramp and into the security of a locked building.

Fulcrum

I checked over the shuttered openings in the wall and was again reminded that I was in Mexico. The hotel took security seriously. If they didn't, they'd be buying new motors every couple of weeks. To prevent that, they'd invested in rolling steel shutters that locked into metal frames. The padlocks that were on each end of the hasps were the real deal. Easily as large as my fist with shackles as thick as my thumb. No way was I breaking in with what I had. Taking a look around from my elevated position, I returned to the beach and moved close to Tiffany.

"Think you could put together another bit of Thermite?" I asked.

She took a long look around before answering.

"I can if I have the materials. But I'm not seeing any iron. Everything is either aluminum or stainless steel because of the salt water."

I looked around like she had, noticing that anything that wasn't made of wood was either shiny metal or painted aluminum. It made sense. If it can be helped, you don't put something that will rust in close proximity to the ocean.

Dog, standing close by my side, suddenly rumbled out a loud growl. He was facing the hotel, and when I looked, I could make out a female figure standing at the top of a flight of stairs that ran up from the sand. Her long hair blew in the wind, streaming behind her as she watched us.

Despite standing nearly a hundred yards away, I could make out the swollen belly of pregnancy. We all stood frozen for a couple of heartbeats, perhaps hoping she couldn't see us in the dark. Then she tilted her head back and screamed into the night.

The North Carolina hovered in the water, the top of her sail 600 feet beneath the surface of the South Pacific Ocean. Still in deeper water, the boat was loitering in the shipping lanes that approached Sydney Harbour. Captain Talbot was in the control room, but Adrienne had the conn or was in command of the submarine.

He was prepared to take immediate control if he felt she was making an error that would place the boat in more danger than they were already in. But, he didn't expect to have to interfere. His XO was every bit as capable as he had ever been when it came to conning a nuclear submarine, and she had earned his trust. But still, he had the ultimate responsibility for the multi-billion-dollar machine and all the lives on board.

They had been overflown twice in the past hour by Russian aircraft on patrol. Neither had deviated from their pattern, having failed to detect the American submarine that was hiding beneath the thermocline. This was where the surface water, warmed by the sun and of varying salinity, mixed with the cold, more stable water of the depths.

The deeper water remained a nearly constant temperature year round, the energy of the sun unable to penetrate far enough to affect it. Where the two strata met, they created a band, or layer, in the ocean that was neither as warm as the surface nor as cold as the deeps. This phenomenon was well known to submariners since it effectively reflected sound waves, and it was used to their full advantage to hide from aircraft and surface ships that might be searching for them.

And this is exactly why Adrienne had parked the North Carolina where she had. At the moment, they were making like a big hole in the water. The boat was rigged for silent running, all non-essential machinery shut down and secured. Personnel that were not actively involved in the operation of the sub were in their bunks. The only way the Russians, or Australians, would detect them is if they had one of their own submarines in the area, beneath the layer.

Even then, unless someone made a mistake that would create a noise in the water, they wouldn't be found by anything other than an active sonar ping. As both the skipper and XO knew, there wasn't a submarine captain in the world stupid enough to be driving around and advertising his position by going active with his sonar. It would only be used once a target had been identified and was being attacked.

"Conn, sonar," came a muted voice over a sound powered speaker.

"Conn, aye," Adrienne answered.

"Surface contact. Closing. Bearing two-oh-oh, range 20,000 meters."

"Speed?" Adrienne asked.

"Best guess at this range is 18 knots, ma'am."

"Is this our girl?"

"Still too faint for the computer to confirm, but it definitely sounds right. It's a big, heavy sucker, and it's on the right course."

"Understood," she said. "Let me know as soon as you can confirm."

"Sonar, aye."

Adrienne checked a digital chronometer mounted to a bulkhead, catching her skipper's eye as she did.

"The timing is right," she said to him in a quiet voice.

He nodded without saying anything. Adrienne reached out and plucked a sound powered phone off its cradle, speaking into it briefly.

"Good luck, Commander," she said, returning the handset to its base.

"SEALs are ready to go on my order, sir," she said to Talbot without looking at him.

"Very well, XO."

A moment later the sonar operator advised her that the computer had positively identified the surface contact as the *Marie Maersk*, a very large container ship the Russians had seized from its home port in Denmark. It was designated as contact Alpha. At 1,300 feet in length with a beam of nearly 200 feet, it dwarfed the North Carolina. And was going to provide them with the perfect cover to sail right up to the mouth of Sydney Harbour, undetected.

The wait for the massive ship to approach felt interminable to Adrienne. Everything was ready to go, she just needed the cover it would provide before she could move her boat again. Finally, it came within a predetermined range. With the sonar operator providing running updates on its position, speed and heading, she ordered the North Carolina to begin ascending.

The Marie Maersk normally had a draft of 40 feet, but she was heavily laden with supplies and the comforts of home for Russia's elite who had taken up residence in Australia. With the added weight, the bottom of her keel was fifty feet below the surface.

Carefully, Adrienne brought the submarine up in the water and slowly added in propulsion until it was pacing the much larger ship. The North Carolina approached Sydney Harbour, directly beneath the keel of the massive container ship. As they progressed, she ordered the boat to stop rising when there was only 30 feet of water separating the top of her sail from the bottom of the *Marie Maersk*.

It seemed as if the very atmosphere within the submarine was vibrating from the powerful, bass pulses of the massive propellers. Frequently, the officers and crew cast involuntary glances upwards, as if they could see the hundreds of thousands of tons of steel that floated just over their heads. Despite their unease, the tactic worked.

The North Carolina was invisible, completely masked by the sounds of the giant ship's propellers, engines and keel slicing through the ocean. As they drew closer to the coast, another sailor began calling out the depth of the water beneath their keel. Adrienne ordered another adjustment, cutting the range between the two craft to 20 feet. This close together, any error could result in a collision and catastrophic damage to the submarine. The vastly heavier ship probably wouldn't even notice.

"Conn, sonar! New surface contact, bearing one-oh-five, 3,000 meters, on an intercept course. High-speed screws, making 30 knots. Marked as contact Bravo. Contact Alpha is reducing speed."

Adrienne acknowledged the report, and as the container ship slowed, she matched its speed. Updates were flowing in regularly now as the submarine continued to slow to stay in its sonar shadow. Bravo approached rapidly, carving a semi-circle until its signature merged with the Marie Maersk.

Checking a readout, she confirmed that they had slowed to five knots for the ship to take a harbor pilot aboard. The pilot knew the channels and currents in Sydney Harbour like the back of his hand and would take command of the 165,000-ton vessel. He was responsible for safely entering the narrow waters and getting it to the dock.

"Notify the SEALs they're GO for lockout!" Adrienne said.

The order was repeated back to her, then she heard the sailor passing it along over a sound powered phone. Within five minutes, she received confirmation that the team had successfully exited the submarine and deployed their RIBs.

She'd done her job, now it was up to them. The *Marie Maersk* would sail right into the harbor with two boats loaded down with SEALs following so close they could reach out and touch the stern hull. It wouldn't be a smooth ride due to the turbulence in the water from the giant propellers, but they would be all but invisible in the dark.

Adrienne took half a second to mutter a prayer for the fighting men, then turned her attention back to conning the North Carolina. It was time to move to slightly deeper water while they waited for the men to return with President Barinov.

Admiral Packard paced on the neatly mown grass that covered the slope, looking up in annoyance as a pair of Marine AH-1 Super Cobra helicopters made another low and slow pass directly overhead. Below him were the blue waters of Pearl Harbor, the USS Arizona memorial gleaming in the late afternoon sun. The water around it held a rainbow sheen from oil that still leaked out of the sunken battleship, even after nearly three-quarters of a century.

Several senior officers stood around him as he puffed furiously on a cigarette. They were having a meeting, and the Admiral hadn't been able to take another minute in the confines of his conference room. Though he'd never admit it, he detested the politics and administrative duties that came along with his rank and position. If he had a choice, he'd let someone else take over, and he'd be back on the bridge of a front-line ship in a heartbeat.

Surrounding the group of officers was a squad of heavily armed Marines. Several times it had been necessary for them to direct personnel in a direction that did not bring them too close. Rumors abounded of the Russians having sent Spetsnaz teams into Hawaii, ahead of the invasion fleet, with the intent of softening up the target by destroying infrastructure and assassinating senior officers.

Marine Captain Charles Black, who was in command of the squad, was in a foul mood as a result. While there was no solid intelligence to support the rumors, he well knew that this was one of the times that the gossip was based on reality. There was a very real probability there were Russian special operations troops already on the ground.

Despite his strenuous protests, the Admiral had overruled him and taken the meeting out into the open. In a scramble, Black had put two helos in the air, posted Marine snipers on several rooftops around the area and assigned two additional squads to patrol a broad perimeter. Even with the added protection, he still wasn't happy. There were just too many places where an assassin could get a shot off at Packard.

So, he stayed close to the old man. Closer than protocol would dictate for a protection detail, but he didn't care. He was prepared to throw the Admiral to the ground and cover him with his own body at the slightest indication of trouble.

The Cobras slowly moved away to make another orbit of the area, and Packard shot an irritated glance at the Marine Captain. Black met his eyes and resisted the temptation to smile. If the Admiral didn't like the increased security measures, he could damn well stay in his nice, safe office.

As the roar of the helicopters' engines and rotors faded, Packard looked around at the assembled officers and resumed speaking.

"I was asking if we've seen any effect on the Russian fleet in response to our broadcasts."

"No, sir. Not so far." One of them answered. "But we've only been on station, transmitting the audio and video for less than an hour. I believe we can safely assume the broadcasts are being received, but we are having to rotate amongst several B-2s so the enemy fleet cannot triangulate the signal."

"How long do you think it will take for an uprising as a result?" The Admiral speared the man with his eyes.

"Difficult to say, sir. But something like that takes time to boil over. And, it's going to depend mostly on the senior NCOs in the fleet. They can't stop it if the enlisted are truly incensed, but they can slow it down. Conversely, if they're of the same mind and lead an insurrection, it could begin at any moment. Commander Marx did an excellent job, and I have a hard time imagining it will not inflame the already simmering tensions within their ranks."

"What's the latest estimate on the Russians making landfall?"

A Marine one-star General stepped forward, preparing to answer Packard's question. Before any words came out of his mouth, one of the Super Cobras began firing its 20mm Gatling gun. The sound was like the very fabric of the air was being ripped apart, and Captain Black responded immediately, slamming into the Admiral.

No one heard the shots over the din of the helicopter firing and the shouts of the protection detail as they faced outwards and backed in to place their bodies between the threat and the senior officers they were guarding. The Marine General's head exploded, a bloody mist spraying the faces of two naval officers standing next to him.

Admiral Packard grunted in pain as he hit the ground, Black landing on top of him an instant later. He struggled to raise his head, but the younger man was stronger and kept him pinned flat on the grass. It took the Captain several seconds to realize there was blood on his hands, and he couldn't tell if it was his or the Admiral's.

Dirk Patton

The Super Cobra ceased firing but remained in a hover above a forested hill that overlooked the area. Men were screaming over the radio and Black roared into his to regain control. Soon, an *all clear* was broadcast by the helicopter pilot. Looking around, the Captain saw that all of the officers were prone on the grass, his squad of Marines in a tight perimeter around the group, each on one knee with their rifles aiming out.

Just because the sniper had been eliminated didn't mean there wasn't another one. Black barked several commands into the radio, a moment later leaping to his feet and bodily lifting the Admiral off the ground. Blood stained Packard's normally immaculate uniform blouse, but this wasn't the time or place to assess his injuries.

With a shouted order, Captain Black charged for the nearest building, one arm around the Admiral. He bore most of the man's weight as they ran, doing the best he could to shield Packard's body with his. The two Marines guarding the entrance to the building saw him coming and ran forward, taking up position behind him to protect the Admiral from the possibility of another shooter.

They charged through the entrance, a few seconds later the remaining officers with the protection detail running in behind them. Black stopped, turning and holding Packard's shoulders in his hands and bellowed for a medic. He was focused on looking for the source of the blood on the Admiral's torso and was surprised when the older man pushed his hands away and took a step back.

"Thank you, Captain. It's only my arm. I'll live," Packard said.

Black gaped at him, having already arrived at the incorrect conclusion that the Admiral had been shot in the chest or back. Packard looked at him for a beat before extending his right hand.

"Captain, my sincere apologies for not having heeded your concerns. I'll not dismiss them again."

Still stunned, Black stared at the offered hand. Finally, he remembered there was an Admiral standing in front of him, and he took Packard's hand.

"No apology necessary, sir," he said. "I'm just relieved you're ok."

Packard released his hand and turned to look through the heavy, glass doors. The body of the Marine still rested on the pristine lawn, blood staining the front of his sharply creased shirt. His eyes narrowed, and he barely acknowledged

383

a Navy medic that ran up and began cutting away his left sleeve to access the bullet wound.

"Captain!" Packard barked as the medic began applying a compression bandage. "Do you have enough men to lock down the base and search for any other intruders?"

"No, sir," Black immediately answered, shaking his head. "We're running a skeleton force. I've got half a dozen squads at my disposal. Every other man is preparing the defenses on Mt. Kaala. Do you want me to pull some back to secure the base?"

"Negative," the Admiral said after a long pause. "Those efforts are more important to our defense. There are obviously advance enemy teams on the ground. We can't afford to have them running around and creating havoc there, too. Advise the defenders at Mt. Kaala of events so they can take additional precautions."

"Yes sir," Black snapped, turning away to speak into his radio.

"Admiral, I need to get you to the hospital. The bullet went all the way through, but you still need to be X-rayed and treated."

"Belay that, sailor," Packard said. "Just wrap it tight. And if you've got some aspirin, I'd appreciate it."

"But, sir..."

"You heard me."

"Aye, aye sir."

The medic suppressed a sigh and did as asked. When he had completed his task, a thick, white bandage encased the Admiral's arm from elbow to shoulder. He dug through his bag and produced a small bottle of Tylenol and handed it to Packard.

Thanking him, the Admiral turned and headed into the building. Captain Black, expecting he would be waiting for an ambulance, rushed to catch up with him.

"No hospital, sir?"

They swept through a security checkpoint and boarded an elevator. The Admiral leaned forward and peered into a retina scanner. When the screen turned green, he pressed an unmarked button on the panel.

"Hospitals are for the Army, Captain," Packard growled.

Black snorted a laugh then fell silent as the elevator car began descending. It kept going for nearly a minute, finally stopping on a level the Marine Captain had rarely been to. When the doors slid open, four heavily armed Marines were waiting. They stepped back, staring at the Admiral when he strode into the large vestibule with Black in tow.

"You'll need to wait out here, Captain."

Packard had paused at a steel blast door. Black acknowledged and backed away as the Admiral submitted to another retinal scan. Again, the panel turned green and with a rumble, the large door slid open. The Captain caught a glimpse of a massive room full of computer terminals before Packard passed inside and the door trundled closed, sealing with a solid *boom* he felt in his feet.

"Is the Admiral OK, sir?"

One of the guards stepped up next to Black.

"He's one tough old sailor, that's for sure," the Captain replied.

Inside the room, several people looked up when the door closed. Several of them did a double take at the sight of Admiral Packard. His uniform was stained bright red, his thinning hair was a mess and blood was already beginning to seep through the thick bandage on his arm. A Navy Captain rushed forward to greet him.

"Sir. I wasn't expecting you. Are you alright?"

"I'm fine, Captain. Point me at Seaman Simmons."

"Yes, sir," the man said, hesitating for a beat before turning. "She's right over there, with Captain West."

Packard nodded and strode across the floor. Jessica looked up and saw him coming, leaping to her feet with a look of concern on her face. Captain West turned and came forward to meet the Admiral.

"Sir? What's happened?"

He took a closer look at the Admiral, assessing his health.

"Russian advance team took a shot at me," Packard said dismissively before turning to face Jessica. "Seaman. How is your work coming? We need our comms and surveillance back."

"Uh, well... sir," Jessica stammered, thrown off by the Admiral's condition. "I just loaded an updated anti-virus program, and it's running. This is my fourth attempt to eradicate the Russian worm. I've gotten some of it, but if I don't get it all, it just rebuilds itself and keeps on chewing through code."

"Are you optimistic this iteration will be successful?" The Admiral asked.

"Cautiously, yes sir. I've learned from each of the past failed attempts. I'm hopeful this one will be it."

Packard looked at her for a long moment, then slowly lowered himself into an empty chair. Pulling out the bottle of Tylenol, he shook four of them into his hand and dry swallowed them.

"Sir, shouldn't you be in the hospital?" Jessica asked, after rushing across the room and retrieving a bottle of water from a small refrigerator.

The Admiral waved off her concerns and drained the bottle without stopping.

"Seaman, forgive my ignorance, but we have a protected copy of the code the Russians infected, don't we?"

"Yes, sir. We do."

"Well, that's good. What I don't understand is why you can't do what the Geek Squad did when my personal, home computer was badly infected a few years ago. They wiped it clean and reinstalled the operating system. It worked fine after that."

Jessica exchanged a quick glance with Captain West before answering. She was concerned that Packard obviously didn't remember that had been the first thing she had tried.

"Sir, that was one of the first things I tried when we found the virus. It didn't work."

"Explain," the Admiral said.

"Sir, because of the nature of the interconnected systems, the worm didn't just infect us here in Hawaii. It was quickly spread to every ship and aircraft that was online. And, while I can't access them currently to verify, I am confident it has also infected all of our remaining communication and surveillance satellites, as well as the Thor System.

"What happened was, I wiped every server in Hawaii clean, and started over with a fresh copy of the Battlespace Software. At first, it seemed as if that would work, but then as soon it made contact with a remote server that was still infected, we wound up right back at square one. If there's a trace of this worm left anywhere, it will rebuild and replicate itself and start spreading.

"The only way to regain full command and control of our assets is to eradicate the worm completely, not just here, but on every server we are in communication with. Failing that, it will not be possible to bring the system back online."

Packard had listened attentively. When Jessica finished speaking, he looked at his aide.

"Captain, I believe you've tried to explain this to me," he said.

"Yes sir, but not near as eloquently as Seaman Simmons."

Packard stood and looked at Jessica.

"Make it work, Seaman. We're out of time. The Russians will be here soon, and it's going to get very bloody."

I raised my rifle, preparing to shoot the bitch that had just given us away, but I never pulled the trigger. Almost immediately, there was an answering chorus of screams, followed by dozens of leaping forms that began pouring over the seawall onto the beach.

"Move!" I shouted.

Dashing to the closest boat, I grabbed a handle set high on the sharply raked bow. Lifting, I started dragging it across the sand, towards the water. The damn thing was heavier than it looked and I wasn't making much progress. More screams sent a surge of adrenaline through my system and I pulled harder as I glanced over my shoulder.

Females were charging through the deep sand, more of them than I could quickly count. And, they were still leaping over the wall onto the beach. The hotel must have been full of them. The only good news was the footing I'd been bitching about was slowing their normally terrifying speed. But not enough.

The boat suddenly surged forward, and I nearly lost my balance. Rachel and Tiffany were pushing on the stern. Dog stood in the sand behind them, facing the coming onslaught of infected. He had to recognize the impossible odds, but wasn't fazed.

Working together, we reached the wet, hard packed sand and were able to pick up speed. I pulled with every ounce of strength I had. Wanting to turn my head to see how close the females were, I resisted the urge. Looking away would slow me down, and if we didn't make it into the water, we were dead. There were way too many for us to hope to make a successful stand.

Three seconds later I met the first wave head on. It crashed against my legs, soaking me to the waist and lifting the bow of the boat. I fought against it but made no progress until its energy was spent. I splashed forward, pulling hard as the bow remained afloat on top of the receding water.

More screams from behind and I heard Dog's savage snarls as he began battling a female. The next wave roared in, lifting the bow above my head and drenching me. Somehow I managed to prevent it from pushing the boat back towards the shore. It rushed under the hull, lifting the small craft clear of the sand.

Spitting saltwater, I screamed at the girls.

"Keep going!"

Fulcrum

I turned for the beach to help Dog slow the infected. I knew the females couldn't swim and wouldn't be able to follow, but they could overwhelm us before we reached water deep enough to stop their advance. The boat had to be out far enough to be safe, then Dog and I could swim out. I hoped.

High stepping through the surf, I moved past Rachel and Tiffany as they struggled against the force of the ocean. Drawing my Ka-Bar, I stepped out of the water and slashed open the throat of a leaping female. I ducked to the side, and her body flashed past. Spinning, I located Dog, who had already killed two and was locked in battle with a third.

I had to twist as another infected charged with outstretched hands. She was young, wearing a tattered gown that looked like she'd fallen victim to the virus during her Quinceañera, or coming of age celebration. When this whole thing started, I might have paused in sympathy for what had happened to an innocent 15-year-old girl. By now, I'd lost all compassion for whom the infected had once been.

Slicing down, with my weight behind it, the blade cut through her wrist and severed her hand. She didn't so much as blink, grabbing a fistful of my sleeve with her other. Continuing the turn, I brought the tip of the blade up and into her throat, ending her life. Kicking her body

393

aside, I moved a step closer to Dog, who was having a harder time than normal.

The female he was fighting was huge. Probably larger than me, and even though he was faster, Dog hadn't succeeded in getting past her thick arms to find a vital spot. I started forward to help him but had to battle two more infected that leapt at me simultaneously.

I managed to avoid the first, inflicting a deep wound across her stomach, but the second one slammed into me, knocking me to the ground. She immediately wrapped me up, trying to reach my face with her teeth, and we rolled into the water.

Unprepared, I inhaled seawater and my throat and lungs locked up. Panic surged, and I frantically began hitting her with the hand holding the knife as I flailed with my other. After what felt like an eternity, I locked onto her throat and squeezed for all I was worth.

My fingers hadn't fully encircled her neck, and as I applied pressure, their tips sank in on either side of her trachea. Pulse pounding in my ears, I dug in until they pierced her flesh, then tore her throat out. Hot blood splashed across my face as she went limp, then another wave inundated me and washed it away.

Fulcrum

Struggling to my feet, still unable to breathe, I whipped my rifle around and slammed the stock into the face of my next attacker. She was stopped cold, dropping dead or unconscious into the water at my feet. Dozens more were right behind her as the main body of the small herd approached the compacted sand.

Aiming, I pulled the trigger just as a wracking cough hit me. My body expelled the seawater, violently, throwing the rifle off. Trying to control my convulsing lungs, I reacquired my targets and pulled and held the trigger. Bodies fell as I quickly ran through a full magazine.

Dropping the empty and slapping in a fresh one, I kept firing, aiming for knees and hips. Right now I didn't care if they were dead. I just needed to slow them down and buy some time.

Dog had finished off the big female and was scrambling off her corpse when he was tackled by a flying body. I shot the three females who were right behind his attacker before they could join the fray. His snarls were loud, drowning out the roar of the surf and my suppressed, full-auto fire, but that was probably because I was focused on him as I kept fighting.

Another magazine change, and I finally remembered to check on Rachel and Tiffany. I glanced over my shoulder, surprised to see the boat floating fifty yards off shore. They both stood, apparently shouting at me that they were clear, but I hadn't heard them during the heat of battle.

Screaming for Dog, I began backing into the surf while still firing. Females were dropping, but there were still more coming than I could handle with a single rifle. A wave crashed into my back, nearly knocking me over and causing me to waste half a magazine that fired uselessly into the sand.

Regaining my balance, I took another step back, now in water above my waist. Firing, I screamed again for Dog but didn't have even a heartbeat to look for him. More than twenty females were in the surf, struggling against the waves as they tried to reach me.

I kept firing, shooting one who was hardly more than an arm's length away. Another step back and the water was to my chest. A wave broke over my head, momentarily submerging me and masking my view of the infected. It passed quickly, and I emerged, blowing water out of my mouth and nose as I resumed firing.

Where the fuck was Dog? I screamed for him again, still not seeing him and no longer hearing his snarls. I took another step back to stand in neck deep water. Spread out to my front, female heads bobbed as they continued wading out to attack me. Firing the rifle was becoming problematic as I had to hold it over my head so it was clear of the water.

My aim suffered, rounds punching into the surface of the water well off target. Hands flailed beneath the surface, grasping for my body. There were too many. If they were able to get a solid hold, I would be dragged under and overwhelmed by their numbers.

With another scream for Dog, I pushed away from the females into water over my head. Letting the rifle drop to hang from its sling, I swam backward, fighting to keep my head above the surface. At least I was now bobbing with the waves instead of having them crash over me.

Somehow, my night vision goggles had remained in place through the fight. I had a good view of the females in the water, and they were already struggling to return to dry land. One of them went under and didn't reappear. I didn't care. I wanted to spot Dog.

I was now more than forty feet from the beach and nearly jumped out of my skin when a hand grabbed the back of my collar and pulled hard. Whipping my head around, I reached for the arm, expecting to see an infected who had been carried out this far and had managed to latch on.

"Get in the goddamn boat!"

Rachel screamed in my face as she hauled on me, nearly pulling herself into the water in the process. Tiffany was next to her, a long handled paddle in her hands as she worked hard to control the boat. Between them, looking like a drowned rat, Dog stood with his head hanging over the rail as he stared at me with his tongue hanging out.

It took some effort, actually a lot of effort, but with Rachel's help, I finally managed to haul my big ass into the boat. As I flopped onto my back, dripping water, Rachel grabbed another paddle and helped Tiffany move us far enough off shore to be away from the influence of the surf.

Dog, also soaked to the skin, sat and looked down at me. Water was steadily dripping off his muzzle, falling on my face, but I didn't care. Reaching up I rubbed his ears, and he slowly lay down until his head was resting on my chest. I wrapped my arms around his neck and hugged him tight.

"Thought I lost you, fur face," I said softly.

His big eyes looked at me for a moment, then slowly closed. As the girls paddled, I closed mine, too.

"What the hell were you doing?" Rachel asked.

I cracked open an eye and looked at her. She was holding her paddle out of the water, looking down from where she was seated on a built in bench.

"Buying us time," I mumbled.

Dog opened his eyes when I spoke, then when he didn't see anything interesting, closed them again with a sigh.

"We were screaming at you. He heard us and swam out, but you just kept fighting. We had to paddle back in and get you."

"Thank you," I said, giving her a grin.

"You really should pay more attention," Tiffany said.

I looked at her and thought about saying something really sarcastic, but she was a bit young for that side of my personality. She'd shown she was more than capable of contributing, and might take my comment as a slight. Nothing would be farther from the truth.

"You're right," I settled for saying.

Moving Dog's big head off my chest, I sat up and looked around. We were more than a hundred yards offshore, bobbing in gentle swells. The beach was full of females. Nearly half of them stood in place, watching us, while the rest paced back and forth. Occasionally, one of them would step into the surf, but would quickly retreat when a wave crashed against her legs.

Fulcrum

We seemed to be slowly drifting south and east. Tiffany frequently had to stick her paddle in the water for a few strokes to keep us away from the shore. The wind was pushing us towards the beach, which was to the east. The southerly drift could only be explained by a current.

Climbing up on the bench next to Rachel, I took a longer look around. Nothing but empty, dark stretches of water in every direction other than east. I knew we were near the northern reaches of the Sea of Cortez, and it was roughly 80 miles to the Baja shoreline.

What I didn't have a good idea of was how the hell we were going to search for the pilot in a rowboat. I sat there, trying to recall what I did know about the Sea of Cortez as we kept slowly drifting south. I knew that in the scheme of things it was a very small body of water. But, scale is relative. Sitting there in the tiny, wooden boat without even a trolling motor, it felt as large as the Pacific Ocean.

"What next?" Rachel asked after several minutes.

I looked back towards the beach, unhappy to see that the females were following us. We weren't far enough out to sea to be hidden from them, and as we drifted, they paced us. Had to do something about that.

"First thing," I said, pointing at the beach. "We need to get far enough out for them to lose sight of us."

"Then what? We can't perform a search in this thing."

I nodded, my attention drifting to the small marina at Rocky Point, still more than a couple of miles south.

"We head straight out so they quit following," I said. "Once we lose them, we come back in, nice and quiet. Paddle into the marina and find a fishing boat. There used to be some nice big boats for sport fishing that ran out of here. Hopefully one of them is still there. It'll be fast."

Rachel looked at me for a long moment, then nodded her head. Without saying anything else, she dipped her paddle and began stroking. Tiffany had heard the conversation and joined the effort. Soon, we were moving at not much more than a snail's pace. But, at least the beach full of females was finally receding.

"Are you just going to sit there and watch us work?" Rachel asked forty minutes later.

I was sitting in the middle of one of the benches, watching the eastern shoreline slowly fade away. Dog was stretched out in the bottom of the boat, asleep on top of my feet.

"My daddy always said, don't take over someone's job if you can't do it better. You two seem to be quite capable."

They were quiet for a moment, then a large splash of water from Rachel's paddle hit me squarely in the face. A lot of it also landed on Dog, and he raised his head with an indignant expression on his face. Before I could say anything, a blast of water from Tiffany soaked the back of my head. I endured their retaliation stoically, figuring I deserved what I got.

"I think we're good, anyway," I said. "Even with night vision, the shore is just a faint line. I don't see how the females could still be tracking us."

"So, time to head in?"

"South for a bit," I said. "I don't think we've drifted more than a quarter of a mile. Let's go about a mile and a half, then with the drift, we should come right into the marina."

Rachel nodded, then handed me her paddle. Smiling, I moved Dog off my feet and slid to the side so I could reach the water. We kept at it for some time. When I could just make out the stone jetty that served as a breakwater for the marina, I turned us to the east.

Having gotten some rest, Rachel took over for Tiffany. The young girl quickly crawled into the center of the boat, curled up with her head on Dog's side and went to sleep. Rachel and I paddled with long strokes, moving us towards the jetty.

"Think this will work?" Rachel asked in a quiet voice.

"Marina may be full of infected," I said.

"Then what?"

"We paddle back north of the hotel, give it a wide berth and take the Tahoe. Drive down the shore and hope."

"Are there more towns south of here?"

"No idea," I said. "Never been south of Rocky Point, but I'd think there probably are. Lots of fishing here. As far as I know, other than drugs and tourism, it was *the* economy for this part of Mexico."

Falling silent after that, we kept working. With painstaking slowness, we drew closer to the jetty. I'd gone fishing here, once, and remembered that it protected a long channel that connected the sea to a sheltered harbor. I just hoped this all hadn't been a wasted exercise, and there were still boats in the marina.

Finally, we reached the curving jetty. Small waves crashed against it, and I steered us wide to avoid the turbulence. Rachel shook Tiffany awake as we rounded the breakwater and entered the calm waters of the channel.

It was perfectly straight and half a mile long. Sand beaches lined both sides, and at least for the moment, they were both empty. Looking around, I signaled to Rachel that it was time to be as quiet as possible.

I wasn't worried about infected reaching us in the water, but if we were spotted, they'd follow along on shore. If that happened, we'd be cut off from any boat we did find. Concentrating on not making splashing sounds with the paddle, I kept a constant scan of both shores going. So far, so good.

As we drew closer to the harbor, I began to make out a few boats tied to the dock. Most of the slips were empty, but there were a few shrimping boats and a couple of sport fishing boats with tall towers sticking up. Either would be perfect, as standing in one of those towers would give a commanding view of the ocean for miles in every direction.

Tiffany tapped me on the shoulder and pointed at a long, wooden wharf. Four figures were standing perfectly still, as if on sentry duty. Fortunately, they were all facing away from us and hadn't detected our presence. Holding up my fist, I signaled for Rachel to stop paddling.

I spent a minute surveying the marina. There weren't any other infected, at least that I could see. The four females that Tiffany had spotted remained stock still. But, to reach any of the boats, we'd have to go right past them. I wasn't confident we could do that without making enough noise with the paddles to alert them.

Turning around, I leaned towards the middle of the boat. Rachel and Tiffany did the same so we could speak quietly. Dog, thinking he was the center of attention, sat up and licked my face.

"I'm getting out here and swimming," I mumbled.

Rachel and Tiffany both looked at me as if I had gone off the deep end. Dog just kept trying to lick me. I pushed him away and held up a hand before the girls had a chance to voice a protest.

"I can move quieter in the water than we can paddle. I'll swim to the boats and find one that will start. While I'm doing that, you two turn around and get outside the breakwater. When I've got a boat, I'll be right there and pick you up."

Rachel was opening her mouth to argue, but I held my hand up again and shook my head to stop her.

"It's the best way," I said. "If I'm spotted, or if I can't start a boat, I'll swim back out."

I didn't wait for either of them to agree. With extreme caution, so I didn't bump or bang against something, I began removing my rifle and vest with its spare magazines. Gently placing my gear in the bottom of the boat, I removed my boots and socks, took off the NVGs and peeled my shirt over my head.

Settling the night vision goggles back in place, I checked the security of my knife and pistol. Tiffany reached out and tapped the goggles on my head.

"Waterproof," I said, giving her a smile.

She nodded and smiled back. I met Rachel's gaze, then silently slipped over the side of the boat into the water.

41

The water was cold, which oddly I hadn't noticed when the waves were breaking over me on the beach. I guess that's what adrenaline will do for you. That, and it wasn't ball shriveling cold, just a low enough temperature to get my attention.

Pushing away from the boat, I began slowly kicking, making sure my feet stayed below the surface. Only my head, from my nose up, was out of the water. I maintained a close watch on the females as I inched my way past. If they spotted me, I planned to go completely still in the water. The head rig and goggles broke up the profile of my skull, and I hoped that the dark water would help me appear as nothing more than a piece of floating debris. In case they saw me.

For once, Mr. Murphy wasn't along for the swim. Maybe the water was too cold, or he was busy fucking up someone else's plan for a change. For whatever reason, I cleared the area where the four infected stood as still as statues and made my slow approach to the closest sport fisherman.

It sat high in the water, thick ropes making it fast to iron cleats on the dock that had about an inch-thick layer of paint covering them. From my perspective at the waterline, it looked as massive as an aircraft carrier but was probably no more than 45 feet long.

Pausing between the boat and the dock, I tread water for a few minutes and listened carefully for the sound of any movement. None. But then there could be twenty females right over my head, and if they were all just standing there as still as the other four, I wouldn't know.

Reaching up, I grasped the edge of the rough, wooden dock and, an inch at a time, pulled myself up for a look. The dock was clear. Turning my head, I checked the open deck of the boat. Also clear. Cautiously, I lifted the loop in the thick line that was over the cleat. Once it was clear, I eased myself back into the water, letting it float on the surface.

Bow line free, I made my way to the rear and repeated the process. The boat was now untethered from the dock, and as long as I could start the engines, it was ready to go. Heading for the stern, expecting to find a platform that would make it easy to climb aboard, I kicked to give myself a push.

I don't know if it was a hunk of concrete, an old piling from a past dock or just a submerged rock, but I managed to kick it straight on with my bare foot. The pain was immediate and blossomed up my leg, causing my stomach to do a flop. Somehow, I managed not to let loose with the string of curses that wanted to come out.

Taking a breath and suppressing the pain, I made my way, without any more kicking, to the stern and grabbed onto a low platform. Lifting myself, I took another look at the deck, then swiveled my head to check the surrounding boats. Nothing was moving, and I didn't see any silent sentinels waiting for me to make a mistake.

Pulling myself out of the water, I crouched on the platform and drew my knife. I waited for an alarm to be screamed, but all I could hear was a steady drip as water drained out of my pants and back into the harbor.

The boat was designed for tourists wanting to fish for a trophy. It had a large, open deck with what was called a *fighting chair*, bolted down near the stern. Equipped with a harness, you would strap in so if you hooked something really big it couldn't pull you overboard. Beyond was a sliding steel door that let into an interior cabin, and probably the engine space below.

Sitting high on top of this was an open air bridge where the boat's captain would sit. Rising up from that was a ten-foot-tall tower with a narrow ladder leading to the top. It would have been used by a lookout who would be charged with spotting a good location for the customer to fish.

I could see the bridge was clear of infected and had already gotten a good look at the open space on the bow when I released the dock line. As long as there were no surprises inside, I was in good shape.

Moving forward in a crouch, I stopped at the door and waited a beat. Nothing other than tomb-like silence. A millimeter at a time, I slid the door open. My knife was up and ready to be plunged into the chest of anything that responded from within. But again, Murphy was giving me a break. No screaming infected leapt at me, and I was able to slip inside without a sound.

Not wanting any uninvited guests, I pulled the door closed behind me and quickly searched several small cabins. All empty. Not particularly clean or orderly, but I didn't give a shit. As long as the damn thing would start and run, I'd be happy.

There was access to the bridge from within the main cabin, and I climbed up. Poking my head into the open air, I looked around. The four females hadn't moved, and other than them, I didn't see anything to worry about. Turning my attention to the boat's controls, I cursed internally when I saw an ignition switch that required a key I didn't have.

I thought about searching below, but doubted it would have been left aboard. Wherever the boat's captain had wound up, it was probably still in his pocket. Not for the first time, I thought about Long. Wished he was here, and chastised myself for not having paid attention when he was hotwiring vehicles. But, I felt that I could start this. The switch looked really simple, and it should only be a matter of prying it out of the panel and connecting the wires behind it.

But, first things first. This boat had been sitting for months. Did the batteries still have a charge, or had they drained in the summer heat? And what about the fuel? Was it still good?

There wasn't much I was coming up with as a way to check the fuel, but batteries are easy. Descending back into the cabin, I flicked a switch mounted on a paneled bulkhead. Bright lights came on, and I quickly turned it back off. OK, I had power. Now, as long as the fuel was good and the engine would start after sitting for so long...

Digging through several cabinets, I finally found a small tool kit that held a couple of screwdrivers and several different sized sets of pliers. I could smell dried blood on them, assuming they were used to remove hooks from fish. Returning to the bridge with them in hand, I set to work removing the ignition lock.

It was easier than I expected, only a simple nut holding it in place. I worked slowly for fear of dropping something that would alert the infected. It came free, and I gently pulled it out of the panel, the wires behind uncoiling smoothly. Expecting only two, I sat and stared when three of them stretched out from the panel.

Why three? I'd already seen a push button on the panel that was for the starters. After nearly a minute, it occurred to me. Just like a car, the boat would have a *key on* position that activated the power, and a second position for it to run. I hoped.

Using my knife, I cut the wires away and carefully stripped the insulation from their ends. Holding the three lengths of copper away from each other, I took a deep breath and another look around. I suspected that as soon as I made the connection, lights would come on all over the boat. And, anything electrical that wasn't connected to an *always on* circuit would start up. If I was right, I'd be noticed the instant that happened.

That meant the boat needed to start quickly and easily. If it didn't, those four females would scream a warning as soon as they heard the starters. I'd have seconds before they could race down the dock and leap aboard, and not much more time before others arrived.

If the engines started, the boat was already pointed at the channel. All I had to do was hit the throttle and motor away from the dock. But, if they didn't, I was going to have to dive overboard and swim to safety before the boat was swarmed.

That wasn't a good option. After I made it back to the small boat, we'd have to spend a lot of time paddling back up the coast, then traipse across the desert to the Tahoe. Then, a slow drive south, looking for another boat. Hours I was worried the pilot didn't have. No, this needed to work. And I had one shot at it before the marina was flooded with females, then we'd have no choice but to fall back to plan B.

Putting my ass into the captain's chair, I looked around again. Still no change. Focusing on the wires in my hand, I pinched the three bare ends together and twisted.

Lights all over the boat sprang to life, and a low pitched whine sounded from deep within the hull. I hoped that was a fuel pump, doing its job. Glancing up, I saw the females look around, then turn in my direction. A second later, from somewhere on the boat, a stereo began blasting mariachi music, loud enough to alert every infected in town.

The females screamed but didn't begin running towards me. For the first time, I noticed that they were pregnant. I started to congratulate myself on that little bit of luck but cursed when what sounded like hundreds of voices answered them from the streets immediately surrounding the marina.

Reaching out, I stabbed the button and pressed hard. Starters whined loudly, even over the pounding music. And they kept whining. The engines didn't start. I released the button as I looked around. Dozens of females were charging, leaping over the low wall that separated the marina from a bordering road.

I pushed the button again, willing the engines to turn over. And they did. Once. Then they coughed and went quiet. Goddamn it! I hit the button again as I stood up out of the seat. The females were coming fast, and I was almost out of time.

The starters whined and this time, the engines began a sputtering, stuttering idle. The lead element of the females rounded a corner and pounded onto the dock, no more than fifty yards away. I had seconds before they would be on the boat.

Engines still loping sickly, I shoved the throttles forward. Either this would work and bring them to life with a roar, or it was time for me to take another swim. They stuttered from the extra shot of fuel and with a curse I started to move for the rail. Before I'd taken more than a step, they suddenly bellowed and the boat lurched forward.

Caught unprepared, I was thrown against the rail and nearly took an involuntary swim. I managed to hang on as the boat rapidly accelerated. It careened off the wooden dock, shoved onto a new course directly for a large group of rocks sticking out of the water.

Fighting the acceleration, I pulled the throttles back and cut the wheel sharply. I don't think I missed the rocks by more than mere inches, but I missed them. Behind, the females were in a full throated scream as they came to a stop at the end of the dock.

Boat back under control, I resumed the captain's chair and pointed the bow at the entrance to the channel. Feeding in a small amount of throttle, I motored forward at a slow pace as more females appeared on the strips of sand that lined the channel and began following me. Waving at them, I accelerated slightly and let out a breath I didn't remember holding.

42

"Sir! It's working!"

Commander Marx burst through the door, ignoring the dirty look he received from one of the nurses.

"What is?" Admiral Packard asked through gritted teeth.

He had finally relented and gone to the hospital to have his injury properly cleaned and treated. Seated on an examination table, he grimaced as the Doctor re-inserted a pair of long-nosed forceps deep into his arm. The Russian bullet had passed through his uniform sleeve, carrying fragments of the material into the wound channel.

"The message we broadcast. Word just came from a reconnaissance flight. A widespread mutiny has broken out in the enemy fleet. Fighting on the ships. Nearly half of them have broken away and are steaming north, for home!"

The man's enthusiasm was infectious, a broad smile breaking out across the Admiral's face.

"What about the remainder?"

"They are still coming, but I'm hopeful the mutiny will spread. Forgive me, sir. I let my excitement get the best of me and ran ahead to tell you. Commander Detmer is on his way with a complete briefing."

"No apology necessary, Commander," Packard said. "That's the first good news I've received in some time."

The door opened, and he looked up to see Detmer poke his head into the room. The Admiral waved him in as Marx stepped to the side.

"I've heard the good news, Commander," the Admiral began. "Now. Give me the bad."

"The Russian fleet, though drastically degraded, still has enough men and firepower to seize the islands, sir. Not as easily as they would have, but we're not out of the woods. However, current assessments of their capabilities indicate we can hold the high ground."

"Holding the high ground is only good for a short time, Commander," Packard growled. "Until they starve us out."

"Agreed, sir. But, if your little surprise doesn't work, that's the best we can hope for at the moment. The Army and Marines have nearly completed the fortification of the old defensive positions and are prepared to meet enemy ground forces in the valleys leading up Mt. Kaala. And, at last count, over ten thousand civilians have joined the defense."

"That is encouraging!"

"Yes, sir, but most are only armed with knives and clubs. We've emptied our armories, but there just weren't enough rifles to go around. The civilians were mostly unarmed because of local gun laws, but they're still willing to face the Russian invaders with their bare hands if need be."

"Understood, Commander. What's the status of evacuating base personnel?"

"Ninety percent complete, sir. Only essential staff remain and we are beginning to move them in phases."

"Any word from Captain West on the efforts to restore the Battlespace program?"

"I just came from there, sir. Seaman Simmons is still waiting for the latest version of her code to complete. She estimates four more hours at a minimum."

Packard glanced up at a clock on the wall.

"What's the latest ETA for the invasion fleet's arrival?"

"We've already begun engaging Russian aircraft four hundred miles north, sir. Losses are heavy on both sides. Unless the mutiny spreads further, or we can find a way to stop them, the first ships will be in range of our land-based guns in twelve hours."

Packard absorbed the information, slowly nodding his head.

"Anything else, Commander?"

"No, sir. And, sir? You're scheduled for the next evacuation wave in twenty minutes."

"Is that the last wave?" Packard asked in a low voice.

"No, sir. There will be four more after that."

"Then I'll be leaving after the last one," the Admiral barked. "The goddamn Russians may have forced us to abandon Pearl, but I'll be damned if I'm stepping foot off this base as long as there's a single man or woman remaining."

"But, sir..."

"I believe I was clear, Commander! Dismissed."

Packard glared at the younger man as he snapped to attention before doing an abrupt about face and quickly departing.

"He has a point, sir," the Doctor said once Detmer had left the room. "We all need you."

"Pardon my language, Doctor, but that's not fucking happening."

"Aye, aye sir," the man said as he began the first stitch to close Packard's wound.

The mariachi music continued to bellow from a large boom box strapped to one of the tower's struts. Not only was it annoying as hell, but it was also sending the females along the sand into a fever pitch of desire to reach me. Motoring along the channel, I finally had enough, drew my pistol and put the damn thing out of its misery. Sure, I could have just climbed up and turned it off, but where's the fun in that?

Rounding the stone jetty, I spotted the small wooden boat, heaving a sigh of relief when I saw Rachel, Tiffany and Dog looking at me. I steered alongside them, cutting the engines to an idle as the two hulls gently bumped. Tiffany came first, then Rachel sent Dog, who scrambled on the smooth fiberglass deck. He would have slipped into the sea if Tiffany hadn't grabbed his shoulders while Rachel shoved on his ass.

He made it aboard safely, then I had to maneuver again to pick up Rachel. When she gave Dog a push, the small boat had moved away, leaving a six-foot gap between us.

"Hold on," I called down to her as I brought the sports fishing boat alongside again.

Leaving the engines idling, I scrambled down to the deck and found a coil of light, but strong, nylon line. Holding an end, I tossed it to Rachel, the rope uncoiling as it flew through the air.

"Tie an end to the handle on the bow," I shouted.

Rachel nodded without asking questions, and while she did as I asked, I made the other end fast to a cleat on the stern of the larger boat. The smaller craft was perfectly good, and there wasn't any reason not to take it along. I couldn't think of a scenario where we'd have a need for it at the moment, but it's always better to have something you don't need than the other way around.

Line secured, I helped Rachel onto the boat. Turning, I wasn't surprised to see Tiffany had already climbed to the top of the tower and had taken a seat on the narrow platform. Dog had claimed a spot on the bridge and sat watching her survey the surrounding sea.

"What was with the music?" Rachel asked, following me to the bridge.

"Crew left a boom box hooked up. It came on when I started the engines."

"Any problems? I heard a gunshot. Did a female make it onboard?"

"No," I said, grinning sheepishly and pointing at the shattered stereo.

Rachel looked at it and started laughing. I slipped into the captain's chair and advanced the throttles, pointing us southeast. My plan was to start at the only point I had been told about. Between the current and winds, once at the location, I believed our best bet was to search along the eastern edge of the small sea.

I called Tiffany down to the bridge. After a brief discussion, she took Rachel's night vision goggles and climbed back up. She understood that she was looking for anything floating on the surface of the water, but also knew to keep an eye out for an infrared strobe. Rachel would relieve her in half an hour, then it would be my turn.

We were all tired, and I didn't want any of us to miss something because we were on lookout for too long and zoned out. Tiffany had protested that she was fine, but I overruled her. We had a man's life as our responsibility, and there was no room for personal ego or pride.

"So how far do you think he may have drifted?" Rachel asked.

"That's the problem," I said. "He's been in the water for more than 30 hours, or at least that's the best information I have. We've got no way of knowing what the winds have been like, or how currents may have affected his drift. Our starting point is 40 miles southwest of Rocky Point. That's all I got before the comms went down."

I pushed the throttles farther forward. Our speed increased to 30 knots, and I did some mental math to figure out how long before we reached the pilot's last known position. Never having been a sailor, calculating distances like this was foreign to me, but at least I understood the concept. If there's a better way, without GPS, to navigate on water, I don't know what it is.

After thirty minutes, Rachel took over as lookout. The sea was fairly calm, but at the top of the tower, every move of the boat was exaggerated. When Tiffany sank to the deck on the bridge, she looked a little green around the gills. I'd found a case of bottled water stored below, and she gratefully opened one and began sipping.

"You OK?"

"Don't like boats," she said in a weak voice, then took another sip. "Can't do roller coasters or anything like that."

I truly felt for her, as I had the same problem. The sickest I'd ever been was one time when Katie and I went salmon fishing in Alaska.

Dirk Patton

We'd gone out on a 26-foot boat the morning after a storm had blown through. The sea had been rough with ten to twelve-foot waves, and by the time we were 12 miles out into the Bering Sea, I just wanted to curl into a ball and die. While Katie fished, I chummed the water with my breakfast and seriously considered just jumping overboard so it would end. We came back with two huge fish Katie had reeled in, and I had sworn never to go back to sea in a small boat.

As usual, when I say I'll never do something again, I wind up doing it anyway. And I wasn't feeling too hot at the moment. The swells were no more than three feet, but there's just something about my innards that doesn't like to be tossed around like a rubber ducky in a bathtub. I was dreading when it was my turn to climb the tower, knowing the motion would be dramatically worse, but I don't like the idea of not pulling my weight.

A little more than half an hour later, if my math was correct, we were in the general area of where the Admiral had told me the pilot was drifting. I cut the engines to idle and shouted up to Rachel to do a slow, three-sixty scan.

She climbed higher until she was standing on the narrow platform intended to be a seat. Taking her time, she spun a very slow circle. Watching her, I debated the wisdom of doing this at night.

Fulcrum

Sure, if my supposition was correct, and the raft was equipped with an IR strobe, we had a better chance of spotting it with night vision. But, if there wasn't a strobe, or it was damaged, the limitations of the NVGs would hamper our efforts. Daylight and a good pair of binoculars would be much more effective in that case.

But, we were racing the clock. The pilot had already been adrift for a long time, with no shelter from the sun and wind. He would dehydrate quickly, floating on a sea of undrinkable water. Perhaps he had some emergency rations with him, but I had no way of knowing. If not, he had maybe another day, or day and a half at the most, before there was no point in us continuing to search.

"Nothing," Rachel shouted after completing the circle.

"OK, let's switch," I yelled back.

She scampered down and noticed Tiffany sitting with her head hanging between her knees.

"She alright?"

"A little seasick," I said, getting out of the captain's chair so Rachel could take over. "You drive. Follow a zigzag pattern. I still think the wind is going to push him to the east. Right now, we should be at the western edge of any area he could be in. Start out going east/southeast at 20 knots for half an hour. We'll turn west/southwest at that point after we change the watch. Got it?"

"I got it, but you don't look so good."

Rachel had pushed the NVGs off her eyes and was peering at me in the bridge lights.

"I'm fine," I said, turning to climb the tower.

"Hold on," she said, grabbing my arm to stop me. "If you're feeling sick down here, it will kill you up there. We can't afford to have you out of commission. I'll go back up."

I looked at her for a long pause, everything telling me just to suck it up and get my ass moving. But she had a point. If the extra motion at the top of the tower pushed me into full blown seasickness... Well, I remembered what that was like in Alaska, and Rachel was right. I'd be next to useless. With a sigh, I nodded and stepped aside so she could climb back up.

"Wow," she said, pausing with her foot on the first rung. "You're getting mellow. You never do what I suggest."

"Go away," I grumbled, giving her a smile so she knew I was kidding.

Fulcrum

She grinned and scampered back up to the top. I glanced at Tiffany, who hadn't moved or even raised her head, and was glad there was one of us who wasn't easily susceptible to motion sickness.

Sliding into the chair, I got us moving as I'd described to Rachel. I had considered trying to do a grid search, a much more effective method for finding someone or something that's lost, but without charts and a GPS, it was essentially impossible. At least for me. There's probably some old sailors out there who could have looked up at the stars and laid out a pattern in their minds, then followed it with uncanny precision. Unfortunately, there wasn't one of those with us.

So, I did the next best thing and drove with one eye on the compass. Rachel stayed in the tower when I made the first turn. Tiffany had climbed to her feet, and offered to change places, but she was wobbly and looked like she'd been hit by a truck. That's the thing about getting seasick, at least in my experience. Once it starts, the only thing that will stop it is to get your feet on solid, dry land.

Rachel had looked down at her and told her just to sit and sip some more water. Tiffany didn't argue, and I had to admit I admired the young lady's grit. When I'd first come across her group, I'd expected a bunch of spoiled princess types. My preconception couldn't have been more wrong, at least when it came to Tiffany. Now, we just needed to come up with a name for her that matched the iron in her backbone.

"Tell me about the girls that were taken by the militia," I said to her after making the next turn.

I was tired and needed the distraction so I would stay alert. Hopefully, Rachel was doing OK. She seemed to be. Every time I looked up, she appeared focused on her task as she continually swept through a full circle.

"The popular girls," Tiffany answered after a long pause.

"What does that mean these days? Well, what did it mean?" I asked, slowly turning my head to scan the horizon.

"We've all been together as a team since junior high. When we got into high school, there were four girls who were just a little prettier and a little perkier. They kind of made their own clique within the team. If not for softball, we wouldn't have all stayed together after high school. Most of us went off to college, but they were too busy going to clubs and parties. A lot of us have rich parents, so…"

"Why aren't you playing for your college team?"

"Cal Tech doesn't have one," she said. "And, I love playing the game, and we're damn good. So there you have it."

"Is your sister one of the popular girls?"

"Wants to be. She's younger than me. Would have been a sophomore in high school this year. Tagged along on the trip with a friend who's the little sister of one of the clique. They were all together when the militia took them."

"I'm sorry we had to wait to go find her," I said.

Tiffany raised her head and looked at me, stretching her legs out. Dog grunted his disapproval at her moving, then stood up, turned a circle and laid down with his head on her lap.

"I get it," she said. "I really do. But, I'm responsible for her. I'm sure my parents are either dead or one of those things by now. That means I'm all she's got left. And she's all I've got."

I nodded my understanding. I had the same feelings about Rachel, I just couldn't talk to her about it. Every time I looked at her, or thought about touching her, guilt came crashing down. Maybe if I had just focused on getting to Arizona, I could have saved Katie. Instead, I got wrapped up with Rachel, then pulled back into the Army. If I had to do it over again...

I shut down those thoughts as my throat began to constrict. Logically, I knew that I couldn't have done anything different. It was only dumb luck that had put me in the same place as Irina, giving me access to a vaccine. If not for that, I'd probably either be dead or one of the stumbling, shambling horde by now.

"You OK?"

Tiffany's voice startled me, and I realized I'd stopped scanning the horizon and had been just staring at a point in space.

"Fine," I said, reaching up and wiping a tear from my cheek.

I checked the compass and clock. It was time to turn back to the west. Gently moving the wheel, I steered for our new course.

"Wait!"

Rachel's shout galvanized me. Sitting forward I slapped the throttles to idle, then stood and looked up at her. She was leaned into the wind, intently staring at a point to the southeast.

"What did you see?" I called out after nearly a minute.

"A single flash of light," she answered. "Tell me again what the strobe will look like."

"White flashes. You only saw a single flash?"

"Yes, and I caught it as I was turning my head, so I didn't even see it straight on."

"Hold your arm out in line with the direction you saw it," I said.

She did, and I looked at the compass, noting the bearing. With a feeling of optimism, I got back in the seat, shoved the throttles forward and steered a course towards the point Rachel had indicated.

"If it's a strobe, why would she only see one flash?" Tiffany asked, coming to stand next to me.

"Maybe both the raft and us happened to be on the crest of a swell at the same time," I said, shrugging. "If he's a long way off, maybe even over the horizon, we could catch a brief glimpse if there was the right combination of waves at the same time. It's worth a few minutes to check out."

I wanted speed. Wanted to get into the area as quickly as possible. But, we couldn't count on that single glint of light. I shouted at Rachel to keep scanning as we progressed.

Fulcrum

She could have seen some debris on the surface, something shiny catching the moon just right. Or it could be a glitch within her night vision goggles. Or any of a dozen other things.

"Saw it again! A bunch of flashes before I lost it. That way!"

I looked up to see Rachel pointing ten degrees to starboard. Feeling better about what she was seeing, I pushed the throttles to their stops and steered to the new course. We were moving fast, and I realized that Rachel was probably getting more of a ride than she bargained for at the top of the tower.

Looking up, I saw her standing on the platform with a firm grip on the surrounding rails. Her long hair streamed behind her as she leaned into the wind.

"Definitely got it! I can tell it's going up and down on the swells. I lose it for a few seconds, then see it again when it comes up!"

She was excited, and the surge of adrenaline had erased the lethargy that had begun to settle over me. Within a few minutes, I started catching glimpses of the strobe as it rode to the top of a wave. I made a slight adjustment to our course, heading directly for it.

In another few minutes, I pulled back on the throttles as we approached the strobe. With the boat at a more sedate speed, Rachel climbed down from the tower. The waves were slightly higher here, probably four or five feet, but we were now close enough only to lose sight of the strobe when it dropped into the very bottom of a trough.

Another minute and I could make out the tiny inflatable raft in my night vision. I thought I could see a form curled up in it, but was still too far away.

"You drive," I said to Rachel, moving away from the wheel.

She took over as I grabbed a long pole with a hook on the end and moved to the pointed bow. Now I could tell there was definitely a human form, balled into the fetal position. He was unmoving, and I hoped that only indicated unconsciousness.

Rachel slowed more as we came within a few yards of the raft. It was no more than four feet across and looked like it was simply an inflated ring with a piece of material stretched across the inside. The pilot was curled up because that was the only way he could fit.

A little closer and I could see that the ring was only partially inflated, causing the raft to ride very low in the water. Either there had been a problem when it was deployed, or it was leaking air. Regardless, this guy was one lucky bastard. I didn't think that thing would have floated another eight hours.

Hooking on to a rope that was attached around the perimeter of the ring, I tugged and walked the raft down the side of the boat to the rear. Rachel, Tiffany and Dog all joined me there, the girls helping muscle it onto the platform.

The pilot stirred once we had him out of the water, looking up at Rachel and blinking several times as if trying to focus.

"Hi, beautiful," he croaked. "I sure hope this isn't a dream."

With that, he lapsed back into unconsciousness.

The pilot was uninjured, just severely sunburned and dehydrated. I'd carried him into the cabin and deposited him on a bunk with not so clean sheets. Rachel had immediately started a saline IV to begin the rehydration process. That, and some salve on his face and hands, and there wasn't much more to be done for him.

"He going to be OK?" I asked when Rachel joined me on the bridge.

I'd already pointed us to the north. The plan was to return to the Tahoe and drive back to the US. I was hoping the pilot would recover quickly, and we could make a stop at Luke Air Force Base in Phoenix so he could fly us the rest of the way. But I needed to know soon, before we committed on a direction. Once we were up into Arizona, there was no way across the river.

"As far as I can tell. He looks to be in very good physical condition and doesn't have anything wrong other than severe dehydration and a really nasty sunburn where his flight suit didn't cover him. Hands and face."

"How long before he should be up and moving?"

Rachel shrugged her shoulders.

"Could be just a few hours, or could be days. Everyone's body is different. But, I'm guessing it'll be pretty quick. He's young, and like I said, he's in good shape, so he should bounce back with the IVs."

"IVs? Plural?" I asked, surprised.

"I hung a second bag of saline. Want to get as many fluids into him as fast as I can. By the way, you were right to keep pushing us. He wouldn't have lasted another day, exposed to the sun."

I nodded.

"Anything else you can do to get him on his feet? As soon as we get to the Tahoe, I've got to decide if we're taking the long way around, or can go find a plane."

"It's all hydration, at this point," she said, shaking her head. "I'd expect him to be conscious soon, but he's going to be weak and feel like he got run over by a truck. I'll know more in a couple of hours."

She trailed her hand along my arm, then turned and disappeared into the cabin below. I sat in the darkness, wishing for a cigarette as I piloted the boat. Not wanting to let my thoughts drift to Katie, I considered how incredibly lucky we'd been to find him quickly and easily. But then, I was due for some good luck about now.

It took us a couple of hours to get to Rocky Point. We were a couple of miles offshore and I cut the engines to idle when the boat came even with the marina. Having felt the change, Rachel climbed up to see what was happening.

"Rocky Point," I said, pointing to the east.

"So how do we get back to the Tahoe?"

"Need to pull the infected into town," I said. "That'll open up things to the north, and we can make a run for it. Is our guest going to be able to move under his own power?"

"He's awake."

There was something in her voice, and I shoved the night vision goggles up and looked at her.

"What?"

She hesitated, then shook her head.

"He's just a bit of an ass," she sighed. "Hasn't stopped hitting on me since he woke up. Tiffany, too."

"We have a problem?"

"Noooo." She stretched out the word as she thought of how to answer. "It's not like that. He's keeping his hands to himself. So far. He just reminds me of some of the really arrogant guys that would come into the club when I was dancing. They've either got money or do something that would make them noticeable. They could never understand why their very presence didn't cause me to go weak in the knees and fall all over them."

"Want me to talk to him?"

I was more than happy to educate the pilot on the error of his ways. It was a shame Martinez wasn't still around. She'd have had no problems shutting him down in no uncertain terms.

"No," Rachel smiled and put her hand on my shoulder. "At least, not yet. I think I got the message across, and I'm a big girl. I can handle it if he gets too obnoxious. So. How are you planning to draw the infected away from the hotel?"

It was obvious she wanted to change the subject. I smiled at her, lowered the NVGs and looked towards shore.

"Sit tight and watch," I said.

Dirk Patton

Accelerating, I angled for a point about half a mile south of the hotel. When we were within a hundred yards of shore, I turned us broadside and cut the engines. Pulling my rifle around, I removed the suppressor and aimed in the general direction of the beach. I wasn't necessarily trying to hit anything, I just wanted to make a lot of racket.

Pulling and holding the trigger, I ran through a magazine on full auto. The noise, as it always is, was brutally loud, and once my ears had recovered, I could faintly detect the screams of the females on the sand. Motoring half a mile closer to town, I fired again, but only used half of a magazine. Our ammo supply wasn't infinite.

I kept this up, moving slowly and stopping every half mile to fire the rifle, until reaching the stone jetty that guarded the marina. Floating fifty yards away from it, I stared at the throngs of females that were quickly pressing in to fill every square inch of dry land. The screams were almost deafening.

"Jesus Christ!" A male voice breathed from behind me.

I turned to see the pilot standing in the narrow entrance to the bridge. He held two IV bags in his hand as he stared across the water at the infected. I could see Tiffany behind him, peering over his shoulders. Dog, who was pretending to sleep, despite all the noise I was making, raised his head to look at the man, snorted and rolled over onto my feet.

"First time you've seen them in person?" I asked.

"Yeah," he said without taking his eyes off the shore.

"Watch and learn," I said, firing another half magazine.

This time, I made a token effort at aiming, and several of the females in the front ranks of the throng fell off the seawall. Their bodies splashed into the water below, unmoving.

I kept us sitting where we were for another ten minutes, occasionally picking off individuals. I wasn't amusing myself, I was giving the females time to keep packing into the town. The occasional shots were simply to ensure I was holding their interest.

"That should be long enough," I said, feeding in throttle and spinning the wheel.

The boat surged as I pointed us to the southwest. We needed to be north, but we also needed to not drag a whole town full of females along with us. I intended to motor in the wrong direction until I was out of sight and hearing of the females. Probably four miles or so to be safe.

443

Only then would I turn north, staying several miles offshore. When we were well north of the resort, I'd turn for the beach and come in slow and quiet. If we were lucky, all of the females would still be in town, waiting for us to return.

"I'm Major John Chase," I said to the pilot.

We had time to talk while I navigated our roundabout course.

"Lieutenant Commander Mark Vance," he said, extending his free hand. "Thank you for coming and getting me."

I waved off his thanks, noticing Rachel and Tiffany moving away to disappear into the cabin. Seems he had already worn out his welcome with them.

"How are you feeling? Going to be able to walk? We're going ashore soon."

His eyes widened as he stared at me in the darkness.

"Are you kidding? Into that?"

He pointed behind us, and I knew he meant the mass of infected.

"Hopefully not," I said. "That's why I was drawing them into the town. Open up a path for us to get to our vehicle."

"You drove here?" He asked, seemingly shocked at the thought.

"Yep. We were near Las Vegas when I got word from Pearl that you were in the water. Took us a bit, but we made it."

He stared at me as if I were crazy, then smiled and looked out across the sea.

"Heard about you in Hawaii," he said after a long pause. "You know. Stories. Rumors. Really crazy shit about some of the things you've done. Guess there might be some truth to them, huh?"

I just sat there, staring at him. Uninterested in what stories might or might not be told about me. Being a folk hero was one of the last things I gave a shit about.

"You didn't answer my question," I finally said. "You able to walk?"

"Yeah," he said, nodding. "Don't feel great, but I can walk."

"What about fly?"

"You know where we can get a plane?" He turned serious when I mentioned flying, and I was gratified to see his reaction.

445

"Luke Air Force Base. Near Phoenix. Take us a few hours to get there once we're in the vehicle. Can you fly something big enough to hold all of us?"

"If its got wings, I can fly it, and if its got a pussy I can pound it!"

The way he trotted this out, I had no doubt it was something he liked to say often. When I was about 19, I might have found it amusing. Cool, even. Now? I think the expression on my face got the message across.

"Hey look, I don't want to step on your toes," he said. "I'm betting that tall, hot babe is yours. No worries. The short one's a looker! A little young, but legal, and I'm not complaining."

It took all of my willpower not to stand up and knock him on his back. Somehow, I managed to keep my ass planted in the seat.

"Commander," I said in a low, perfectly calm voice. "If you lay one, single finger on that little girl, I will feed you to the infected, one piece at a time. Be sure you understand me because I will not warn you again."

Dog, picking up on my mood, sat up and stared at the Navy pilot. He growled softly, curling his upper lip to show his teeth. Vance looked at me, the smile on his face vanishing as

446

he understood I wasn't kidding. After a long beat, he nodded and disappeared into the cabin without saying anything else. I blew out an irritated sigh and adjusted our course to head north.

I dropped the boat's anchor half a mile offshore. We were, what I estimated to be, a mile north of the resort, and I didn't want to go any closer and risk the engines being heard. Climbing down from the bridge, I made my way to the stern deck and hauled on the line that was tied to the wooden boat.

Standing on the platform, I held it steady as Dog jumped in, followed by Tiffany, Vance then Rachel. The pilot had removed his IVs and seemed none the worse for wear. He also hadn't spoken to me since our chat and seemed to be making a concerted effort not to look at me.

Once we were aboard, I reminded everyone to stay as silent as possible. Releasing the line, Rachel and I began paddling towards the beach. It didn't take long as we got some help from the wind, then the surf caught us and propelled the boat forward. At that point, all we could do was use the paddles to try and maintain our course.

I was in the front, and when I felt the keel scrape against sand, I dropped my paddle and jumped over the side. The water was hip deep, but with the waves coming in I got dunked a couple of times as I dragged the boat forward.

Rachel joined me in the water, and between the two of us we pulled until the bow was resting on smooth sand.

Dog jumped out, twisting in the air so when he landed he didn't get his feet wet. He stood there panting, almost as if he was laughing at me, then turned and raised his nose. No growls followed, but the wind was coming in off the water. He wouldn't be able to smell any infected that were waiting for us in the low dunes.

Vance was the next one out, splashing into knee deep water. He turned to help Tiffany, then caught himself and glanced at me. I guess he had taken my message to heart. I nodded that it was OK for him to help her, then moved a few yards up the beach and scanned with my rifle. Everything looked clear.

A minute later, we were formed up and moving in single file towards the desert. Dog and I were on point with Vance and Tiffany right behind. Rachel brought up the rear. It was a long walk to where I'd left the Tahoe, but we made it in just over 90 minutes without encountering any problems.

Apparently, my distraction had worked. When we came to a point where the resort was upwind, I expected Dog to growl to let us know he smelled infected. But, to my pleasant surprise, he remained quiet.

Reaching the Tahoe, I took a few minutes to replenish my ammo from the stock in the back. While I did this, Rachel put Vance in the back seat and started a fresh IV. He was on his feet, but he was still dehydrated. When Dog jumped in and sat down next to him, he shrank away against the door. Tiffany climbed in on the far side and pulled Dog to her, gently stroking his head.

"I'm driving," Rachel said when I closed the rear hatch and headed for the driver's seat. "You've expended a lot of energy since we left Nevada. You've got to be tired. You need some sleep in case we run into more trouble."

I stared at her for a long time. Thought about protesting. But, she was right. I was exhausted, and just about every inch of my body hurt. I wasn't even sure I had the energy to argue with her.

"OK," I finally said. "You know where we're going?"

She nodded and smiled at me.

"When we get close to those little border towns, I was planning on cutting through the desert and circling around, so we didn't have to push through the infected."

"I can do that," she said, taking my arm to escort me to the passenger seat. "If I have a problem, I'll wake you up."

We paused outside the door, and she held onto my arm, looking into my eyes. When I didn't look away, she leaned in and kissed me. Soft and gentle. Pulling away, she opened the passenger door and flapped her hand. With a tired smile, I got in and wiggled on the leather upholstery until I was comfortable. Apologizing to Tiffany in advance, I reclined the seat back, and already had my eyes closed by the time Rachel was behind the wheel.

I opened my eyes when Rachel shook my shoulder and called my name. Brilliant sunlight made me squint and raise a hand to shade my face.

"Where the hell are we?" I asked, my mouth gummy from sleep.

"I think we're about half an hour from the air base," Rachel answered.

Blinking, I looked around and recognized the stretch of Interstate 10 we were driving on.

"Where do I turn?" Rachel asked.

I told her which freeway to take, then raised my seat and looked into the back, coming face to face with Dog. He gave me a lick before sneezing on me. Well, that's one way to wake up.

Vance was dozing with a half empty IV bag still dripping into his arm. Tiffany was in her own little world, staring out the side window. I turned back to the front and opened a bottle of water. It was warm, but I didn't care. After drinking most of it, I was able to wash Dog snot off my face with the remainder.

"Think we'll have a problem with the guy we ran into on the way down?" Rachel asked.

"Don't think so," I said. "He didn't seem crazy or stupid. Just didn't know what he was doing. I think he's got his family hiding out somewhere on the base and now that he knows we don't mean him any harm, will just steer clear. If he even sees us."

Rachel nodded and turned onto the new freeway. We covered the last few miles quickly, despite the number of abandoned cars that created an impromptu slalom course. I pointed out the proper exit and Rachel turned onto it, making a left at the bottom of the ramp.

"We're going straight to the flight line," I said as we progressed down the street that ran past the main gate.

Fulcrum

Turning around, I made sure Tiffany was alert and woke the pilot, telling him it was time to go to work. He nodded and quickly removed the IV needle from his arm. His eyes were much clearer than the last time I'd seen them, and he no longer looked as haggard. Filthy, sunburned and in need of a shave, but then I wasn't any better.

Rachel slowed and drove through the gate, the Tahoe bouncing as it rolled over the tops of the bollards that Tiffany had retracted on our previous visit. I had my rifle up and ready as we progressed, but didn't see anything to be worried about, even after scanning all of the rooftops.

After a wrong turn, Rachel retraced some of our path, then we were approaching the gate that protected the flight line. It was still closed and locked, just like last time.

"Ram it," I said when Rachel started to slow.

I'm sure there was a time when she would have been hesitant to do what I'd just told her. Those days were long gone. The big SUV surged forward, and the gate tore apart from the impact. A grinding noise started up from behind, and I looked into the side mirror. We were dragging a section of chain link. Oh well.

"Commander, take your pick," I said, waving my hand at the parked aircraft in front of us.

"How far are we going?" He asked, leaning forward for a better look.

"Groom Lake."

"Area 51? Really?" He asked in surprise. "OK, let's take an Osprey. That's the only thing I see that will carry all of us."

By now, Rachel knew what the aircraft looked like. She drove another few hundred yards, then came to a stop beside four of the V22s that sat gleaming in the sun.

"What do you need us to do to be ready to go?" I asked as we all climbed out onto the tarmac.

"Nothing," he said, striding for the closest plane. "As long as its got fuel and isn't red-tagged for a maintenance issue, we're good to go."

Following behind, Rachel and I scanned our surroundings as we walked. Dog trotted to the Osprey's landing gear and relieved himself on a tire. I hoped that would bring us good luck.

We waited outside while Vance did whatever it is pilots do before taking off. I kept waiting to hear one of the big engines come to life, but they remained still and silent. A minute later he emerged, shaking his head.

"Batteries are dead. Let's try another."

He led the way to the next aircraft, disappearing inside as the rest of us took up station at the nose. Glancing through the windscreen, I could see him in the cockpit, flipping switches, and checking instruments. A moment later there was a loud whine from the left engine nacelle.

The noise rose in pitch as both rotors slowly began to turn. They were horizontal, making the plane look like a twin-rotor helicopter because they're too long to be oriented vertically, in flight mode, when the Osprey is on the ground.

As the left engine spooled up, thick, white smoke poured out of the exhaust. We had to step back to avoid being engulfed by the cloud, but the rotors continued to accelerate and quickly cleared the air. They spun faster as the engine roared, then the right one came to life. More white smoke poured out but was instantly whipped away by the rotor wash. Vance looked at us through the windscreen and flashed a thumbs up.

Running around the Osprey, we gave the engines plenty of room. The rear ramp was coming down as we arrived, and I led the way inside. When Dog and the girls were aboard, I slapped the button to raise the door and headed for the cockpit. Rachel and Tiffany looked around for a moment before taking a seat on the deck. There weren't any seats for passengers.

"Ready?" I shouted over the bellow of the engines when I stuck my head into the flight deck.

"Good to go," Vance said. "Might want to take a seat. I haven't flown one of these in about five years."

Oh, crap. I rushed back and dropped to my ass as the aircraft lifted off, the deck tilting to the side. Dog started to slide, and I grabbed him and held on as the vibration increased and for a moment we tilted even farther. But, Vance eventually got us leveled out, and it felt like we were in a static hover.

That lasted for a few seconds, then he began to accelerate, the deck tilting back as we gained altitude. Checking on the girls, I saw a terrified look on Rachel's face, but she was holding it together. Tiffany, on the other hand, was smiling from ear to ear.

Fulcrum

"Think they'd teach me how to fly one of these?" She shouted when she saw me looking in her direction.

"You can't do roller coasters and you get seasick, but you want to be a pilot?" I shouted back.

"Yes!"

She smiled, expecting that one word to explain everything. Shrugging, I smiled and nodded. It just so happened I knew the man that could make that happen, and there was no doubt we were in desperate need of pilots.

The smile vanished from my face when the deck suddenly tilted without warning and Vance shouted for us to hold on. A vibration strong enough to rattle my teeth started up, growing worse as we banked and began rapidly descending. Rachel and Tiffany looked terrified, and frankly I wasn't feeling too confident at the moment, either.

A couple of minutes later there was a brutally hard impact as we reached the ground. Somehow the aircraft held together and began taxiing.

"Still wannabe a pilot?" I asked Tiffany before scrambling forward into the cockpit.

"What the fuck was that all about?" I shouted.

"That's called a good landing," Vance grinned.

"What?"

"Still alive, aren't you?" He chuckled.

"Funny, asshole," I grumbled, climbing to my feet and looking out the windscreen. We were near the end of a runway on Luke Air Force Base. "What happened?"

"Something wrong with the port engine," he said. "Felt like the rotor was running slower than starboard. Other than that, beats the fuck out of me. I just fly 'em."

"So what now?" I asked, watching as we slowly approached the flight line where the Osprey had been parked.

"Check the others," he said. "No way in hell I'm going back up in this egg beater."

I nodded, then went to the back to fill in the girls. Vance pulled to a stop a few minutes later, the engines going silent as the rear ramp descended. He stepped out of the cockpit and I held up a hand to slow him down.

"We're on security," I said to Rachel and Tiffany, leading the way out.

While the pilot checked the remaining Ospreys, we kept an eye on the surroundings. To my great relief, nothing and no one appeared to bother us.

"None of the V-22s are going to fly," Vance said after nearly ten minutes of checking them. "There's two of them with juice in their batteries, but no fuel."

"Can't we transfer the fuel from this one?" I asked without taking my eyes off my area of responsibility.

"We can, but it will take a lot of time. I'm starting to wonder if these should have been red-tagged, and were left behind for a reason."

"Any bright ideas, or are we driving again?"

"Saw some helos from the air, on the far side of those hangars," he said, pointing. "We should check them out before we make a decision."

I thought about that for a moment, then nodded agreement. We all piled into the Tahoe and drove down the flight line before cutting between two massive hangars. Behind them was a secondary flight line for rotor wing aircraft.

There was a lot of empty space, and the only helicopters remaining were five hulking Chinooks.

"Can you fly one of those?" I asked, staring at the twin rotor behemoths.

"They're actually easier to fly than an Osprey," Vance said as I pulled to a stop next to one. "Let's hope they're airworthy."

We repeated the process, the girls, Dog and I standing watch while he checked out the closest aircraft. I turned when he shouted from the hatch.

"Sit tight. I'm going to take it up and make sure we don't have another problem."

I gave him a thumbs up and we moved away as the engines came to life and began turning the long rotors. Soon, they were at takeoff speed, and he lifted into the air. For several minutes he circled the area, banking and changing altitude. Finally, he landed the huge helicopter in a stinging swirl of dust. I could just make out the thumbs up he flashed through the windscreen.

"Let's go," I said, heading for the rear ramp that was already on its way down.

Rachel, looking dubious, mumbled something I didn't catch over the roar of the idling Chinook. After a moment, she fell in behind me and we boarded the waiting helo. Tiffany dashed forward and disappeared into the cockpit. When I checked on her, she was strapped into the co-pilot's seat and grinning from ear to ear as she watched Vance work the controls.

"Sir! Battlespace is coming back online!"

Admiral Packard had fallen asleep at his desk. He jerked awake when his aide delivered the news from the outer office in a very unprofessional manner. Packard didn't care. Leaping to his feet, he charged across his plushly carpeted office and through the door.

"CIC!" He roared at his Marine guards.

As two of them dashed ahead to clear the way, Captain Black radioed a heads up to the enhanced protection detail spread around the building. The rest formed a bubble around the Admiral, matching his pace.

It was still dark when the group pushed through the building's doors, the sun just beginning to lighten the eastern horizon. Walking so fast it nearly counted as a double-time jog, Packard turned and headed for the Combat Information Center. All around him was movement as more Marines fell in to join the procession. A pair of Super Cobra helicopters hovered above, constantly scanning the area with their FLIR systems. Captain Black wasn't about to let any more harm come to the Admiral.

Fulcrum

Pushing through a set of doors, Packard ignored the elevator and raced down a flight of stairs to the subterranean levels of the operations building. Without breaking stride, he burst into the CIC, which was a hive of activity.

All around the room, screens that had been dark were coming to life. Data scrolled across them as the servers in Hawaii reestablished communication with the handful of ships the US Navy still had operational around the globe. One by one, the system began updating their position and status, plotting them on a single, massive display that covered an entire wall.

Still more screens brightened as surveillance feeds from aircraft and satellites began working again. The Admiral breathed a sigh of relief before shouting for a status update on the Russian fleet. While he waited impatiently for a console operator to answer his request, the steel door from the stairwell behind him slammed open, banging loudly against the concrete wall.

Captain Black was the only Marine that had accompanied Packard into the CIC, and he reacted immediately, spinning and raising his rifle as he placed himself between the Admiral and the door. Jessica, flushed by a sprint from where she'd been working, froze in her tracks when she saw the weapon aimed at her face.

"Stand down, Captain," Packard said, pushing past the Marine to greet Jessica.

Black lowered his weapon but didn't take his eyes off the new arrival.

"You did it!"

The Admiral extended both of his hands to shake Jessica's. She smiled at his praise.

"Sorry it took so long, sir," she said. "And, I've got one more thing to do. Thor didn't come back online automatically. I've got to give it a little nudge."

"By all means, carry on," Packard said, stepping out of her way.

As she dashed for a vacant console, another screen came to life. It showed a crisp image of a fleet of ships spread across a large swath of ocean.

"Admiral, the Russian fleet," the operator called.

Packard stared at the display, counting the number of ships still bound for Hawaii. Before he finished, Commander Detmer ran into the room, breathing hard. He stood beside the Admiral and quickly counted, then dropped into a seat and began working on a console.

"They're down four more ships since our last report, sir," he said. "All four were civilian cargo ships that we believe were carrying ground troops. That's the good news. The bad is that there's still some serious firepower heading for us. Three guided missile cruisers, four guided missile destroyers and four guided missile frigates. There's also ten landing ships and two more civilian cargo ships remaining."

"Range?" Packard asked, glaring at the screen.

"Two hundred nautical miles northwest of Oahu, sir. They are well within range for all of their missiles to strike any target on the island."

"Why haven't they started softening us up, yet?"

"All I can surmise, sir, is that they want Oahu intact. There's not much of the world left that's habitable, other than Australia. Maybe this isn't about finishing us off so much as seizing the island for themselves. It's definitely better weather than Moscow."

"And, they'd have the entire civilian population to pick and choose from for a captive workforce. Slaves, if you will."

Captain West hadn't been able to keep up with Jessica and had arrived in time to offer an opinion on the Russian's motives.

"It's time to show our hand," the Admiral said. "Bring the subs up and feed targeting data to them."

"Aye, aye sir!" The CIC duty officer responded before turning and snapping off a string of orders.

Five minutes later, four American guided missile submarines each received a two-character message over ELF. The two letters were *GO*. Eighty miles due north of Oahu, they had been maneuvering silently in the ocean, steering racetrack patterns 800 feet beneath the surface for several months. Never believing that Hawaii wouldn't become a target for a Russian invasion, they were Admiral Packard's holdout Ace.

The submarines, all Ohio class, had been sorely needed in the various naval engagements that had been fought with the Russians. But the Admiral wasn't one who liked to put all his cards on the table until there were no other options. Now, he was going to use them, and the more than 600 Tomahawk cruise missiles they carried.

While the submarines were about to send a veritable swarm of missiles towards the

Russian fleet, he also knew that only a small percentage would actually succeed in penetrating the enemy's defenses. But, it wouldn't take many. The idea was to overwhelm the approaching warships' ability to knock them out of the air.

The four subs, already spread across thirty miles of ocean, quickly responded. Each ascended to periscope depth and extended an antenna mast above the waves to receive more detailed orders as well as targeting information from Pearl Harbor. Once this had been completed, the captains ordered the commencement of the cruise missile attack.

Within minutes, dozens, then hundreds of missiles erupted from the dark surface of the Pacific Ocean. Each was launched vertically by high-pressure gas, a solid-fuel rocket booster igniting to lift it clear of the water and quickly accelerate the weapon. Transitioning to horizontal flight, the wings deployed and a jet engine took over, propelling the missile at well over 500 miles per hour.

Each had received targeting coordinates seconds before launch, and the onboard guidance systems turned them to streak towards the Russian invasion fleet, less than fifty feet above the gentle swells.

"Lead missiles will arrive on target in nineteen minutes, sir," the CIC TAO (Tactical Action Officer) reported to Packard.

He nodded, eyes fixed on the screen that gave him a view of the ongoing launches. It wouldn't be long before the Russians detected the inbound weapons. This was when things could go horribly wrong for Hawaii.

The enemy still had plenty of nuclear tipped, tactical missiles, and the Admiral had no idea what the fleet commander's orders were. Was he to take Oahu intact, at all costs? Or, if he was met with insurmountable resistance, had he been given the authority to launch on the Americans?

Worry over that possibility had caused Packard to hold back a damaged Arleigh Burke class destroyer. It was seaworthy, barely, but he'd kept it at anchor in the middle of Pearl Harbor. With its SPY radar system and anti-missile missiles, it was the last line of defense for the island. Linked into the Battlespace network, it also had control of multiple missile batteries that had been set up on the summit of Mt. Kaala.

"Sir, the Russians are maneuvering!"

He looked at the real time image of the enemy fleet, seeing every ship accelerating and turning their bow to the attacking missiles. The idea is to present as narrow of a profile target as possible, hoping to avoid a direct hit by any weapon that leaked through the ship's defenses.

"Admiral, Thor is online!" Jessica called from the far side of the CIC.

The duty officer shot a dirty look in her direction for the severe breach of procedure, but both she and the Admiral ignored him. Packard quickly strode to where she was working.

"Can Thor hit a moving target?" He asked as he approached.

"No sir," she said, shaking her head. "It makes slight targeting adjustments to the rods when they're dropped, but after that, it's no better than a dumb bomb."

Packard cursed softly, cutting his eyes back to the screen displaying the Russian fleet. Dozens of fires bloomed briefly across all of the ships as defensive missiles began leaping off their rails to meet the incoming wave of Tomahawks.

"Will they stay on a straight course, sir?" Jessica asked.

"The Russian ships? They should, at least until the attack ends. Why?"

"Because," Jessica began, spinning and typing furiously. "I think, if I know where they are, their course and speed, I can calculate where they should be when a Thor rod arrives."

Captain West and Commander Detmer had followed the Admiral, and both immediately began encouraging him to let her try. He nodded, which was all Jessica needed to keep working on the targeting solution.

"How are you accounting for the change in target position that occurs in the time necessary to perform the calculations?" Captain West asked, leaning over her shoulder.

"Here, sir," she answered, briefly tapping a line in the code she was creating on the fly.

He looked at the indicated point, then straightened up and smiled at the Admiral.

"Think it will work?" Packard asked quietly, not wanting to distract Jessica.

"She knows what she's doing, sir. As long as the Russians don't change course or speed, she's got a good shot at dropping a rod right on top of the bastards' heads."

"So far, so good," Vance said when I stuck my head into the cockpit.

We were airborne, again, just starting to turn north to head for Nevada.

"I have a favor to ask," I said.

"What's that?"

"If we've got enough fuel for a side trip, I'd like to head east. Far edge of the city."

"What for?" He asked without taking his attention away from the flight controls.

I sighed before answering.

"My house. What's left of it. I'll probably never have the chance again, and there's something I'd like to get."

He was quiet for a moment, his eyes scanning the instruments.

"What?"

"It's personal," I said, not feeling like telling him my life's story.

He turned to look at me for a few long seconds, finally nodding. A moment later we banked to the right.

"Where am I going?"

I leaned forward over Tiffany's shoulder to see through the windscreen, looking for landmarks.

"See that freeway to the south? The one running east-west. Follow it until I tell you."

He did as I asked, paralleling the multi-lane stretch of Interstate that ran through downtown Phoenix. Soon, we overflew the airport, continuing east.

"About thirty more miles," I said, looking down at all the burned out neighborhoods.

There weren't any vehicles moving. No people, infected or not, on the streets. Just another of the thousands of ghost towns that was all that was left of America.

It didn't take long to reach the general area of my neighborhood, and I gave Vance directions to get us over a stretch of empty desert that bordered the small community of homes. We'd overflown the burned out husk that had once been my house, and it looked even worse than I remembered seeing it from the bomber on the way to Los Alamos.

Fulcrum

Vance gently brought us down, a barely perceptible bump as the landing gear touched the ground. A huge cloud of dust, kicked up by the rotors, enveloped us and blotted out the view through the windscreen. I headed for the back.

"What are we doing?" Rachel looked up and asked as I passed her.

"My house," I said, knowing she'd understand. "I'll be back."

I hit the button to lower the ramp, walking out and jumping to the sand. The rotors were still spinning, kicking up a storm of stinging debris, but I ignored it and jogged away towards the wall that encircled my development. I was halfway there when I realized Dog had followed and was trotting next to me.

The wall was down in several places, apparently having been rammed by large vehicles. I picked my way through the shattered blocks, into a neighbor's back yard. By now I had my rifle up, just in case there were any infected or survivors that might take exception to my presence.

Dog stayed next to me, moving easily and remaining silent. Moving through the side yard, I emerged onto their driveway and came to a stop. My house, or what was left of it, was directly across the street. It had burned completely, the wooden frame collapsing in on itself. The roof had been covered with clay tiles, and the exterior walls had been stacked stone. Without the structure of the framing, all of this had collapsed until there was nothing other than a pile of rubble.

I moved closer, stopping in the street for a moment, then made a slow circle around the property line. The debris was mounded deep, and it was heavy. The safe I wanted to access had been in a room that was near the middle of the house and that area was completely buried under several tons of what was left of my home. There was no way, without time and heavy equipment, that I'd ever be able to get to it.

Standing there, I couldn't help but let my mind drift to the past. All of the time I'd spent here with Katie. Some of them bad, but those had been very few and very far between. We'd been happy. Enjoyed every minute we spent together. And we spent as much time together as we could. We'd never been one of those couples that seemed to need time apart from each other.

Lost in my memories, I looked down when Dog bumped my hand with his nose. He was sitting by my foot, staring at me. I ruffled his ears, and with a tear in my eye I took a last look at my house before turning and running for the waiting helicopter.

Fulcrum

"Find it?" Rachel asked when I climbed aboard.

I pressed the *close* button for the ramp and shouted for Vance to get us in the air, then sat down close to Rachel.

"Too much debris," I said. "Couldn't get to the safe."

"I'm sorry."

She reached out and took my hand. I squeezed back in response, then she scooted across the deck and wrapped me in a hug. Together, we laid back and soon I was asleep in her arms.

Some time later, my eyes snapped open when Tiffany shook my shoulder.

"Vance needs you," she said.

I disengaged myself from Rachel and stiffly made my way to the cockpit.

"Check that shit out!"

Vance pointed through the windscreen. I took another step forward and looked to the side. We were over Nevada, not too far from Hoover Dam. The view of the shattered top was awe inspiring from the air, especially with the massive plume of water that was still pouring through the breach. But, that wasn't what he wanted me to see.

Several miles north, heading towards the shoreline of a partially drained Lake Meade, dozens of vehicles raced across the desert. Dust boiled into the air in their wake. I wouldn't have cared if it wasn't for the Humvee that was only a few hundred yards in front of the main group. It might have been their leader, but it sure looked like it was being pursued.

With a bad feeling in my gut, I activated my radio and made a call. Nothing. I repeated myself, a moment later Igor's voice sounding over my earpiece. I could hear a roaring engine and rattling vehicle in the background.

"Battlespace comms with Pearl are restored, ma'am!"

Lieutenant Commander Adrienne Cable rushed to the side of the sailor who had just reported, double-checking the monitor he was looking at. She stared for a couple of seconds before turning away.

"COB," she shouted to the Chief of the Boat, the most senior NCO aboard. "Inform the skipper."

"Ma'am," the communications specialist continued. "Pearl is requesting a status update on our mission."

"Stand by," she said, waiting for the Captain to arrive and dictate their response.

While she waited, she moved out of the control room, past the sonar station and to a cramped space where another sailor was working on a console. He was responsible for communications with the SEAL team that had gone into Sydney, and now that Battlespace was back up and running, he was working furiously to establish a link with them.

Dirk Patton

The North Carolina had heard nothing since the SEALs departed, but there had been no other options. Even now, reaching them on the encrypted, digital radio was proving to be problematic. This was mostly due to the fact that the sub was still submerged, with only a few inches of antenna, supported by a buoy, floating on the surface. The buoy was tethered to their sail and could be reeled back in at a moment's notice.

A high-gain satellite antenna comprised most of it, with only a stubby, black fiberglass mast sticking up for local area comms. The whole unit was stealthy as hell, and extremely difficult to spot in the daytime. And if anyone who didn't know what it was happened to see it, they'd pass it off as a small chunk of debris. At night, it was invisible, floating on the waves. But, its range for anything other than satellite comms was very limited and intermittent.

When a wave passed under it, lifting the antenna higher in the air, they had a good shot at reaching out several miles. But when it slipped into a trough between the swells, it was completely masked, and the signal would drop. The only consistent link was from an orbiting satellite that was looking directly down at the point in the ocean where the buoy floated.

"Anything?" She asked the sailor.

"No, ma'am. Not yet," he said, never taking his focus off the equipment he was manipulating.

"Let me know the instant you have something," she said, turning and dashing back into the control room before he could acknowledge her order.

Commander Talbot was arriving as she stepped through a narrow hatch, the COB calling out loudly that the Captain was present.

"Battlespace is back up, sir," Adrienne said. "Jones has a message from Pearl, requesting a sitrep. Figured you'd like to handle that."

"You figured right, XO. Any word from our SEALs?"

"No, sir. Not yet."

Talbot nodded and moved to the secure comms console, quickly read the message from Hawaii, then began dictating a reply in a low voice. As he spoke, the sailor transcribed his words into a computer that would first encrypt them, then compress the entire message into a data file that would be sent out in a burst transmission that would last less than half a second.

"Conn, radio room. I've got Fulcrum team!"

The shout galvanized both Adrienne and Talbot, and they dashed through the hatch to where the sailor was seated. There wasn't room for either of them to enter the small workspace, so they stood in the passageway and leaned in. The operator was pressing one side of his headphones tighter to his ear as he spoke into a microphone in a loud voice.

"Fulcrum one, repeat last. Repeat last!"

"On speaker!" Talbot ordered.

The operator flipped a switch, an overhead speaker blaring to life with the sounds of a raging battle. Rifles were being fired, and men were screaming at each other.

"We're in contact with…" Commander Sam began to broadcast, his voice rough as he was obviously running, then the transmission cut out and there was only silence.

"Buoy's in a trough," the operator said, though both officers knew what had happened.

The wait for the next swell to lift it high enough to restore the link was excruciating, but they endured the time stoically. With no warning, the sound of a weapon firing on full auto suddenly blared out of the speaker.

"...Bay. We're trying to..." there was a much shorter interruption. "... men down. We're trying to reach... sulate."

The transmission went silent again, and Talbot suppressed a curse. He wasn't one to let the crew see his frustration.

"They're trying to reach what?" He asked.

"I didn't get it, either, sir," Adrienne said, shaking her head.

"Begging your pardon, sir, but is there an embassy in Sydney? One of ours, I mean."

The operator looked over his shoulder at the skipper.

"Sulate is consulate?" Talbot asked when he realized what the sailor meant. "Maybe..."

He was cut off when the transmission restored.

"...you copy? We... off from the RIBs... ... ... in Royal Bo... Gard..."

"Get me a map of Sydney!"

Talbot shouted towards the control room. Thirty seconds later, COB appeared and extended a large, paper map, folded over to show the area where the SEALs had landed.

481

"Here, sir," he said, pointing at a spot on the map. "Sounded like he was saying Royal Botanical Gardens. And here's the US Consulate. They're making a straight line for it, cutting through the Gardens, from where their target is located."

He tapped locations on the paper as he spoke, Talbot and Adrienne looking closely.

"Thank you, COB," the skipper said. "XO, stay with the radio and find out as much as you can. I need to get this message out. Maybe Pearl is in contact with the consulate and can give them a heads up about what's heading their way."

He rushed down the passageway to the control room as the signal restored. Commander Sam was no longer speaking, but his breath sounds were heavy from running, gunfire loud over the speaker.

"Are we armed?" I shouted at Vance.

"Negative," he said, looking around at me. "Aircraft is naked."

"Shit! OK, see that Hummer? That's one of us, and he's in trouble. Get over him. I'm going back to the ramp and see if I can slow those assholes down with a rifle!"

"Oh, hell yeah!"

His enthusiasm surprised me, but then he was a combat pilot. I held on as he banked sharply and began descending towards Igor. The Chinook had just leveled out when an alarm in the cockpit began screaming.

"Fuck me, they've got a lock on us!" Vance yelled.

Before I knew what was happening, the helicopter tilted far to the side and only the firm grip I already had kept me from being thrown around like a rag doll. It felt like he kept rolling until the deck was vertical, then twisted to the side and dropped alarmingly. Tiffany, already strapped back into the co-pilot position, fared much better.

There was nothing I could do other than hold tight. A second later, in my peripheral vision, something trailing fire and smoke flashed past our nose.

"What the fuck was that?" I shouted.

He didn't answer, just kept bouncing us all over the sky as he brought the big helicopter down and into the cover of a series of tall hills. With a vibrating roar, our speed bled completely off, and we came into a hover.

"SAM," he said in a much calmer voice than I could have imagined at the moment.

Shit. I'd seen these guys raiding the armories at Nellis. Not only had they gotten their hands on a Surface to Air Missile, but they also had someone that knew how to use it.

"What can we do?" I asked, not releasing my grip in case he had to make any more sudden maneuvers.

"Do? Not a damn thing," he said. "We don't have any countermeasures, no weapons... nothing. We're a fucking sitting duck up here. We just got lucky as hell, and can't count on it twice."

I looked around in frustration, seeing Rachel peering around a bulkhead at me. She was on the opposite side of the aircraft from where I'd left her.

"You OK?" I shouted over the roar of the engines.

"Bumped and bruised, but OK," she shouted back. "What's going on?"

"Bad guys got some air defense," I answered, not taking the time to go into details.

"Vance," I said, turning back to the pilot. "Can you circle around, staying low, and come in over the lake? Pick up our guys at the shore?"

"I can do that," he said, shaking his head. "But, while were sitting there loading, the bad guys are going to close in and blow our asses off."

I was quiet for a bit, chewing on my lower lip in thought.

"Did you see that marina?" Tiffany asked.

"What marina?"

"About four miles south of where the Hummer is heading, there was a marina. If they can get there and escape on a boat, maybe we can pick them up once they're clear of the area."

"There were boats?" I asked in surprise.

I had noted that the level of the lake had dropped significantly. But, it was still draining. Maybe it hadn't dropped so much that a floating dock wouldn't still be serviceable.

"Looked like it," she said. "Only saw them for a second, but it looked like at least a dozen tied to a dock."

"Think we can get there without getting shot down?" I asked Vance.

"Maybe. What you got in mind?"

"Drop me, then get clear. I'll get a boat ready to go. All they've gotta do is pile out of the Humvee and jump in. It'll save them time they don't have. I'll head up the lake and find a place that's in cover so you can pick us up. Now, can you get me to the marina?"

"Hold on to your ass," he said, grinning.

The deck tilted as he spun the helo around. Accelerating, he kept the hills between us and what I was pretty sure was the militia. I watched through the windscreen for a minute, not liking seeing the ground rushing past, seemingly close enough to scrape the aircraft's belly. Vance was keeping us low.

As he flew, I called Igor on the radio and told him what his new destination was. He responded with a long string of Russian curses, then confirmed in English that he understood.

Moving to the back, I kept a grip with my hands in case of any sudden maneuvers. Rachel looked like she'd been through a washing machine on spin cycle. She sported a bruise on her cheek that was already spreading and would become a nice shiner before it was done. But, she wasn't bleeding, and there weren't any broken bones. Dog lay on his belly, legs splayed out in anticipation of his world turning upside down again.

I spent half a minute filling in Rachel, then returned to the cockpit. As I stepped in, we banked hard to the left and if I hadn't been gripping an overhead handle, would have wound up on my face.

We were over the lake now, and it felt more like riding in a really fast boat than a helicopter. The water couldn't have been more than ten feet below the Chinook's belly. Ahead was the marina Tiffany had spotted. From this perspective, I could see that it would soon be unusable.

The dock was one of the floating variety, tethered to the rocky shore. The chains were stretched to the limit, and most of it was already resting on dry lakebed, along with a large number of boats. Only the outer twenty feet was still afloat. Fortunately, there were three boats that still had water under their keels, tied to the outermost edge.

A couple of miles to the right, I could see the dust plumes made by the approaching vehicles. They were coming fast, and would be at the marina within three minutes.

"I'm coming in hot," Vance said. "Brace yourself, then as soon as we're in a hover, get your ass out the door."

"Got it," I said, slapping him on the shoulder and running for the back.

Rachel saw me activate the ramp and reached forward to wrap Dog in her arms. I was glad she did as there was a good chance he'd follow me out.

The ramp reached its lowest position, and I dropped to my knees, grabbing a handle next to the opening. I was braced none too soon, the helicopter suddenly flaring and whipping around, nearly tearing my grip free. A few seconds later the deck leveled out, the edge of the ramp only a foot above the wooden dock. Standing, I raced to the edge and jumped.

My boots had barely thudded onto the wooden planks when the Chinook roared away, skimming the lake's surface. I ran for the closest boat, a large craft set up for water skiing. It would have a huge engine and be fast, and once Igor and company were on board, we needed all the speed we could get.

Of course, there were no keys in the ignition, but I was getting to be an old hand at this. Whipping out my Ka-Bar, I pried the lock cylinder free and cut the wires attached to its back. Twisting them together, I hit the starter and breathed a sigh of relief when the engine rumbled to life and settled into a steady thrum.

"Igor," I shouted into the radio as I released the lines holding the boat to the dock. "I'm in position!"

"Cannot see!" He shouted back.

I looked up and saw the problem. I was well below the level of the surrounding desert. If the lake was full, the marina would be several feet higher and visible over the lip of terrain. Now, unless you were standing on the edge, it was hidden.

Tearing through the boat, I found an emergency kit and ripped it open. A bright red flare gun was held to the inside of the lid by two spring clips, four shells neatly contained in the lower section. Yanking it free, I loaded in a shell, held it at arm's length above my head and pulled the trigger.

"I'm the flare!" I shouted as it streaked skyward, trailing a brilliant, fiery tail that was clearly visible even in full sunlight.

"See you," he answered.

Ten seconds later I could hear the Humvee's straining engine, punctuated by distant gunfire from the pursuers. The boat had drifted a few feet, a current created by the continuing outflow of water pulling it towards the dam, so I bumped the throttle and steered until it nudged the dock. With the nose against the wooden planks, I left the throttle partially advanced to keep it in place for boarding.

There was a screeching of tortured brakes and the grinding of tires on sand and rock from above. A huge cloud of dust boiled up, slowly starting to drift towards me. An instant later, Igor appeared at the top of the slope and stopped, turning to wave at someone to hurry.

I recognized Chelsea when she ran down the steep embankment, then had no idea who the next girl was. Right behind her came another I didn't recognize, and it dawned on me that Igor hadn't been sitting on his hands while I was gone. He'd rescued the captured girls.

They kept coming, Chelsea pounding down the dock as the last one crested the top and started down with Igor right behind her. Holding the boat as steady as I could with the throttle, I glanced to the side and recognized another problem I'd overlooked. The other two boats! What was to stop our pursuers from using them to chase us out onto the lake? And if they brought a SAM with them, Vance would be a sitting duck when he came to pick us up.

Tearing two grenades off my vest, I pressed them into Chelsea's hands and held on as I met her eyes. She looked back at me like I was deranged.

"When I tell you, pull the pins and throw them into those boats," I said, turning my head to look at the targets.

"I... I..." she stammered.

"Pull a pin and throw, then pull the second pin and throw. Underhand, just like a softball! You'll be fine. You've got five seconds once the pin is out."

She nodded, appearing less than confident. I released her, looking around as the last girl jumped in, landing on top of the pile of girls that had already boarded. We were overloaded, the boat riding low in the water, but at the moment I didn't care.

Igor came running backward, rifle aimed at the top of the slope. Turning at the last possible instant, he leapt and crashed onto a cushioned seat at the stern.

"Now, Chelsea!" I shouted.

A spoon clanked as it hit the deck, then the first grenade arced across forty feet of open water and landed in the cockpit of one of the boats. A heartbeat later, another clank as the second spoon hit the deck and I jammed the throttle forward. By Chelsea's excited shout, I was pretty sure she'd put both grenades exactly where she wanted them.

The ski boat's engine roared, but our acceleration was sluggish. Either it wasn't as powerful as I'd expected, or we were even heavier in the water than I'd thought. Glancing around, I saw all the bodies crammed in, then looked up as the first grenade detonated.

The boat that had been next to the one I'd taken shuddered, chunks of debris ripping through the air, then flames began to appear as it started to settle in the water. That left the boat at the opposite end of the dock, and I kept waiting for the blast that would take it out of commission. And waited. It never came.

It's a rare thing, but not unheard of, for a grenade to have a faulty fuse. I knew this wasn't Chelsea's fault as I'd clearly heard two spoons hit the deck of our boat. She'd pulled the pin, there was no doubt, but the grenade hadn't done its job.

There wasn't time to turn around and try again. As we slowly accelerated out into the lake, dust billowed above the marina as the bad guys began arriving. Quickly, figures appeared along the edge of the overlooking terrain.

Immediately, I began sawing the wheel back and forth to present a more difficult target. I don't know if they started shooting at us, but that's what I would have done. Regardless, a little insurance never hurts. And if they were firing, it must have worked. Neither the boat nor any of the people in it took any incoming fire.

"Here come!" Igor shouted.

I threw a glance over my shoulder. He was lying across the stern, body on top of the engine compartment, aiming towards our pursuers. At the marina, men were swarming around the boat that hadn't been destroyed.

"Chelsea, drive!" I shouted.

With a frightened look, she slipped behind the wheel when I jumped up and headed for the stern. I had to climb over the girls that were still trying to sort themselves out, then stretched across the engine cover next to Igor.

"Pissed off the natives, didn't you?"

I yelled to be heard over the bellowing motor. He looked at me and grinned.

"Igor need fun, also," he said, then it was time to get serious.

We had opened up close to three hundred yards of space from the dock, but I could clearly see the activity through my rifle scope. They had the boat started, and four men climbed aboard as those remaining behind released the lines and shoved it clear. I wasn't terribly concerned over most of them but didn't like it when I saw what one asshole had carried with him. He had a Stinger.

The Stinger is a shoulder fired, heat seeking, Surface to Air Missile. The launcher consists of a long tube that houses the missile, with a box-like housing near the front that contains the targeting system. They're simple to use, with minimal training, and the sight of the weapon reminded me how incredibly lucky, or good, Vance had been to avoid the one that had been fired at the Chinook.

"Rachel! Can you hear me?" I shouted into the radio.

I had to try three more times before she answered.

Fulcrum

"Tell Vance there's a boat chasing us, and they have a Stinger. He'll know what that means. He has to stay clear!"

As I was speaking, Igor began firing. He no longer had the sniper rifle I'd taken from Groom Lake and was having to make do with an M4 rifle with a low power scope. But, after his third shot, the boat suddenly swerved, losing a little bit of ground. I don't think he'd hit any of the occupants, but he'd apparently given them something to think about.

I heard Rachel answer my message, but was too busy trying to sight in the man holding the Stinger. Everyone else was only armed with rifles, and while they couldn't be dismissed, they didn't present much, if any, danger to the Chinook.

"Shoot the fucker with the Stinger!" I shouted to Igor.

He grunted, and both of us began firing slow and steady, aimed shots. If we could take out the SAM, we could throw out enough suppressive fire for Vance to come in and pick us up.

We kept at it but weren't having any success. There was some wind creating small waves on the surface of the lake, and while the ski boat wasn't bouncing too much, it was enough to throw us off. Even if we'd had a stable platform to fight from, the pursuers' boat was also jinking around in response to the water conditions.

The boat suddenly slowed, catching Igor and me by surprise. But a second later that surprise changed to an *oh fuck* moment. The guy with the Stinger stood up and pointed the business end of the missile tube directly at us.

"Will work?" Igor shouted.

"Shoot that fucker!" I screamed, switching to full auto and sending a stream of bullets towards him.

No, Stingers are not designed to attack ground based targets. But, the targeting system doesn't know that. Right now, the infrared seeker head in the missile was attempting to lock on to the heat of our engine. If it succeeded, the operator would be notified and could fire the weapon.

While I didn't have first-hand experience with using one against anything other than an aircraft, I'd heard stories of it being successfully done. As long as the target was hot enough for the missile to achieve lock, and there wasn't anything blocking the flight path, in theory, it should work.

Fulcrum

My only hope was that the heat being emitted by our engine wasn't enough for a missile that had been designed to home in on jet engines to achieve a lock. But then, we were floating on water that would present a nice, cool background to the seeker head. And, we'd be the lone hot spot in all that coolness.

While I kept emptying magazines at the boat, and getting a few hits that sent shards of fiberglass into the air, Igor maintained a steady rate of fire. One round at a time. I dropped an empty mag, slapped in a fresh one and took careful aim. We were drawing away from the boat as it bobbed in the swells, waiting for the Stinger to lock on so they could finish us off.

Igor and I both fired at the same moment. He, a single round, while my rifle kept chattering. A couple of seconds later, the man with the Stinger pitched backward. The missile flew out of his hands and tumbled once in the air before splashing into the lake and sinking.

I released the trigger and Igor and I stared for a moment, hardly able to believe our luck. We traded smiles, then looked back to see the boat surge forward in pursuit. It was at least three hundred yards behind, probably closer to four, and within a very few seconds it was obvious it was much faster than we were.

"What the hell did you do to these guys?" I shouted, a little surprised at their determination to catch us.

"I kill many," Igor said, shrugging.

Grinning, I called Rachel with the news that the Stinger was out of commission. Vance answered instead.

"Took you long enough," he cracked.

"Fuck off, flyboy," I said. "I've still got a boat on my ass, and he's faster than I am."

I flinched when a bullet struck a few inches to my right, pinging off a stainless steel rail. From within the boat, there was a cry of pain as the ricochet found one of the girls. I started firing again, in full auto, Igor joining in. It must have helped as no more rounds found us, but our pursuers were gaining. They were inside three hundred yards and drawing closer.

"On my way!"

I heard Vance's voice on the radio but didn't have time to respond. Changing magazines, I began firing three round bursts. One of the occupants slumped to the side and stopped moving, but the remaining pair kept shooting. A moment later there was another cry of pain from within the boat, then a round slammed into my rifle.

498

Fulcrum

The impact was vicious, shoving the weapon into my face as pieces of the receiver turned to shrapnel and tore into my arm and shoulder. I was briefly stunned, then looked down at the ruined rifle still gripped in my hands. Only one eye was working, and I reached up to touch my face, my hand coming away covered in blood.

Before I could check myself further, a roar from behind caught my attention, and I looked up as the Chinook overflew the boat that was chasing us. Vance was low over the surface, the huge rotors kicking up rooster tails of spray. The bad guys disappeared in a cloud of water, then it was our turn.

Vance came right over us, continuing on without slowing and rapidly pulling away.

"What the fuck are you doing?" I screamed into the radio.

"Gonna scoop you up, dogface," he answered. "Keep going straight."

Now far ahead, I saw the Chinook slow to a hover and descend. The rear ramp was all the way down. I could make out a figure that I was sure was Rachel, standing at the top of the ramp. As we approached the now static aircraft, Vance continued to descend until the ramp was submerged and water was washing into the interior. I finally realized what his plan was.

"Grab something and hold on!"

I shouted the warning to Igor, then slithered backward off the engine cover and onto the top of a girl. Scrambling over legs, arms and heads, I made it to the wheel and grabbed Chelsea's arm, pulling her out of the seat. Dropping in, I swiped at the blood that was starting to block my one good eye, then shoved on the throttle. It was all the way forward. We couldn't go any faster.

Through the stinging spray of water, I squinted at the open maw of the Chinook with my good eye. From behind, Igor's rifle began firing again. The bow of the ski boat reached the ramp with a jarring impact. The tail dipped as our weight came onto the ramp, then we screeched our way up and into the aircraft, slamming against the bulkhead that protected the cockpit. Hammering the throttle to idle, I ripped the wires apart that were keeping the engine running.

The Chinook shuddered and tilted back and forth as Vance struggled to regain control after the sudden change in weight and balance of the aircraft. The rear ramp whined audibly over the roar of the rotors, finally sealing with a dull thud.

Fulcrum

The ski boat, with a sharp keel, was leaning to the right at a 45-degree angle. I sat there, my body having decided it was time for a break. Rachel, Tiffany and Dog were looking at me from the protection of the far side of the bulkhead, then all three hurried forward.

Rachel came around to the low side of the tilted boat and leaned in. I smiled at her, but it felt like it was someone else in control of my face. I couldn't see out of my right eye, and my left was looking through a red film of blood.

"Sit still," Rachel said, a grim expression on her face. "You've got a bullet sticking out of your head."

Despite her warning, I raised my hand, intending to find it and pull it out. She grabbed my hand, stopping me, then I fell down a deep, dark hole and didn't know anything else.

The Thor satellite, in geosynchronous orbit over the north Pacific, woke up and responded to Jessica's command. It only took a few seconds for the targeting data to load, then eleven rods were pushed out of their tubes. Small guidance pods on the base of each gave them an initial downwards thrust, also making slight adjustments to their trajectories.

"Rods are away, sir," Jessica said to Admiral Packard. "Eight minutes, twenty-seven seconds to impact on target."

Packard looked at the main screen in the room, verifying that the Russian fleet was staying on course, the bow of each ship pointed directly at the inbound Tomahawks. In the lower corner, a small clock counted down the time to target for the lead missile. -00:09:18. The Thor rods would arrive fifty-one seconds before the first cruise missile.

"Admiral! Message from the North Carolina, sir!"

Packard turned as a young Lieutenant dashed up and held out a piece of paper, still warm from the laser printer. He read it quickly, then looked up at Captain West.

"Get a message to our consulate in Sydney," he said, handing the paper to his aide. "They've got Marines. It's time for them to earn their pay. I want them out the gate and helping our boys."

"On Australian soil, sir?" West asked in surprise.

"Don't give a shit about anyone's panties getting in a bunch," the Admiral growled. "Help our men!"

"Aye, aye sir!"

The Captain raced away, heading for the closest communication terminal.

"Seaman," he said, turning to Jessica. "Can you show me our Sydney consulate?"

"Yes, sir," she said.

She worked quickly, taking over a display on the side wall. It took her a couple of attempts, but she persisted, succeeding in establishing a real-time link with an NSA satellite over Australia. Manipulating the imaging feed, she paused to look up the coordinates of the US consulate. Plugging them in, the image smoothly zoomed until the large building was centered on the display.

"There," Packard said immediately.

He pointed at a large swath of ground that was a black splotch in the middle of the densely concentrated city lights of Sydney. Within the darkness, bright pinpricks of light could be seen. There was one area where they were tightly concentrated, then a long line of them to the east. They were seeing the muzzle flashes from lots of rifles being fired.

Jessica zoomed some more, then made adjustments to the software that allowed them to clearly see the battle being fought. Packard stepped around a console for a closer view of the screen.

Eight SEALs were running across a broad, grassy field. Three of them were obviously injured but were still fighting as they all fired towards a broad skirmish line of soldiers that were in pursuit. Packard squinted, looking at the attackers. They were all in Russian uniform.

The SEALs were making for a narrow street that bordered the Royal Botanical Gardens, separating them from a large hospital complex. After that, there were three blocks of downtown Sydney before they would make it to the skyscraper that housed the consulate.

"Sir, the consulate is sealed off by Australian police," Captain West said, hurrying to Packard's side. "The Marines can't get out without fighting."

"Show me!" The Admiral snapped to Jessica.

She adjusted the satellite view slightly to the west, then put a red marker on the top of the tall building that housed the consulate. An entire city block surrounding the location was closed off, dozens of official vehicles filling the streets. At least fifty armed men, wearing police uniforms with body armor, formed a cordon around the area.

"They can't stand to our Marines, sir," Captain West prompted.

"No, but they can," the Admiral said.

He pointed at a convoy of military trucks that was moving through the city streets at a high rate of speed. Several of them stopped at the north edge of the consulate building to disgorge Australian soldiers, the bulk continuing on past the hospital and spreading along the street that bordered the gardens. Over a hundred men jumped down and quickly formed up to prevent the Americans from exiting the open field.

"Get the Australian PM on the phone," Packard said. "Now!"

He kept watching as Captain West dashed away to place the call. The SEALs were still fighting, but they'd slowed when they saw the Australian forces formed up to cut them off. One of them fell, having been shot, before they all dropped to the ground and continued firing at the advancing Russians.

The Aussies weren't there to join in the fight, just to make sure it didn't spill into the city center. And, almost assuredly, to make sure the Americans didn't escape.

"Sir, the Australian PM," Captain West said, extending a headset towards the Admiral.

Packard snatched it out of his hand and settled it in place without taking his eyes off the screen. The SEALs, apparently out of ammo, had stopped firing and were running at the line of Australians. The Russian troops, with no more fire coming their way, began charging across the open ground. The Americans came to a slow halt when the local soldiers guarding the edge of the field raised their weapons to prevent them from coming any closer.

"Mr. Prime Minister, are you aware of what's happening in Sydney?" The Admiral said through clenched teeth.

"If you are referring to the illegal incursion onto Australian soil by the American military, Admiral, yes I am."

"Then arrest them, Prime Minister! Do not allow the Russians to take them."

"I'm afraid that's out of my hands at this point," the PM replied smugly. "My understanding is that your men were attempting to gain entry to the residence of President Barinov. That makes this a matter best handled between the United States and Russia."

"You son of a bitch!" Packard said, no longer attempting to control his anger.

The PM was saying something in response, but the Admiral's attention was drawn fully to the screen. The SEALs were now completely surrounded and on their knees as Russian troops held them at gunpoint. Motion to the side resolved into a Hind helicopter entering from the eastern edge of the view.

It was flying low and fast, flaring into a hover and touching down in the middle of the large, open field. The side door opened, and several uniformed Spetsnaz jumped down to set up a defensive perimeter. A moment later, a squat figure with white hair stepped out and paused to adjust his suit. Barinov!

The Australian PM was still speaking, but Packard stabbed a mute button on the headset and whirled to Jessica.

"Do we have a Thor platform over Australia?"

She spent several seconds working on her console before answering.

"No, sir. We can hit parts of southeast Asia, but Sydney is too far south. Guess no one ever thought we'd need to attack the Aussies."

He grimaced, then took a second to check the screen showing the progress of the Tomahawk missiles. -00:02:31. A little over a minute and a half before the Thor rods arrived on the Russian fleet. Another second to satisfy himself that the enemy ships had not changed course, then he looked back at the screen as Barinov strode across the field towards the captured SEALs. He was accompanied by three aides and surrounded by a large squad of soldiers.

"Sir, targets are launching defensive weapons," the duty officer called.

A glance back at the Russian fleet. Blooms of fire and thick smoke from every ship as anti-missile missiles were fired. Noting the time to target, he turned back to the view of Sydney and noted that the PM was still talking. He listened for a moment as the man continued to try and justify his complete capitulation to the enemy. Packard unmuted his headset.

Fulcrum

"Mr. Prime Minister, shut the hell up!" He barked, silencing the protestations of the politician. "You have troops standing less than two hundred yards away from my men. It is time for you to make a decision. Sir, if you allow the Russians to take them, or harm them, I will consider it an act of war by Australia against the United States of America.

"We're hurt, as you well know, but we're not out by a long shot. If you don't believe me, I suggest you have one of your aides set up a satellite view of the ocean, 200 miles northwest of Oahu. But, you'd better hurry, or you're going to miss it."

For a moment, all he could hear was the soft breathing of the man on the other end of the call. Then there was a muted click as he was put on hold. Packard stood waiting, watching as Barinov stepped through the ranks of his men and stood looking down at the captured Americans. He seemed to be talking to them.

Turning his attention to the main screen, he watched as more defensive missiles were fired. By now, the majority of the enemy fleet was obscured by dense clouds of smoke from repeated launches. He glanced at the timer, then back at the vague shapes of the Russian ships.

Three seconds later, the first Thor rod arrived on the lead ship, a guided missile cruiser nearly as long as an aircraft carrier. From within the blinding smoke, there was a brilliant flash, then a concussive wave raced out in all directions, blasting the air clean of the rocket motor exhaust. Three more flashes heralded additional strikes, then there was a sudden burst of atomized seawater that completely hid the entire fleet.

Another flash, then two more eruptions from the ocean as millions of gallons of water were instantly boiled to steam. A few seconds later, three more flashes within the roiling aftermath of the Thor strikes. The entire CIC was silent as the men and women intently watched the screen, waiting for the air to clear.

"Seaman?" Packard spoke quietly to Jessica.

"That's all of the Thor rods, sir. From what I saw, I believe we had eight direct hits and three misses. The misses should be what put all the water into the air. I'm switching to thermal so we can see through it."

The screen blinked, but before the imagery could update, the Tomahawks began arriving on target and detonating. The Russians had successfully shot down slightly more than 100 of the inbound cruise missiles, and would have perhaps splashed most of the remainder of the weapons were it not for the Thor attack.

Fulcrum

Now, in rapid succession, missile after missile screamed into the maelstrom and detonated. There was so much heat energy expended, and additional smoke and atomized water thrown into the air, that all modes of surveillance were useless.

The barrage of Tomahawks continued for several minutes. When it was over, a dense layer of smoke and water vapor covered more than forty square miles of the ocean's surface. The mist quickly cooled the area, and the satellite's thermal imaging began to give them a view through the cloud.

Everyone waited, holding their breath and riveted to the screen. Jessica changed back to normal mode when nothing substantial was visible on thermal. Water and smoke still obscured the view, but it improved by the second. Initially, no one understood what they were seeing. Or not seeing. Commander Detmer was the first to recognize it for what it was.

"There's only debris left," he began in a quiet voice that rose in excitement, loud in the stillness of the CIC. "All of their ships have been destroyed and sunk!"

Stunned looks were exchanged, then shouts and cheers suddenly erupted throughout the room. Hugs were exchanged by people with expressions of relief and joy. Admiral Packard took a deep breath and slowly let it out before turning back to the view of his SEALs.

Barinov was apparently in the mood to hear himself speak. He was walking a slow circle around the captives, his hands behind his back. His head was turned to face them as he moved. As he was finishing a circuit, an aide with a phone to his ear dashed forward and leaned close to speak.

The Russian President's body language showed shock and surprise as he leaned away from the man, then thrust his head back forward with what had to be a question. The aide spoke briefly into the phone before nodding his head to confirm the news he'd just delivered.

"Merry Christmas, asshole," Admiral Packard said under his breath as he watched Barinov learn of the destruction of his invasion fleet.

He saw several more exchanges between the two men, taken aback when Barinov suddenly looked straight up. The image was so crisp, Packard could see his rheumy eyes searching the sky. So, the bastard knew he was watching.

The Russian stared for several, long seconds. The Admiral experienced an eerie feeling, as if his enemy was able to look through the satellite camera and see him standing in the CIC.

Finally, Barinov turned away and strode to the closest soldier. Reaching out, he snatched the man's sidearm out of its holster and strode towards the captive SEALs. Packard watched in horror as he walked behind the Americans, methodically shooting each one in the back of the head.

"Captain West. Order the North Carolina to put a Tomahawk on Barinov's location. Now!"

"Captain, flash traffic coming in!"

Talbot and Adrienne rushed to the console and leaned in as a high-speed printer chugged out the message. The skipper reached past the sailor manning the station and ripped it free the instant it was completed. Adrienne moved next to him, reading over his shoulder.

With Battlespace restored, they had been able to access the feed from the satellite and had seen what had happened to Fulcrum team. Expressions in the control room were grim as the Captain and XO read their orders. Tears were in Adrienne's eyes, as well as many of the sailors who had watched in horror as their brethren were executed.

"XO?" Talbot asked quietly.

"I'm good, sir. I recognize this as a valid order."

"Very well," he said.

He was turning to issue the orders necessary to launch their Tomahawks when a shout from the sonar operator stopped him.

"Conn, Sonar! Multiple surface and airborne contacts approaching at high speed. They're on a bearing to our current position."

"XO, get us to deep water!" Talbot barked then turned around as she began issuing navigational orders. "TAO, spin up two missiles and enter the targeting data we received from Pearl in the flash traffic!"

The control room was suddenly a hive of activity as everyone jumped to execute the orders that were being issued. Talbot grabbed an overhead handle as the deck tilted in response to Adrienne's orders to move them farther offshore and away from the approaching threats. It leveled a moment later, a slight vibration starting up as the submarine accelerated to flank speed.

"Captain, missiles are ready! Doors are open!" The Tactical Action Officer called out.

"This is the Captain. Release of missiles is authorized!"

"This is the XO. I concur. Release of missiles is authorized!"

The two officers stepped to the weapons console, each inserting a key that hung from a chain around their necks. After a brief countdown, they turned them in concert. A light flashed on the panel, and a moment later the boat shuddered as a gas generator shot two missiles out of the top of the submarine.

"Close outer doors!" Talbot snapped. "XO, take us deep before the goddamn Russians put a torpedo in the water."

"Aye, aye sir!"

Twin geysers appeared in the water, only ten miles from the entrance to Sydney Harbour. A second later, blooms of fire lit the dark surface as the Tomahawks' rocket motors ignited. They swiftly gained altitude before turning over and streaking towards the city.

Quickly, the rockets burned out and jet engines took over. Approaching North Head, the point of land that guards the northern entrance to the harbor, the two missiles began to descend, their speed increasing to just over 500 miles an

515

hour. Six miles remained to reach the Gardens where Barinov was standing, which they would cover in slightly more than forty seconds.

The launch had been detected by two Russian guided missile boats sitting in Sydney Harbour for the sole purpose of protecting their president. Before the Tomahawks passed North Head, both of their targeting systems had locked onto the approaching threats. Seconds later, the computers that controlled the defensive weapons, which were in automatic mode, ordered the release of anti-missile missiles. Each boat fired four.

The eight Russian missiles screamed to meet the inbound American weapons, constantly adjusting their flight based on a real-time data link from the ships that fired them. Even with this advantage, several of them missed and continued on to fall harmlessly into the ocean when their fuel was expended.

The last three successfully destroyed the pair of Tomahawks over the still waters of Sydney Harbour. The twin explosions rattled windows all across the city and caused Barinov to pause and look up into the night sky.

"American missiles were just intercepted, sir." His aide stood next to him, a secure radio pressed to his ear. "No other inbound weapons detected at this time. We are in pursuit of an unidentified submarine, east of the harbor entrance."

Barinov grunted, then took a moment to look back at the bodies of the American sailors he had personally killed.

"They are children, no?" He asked his aide, referring to Americans.

"Yes, Mr. President. They are, but they are dangerous children. And they will come for you again."

Barinov snorted in response.

"Let them come, Yevgeny. Let them come."

Dirk Patton
Continue the adventure in Exodus: V
Plague Book 13, available now from Amazon.

Made in the USA
Monee, IL
19 April 2020

26643161R00285